Jane Pek

THE RIVALS

Jane Pek was born and grew up in Singapore. She
holds a BA from Yale University, a JD from the New
York University School of Law, and an MFA in fiction
from Brooklyn College. She is the author of the novel
The Verifiers, and her short fiction has appeared twice
in *The Best American Short Stories*. She currently lives
in New York, where she works as a lawyer at a global
investment company.

ALSO BY JANE PEK

The Verifiers

THE RIVALS

THE RIVALS

THE RIVALS

Jane Pek

Vintage Books
A Division of Penguin Random House LLC
New York

A V I N T A G E B O O K S O R I G I N A L 2 0 2 4

Vintage and colophon are registered
trademarks of Penguin Random House LLC.

This is a work of fiction. Names, characters, places, and incidents
either are the product of the author's imagination or are used fictitiously.
Any resemblance to actual persons, living or dead, events,
or locales is entirely coincidental.

Library of Congress Cataloging-in-Publication Data
Names: Pek, Jane, author.
Title: The rivals / by Jane Pek.
Description: New York : Vintage Books,
a Division of Penguin Random House LLC, 2024.
Identifiers: LCCN 2024006466 (print) | LCCN 2024006467 (ebook)
Subjects: LCGFT: Detective and mystery fiction. | Novels.
Classification: LCC PS3616.E3556 R58 2024 (print) |
LCC PS3616.E3556 (ebook) | DDC 813/.6—dc23
LC record available at https://lccn.loc.gov/2024006466
LC ebook record available at https://lccn.loc.gov/2024006467

Vintage Books Trade Paperback ISBN: 978-0-593-47015-2
eBook ISBN: 978-0-593-47016-9

Book design by Christoper M. Zucker

vintagebooks.com

Printed in the United States of America
10 9 8 7 6 5 4 3 2 1

For my siblings, Pek Li Jun and Pek Wenjie

PART ONE

PART ONE

I.

20xx New Year Resolutions

1. Visit Mom every ~~two~~ three weeks
2. Finish reading *The Analects*
   (abridged version okay)
3. ~~Ask Becks out on a date~~
4. ~~Start dating~~
3. Go on [three] dates
4. Stop correcting Coraline's malapropisms
   (or at least be less obnoxious about it)
5. Be less judgmental

II.

MASON PERRY STROLLS into Veracity on a permafrosted January morning to tell us about his case, tripping all my Pavlovian dislike responses as he goes.

As he talks, I gradually figure out why. He's too sure. Of himself, because he's handsome and urbane, and also well-off and successful—we know from our precheck that he played lacrosse at Dartmouth and works in investment banking. That we'll be only too ready to help him, because of all of the above. That the world is a place where he can have whatever he wants, because he's never had an experience to the contrary. For an instant I wonder what it would be like to be Mason Perry, someone like him, if I would also be going around bestowing my winningly asymmetrical grin on all and sundry, projecting a force field of confidence that a ballistic missile would bounce right off of.

"How long will that take?" he asks, and eases back into his chair.

I refrain from looking at Becks, seated next to me, to see why she hasn't started machine-gunning through our list of intake questions as she typically does. Mason Perry interrupted our latest disagreement—rather, the latest episode in our interminable epic of a disagreement—and I don't want her to interpret that action as a sign of détente.

Becks begins tapping a fingernail on the surface of the table, a slow, considering sound—and kicks my shin beneath it. I jolt. Mason Perry, who so far has been floodlighting Becks with his attention, blinks at me.

Right: *my* turn to lead the client intake session.

I sit up straight, as if better posture can compensate for the fact that I stopped listening to what Mason was saying two sentences in, and ask, "Were your parents really into Erle Stanley Gardner?"

Across from us the robust glow of Mason's face dims into confusion.

"He wrote the Perry Mason novels," I say.

"That show came from a book?" says Mason Perry. "I had no idea."

"I think you have your answer," Becks says to me. Rather, those are the sounds she's making—what she's really saying is: *Jesus Christ, I would fire you if I could.* She turns back to face Mason Perry. "What's the woman's name?"

"Amalia," says Mason. "Amalia Suarez."

Becks says, "Any reason to suspect she might not be telling the truth about anything?"

He pauses. There's a staginess to it—to his entire manner, as if he's imagining an invisible film crew trailing behind him, recording his every hand wave and head tilt.

"There must be something," says Becks. "Otherwise you wouldn't have come to us."

"That right?" he says. "You don't get people coming to you just to . . . make sure?"

"They generally have better things to do with their time and their money."

Mason says, his gaze floating past us like his inner director has asked him to turn up the pensive dial, "You meet someone and she's the girl of your dreams. What's more important than confirming that she's really what she seems to be? That you're not going to end up destroying your life over something that doesn't even exist?"

I must admit, he does pensive well.

Now I do glance at Becks, to see what she's making of all this. Her profile is sharp enough to cut. She's wearing her default expression of disapproval inflected with boredom. It's annoyingly elegant, as is everything else about her.

"How do you know?" I ask Mason, because that kind of all-in declaration always intrigues me. "About her being the girl of your dreams?"

He continues looking into the middle distance for another beat. Then he breaks out the dentist's-dream smile, and says, "You just know."

There are a few different ways to describe Veracity LLC and what we do as verifiers.

When I'm at a party and someone asks me about my job: *I work at a small company that conducts independent research for matchmakers.*

What Veracity's founder and ex–big boss Komla Atsina said when he hired me: *Think of us as a personal investments advisory firm.*

What all our clients think: we're an online-dating detective agency, sussing out whether the people they meet on matching platforms are lying about themselves.

What I learned after I made some questionable decisions around disregarding company policies and the like (although, hey, good thing I did in the end): Veracity was set up to verify not only individual daters but also the matchmakers themselves. In furtherance of their corporate mandate of profit maximization, the Big Three matchmakers—which together account for four-fifths of the market—had taken to seeding bot profiles within their own systems, at first to increase their subscriber numbers and subsequently for even more dubious purposes. Last year we found out that Soulmate, the Walmart of dating platforms, had developed bots capable of passing as your average socially obtuse human; and the people in charge of Soulmate were raring to start using them to manipulate subscribers' behaviors and preferences.

What Becks and I have been tussling about ever since Komla exited almost two months ago, leaving us, along with our resident misanthropic tech savant Squirrel, as copartners of Veracity: what to do with this information. After all, what sort of self-respecting detective story stalls out with: *and they sat back to watch the bad guys continue on forever after?*

Whenever we get on the hamster wheel of that argument, Becks will start racing to inform me yet again, like the character saddled with bringing the reader up to speed in chapter one of a sequel, why it's too risky for us to do anything except exactly that: watch, and wait. She'll lead with how the Big Three are billion-dollar companies, versus our two-and-a-half-person operation mucking around on the third floor of a town house in Tribeca. (Here she'll sneak in something snide about Squirrel, wasted because he's never around to hear it.) She'll expound on how Veracity is already hacking into the matchmakers' systems in order to keep tabs on the synths, as we refer to this new generation of bots, and we don't want to give them additional opportunities to learn about us. Finally, as if I could ever forget, she'll remind me that the person running Soulmate's synth program, the very brilliant and very disturbed Lucinda Clay, went so far as to murder a journalist who was trying to write an exposé—and she knows I'm going to say we don't need to worry about Lucinda anymore, which is blatantly wrong for as long as Lucinda herself isn't dead, and regardless there'll be plenty of other people at the matchmakers willing to adopt Lucinda's problem-solving approach, because human beings are a fucked-up species.

Earlier today, when Becks used three variations of the word *risk* in the same sentence, the impulse control gateway of my brain—never too securely latched at the calmest of times—clanged open, and I said, "You're not scared, are you?"

And thank goodness that right then both of our phones pinged to indicate someone was outside the building buzzing to be let in, and our screens brightened with Mason Perry's visage, and so instead of proceeding to eviscerate me like she obviously wanted to do, Becks tapped the ENTRY button on her phone screen and headed into the conference room.

III.

I MAKE MYSELF a second mug of milky tea, settle into my gratifyingly ergonomic chair, pull up the new Symposium album on Spotify, plug in my earphones, and get down to desktop-diligencing Amalia Suarez.

First, what's available in the official public domain. Amalia's LinkedIn profile provides a nifty summary of her educational and professional résumés: high school in Mexico City, UCLA for college; currently a product manager at Vroom, described as *the fastest-growing urban e-mobility company in North America*. I'm able to find backup evidence of her time at UCLA: she won a comp lit department award her junior year for a paper she wrote comparing the Latin American and Japanese traditions of magical realism through an analysis of the detective in the fiction of Jorge Luis Borges and Haruki Murakami—as she should have, because that is indeed an inspired idea. I also confirm her employment from Vroom's website, where her name and picture are included in the *Team* section and where I learn that *urban e-mobility company* means her employer is to blame for the infestation of e-bikes and e-scooters on New York City bike lanes.

Next, the much-less-official public domain. I open up Match Insights, Veracity's custom-built program that indexes online-dating profiles across all the matchmaker platforms we know of. Once upon a time, I thought Veracity licensed this information from the matchmakers; now I know we very quietly siphon it off their systems. Amalia has profiles up on two matchmakers, using the same handle of Amalzz: Let's Meet, where she and Mason matched four months ago, and I Heart You. The information in both profiles is consistent—twenty-nine years old, Mexico City to New York by way of California, loves beaches and spicy food and something called the Somnang Files—and she hasn't logged in to either platform for the past two months.

Because Amalia has linked her Let's Meet profile to her Instagram account, I can look at what she posts on the latter as well. Pictures of her on beaches. Pictures of her at Thai, Indian, and Mexican restaurants. (I take a few personal notes: some of these dishes look amazing.) Pictures of her drinking margaritas with groups of friends. Pictures of an ethnically ambiguous middle-aged man—combination of white and some kind of Asian is my guess—who possesses a beautifully Brylcreemed head of hair and a hell of a broody expression; these are paired with enigmatic quotes (for example, *You only succeed by becoming the enemy you hunt*). The last category confuses me until, with Google's help, I realize that this is Simon Somnang Meade, fictional MI6 agent and star of a series of spy movies set during the Cold War that are collectively known as the Somnang Files.

I'm humming along to the acoustic version of "Eurydice Gets Mad," reflecting on how Symposium has truly outdone itself this time—every song on this album, so good—when I'm startled by a hard double tap on my shoulder. I jump and spin around.

Becks glowers down at me from what feels like an even greater height than usual. Then I realize how low I've slid in my chair. I wiggle upright and pull out my earphones.

"—destroy your eardrums if you keep blasting music at that volume."

I cup one hand around my ear and say, "What? I can't hear you."

The edge of her mouth twitches, which I'll count as a victory—from Becks, that's the equivalent of a laughing-till-crying emoji. Then she says, nodding at my screen, "Anything interesting?"

"Amalia Suarez is really into this indie film franchise about a British-Cambodian spy." So much so that I took an online detour to find out more about the Somnang Files, just in case I've been missing out this whole time, which has included signing up for Somners of Gotham, a mailing list for Somnang fans in the New York metro area. Simon Somnang Meade seems like a secret agent in the Graham Greene mold, a core of existential despair contained within a fractured shell of duty and faith. His following is as tiny as it is devoted. There are meticulously constructed timelines and family trees (Somnang, as he's known, has blood relations conveniently placed throughout the British aristocracy and the Cambodian countryside, all jockeying to either defend or betray him), long-running arguments about various plot points, enough fan fiction to drown in. I get it. My favorite protagonist, Inspector Yuan Lei of the Ming Dynasty Chronicles murder mystery series, is similarly underappreciated, and I love proselytizing about him to everyone while knowing that if he ever went viral I would immediately go look for a new obscure fictional detective to fawn over.

"In other words," says Becks, "no."

"She doesn't seem to be lying about anything." As I say that I feel a twang of disappointment, because I'm an awful person who wouldn't have minded if Mason Perry hit a traffic snag on the no-speed-limit autobahn of his life. "From the desktop work, everything checks out."

Except . . .

There's usually a moment, as I'm learning about a target—how they describe themselves and the type of person they're looking for, how they flirt and banter (or not) on the matchmaker's chat app, what they share on their social media accounts, what is provided through third-party sources like company websites or pictures of public events they have attended—when all this information gloms together into the shape of a person. It's like reading fiction, actually, and getting to a point when the characters finally shake off the writer's words and meet you on their own terms.

And when I had my Amalia Suarez moment, which took place as I was reading through her posts on the subreddit r/Somnang-theSpy, what I thought was: *I don't see her and Mason Perry together. Not at all.*

I almost say that to Becks, but she'd just dismiss it as me being overeager. I'll carry out my observation, and if I find anything to corroborate my intuition I'll bring it up then.

"Also," says Becks, "are you coming in Tuesday and Wednesday next week?"

"Why wouldn't I?"

"It's Lunar New Year."

Is it? But that would mean Monday night is the reunion dinner, and if we haven't made a reservation at Golden Phoenix yet, there's no way in all eighteen levels of Chinese hell the restaurant will be able to cram us in—

"You knew that, right?"

"Yeah," I say. "Of course."

Surely Charles has already taken care of this: he's Mr. Responsibility. Or Coraline, who actually goes to the trouble of helping our mother with LNY prep each year. Although neither of them has said anything about it on our sibling chat group, the Three Cs—or anything at all, come to think of it, in the past couple of weeks.

And: our mother. She's obviously been aware of the dates this whole time but said nothing because she's waiting to see if we'll screw up.

I grab my phone from the desk so I can panic-text my siblings, then think to ask, "Um—was there anything else?"

Becks is already walking away. "I'm stepping out," she says. "I'll be back by two."

IV.

FOR FOUR DAYS, Amalia Suarez is exactly where she's supposed to be at any given time. She goes to work at Building 93 of the Brooklyn Navy Yard, where Vroom is located—from her route, as well as the speed at which she travels and how it doesn't deviate across elevations, I'd guess she's commuting by e-scooter. Afterward she's off to one engagement or another, all consistent with the schedule Mason has given us for her: coed soccer league game, dinner with Mason and another couple, trivia night at her local bar in Crown Heights, date with Mason. Just watching this level of activity makes me feel like taking a nap on the couch.

Mason has requested that we provide a daily accounting of Amalia's whereabouts the next time he comes in to Veracity for an update, which seems a tad stalker-ish to me, although I guess I'm not really in a position to comment. When we asked why, he dimpled at us and said that since he was going through all the trouble of getting this verification done, he might as well have it be comprehensive. "I mean, assuming it's something you can do?"

"Of course," said Becks, and then quoted him a supplemental price that made my eye twitch. Mason simply looked pleased.

"Not a problem," he said. "You have to pay for quality service, I know that."

Just as well he doesn't know how easy it actually is for us to deliver this quality service. All I have to do is pull up the Finders Keepers app a couple of times a day, see where Amalia currently is and has been in the last several hours, and log that in my spreadsheet.

Finders Keepers. That's the one tool we use as verifiers that gives me the sensation of stepping from tolerably squishy moral ground into what could very well be a patch of quicksand. It's a geolocation-tracking app: if we have someone's phone number and they keep their GPS function on—which everyone does, because then your Lyft driver can find you, and you can get accurate directions on Google Maps, and for a thousand other reasons—we can see where they are. I used to believe what Komla told me, which was that we technically had our targets' consent. Users on dating platforms agreed to share their locations via phone GPS with the matchmakers, in order to improve matching results, and the matchmakers in turn had an arrangement to sell that data to third parties like Veracity. Then I found out nobody knew what the hell we were doing. For now, I'm dealing by not thinking about it, which I've heard is the adult way to handle things that make you uncomfortable.

On the fifth day, over the weekend, Amalia vanishes.

I first notice late Saturday morning, after my usual pickup game of Ultimate in Prospect Park. Our side wins, thanks in part to a dive-across-the-grass intercept by yours truly, and so I'm equal parts filthy and triumphant when I pull on my hoodie and take out my phone and do a quick Finders Keepers check on the two targets I'm currently observing. The first is at his parents' house in Westchester; Amalia is MIA. When I look at her location history, I see that Finders Keepers last recorded her at her home, at 8:39 a.m. She probably forgot to charge her phone after she got home last night—she was out until three a.m. at a warehouse party in Bushwick—it died, and she's still asleep.

Seven hours later, she still hasn't popped back up on Finders Keepers.

I consider the options. Her phone suffered a more permanent death. Or she could, for whatever reason, be choosing to leave it off. Maybe she's embarked on a digital cleanse? That would be commendable of her, but it's going to leave a sizable gap in my spreadsheet of Amalia Suarez's whereabouts—and I hate the thought of having to tell Mason Perry that it turned out keeping track of his girlfriend was something we couldn't do after all.

I pace up and down in my living room, in the hope that movement will activate my little gray cells. In *Inspector Yuan and the Sichuan Seven*, one of the prime suspects is a *bian lian* opera artist, a face-changer who switches through hundreds of masks in the course of his performances. The inspector has no idea of the actor's true appearance, not until he sends Constable Zhang to follow the suspect's mother during the Qing Ming Festival and note the man who shows up to help her sweep the ancestral grave. (Of course, the fact that this suspect exhibits such filial piety is a clue to the reader that he cannot be the vicious killer.)

Mason told us he and Amalia would be spending all of Saturday together, and we haven't received any updates to the contrary. So: if I find him, I should be able to find her.

When I enter in Mason's number, he shows up just south of Union Square, at a place called What the Pho? Yelp and Google checks confirm that What the Pho? is the type of establishment that primarily caters to the overlapping Venn diagram of the budget conscious, people who are awake and hungry at one a.m., and college students. An unusual Saturday dinner date choice for a professional couple in their late twenties.

I stare at my screen and think of the disbelief that's sitting like a pebble in my shoe, continuing to chafe until I shake it out. Also, that I'll have to be in Manhattan anyway, for dinner with Maddie and Julia.

I text my friends to say that I'll be late—luckily they have suffered me since high school, so are used to my elastic treatment of time—and then begin the layering process for my bike ride.

As I attempt to lock my bike to a sign pole using the blocks of ice masquerading as my hands, I ask myself, the way I do at this point every winter, whether I should just give in and get the lobster gloves that all the delivery guys seem to have taped to their handlebars. I said once to my roommate, Max, that I was afraid I would start being mistaken for a Chinese food delivery person; his reply was "Don't worry, I think the scale has already been tipped," which was consternating enough for me to forget to point out the pun.

At last I wrangle my U-lock shut. I'm on University Place between East Eleventh and East Twelfth; What the Pho? is across the street. It looks exactly like it does in the photos: big neon signboard and posters advertising 20 percent off this and that, waving cat figurine in the window, basket of take-out menus hanging by the door, condiment caddies on every table. Busy, too, with people walking in and out every few minutes. I study a DoorDasher as he parks his e-bike on the sidewalk and enters, insulated carrier strapped to his back. Hmm. I'm going to assume Max has no idea what he's talking about.

I back up against the wall behind me, into the shadow cast by the pyramid of wilting bouquets outside the neighboring bodega. For anyone else this might come across as suspicious lurking, especially with a feels-like-twenty wind chill, but one feature of being a petite, soft-spoken Asian female is selective (and sometimes not-so-selective) invisibility. I do hope I won't have to hang out for long; according to Google, people typically spend thirty to forty minutes here.

As it is, I'm still slouching into position when Mason leaves the restaurant. Not that I notice, amid the constant in-and-out march of diners and people picking up to-go orders. I get the Finders Keepers triple-buzz alert that my target is moving, and when I check, I see that Mason is already south of me on University Place and heading farther away. I start walking as well, trying to monitor the other side of the street without tripping over myself. Everyone is swaddled in winter paraphernalia, their faces dim and indistinguishable in the darkness. I'm not going to be able to pick him out unless I get uncomfortably close.

I'm trying to decide how long I should follow his pulsing blue dot for when I see it zag—across the street, in my direction. Crap, could he be onto me? Then I register the man pulling open the door of the shop several feet ahead of me, and the girl with him. The light from the store's interior falls upon them and I recognize the patrician angles of Mason Perry's profile.

After they enter I wander past. It's an ice-cream shop, and, unsurprisingly, they're the only customers. I don't have time to get in more than a peek at the girl, as she's inspecting the display cabinet with the gravity of someone selecting an engagement ring, but what I log—medium-brown curly hair, wide eyes, a strong nose, a plushness to the mouth—all fit with the pictures of Amalia Suarez that I've been reviewing.

I install myself in another patch of shadow nearby. While I wait for them to come out I google the Milky Way's menu, and understand Amalia Suarez's equivocation: the place has more than twenty flavors. Honey sriracha? I'll have to come back for that one.

There's the ding of the door closing behind them and then they're strolling down the street, toward me. I keep staring at my screen and start moving my thumbs like I'm composing a treatise in text.

Mason: "So? Is it disgusting?"

Amalia: "It's . . . interesting."

As they pass me, I glance up. They're walking side by side, not touching. Mason is holding a cup; Amalia has gone for the superior option, a waffle cone.

"Sounds like maybe you're having some regrets."

"No! I stand by my choice."

I wait for one of them to offer their ice cream for the other to sample, or to ask to have a taste. Instead, as they step off the sidewalk to move around a group of kids in NYU sweatshirts, Mason says, "Determining compatibility through favorite ice-cream flavors. How's that for a start-up idea? You could set up partnerships with local ice-cream shops . . ."

I follow, cutting through the NYU gaggle. Unfortunately a girl lets out a supersonic shriek of a laugh right as I sidle past her and I don't hear Amalia's response.

When I can see them again, Mason and Amalia are standing at the street corner waiting for the light to turn. I study them from behind. What would I think, without context? Two people who are comfortable enough with each other, who get along. Friends, sure. But lovers?

The WALK sign blinks on. Amalia tosses the remnants of her waffle cone into the trash can. "Although . . ." I hear her say as they start to cross, and I move closer; I'm done following them tonight, but I might as well listen to this. ". . . if I ever meet another person who also goes for the honey sriracha, I might have to marry them."

V.

IT'S FUNNY HOW I can tell, across the crowded length of the restaurant, in anemic lighting, with only the back of her head and the set of her shoulders visible to me, that my mother is Pissed. My body knows it before I do: a corkscrewing in my stomach, an ancient, familiar, momentarily unbearable sensation. What if I turned around and walked out again? No one has seen me yet.

My phone buzzes in my jacket pocket. It's Coraline: *Don't even think about it.*

I look over again and see that my sister has stood up from her seat at the table, all the better to glare at me. She waves in my direction and three separate servers swerve toward her. I call it the C-field: the geomagnetic force of Coraline's beauty. I've witnessed its effects since I was a kid—the way others look at her, the things they say, how they maneuver to be around her—but it's still always impressive, and also residually disturbing. Maybe I even notice it more now that I'm working at Veracity, where so much of my time is spent with our targets' virtual personas, mapping them to how these people move through the physical world. In the beginning I looked for gaps between the two. Now I know there will always be gaps. What matters is how wide, and how deep.

"Welcome to the Blue Lotus. Do you have a reservation?"

The doubt in the maître d's tone is as exquisitely faceted as a twenty-four-carat diamond, and despite my misgivings about committing myself to this dinner, I derive some satisfaction from being able to point and say, "I'm with that table."

He turns around and then back again. "Excellent. You are the final outstanding member of your party." He picks up a menu. "Would you like to check your coat?"

I try to remember the last time I dined at an establishment where that question was asked non-facetiously. "I'm fine."

I follow him past table after table of sleek, well-dressed, predominantly white people sipping from wineglasses and cutting into the pastel-hued dumplings on their plates with forks and knives. What was Coraline thinking? The dumplings do pique my appetite—they're very plump—but an Asian fusion restaurant in the West Village named after a Tintin comic book is so not a venue where real Chinese families gather to celebrate their most culturally significant meal of the year.

We arrive at my family's table, which is obviously a table for four with an extra place setting squeezed in next to a man I have never before seen in my life.

I glance around to check if anyone else seems perturbed by this. My mother is squinting at her menu as if reviewing it—except she isn't, because her reading glasses remain lodged right above her hairline. Charles, to her left, hunches over his phone typing out some asap work email. Becks would have something absolutely scathing to say about his posture. I'd been wondering if his girlfriend, Jessie, would join us: guess not. Maybe she needs a break from the Lin family circus.

Across from my brother, Coraline lowers herself back into her chair. Now that I'm closer, I can sense the current of anxiety zapping off her. The C-field is under some strain this evening.

Last month Julia bullied me and Maddie into accompanying her to an improv class. It wasn't my thing—I embarrass myself around random people enough as it is—but now I find myself thinking of what the instructor told us: *Yes, and . . .* Accept the reality you have been presented with and build on it.

"I'm glad we're trying something new," I say. "This place looks amazing!"

"Doesn't it?" says Coraline. "It only opened last year and it already has a Michelin star."

Our mother says, without looking up, "What does that mean? Western people think this is good Chinese food?"

I say, "Coraline, do I get an introduction to your gentleman friend?"

"Oh!" says Coraline, like she's forgotten all about this large male sitting in her personal space. "Yes. This is Richard." She turns to him. "My sister, Claudia."

Richard smiles at me, bright and guileless, unaware that the floor beneath him is really a covered pit of poison-tipped spikes. He could be a fraternal twin of any number of my sister's exes: tall, fair, well groomed, assured, B-list actor handsome. "Lovely to meet you. Coraline tells me you're an intrepid New York City cyclist."

His British accent is crisper than a Granny Smith. My inner Anglophile upgrades his attractiveness by a notch. As I make my way around the table, I say, "Just foolhardy, I think."

"I'm very impressed. When I was at Oxford I cycled everywhere, but I'm too much of a melt to face the traffic here."

Another notch. "I'll take traffic any day over five-hundred-year-old cobblestones." That's one of my gripes with Tribeca, where I bike to every morning for work. Perfectly serviceable roads are constantly being torn up and cobblestoned for maximum quaintness—and real estate prices—and juddering over them always makes me worry that I might knock a filling loose.

"My secret was loads of seat padding." Richard pauses. "I meant the bicycle seat."

Coraline flaps her menu over the center of the table; Richard discreetly shifts her cocktail to safety. "Let's order. Mom? What do you want?"

"You order," says our mother. "I don't know anything on this menu."

"You do, they just use a lot of words to describe everything. There's *shao rou*, duck, tofu—"

"Dumplings!" I say.

"Should we order the fish?" asks Richard. "For *nian nian you yu*?"

Even Charles lifts his head at that: the rising and falling sounds of Mandarin uttered so fluently by this literally and figuratively exceedingly white man. Beside Richard, Coraline is smirking like she's Henry Higgins presenting Eliza Doolittle at a royal ball.

"You know Chinese!" I say—and thank god our mother didn't start commenting about him in Mandarin prior to this revelation.

"I'm learning." He's pinking a little at our attention. "It's a difficult language."

"The way you speak," says our mother, "is good. Much better than Claudia."

"You're too kind. I'm sure Claudia—"

"No. She is hopeless."

"In more ways than one," I agree. "Okay, are we ready?"

The ordering process rapidly devolves into chaos, as it tends to whenever my family dines at any restaurant that is not Golden Phoenix, where we've had decades to codify our order. Coraline quizzes the server for recommendations and then disregards all of them. Our mother, despite her initial abdication of responsibility, starts asking why we're not adding this or that, including dishes that aren't even available here. When the server reads back everything to us, Charles says we have ordered way too much. We start negotiating over what to eliminate. I offer to give up the dumplings, but everyone else objects: it would be sacrilege not to consume *jiaozi* during Chinese New Year. Finally we send the server off to see if the kitchen can give us a half portion of the duck dish—"And if not," says Coraline, "then we still want it, the whole thing—but we'll take out the fried rice."

I'm hopeful that this frenzy of activity has tired out our mother, or at least diverted her sufficiently from the prior *look at my lousy Chinese daughter* topic of conversation, but she leans forward and says to Richard, "You can also read? And write? In Chinese?"

Of course he can. "Although my *fan ti* needs work," he clarifies.

Our mother's gaze levels from him to me and back again as she says, "And it's not even your culture."

"It's one I admire greatly. The history and the civilization, of course, but also how much beauty there is in it. I lived in Shanghai for several years. I taught English, did some translation work on the side. Traveled as much as I could. The more I experienced of China, the more I—"

Charles scrapes his chair back and stands; we all stare at him. "Sorry," he says. "I have to take this."

I watch him excuse his way through a large party toward the doors of the Blue Lotus, phone pressed to his ear. Charles is a manager at Precision Consulting, one of those professional services firms that companies pay lots of money to so kids a few years out of college—including a bunch of people I knew at Margrave, now sleep-deprived PowerPoint wizards at McKinsey and Bain—can feed them elaborate gibberish about how to better run their businesses. He's in the social-tech group, which covers the matching industry, and his big project for the past several months has been for a matchmaker client. I've been trying to find out more about it when I can, on the principle that any activity involving a matchmaker and NSA-clearance levels of secrecy—Charles won't even tell us which matchmaker this is—must contain at least a tiny bit of nefariousness.

Our server approaches with our appetizers. I'm disappointed by the surface area ratio of plate to edible content. As he's refilling our water glasses, our mother says to us, like she's making a joke, "Such a long time to cook so little."

I remind myself: *Yes, and* . . . "It looks really busy in here. The kitchen is probably backed up."

"But they have space for us. Not like other Chinese restaurants."

"Actually, they didn't." Coraline leans forward and says, lowering her voice, "We took someone else's reservation."

"What?" I say.

"But, like, legally. I know the guy who owns this place, so I asked if he could get us a table for tonight and he moved some things around. The other people can just eat here another day."

Our mother turns her fork around in her hand like she has no idea how to use this implement. "You shouldn't ask for favors. He will want you to pay back."

I say, "Let's eat before the food gets cold."

It takes us all of three minutes to finish the appetizers—which, as it turns out, are chilled—but at least during that time no one speaks. I'm about to try to reset the mood by sharing a universally adorable video of sunbathing capybaras when our mother says, "Richard."

He looks up from his plate. "Yes?"

"Why did you leave?"

"I beg your pardon?"

"China. If you love it so much."

Richard nods as if she's asked the most insightful question of the century. This dude really is exemplary meet-the-Asian-parent material. "There were a few different reasons," he says. "But the biggest one, well . . . I suppose I came to feel like I would never belong, not the way I wanted to."

"I see," our mother says. "Is that why you date Chinese girls? Try to get as close as you can?"

We're sitting in the miasma of mortification generated by our mother's questions when Charles rejoins us. "Food's still not here?"

"You missed the appetizers," I say. "Now we're waiting for the entrées. Was that work?"

Coraline picks up her cocktail and says to it, "I'm going to need another five of these."

"My brother has been really busy with a big consulting project," I explain to Richard, whose hue is beginning to ebb from tomato to salmon.

"What's it about?" he asks Charles, exactly as I'd hoped he would.

"Did you meet my sister online?"

Richard's face reddens back up as if he's already anticipating our mother's next salvo. Beside him, Coraline tosses her hair back and says, "Of course. Who meets offline anymore?"

"Which platform was it?"

Richard and Coraline glance at each other in that bashful-coy way that new couples do. He says, "Partnered Up."

"I won't ask what your comp score—"

"Ninety-two percent!" says Coraline.

"Okay," says Charles. "Basically, my client's goal is to improve the accuracy of that rating by taking a more sophisticated approach to the types of data that go into generating those scores."

"Hold on," says Coraline. "Are you saying that our rating isn't accurate?"

"The margin of error isn't insignificant. How do matchmakers develop their comp scores? They—"

"Is *not* insignificant . . . so it's significant! The error."

"Not quite. *Significant* would be an order of magnitude up, like a thirty- or forty-basis-point deviation. *Not insignificant* is more—"

Sometimes I think if I were to read the things my brother says on a matching app chat, I'd flag him as a synth failing to pass as human. I say, before Coraline can spiral into preemptively break-ing up with Richard right now, "Isn't it better that the match-makers aren't, like, super accurate? That would take all the fun out of dating."

My siblings glance at each other, and I can tell what they're thinking: so says smartass baby sister, who has never tried match-ing herself and hasn't even been able to level up from the short-term hookup stage of the relationship game. For an instant I wish I could bolster my position with everything I do know. About the matchmakers, but also about all the people who rely on them, who walk into Veracity and talk to us about their matches—how excited they are, and afraid, and hopeful.

But, and this is definitely for the best, my family has no idea about what I do at Veracity, or that I work there in the first place. Originally, when I thought I was just playing online-dating detec-tive, I didn't want to tell them because they would disapprove of how eccentric that was, and also unconducive for any sort of respectable career progression. Now, all those reasons still apply, plus there's the issue of the associated body count and—probably worse in my family's view—the around-the-fringes-illegal nature of some of the things we do.

Coraline says, "There's nothing fun about wasting years of your life on a douchebag."

Typical Coraline exaggeration: she was with her ex Lionel for only a year and a half. (Although he *was* a douchebag, and an even drippier one than she knew.) "All I mean," I say, "is that maybe falling in love should be like a mystery. Something you solve together as you go along." Suddenly I hear Becks in my mind, that impatient tone, slightly scratchy like she's on the perpetual cusp of a sore throat (without, alas, ever actually contracting one and losing her voice): *That analogy makes no fucking sense.* "Like, whether the two of you can actually be together. Or it's just some weird attraction that's going to go nowhere."

The entrées arrive, barely more substantial than the appetizers. I wait for our mother to make another snide remark, but she's silent as she watches the server set them down on the table.

After the server leaves, Charles says, "No leftovers, that's for sure."

"I didn't hear anyone else say they would make a reservation."

If voices were weapons, Coraline's would have sliced him right in half. My brother blinks. Then he says, "Chill out, Cor. I was just making a comment. You don't have to be so sensitive about everything."

"Do you know how hard it was to find a legit Chinese place for tonight?"

Now our mother joins in, like the *wuxia* grandmaster floating down into the quarrel between her underlings, except instead of calling for harmony she maims them both. "You said you specially planned for us to come here."

I say, "We did"—that being the cover story up until fifteen seconds ago. "We always go to Golden Phoenix. We thought we would shake things up, try a restaurant with a different color and Chinese motif in its name."

Richard chuckles politely. No one else reacts.

"Not because you all forgot," says our mother. "*Tuan yuan fan* doesn't mean anything."

Our server leans in over our table. "How is everything?"

"It's great!" I say, just as Richard says, "Just marvelous."

Coraline says, "If we forgot, we wouldn't be sitting here right now."

"Then this is on purpose," says our mother. "Sitting here the only Chinese people stupid enough to pay this kind of money to eat this food. At this table where Claudia doesn't even have a proper seat."

"That's what she gets for being the latest."

Which is rich coming from the woman whose friends will tell her they're meeting up thirty minutes earlier than they in fact are, but I'm not about to start an ancillary dispute with my sister. "I'm totally fine," I say.

Our mother sits back. "I'm tired," she says. "I think I'm ready to go home."

Charles, Coraline, and I take turns looking at one another, tracing out a little Bermuda triangle of consternation: this isn't a ploy our mother has tried before. Charles says, "Okay. We'll finish up and then I'll drive you back."

"I mean now."

"And leave all this?" says Coraline.

"That's what you want, right?" says our mother. "All of you don't want to be here."

I say, "Of course we want to be here."

"Charlie, what street did you park? I will go to the car first."

"What? No," says my brother. "We'll all leave together. Let me just get the check."

I'm thinking about how glad I am that I was able to lock my bike right in front of the restaurant, so once we get outside I can make my farewells and escape, when Coraline says, "This is so stupid! We pay for all this food and then walk out without trying it? I'm staying." She glares at Richard. "We're staying."

Charles, who has been glancing about trying to get the attention of a server, looks at her. She says to him, "You should stay too."

None of us moves, but suddenly I feel like the one still standing after the music has cut off and everyone has rushed for the chairs. That's the way the game always goes. My brother and my sister, together, and me. I can't blame them for it: so much of what holds Charles and Coraline together is the experience of being forcibly transplanted from rural Taiwan, away from our grandparents and a bucolic setting worthy of a Studio Ghibli anime, to the confined chaos of New York, with a disappearing act of a father and a mother who made it clear, through a thousand cuts, that they were here only because she had no other choice. Still, when I was younger, I would sometimes pretend, only to myself, that I had also been sent off when I was born and then brought back when my grandparents became too old to continue taking care of us, and it was just that no one knew about it, so I could feel like I belonged with my siblings.

Our mother rises. Her expression is subway-commuter blank, the look of someone about to get off at her stop. She lifts her coat from the back of her chair and puts it on. Of course she wouldn't have checked it, to save on the tip.

Coraline says to Charles, "Just order a car to take her back. You're not her driver."

My brother opens his mouth, and I realize, with that same corkscrewing feeling as before, everything in me winching tighter and tighter, that I have no idea what he will say.

"Disappointment," says our mother, "all of you."

Coraline says, "Maybe people get what they deserve."

"Everything I did—"

"Can we please, for once, not be this family? Please?"

Everyone turns to me. I can see the alarm flickering in their expressions, as if they're afraid I might start bawling, which is absurd because since age ten the only time I ever cry is when I'm watching emotionally manipulative Disney movies.

"Okay," says Charles, like he's trying out the pronunciation of an unfamiliar word. "Okay."

Coraline spears a cube of roasted pork. She's not looking at our mother when she says, "You want to talk about all the things you did?"

Richard says to her, gently, "Why don't I stay and settle the bill? You can head out first with your family. I remember you made the reservation on the earlier side in case it took a while to drive back to Queens."

She doesn't say anything.

"I'll ask them to pack the food for takeaway." He smiles at her like they're the only two people at the table, in the restaurant, in the world. "We can spread it out over all fifteen days of the new year."

Lunar New Year is really fifteen days long? So glad it's such a nonevent here.

"Cor, I can drop you off on the way to Flushing," says Charles.

Coraline shakes her head. "I'll wait for Richard."

"I'm going outside," says our mother. "This place is too noisy."

Charles gets up when she says that, but when she turns and walks away he doesn't move. She has to squeeze her way through the people gathered at the bar, and I can see how none of them even notices her, the small older Asian woman in the puffy coat, her head down, her arms hemmed to her sides. They shift aside, barely, and then close the gap again, and it's like she was never there.

My brother is still standing at his seat, clutching his precious phone. He says, looking down at Coraline, "*Ta jiu shi ze yang ma*"—that's just the way she is.

I don't understand Coraline's response, but I don't have to: she flings it at Charles like a Molotov. Richard glances between the two of them, and it's weird—as in sickening—to think that this almost stranger can be a part of my siblings' exchange in a way that I can't.

Then Charles turns to me and tips his head in the direction of the Blue Lotus's doors. "Come on, Claw," he says.

I don't look at my sister as I follow him out of the restaurant.

VI.

I'M AT THE OFFICE by eight the next morning, which is the earliest I've managed this year by a generous margin. Becks isn't in yet. I turn on the lights, disarm the alarm system; Squirrel has rigged everything up on our phones, so all I need to do is tap icons. From the outside our building looks like the other Federal-style town houses on Harrison Street, three stories of stately redbrick and symmetrical windows, but Veracity's decor is all modern minimalism. White walls and ash wood floors, unadorned desks and chairs. Everything about it whispers *discreet*.

I dump my bag on my desk and then take my time making my tea in the pantry in the back. I even go into the room I still think of as Komla's office to water his overgrown-yet-still-growing potted plant, and end up standing by the windows for a few minutes. A pair of workmen are unloading a van, the only movement on the street. The lemony morning light slants across the cobblestones, and I must admit they look charming from where I am. It's soothing, being here alone like this, after last night's drama—I'm a literary contrarian when it comes to Hemingway, but right now I'll give him his clean, well-lighted place.

After Komla left Veracity, Becks asked if I wanted to take over his office, rather than continuing to sit out front like a glorified receptionist. I said no. I like watching our clients come in through the door—you can tell a lot from how they walk, the way they look around, whether they hesitate at all. (Mason Perry, for instance: entitled as a viscount.) Also, I guess there's a bit of superstition on my part, of trying to bargain with the universe: if we leave Komla's room empty, maybe he'll be more likely to come back.

Becks arrives a little after nine. When she sees me she says, like I've let her down, "Aren't you out today?"

I had originally told her that I would take the first day of Lunar New Year off, with the idea of visiting my mother. I've already fallen behind on my every-three-weeks resolution, which just goes to show why I should stop making resolutions: I don't adjust my behavior, but I feel guiltier about it. I say, "I changed my mind."

She transfers her thermos to her other hand. "Is your family that insufferable?"

"What?"

"You'd rather come to work than see them."

"I like coming to work," I say. "I mean, not that I don't like my family, too. I like them both. Just saying that one has nothing to do with the other."

She considers me. She's brought the cold in with her, lingering like a scent around her hair and her coat. "Good for you," she says. "Mine is a huge pain in the ass."

Then she turns around and walks back out through the front door.

I stare at her through the glass. She's raising her phone to her ear as she steps into the elevator and out of view. What just happened?

It's only when I sit back down at my desk that I register the truly bizarre part of that exchange. Her *family*? Becks Rittel and

I have worked together for seven months now, during which time we've solved a murder, gate-crashed a gala, uncovered a corporate conspiracy, and become co-owners of an online-dating detective agency, and she still acts like disclosing anything personal could launch a nuclear war. Pretty much all I know about her life, based on daily observation, is that she has a monochromatic wardrobe and reading tastes wide-ranging enough to stock a library. And, now, a pain-in-the-ass family. Unsurprising, on one hand, given what a pain in the ass Becks herself is; but also semi-shocking, that the concept of family is applicable to her at all. She puts me in mind of Athena, sprung fully formed from some divine source, regal and wrathful. Not that I'll ever tell her that.

Becks returns in the early afternoon with the news that we have a client intake meeting in thirty minutes. "Pradeep Mehta," she says. "He's in the calendar for tomorrow, but he's been harassing me for an earlier slot. Since you're here today, I figured we could move him forward."

"You don't usually care about what our clients want," I say.

"I don't. But if that man sends me one more whiny email I'm going to punch him when he shows up."

Pradeep Mehta gives me the impression of having run all the way from the subway station on Chambers Street and up the two flights of stairs to our office. He pulls open the door, steps inside, and says to me from several feet away, "Excuse me. I have an appointment."

He glances at his watch, taps it, looks back at me. He's a slim man, medium height, with a cap of wavy black hair and large, intent eyes. There's a jitteriness about him, like he's either over-caffeinated or inordinately anxious. Maybe it's the fact that he's here, ready to hire us to audit whomever he's dating without their knowledge or consent. It makes almost all our prospective clients uneasy, to some extent, and the ones who are unfazed we reject. As Becks pointed out: "The worse they feel about what they ask us to do, the less likely are to ever blab to anyone about it."

I get up from my desk. "Yes," I say. "Pradeep, right?" He's ten minutes early, which means the ten minutes I intended to spend looking over his precheck results no longer exist and I'm heading into this session knowing nothing about the guy except that he's in full-on crisis mode. Luckily, Becks will be prepared—she always is. "I'm Claudia. Let me go get Becks."

Pradeep starts talking the moment we enter the conference room. "My identity's been stolen. I need your help to stop it." The rolling slope of his accent is slight but distinct: he didn't grow up speaking American English.

Becks and I look at each other. She clicks the door shut behind her. "Do you even have any idea what we do?"

"Yes, of course. You check up on people who are dating online. Breon Jones told me about your service."

So Pradeep is Breon's referral. I remember Breon Jones well. He contacted us the week before Christmas, having impulsively invited the man he'd been dating for three months to spend the holidays with his family in Atlanta. *I don't so much mind if he's lied here and there*, he told us. *I mean, I have, right? Nothing too big, but, you know. I just need to know what he lied about, because my mom and my sis* will *find all that out once they get their hands on him, and I need to be ready.* Becks gave him hell for jamming us on the deadline, but we completed our verification in time, and he was so grateful that he delivered a hummingbird cake as a thank-you. Custom made—he owns a bakery up in Harlem. I still dream about that cake.

Becks says, "Then why are we even talking right now? Go put a freeze on your credit cards instead of wasting our time."

"It's not that kind of . . ." Pradeep shakes his head. "Maybe I'm not being clear. This is my online identity—my Let's Meet profile. Someone stole it."

I ask, "Someone has taken over your dating profile?"

Another head shake. "Cloned it." He digs into the pocket of his jacket. "I'll show you."

What Pradeep shows us, holding out his phone like an entry pass, is a picture of a South Asian man around his age, with the same milky-tea skin tone. I glance from the screen to Pradeep's face and back. They do look similar, like two permutations of the same set—although once I think that I worry that I'm just being racist—but these are clearly two different people. Handle: *Silent G.* Last active: *Two hours ago.*

I hear Becks take a breath. I say, before she can lead with anything too rude, "That's, um, not your picture."

"Not the pictures. The information." He points at the text right below the photo. "Thirty-three years old. Midtown, New York. Same as me."

"I didn't know anyone actually *lived* in Midtown," I say. Or would want to.

"It's close to my work. That, also." Pradeep flicks a finger across the screen. "Works in commercial real estate. Came to New York four years ago. Vegetarian." Another flick. "Cricket player. Likes action movies and video games. And this."

I read: *On my life to-do list: Cycle the Friendship Highway.* "What's the Friendship Highway?"

"A cycling route. Through Tibet—you go from Lhasa to the Nepal border. This isn't even in my profile."

Seems like something I should include on my own currently nonexistent life to-do list. "It sounds epic," I say. "How long is the ride?"

"Google it later," says Becks. To Pradeep: "If that wasn't in your profile, how could it have been copied *from* your profile?"

"It wasn't. He already knew about it. I told him. That's why he put it in."

This is reminding me of the Shadow Fist sequence in *Inspector Yuan and the Chrysanthemum Palace*: the more practitioners learn of that skill, the less they can recall of it. (Which seems at once profound as a life philosophy and unworkable as a martial art.) What follow-up question to even ask here?

"Are you being incoherent on purpose, or do you really not know how to talk to people?"

Definitely not that. I grab Becks's arm as the slightly more acceptable alternative to telling her to shut up. Pradeep's restless manner, together with those Bambi eyes, makes me think of an injured deer. He's stumbling toward us now—emphasis on *stumbling*—but he could just as easily panic and flee.

Becks glances at me, one eyebrow arched. I immediately let go. Very warm in this conference room, all of a sudden. I say to Pradeep, "What you said just now. That *he* already knew about it. Who are you referring to?"

He lowers his phone. "He's . . ." For the first time in the conversation, I sense him pausing over what words he should use. "We were . . . together. Not anymore."

"When you say *together*," I say, "you mean you were dating this person?"

Pradeep shifts his feet. "Yes," he says. "I guess so."

"The profile picture you showed us. Is that him?"

"No. Matthew is American."

After a moment I say, "And when you say *American*, you mean . . . white?"

"Yes."

I would be more irked by these staunchly uncooperative responses if not for the feeling I'm getting that, to Pradeep, this relationship—or this man, or both—was a danger to him, such that he's only able to talk around it, even now. "So, it sounds like you think your ex—Matthew, that's his name?—set up this Silent G profile with your information in it?"

"Yes, yes. That's what I've been saying this whole time. That's why I came to you."

"Why do you think he would do that?"

"That's not important. He is, so I have to stop it."

"Who's asking for help here?" says Becks. "Answer Claudia's question."

Again, that pause: selecting his words, and his story. Then he says, "I ended it. Between us. It made Matthew angry."

Becks says, "That doesn't mean he's behind this."

"Of course he is." Pradeep gestures at his phone with his free hand. "He knows all these things about me, and he put it on Let's Meet, and—"

"What does the fact that it's Let's Meet have to do with anything?" says Becks.

"Matthew works at Let's Meet."

"That's called a coincidence."

"No," says Pradeep, "it's not. He has access to the back-end systems. He changed the . . . What is it called? How you rank with other people."

"The compatibility score," I say. Now there's an industry term I wish would be replaced. The idea of a points system feels antithetical to romance, although that might also just be my visceral reaction from a lifetime of mediocre grades.

"I have a one hundred percent score with Silent G."

"That's not possible," says Becks. "The algorithms never go above ninety-six."

He taps his phone screen and then turns it to us. His matches are ordered in list view. Silent G's thumbnail picture is at the top, and the badge icon next to it that Let's Meet uses to display its comp scores indeed says *100%*.

Becks takes out her own phone. After a few seconds she says,

"Hmm." She tilts the screen so I can see. She's pulled up Pradeep's Let's Meet profile (handle: That's Deep) on Match Insights—same comp score.

That was how he came to know about Silent G, Pradeep tells us: the profile showed up in his matches. Once he viewed it, he realized Matthew had set everything up. "You see. He's messing with me."

Becks is still scowling at her screen. "How do we know this Matthew even exists?"

"What? Of course he exists. Why would I make up all this?"

"Any reason. No reason. Veracity wouldn't be here if people didn't go around making up dumb shit all the time."

I say, "Not that we think you did"—the accusatory edge of Becks's tone notwithstanding.

"What's his full name?" says Becks. "As a start we can look at his LinkedIn profile and see what it says about his role at Let's Meet."

"He's not on LinkedIn," says Pradeep. "He doesn't like social media."

"Smart of him. And convenient for you."

"I'm not . . ." He pulls his shoulders back. "I'm not crazy, and I'm not lying. Matthew is real. He's real and he's doing this to me."

This is one of those times when I wish Komla were still here, not simply because I miss him, his magnificent smiles and his unflappability and the way he had of making you feel like what you had to say was important, but also because he was our client whisperer. If he were running this intake, Pradeep would be reading us entries from his diary by this point. But it's just me and Becks now, and without a personality reboot Becks wouldn't be anyone's last choice for a confidante.

I nod and say, "That's exactly why it's important for us to have a better understanding of who he is." One of Inspector Yuan's maxims in witness interviews and sword fighting showdowns alike:

use your counterparty's momentum to move yourself forward. "He's at the center of this situation. We won't be able to assess your situation without information about him as well."

Pradeep looks from Becks to me and back again. I find myself willing him to be convinced. There's a mystery here—what really happened between him and Matthew, what's happening to him now—and I want to find out.

"Matthew Espersen," he says. "That's his name."

I spend the next ten minutes tweezing additional splinters of information out of Pradeep: Matthew has been at Let's Meet for the past three years, as an IT infrastructure specialist; Pradeep met him on Ballsy, a boutique hookup app for gay men; they dated for a year; they broke up in December, shortly before Pradeep flew back to India to visit his family. "It was the right thing to do," he says. "Yes."

He looks down at his phone. He taps the screen a few times, stares at it, and then abruptly holds it up to me. "This is him."

There's an ascetic air to Matthew Espersen, despite his smile and his comfortably baggy T-shirt (the quote on it: I KNOW A DEEP LEARNING JOKE BUT IT'S SHALLOW). The close-shaved head, maybe, or how his skin looks vacuum-sealed to his bone structure, or his vampiric pallor. He reminds me of a monk let out from his cell after about a decade of prayer and fasting. Pradeep is next to him, shoulder to shoulder. The sun is bright on their faces. They're on the High Line. I can tell it's the West Twenties stretch of the park from the wedge of the Chelsea Piers facade visible behind them, and summertime from how intrusively green everything is.

And, Pradeep—he looks all woozy with happiness, as if to be where he is, with this man, like this, is more than he could ever have thought to ask for. It makes me think again about his reticence when it comes to Matthew. Maybe the danger he feels he has to skirt around is really himself.

"That was on my birthday."

Pradeep presses a button on his phone to dim the screen. He holds up his wrist. The face of his watch gleams at us: another, smaller screen, crowded with icons. "He gave me this. To help monitor my physio KPIs."

Now that I'm up close I can appreciate what a fancy smart-watch it is. Even the strap looks futuristic, made of some meshy material with a squiggly logo embossed on it. This device should be communicating with other galaxies, not monitoring heart rates and calories burned. "Are you a physio-quant?" I ask. It's a con-cept I inadvertently became familiar with while verifying a target who was an endurance-event enthusiast. Three days of observa-tion in, I realized that when she talked about *tracking my macros*, she was referring to her daily intake of fats, carbohydrates, and proteins, which she carefully regulated for *performance optimization*. She seemed like she might be a troublesome dinner date, and in the end our client agreed as well; at our final debrief, he told us he didn't think it was going to work out. (It took every ounce of my self-control, plus Becks giving me the Medusa stare, not to shout out the pun.)

Pradeep shrugs. "The approach makes sense. Your body is like a machine. You need to know the inputs, and how to adjust them, so you get the outputs you want. Most people operate at a sub-optimal level and they have no idea why. It's exercise, nutrition, rest—everything."

"But," I say, "at what cost?" Giving up refined sugars to extend sentience by a few years at the scraggly tail end of things really doesn't seem worth it.

Becks, who has been on her phone during this time—researching Matthew Espersen, I suspect—says, "Can we focus?" She looks at Pradeep. "What are you expecting us to do here?"

He opens his mouth.

"Stop whatever you believe is happening to you. I get that, you've said it seventeen times. But how?"

He closes his mouth, then opens it again. "You find out the truth about people. What they put on their profiles. And I'm telling you, this Silent G profile, it's fake—"

"That's my point," says Becks. "We verify the target and we tell the client if there's anything false. You already know Silent G isn't a real profile. There's nothing more for us to do."

"Maybe . . ." I say.

She glares at me and I shut up. She's right, much as I dislike admitting it. This might be a mystery, but it's not a case. At least not one that Veracity can take on.

Pradeep blinks at us like he's been spun around. "Breon said you could help."

"And I'm guessing you didn't tell Breon what you actually wanted help with."

He's silent.

"Look," says Becks. "Just report Silent G to the matchmaker as a spam profile."

"I don't want to draw attention to this. I just want the profile to be taken down."

"If you want the profile to be taken down, you need to draw attention to it. Let's Meet will only take action if you make it too annoying for them not to."

"You don't understand. I can't have that profile out there like that."

Becks steps to the door and opens it. "*You* don't understand. We can't do anything for you."

I say, because Pradeep is looking through the doorway as if he's being ordered into the Battle of the Somme, "I know it's, um, frustrating, having that profile out there, based on your information. If you're concerned that it could mess with your matching results, you could switch to another platform?"

"I don't care about that," he says. "It's how he could use it to . . . If people saw, if they thought . . . It's just—it's bad."

Before I can ask, *Bad how?* Becks says, "If you can't live with that profile being up, then report it, for Christ's sake. This is something for the matchmaker to deal with, not us."

"He knows," says Pradeep. "That's why he's doing this. He knows exactly how bad this is for me."

He keeps his gaze ahead of him as he walks out of the room. Becks doesn't say anything, and so neither do I.

VII.

ON MY SECOND MOSEY down East Tenth Street between First and Second Avenues, I notice the group milling about on the opposite sidewalk. Specifically, what's on their heads: Panama hats, safari helmets, fedoras, even one of those conical straw hats that I associate with rice paddies and irreversibly back-damaging exertion. I check Finders Keepers. Amalia Suarez resurfaced last Sunday, after a twenty-four-hour blackout, and since then I've had no further issues tracking her. Right now it looks like she's at Houston and First Avenue—on her e-scooter, it will take her only a few more minutes to get here.

Yesterday Mason Perry emailed us what he knew of Amalia's weekend schedule. On Saturday, his note said, she would be in New Haven visiting her cousin. Reading that sentence, I thought of what Inspector Yuan would sometimes say to his sidekick, Constable Zhang: *This feels like walking into a house with bad feng shui.* (To which loyal, bovine Constable Zhang would respond with something like: *But we're in a forest.*) I only figured out why when I received that day's Somners of Gotham digest email, which included a reminder of Saturday's *A Gentleman's Game* screening—an event several members, one Amalia S. included, had already proclaimed their excitement for.

I cross the street and ask one of the helmets, who's standing by the curb, "Is this for the *A Gentleman's Game* screening?"

"Yep." He's a stout man, middle-aged, with a nose like a capillaried light bulb. The headgear makes him look like one of those colonial explorers basking on the veranda of a bungalow built with forced labor, perpetually sloshed, complaining about the laziness of the natives. He points at the building we're all gathered in front of. It's a beige-colored low-rise that has several decades' worth of New York City filth grimed onto its facade, unmarked, residential; I had walked right by it earlier. "Down the stairs."

I can see, in between another helmet and a trench coat, a half flight of steps leading down to what looks like a garden-level service entrance. "That's the Firefly Theatre?"—which was what the Somners of Gotham website listed as the location for this event, indicating, I had assumed, a venue that was actually a theater.

"Sure is."

I have a vision of myself stepping through that door and my bones being found fifty years later, bricked up into a basement wall. What are the chances that this movie fan club turns out to be an operation reenacting Edgar Allan Poe's gruesomest stories?

Which is when I realize: "Operation Firefly."

To prepare for this afternoon, I spent last night binge-watching the Somnang Files. Admittedly I kept dozing off—Somnang spends a lot of time walking around in different Southeast Asian cities that all look the same after a while, either dusty or deluged, always hot and chaotic; he's perennially tailing someone unspecified or being tailed by someone unspecified—but I do remember Operation Firefly in *A Gentleman's Game*. Somnang's mission to identify a Communist mole in the British embassy in Saigon implodes, and he's forced to hide in a local family's basement unit while a North Vietnamese assassin known only as "the Dream" searches for him.

The man nods like I'm his spy cadet protégée. The screening before this, he tells me—*With Other Means*, the first film in the franchise—took place at the Yale Club, an homage to Operation Sundial, where there's a handoff of incriminating papers in the library of a Belgravian gentleman's club.

It occurs to me: "Have you thought about serving themed snacks as well?"

"The purists among us believe it would be a distraction from the film."

We turn around. Amalia Suarez is standing on the road behind us, wearing a black fur hat that's at least three sizes too large. Next to her, her e-scooter looks like a long-necked mechanical pet.

"Not me," she adds. "I'm too sloppy to be a purist about anything."

"I don't know you at all," I say, "obviously, but your hat suggests otherwise. It looks exactly like what Petrovich was wearing in *Sons in Exile*." On Somnang's Soviet nemesis, the headdress seems to serve as a substitute for character development. On Amalia, it just makes her look ridiculous. But also, very cute.

The man with us says, with the air of an art appraiser faced with a dubious Warhol, "Shape's off. Petrovich's ushanka is flatter on top."

"Pete's the purist," says Amalia. "I'm Amalia, by the way."

"Jiayi," I say—my Chinese name, which no one outside my family uses or even knows about.

Amalia collapses her e-scooter into a package with practiced quickness, picks it up, and says to us both, "Shall we descend?"

The building's basement is shabby, paint peeling off the walls and randomly exposed pipes, but reasonably clean and so brightly lit my pores feel like they're under scrutiny. I follow Amalia and

Purist Pete down a corridor to our cinema, which turns out to be the laundry room. It's an ingenious setup: a projector on a table at one end, the wall opposite for the screen, and the washers and dryers that line the length of the room as seating. When we enter, a fedora is hanging a blackout curtain over the window. Another fedora pokes at the screen of the laptop that is plugged into the projector. Everyone else appears content to be utterly unhelpful, so at least I won't stand out in that respect. I station myself on top of the dryer closest to the door and watch Amalia chatting with a couple in matching tweed caps. She's removed her own hat, possibly because it's ninety degrees in here.

When I purchased my ticket to this event—the price of which feels even more outrageous now that I'm sitting here with neither back support nor seat padding, so good thing I expensed it to Veracity—I figured there were three possible outcomes. Amalia wouldn't show after all; she'd changed her mind about attending. Or she would arrive with someone who wasn't Mason. Or she would meet not-Mason at the venue.

Except, from what I can see, it's none of those. So then: Why the lie?

The gray rectangle being projected on the laundry room wall changes to an opening credits image: VOYAGER FILMS PRESENTS. The lights click off and the darkness flattens us into shadows. There's a scattering of applause; someone says, in an accent stretching all the way from England to New Zealand, "About bloody time!" People shuffle about, ducking out of the way of the projector's dusty swath of light, claiming whatever butt space remains available on the machines.

"Welcome to the first Somners of Gotham screening of the new year!"

Now we all look to the back of the room, where the two fedoras are standing, one on either side of the projector. A couple of people whoop. Taller Fedora says, "It's great to see so many old faces—"

"Old as in familiar," says Shorter Fedora.

"Thank you, Hannah, for rescuing me from my faux pas, as usual. So many familiar faces, and some unfamiliar ones as well, which is always exciting. All looking very youthful in this dim lighting."

Taller Fedora fanboys about the Somnang Files for a few minutes—its nuanced, devastating exploration of war and politics and colonialism and morality, what a compelling protagonist Somnang is, how every single one of these movies is both a stab through the heart and an exquisite drowning—Shorter Fedora thanks a Somner named Raymond for securing us such an atmospheric space, and then, finally, the film begins.

Amalia's voice, right in my ear: "I can squeeze in here next to you?"

I jump: I'd thought she was at the front of the room, with her friends, not leaning against the side of my dryer. "Oh—sure," I say, and scooch to my left.

She hoists herself up. Her shoulder brushes mine as she sits back. I stare at Somnang startling awake in his hotel room. He sits up and swings his legs off the bed. It's a shot from behind: he's shirtless, his back a pale, welted canvas.

"Also . . ."

Somnang stands, stretches, walks to the window. He pushes it open and leans out—keeping tabs, we'll learn in ten or so minutes, on the man who's keeping tabs on him. I turn as the camera pans to the street below, teeming in the glare of a tropical sun. The brightness of the screen clarifies Amalia's smile, her dangly earrings, the take-out box in her lap, and the individually wrapped green-and-yellow slices of cake packed within it.

She tilts the box at me, an invitation. "Themed snacks!" she says.

———————

The camera retreats from Somnang sitting on a bench in Hyde Park in an autumnal drizzle, having just received news that the family who sheltered him in Saigon has been found dead, their necks identically broken, all thirteen members across three generations. It pulls up and away: the yellowing rectangle of the park, a teasing gleam of water, the spread of brown and gray buildings, an empire's failing heart. Then a black screen, and the closing credits rolling as Karen Carpenter's warm contralto sings that song about longing to be close to you.

The room remains dark, the audience motionless. I feel all goosebumpy. Last night I'd actually stopped the movie with five more minutes to go. Somnang had returned to London and was spending his time drinking alone in pubs or lurking outside his ex-wife's house, watching her and their daughter through the window— nothing more was going to happen, obviously. Well, now I know.

Beside me Amalia Suarez sighs, softly, like she has been holding her breath.

The lights come on only after the credits have concluded. There's still a residual sorrow in the air, as if the world of the film has seeped into the one we're inhabiting.

"Fuck," says Amalia. "That last scene. Gets me every time."

"Me too," I say.

"Especially given what we find out in *Bearers of Gifts*."

Oops: haven't watched that one. Around us people are standing, stretching, talking in hushed voices as if they've just shared a religious experience, which maybe they have. I hop off our shared dryer and say, like the infidel that I am, "Those cakes—or whatever they are—are super tasty. Where are they from?"

"They are, no?" she says. "It's a Vietnamese dessert shop in Sunset Park."

"That's where you live?" I'll have to double-check my spreadsheet, but I'm fairly certain Amalia hasn't been in Sunset Park since I've started tracking her.

"No, I'm in Crown Heights." She waves at someone passing by behind me. "I just find excuses to go there." Her smile reorients on me. "Or, in this case, make my long-suffering boyfriend go there for me."

Long-suffering and Mason Perry: two concepts that don't seem to belong on the same continent, let alone in the same sentence. I say, "That's nice of him. Especially when I'm guessing he's not a Somnang fan like you."

She tilts her head. "What makes you guess that?"

"He's not with you." I pause. "And when you arrived, earlier, Pete wasn't surprised that you were by yourself, and he didn't ask where your boyfriend was or anything like that. Implying that your boyfriend isn't part of this group."

Amalia laughs. "Amazing. You are like a detective."

I'm tempted to impress her further by unfurling a Sherlockian deduction—that I can tell she's a soccer player from her stride, maybe. Then I regain my sanity. "I read a lot of murder mysteries."

"It's working, because you're right. My boyfriend's not into the Somnang Files. He's watched them all, but only because I'll stop dating someone after three months if they don't."

"Really?" I say. "That's your relationship rule?"

"One of them. I don't need the person to love the series, or even like it at all. I want to see if they'll give it a try." Amalia slides off the dryer. "Which Mason did, and he thinks the Somnang Files is boring as hell and I'm too invested in the lives of fictional people."

"But sometimes it's because people are fictional that you can feel so close to them," I say.

She tilts her head again. "Say more."

A heavyset Black man comes up to us. "All right, let's move this over to the Forester," he says. "My super is going to kill me if we're not out by five."

This must be Raymond of the laundry room largesse. I look around to see Taller Fedora hoisting the projector out through the doorway and everyone else gone.

Amalia winces. "I can't join this time."

"Come on. Half an hour."

"I need to get back to Brooklyn. It's my roommate's birth-day—"

"Invite her."

"No offense, but the last thing she'll want is to spend it in a random pub arguing about whether the Dream and Liên Duong are really the same person."

I say, "What?"

"You haven't heard that theory before?" says Amalia.

Raymond says, "They're the same height, same build. Liên leaves the party early; Le Roff is murdered that night."

"God forbid there should be two interesting female characters in the same movie," says Amalia.

"You may not like it, but the evidence is overwhelming."

"Such BS. Give me one thing that's more than just coincidence."

While they quibble, I think back on the scenes I remember of Liên Duong, the grave, beautiful, Sorbonne-educated intellec-tual who returned to Saigon in the wake of South Vietnam's 1967 presidential election to work in the Nguyen administration. One in particular struck me: at the party hosted by the French ambas-sador, Somnang steps out into the garden to get away from an odious diplomat (American, of course) and encounters Liên, stand-ing under a tree laden with white blossoms, smoking. It's a scene that's pure mood, lush, dreamy, an unexpressed longing for things to be different in impossible ways from what they are.

"Liên is left-handed, isn't she?" I say. "There's that scene where she lights Somnang's cigarette in the garden and they joke about it. But the police report on Le Roff's death describes an attack by a right-handed person."

Amalia and Raymond are staring at each other like I've just solved the moving sofa problem. "Oh, shit," he says. "If that's right . . ."

She says, before I can, "Pun unintended." She looks at me. "I am starting to think you *are* a detective."

"You're a detective?" says Raymond. "Police or private?"

"Neither," I say. "But the southpaw killer is a common mystery trope. I think writers like it because it's an easy way to narrow down the list of suspects."

The three of us exit the basement and climb up into a flinty winter dusk. Across the street, the pocket-size storefront of a ramen shop glows out at us. A young Asian man sits alone at the counter along the window, head down, slurping from his bowl. He looks like the subject of a Hopper painting, updated for the twenty-first century.

Raymond heads off to the Forester, after trying one more time to cajole us into coming along. (I pretend I also have another appointment I need to rush off to.) As he walks away, Amalia says, "What about the group theory? For the Dream's identity?"

Oh man. The next time I go undercover like this, I need to be so much better prepared. "What about it?"

"Your powers of deduction, what do they tell you? Thumbs-up, thumbs-down?"

"Well . . ." I say. *Group theory*—what could that refer to?

If one school of thought is that two characters are in fact the same person, maybe this is the opposite: what appears to be one character is in fact two or more.

"Are we thinking of the same thing?" I say. "The idea that the Dream is actually multiple people?"

Amalia nods. "Exactly."

"I think it's possible." Time for the redirect. "What do you think?"

She smiles. "That's the reveal I'm putting all my money on."

The more imminent reveal, if we spend any more time talking

about Somnang, is what a fraud I am. "I don't want to keep you from your roommate's celebration," I say.

"It's more like a diversion," she says. "She and her boyfriend broke up a few weeks ago and she's in a major slump."

"I'm sorry to hear that."

"Oh, I'm so relieved. He was gross. Cocky finance bro who walked around acting like the world was there to do him a favor. He was always talking about going out to the Hamptons for the weekend, like anyone gives a shit."

I say, slowly, "I'm familiar with the type."

"Oh no," says Amalia. "Does *your* boyfriend work in finance and love going to the Hamptons?"

"No!" I say, appalled. "God, no."

"The way you said that, I thought . . ."

"It just reminded me of someone I know," I say. "I don't even have a boyfriend; I wouldn't. I mean, because I'm gay. Not because I'm planning to become a nun or anything like that."

Amalia pauses, like we've been tossing a Frisbee back and forth this whole time, long lazy arcs, and now I've gone and flung it into the bushes. People are often surprised when they find out I'm gay, which doesn't seem to bode well for my romantic prospects.

"Then—girlfriend?" she asks.

I'm about to make a joke about my permanently single status— *Well, maybe I am planning to become a nun!*—when I realize: this could be an opportunity. "Yes, and she's not a Somnang fan, either. Like your boyfriend. I didn't even tell her I was coming to this screening."

"Why?"

"She would get upset that I'd choose to watch this movie again for the fifteenth time instead of spending Saturday afternoon with her."

Amalia's eyebrows draw together as if she's thinking my made-up girlfriend sounds rather controlling.

I add, "Your boyfriend, he doesn't mind?"

She laughs. "Definitely not. Mason is happy to have the time to do his own thing."

If *she's* not lying, and I don't believe she is, then that must mean—

"But you're right," says Amalia. "I should get going. I have to drag my roommate to the restaurant where we're all meeting for dinner. You are walking to the subway?"

—Mason Perry lied to us about his girlfriend's plans. "Just to my bike over there." Which makes the question of why all the more interesting.

"A bike commuter!" Amalia sounds like a birder whose favorite species has just fluttered down onto a branch right in front of her. "Is it okay if I take a look at your bicycle? I work at an e-mobility start-up, and we're always trying to get additional data points on the cyclist demographic."

Or a missionary seeing an opportunity to rescue a soul from damnation.

We walk halfway down the block to the hoop rack where my secondhand Trek is keeping company with a fixed-gear bicycle with baby blue wheel rims. "Not the fixie," I say, before Amalia can mistake me for someone more hard-core than I really am. "I love how clean their lines are, but I need gears in my life."

"Your bike has seen a lot of action."

"I figure the more banged up it looks, the lower the chances someone would want to steal it," I say, which sounds better than the fact that I'm too lazy to ever clean it.

"Fair enough. You have to go over bridges a lot?" She looks up. "Nice to get a bit of a boost on the upslope, no?"

"Are you trying to entice me over to the dark side?"

"Are you open to being enticed?"

She's smiling at me, and my mind is suddenly as unyieldingly blank as that laundry room wall before the projector started up. I glance away. "Um, I'll think about it."

When I look over again, Amalia is crouched next to my bike unfolding her e-scooter, which takes a bit longer than the inverse. Eventually she stands and shakes her hair out of her face. "It was so nice meeting you," she says. "See you at another Somners of Gotham thing soon?"

I nod vigorously. "Yes. Same."

She bumps her e-scooter off the curb and onto the road. I watch her hum off, heading the wrong way on East Tenth, and a thought finally flashes up on that empty screen: I would indeed like to see her again soon.

VIII.

"YOU GOT ME." Mason Perry sounds quite delighted. "I lied."

"And what inspired you to do that?"

Most people, upon having that question shurikened at them by the Blonde Assassin—my nickname for Becks, only ever uttered out of her presence—would at minimum flinch. Mason's smile just gets wider, and more lopsided. "I wanted to see if this outfit was for real."

"We get a lot of self-sabotaging clients," says Becks, "but this deserves a prize."

He shakes his head. "It's not a sabotage. If you hadn't caught this, then obviously the verification wouldn't be worth much in the first place. There would be nothing to sabotage. And if you did catch it—which you did, so kudos to you—then there'd be no sabotage."

I say, "It still feels like a sort of cavalier attitude to take toward the verification, especially given what you told us earlier about how important Amalia is to you."

"It's exactly because she's so important to me that I needed to make sure you knew what you were doing." Mason props his forearms against the edge of the table, lacing his fingers together. "So how did you keep track of her like that?"

"We don't disclose our methods," says Becks.

"Let me guess. There has to be some digital component to it; your business model wouldn't be scalable otherwise. Do you try to triangulate across a target's social media accounts? And then combine that with—"

"You can guess all you want," says Becks, "but it'll be less annoying if you do it in silence."

"Of course, of course," he says. "I was just curious."

Becks starts reciting our boilerplate closing language like she hasn't heard him: the verification is now complete, the invoice balance is due within fourteen days, the client's confidentiality obligations regarding this engagement, all related discussions, and the existence of Veracity LLC itself remain perpetual.

As we stand up, I ask Mason, "What do you think of the Somnang Files?"

"The movies that Amalia likes so much? They're okay. I'm not really into all that spy stuff. Too many shades of gray. I prefer to know who my heroes and villains are."

"Some people get confused by ambiguity," I agree.

He gestures for me to precede him out of the conference room. As he exits behind me, he adds, "I haven't even gotten around to watching the second one."

———————

The elevator closes on Mason's face, and Becks says, before she even turns around, "Don't make contact with a target again."

"If I hadn't done that—"

"You would have seen from Finders Keepers that she didn't

go to New Haven like she was supposed to. You would have conducted an observation. You would have told Mason that there was a discrepancy in the information he gave us about Amalia's schedule and where she actually was. We would have done our job."

"We wouldn't have known that he was the one lying, or why."

Becks says, as we walk across the elevator bank and back into the office, "We don't concern ourselves with motivations. Remember?"

That was one of Komla's mantras. Under his watch, the verifier's role was to report on what was objectively observable. No delving into the target's state of mind or speculating on the reasons for their behavior. Sometimes clients would ask us to—what did we think it meant, could the target have intended this or that, was it possible, why—and Komla would chuckle and say that the verifiers were in no position to opine. No one can know except the person who has acted, he would say, and even then they very well might not.

"Maybe we should," I say. "You don't convict a person of murder if they trip while they're holding a knife in their hand and the knife flies off and lands in someone's heart."

"That's the most elaborately ludicrous analogy I've heard from you yet."

I follow her into her room. "Okay, forget the analogy. The Samuel Chu case, then."

"Jesus Christ. Can you not let that go."

I will concede that Samuel Chu affected me like an especially virulent strain of the flu, leaving me wheezing in my sleep long after I should have recovered. It was that pensive, interstitial week between Christmas and New Year's, the sun went into hiding for three days straight, things were otherwise slow at Veracity. And we had just found out that Lucinda Clay might have murdered a second person.

Cameron Keller was a Soulmate employee based in San Francisco who worked on the company's synth program, reporting directly to Lucinda. He was also, we believed, feeding information about the synths to Sarah Reaves, the journalist whom Lucinda killed. He died in mid-December of a cardiac arrest, very surprising for someone who was in his thirties and, according to the brief obituary in the *San Francisco Chronicle*, an avid tennis player. St. Elmo, the name that Sarah's source went by, started sharing with Sarah materials relating to Soulmate's plans a month after Cameron joined Soulmate. The last upload from St. Elmo took place two days before Cameron's death. All of which coincided with Lucinda's business trip to San Francisco that week. Coincidences all the way down.

In any event, Becks was insistent that there was nothing we could do. Cameron had died on the other side of the country. We had no connection to him. And even if Lucinda had done it—well, we had recorded her confession to Sarah's murder, so it wasn't as if she was getting away. The only thing I was able to convince Becks to agree to was requesting a copy of Cameron's autopsy report from San Francisco's Office of the Chief Medical Examiner, since those records are public in California, and I came away from that discussion feeling like I'd arm-wrestled with a gorilla.

So when Pauline Gould came in two days after Christmas and asked us to verify Samuel Chu, I was all over it. I wanted to divert myself from how another year was ending, and what things would be like with Komla gone, and what the hell we were going to do about the synths. A case like Samuel Chu's could afford me the satisfaction of a task I could actually complete.

And, maybe, the guy looked like the type of older Asian man who, when I was younger, I would sight on the playground or in a store, tending to his own children, and think about how in a life only infinitesimally different he could have been my father, instead of the *see you later I mean never* scumbag I apparently inherited the shape of my nose and my intolerance for spicy foods from. Samuel had a New York Philharmonic subscription and volunteered at the Wild Bird Fund. He let people cut in front of him if they said they were in a hurry. He wore wire-rimmed glasses and orthopedic shoes. He still spoke English with a Chinese accent after twenty-five years in the States, and his favorite author, at least according to his matching profile, was Milan Kundera.

Anyway. I tracked him for two weeks and established that not only did he not go up to Boston to visit his sister's family—as he had told our client he did, which was why he couldn't meet her children while they were in town for the holidays—he didn't once leave the Upper West Side or, as far as I could tell, interact with another person except the baristas at his local coffee shop.

I say, "I feel like we were responsible for that relationship ending."

"So?"

The one time I wouldn't mind if Becks contradicted me and she refuses to oblige. "And maybe that wasn't the best outcome."

She moves to stand behind her desk. "According to you. The client thought it was."

"Yes, but . . ." Pauline Gould had been impassive throughout our debriefing. At the end, when Becks asked if she had any questions, she shook her head. *Very helpful*, she said. *Thank you.* She had originally engaged us for a four-week verification, but she told us there would be no need to continue. *He's a nice man*, she said, *but he's also a coward, and that's not what I need in my life right now.*

"But you know better."

"No. But if we had found out more about what he was thinking, why he lied, we could have given Pauline a more complete picture."

"We gave her the facts. That's what we're supposed to do."

"The facts aren't enough without context."

"That's why we cover our asses with disclaimers."

I stare at the miscellaneous ruins pictured on the cover of *The History of the Decline and Fall of the Roman Empire: Volume 1*, which has been sitting open on Becks's desk—at the same page, I'm pretty sure—for the past several weeks now. Yes—but Samuel Chu seemed so alone. And now, thanks to me, he is, even more so than he was before.

"It's dangerous to try to get to know our targets."

I look up. "What do you mean?"

"Not in whatever implausible, histrionic way you're imagining." She's frowning at me, but there's an inwardness to her expression, as if she's unsure of what to say next: very un-Becks. "It can make you feel . . ." An additional line etches itself in between her eyebrows. "Like you have a stake in what happens. When you don't. Not at all. What our targets, and our clients, choose to do—that has absolutely nothing to do with us."

I think of Amalia telling me her boyfriend has watched all the movies in the Somnang Files series, and then, just fifteen minutes ago, Mason confirming that he in fact hadn't. Another loose stitch in a tapestry that, according to Becks, I should never have gotten close enough to view.

"Anything else?" says Becks.

I shake my head. "I'll go write up the summary case memo."

IX.

I SPEND VALENTINE'S DAY observing a target who canceled dinner plans with our client on twenty-four hours' notice, claiming a stomach bug, and went bowling with a trio of friends instead.

The arcade is in the West Thirties, and when I exit I find myself marveling at how many people this city must hold, like gut bacteria swilling about in the intestines of a concrete monster. It's hard to think of an area in New York less romantic than where I'm standing, a garishness of billboards and discount stores and fast-food outlets, and still everyone I see looks like they're on a date or hustling toward one. The number of bouquets being cradled around me—if an alien were to alight right now, it might conclude that flowers have manipulated human beings into a state of unquestioning service and reverence. I mean, maybe they have.

I wonder what Amalia and Mason are doing tonight, and for a moment—a three-minute-long moment, while a cabdriver decides to rest his elbow on his horn because that always works when traffic is backed up for blocks—I think about finding out.

The crash and clatter from the bowling alley echoes after me all the way home. Max is out, of course; my roommate contracted a virulent strain of monogamy a couple of months ago after he met a boy on Soulmate, and since then he's been using our apartment primarily as a storage unit. Not that I mind—I'm looking forward to letting out my inner sixty-five-year-old, curling up on the couch with a mug of hot chocolate and the new Inspector Yuan novel, falling asleep at ten.

For once, though, I can't get into the mystery. The victim is killed by a poisoned needle rigged to shoot forth from the mouth of a statue of Confucius, and this happens as she's walking along a thoroughfare during, it's repeatedly emphasized, the most crowded time of day—it all requires a suspension of disbelief greater than the Brooklyn Bridge. Eventually I give up and switch over to Netflix.

I'm intending to rewatch *The Philadelphia Story*, in acknowledgment of V-day, but at the top of my recommendations list is the latest movie in the Somnang Files franchise, *Bearers of Gifts*. I imagine Netflix's predictive algorithm gyrating to account for the whiplash in my tastes from classic rom-coms and Agatha Christie adaptations to fatalistic Cold War noir. I'm about to help out the algorithm and reject the selection, but then I remember Amalia's remark to me in the laundry room: *Especially given what we find out in* Bearers of Gifts. All right, let's find out.

Bearers of Gifts is set in Malaysia during the Communist insurgency of the late 1960s. The country has gained independence but the British are still around, like the waking dregs of an unpleasant dream, anxious to maintain some degree of influence. There are a lot of tedious, oblique backroom discussions about Malaysian political parties, all referred to by similar-sounding acronyms, and the upcoming federal elections. Two-thirds of the way through, the reveal about the events in *A Gentleman's Game*—the death of the Vietnamese family who sheltered Somnang—is shuffled into the narrative and out again like a trick card, a surprise to the viewer but not to Somnang.

Somnang's MI6 contact in Kuala Lumpur tells him that his cover as a commodities merchant has been blown, and proposes that Somnang stay with a pro-British Chinese family until he can be safely removed back to London. Somnang refuses, saying it will be too dangerous for the family. The contact assures him that they will be kept safe from Communist retaliation. *It's not the Commies I'm concerned about*, says Somnang. *It's our own bloody government. Someone somewhere will decide we can't risk the locals betraying us and so we have to betray them first. They did that in Saigon. They'll do it again. That's how power works, see? You do what you want, because you can.*

The actor portraying Somnang delivers the indictment with a flatness that could be construed as either resignation or irony, and listening to him, I have the bizarre thought that Amalia intended it for me as some sort of message. As if she could tell I was faking it somehow, and so directed me to this sound clip of cynicism and perfidy.

I stop the movie: all right, someone is either watching too many spy films that hinge on intelligence being relayed via cunningly circuitous methods, or feeling guilty about what she did, or both. As I navigate back to the Netflix home screen and select *The Philadelphia Story* like I should have in the first place, I remind myself that Amalia will never know that I was lying to her when we met. And, regardless, so what? It's not like I'll ever see her again.

PART TWO

1.

Reasons to Stop Thinking About X

1. Straight (according to matching profiles)
2. Even if not irrevocably straight, already dating someone else
3. Someone else, aka an ex-client
4. Believes I have a girlfriend
5. The Somnang Files *is* boring as hell

II.

AT FIVE O'CLOCK on a blustery afternoon, the line for *Norah Simmons: Refracted Selves* commences on the sidewalk, straggles up the low flight of steps outside the Whitney Museum and along one wall of the building to the doors, and then tightens into a disheartening sinuous trail across the museum lobby. At least we've now made it to the warmer side of the glass, so I can stop staring enviously at my fellow supplicants removing their hats and gloves and unzipping jackets as they move indoors.

"A timely reason to fall back, question mark."

Benny and I, standing on either side of Max, squint at each other. "Defeat?" he says.

"It's . . . fifteen letters," says Max. "No, sixteen. No, fifteen."

I say, "Maybe someone else should be reading out the clues."

"Benny can't do it because he'll just solve everything right away, and you get distracted too easily. Longest river in Europe. Five letters."

"Volga!" says Benny.

Max types that in. "Sleight of hand. Eleven letters. Third letter is a *g*."

"Wouldn't it be funny," I say, "if this line was like a Möbius strip and we're just going round and round in this lobby? Funny as in tragic."

"Legerdemain," says Benny.

It takes us a Sunday puzzle to arrive at the stairwell at the far end of the lobby, and then a Friday to ascend to the fourth floor. While my feelings about Benny's presence in Max's life—and by extension mine—remain as conflicted as the Kashmir border, there's no denying he's drastically upped our crossword game. Max is cooing at Benny about what a genius he is when we finally get close enough to the entrance of the gallery for me to comprehend what awaits us within. What comes to mind is something I read once about intensive shrimp farming in Thailand, where the poor little crustaceans are packed so tightly in their ponds that the ones positioned at the rim all end up getting their eyes rubbed away over time, a horrific image that caused me to swear off shrimp until the next time I had a craving for pad thai.

I glance around at the boys. "What do you think about skipping the cultural enrichment part of the evening and moving straight to caloric enrichment?"

"Really?" says Max. "This is like the first art show you've ever asked me to go see with you."

"It's probably not worth the risk of death by asphyxiation." Especially since I'm interested in this artist not because I actually like her work or even know anything about it, online research aside. From the Whitney website: *Simmons is equal parts inspired and unflinching in her quest for emotional authenticity through the digital construction—and deconstruction—of artifice.* Based on the samples I've scrolled through online, I'd rephrase that as: *She takes portraits of people and then photoshops them.*

"I'm fine with whatever," says Benny. "She's supposed to be the artist of our zeitgeist, and we've already spent the past ninety minutes waiting. But I understand if it's too stressful for you, being around so many people."

So says the transplant from small-town North Carolina to the Queens native. "That's how Max and I ended up in Gowanus right next to a Superfund site," I say. "No one else living there."

Max says, "Also we thought all those toxins might give us superpowers."

Benny squeezes him around the waist. "Is *that* why you're so irresistible?"

I say, because dear god, "It was just a suggestion. I'm fine sticking with the original plan." Which is really the original-as-modified plan, since my original-original plan featured just me and Max, the kind of tête-à-tête we wouldn't be able to have with Benny present, and splitting a meatball parm hero at our favorite sandwich shop in Greenwich Village. It's not that I dislike hanging out with them both, but after a while I start to feel like the straight best friend in a queer rom-com, which is unsettling on multiple levels. "Why don't we set a time to meet in the lobby downstairs?"

Max looks at his phone. "When's our reservation?" he asks Benny.

"Seven thirty."

"We have a reservation for dinner?" I say. "Where?"

"The Chubby Sunchoke," says Benny. "It's a gluten-free raw food restaurant."

"And you felt reservations were necessary?"

"So we'll meet at . . . seven ten?" says Max.

I guess I can always duck out before then and find somewhere to sit and finish reading *The General in His Labyrinth* on my phone. "Sounds good," I say. "Gentlemen first."

I'm hoping that I can draft off of Max and Benny as they press on into the gallery, but almost immediately someone mashes himself in between us. This is like being at a concert, sans access to beer or weed, subject to the consolidated roar of the crowd's views on Norah Simmons in lieu of anything remotely auditorily pleasing. I'm bumped this way and that by all the people around me—everyone else seems to have definite ideas about where they want to go, even if, as far as I can tell, it's backs of heads and shoulders all the way.

"She really makes me feel *seen*, you know?"

"—a bit derivative, don't you think, of that other artist, what's their name, god, it's killing me—"

I learned about Norah Simmons during my very first verification at Veracity: the target brought up Simmons's name as an artist he said our client might like, based on the other artists she had listed as favorites in her Soulmate profile. That was last August, when no one else seemed to have any clue about Simmons. Her work had only ever appeared in one gallery, part of a group show in Bushwick; according to Google Trends, searches for *Norah Simmons art* or *Norah Simmons artist* were flatlined until the start of this year. Now we're talking solo exhibition at the Whitney Museum—that *my mother* asked me if I knew about because she had heard of it from *her mah-jongg group*. Everyone else's children, she told me, after having been inundated by news of Simmons's art on their social media accounts, ferried their respective mothers from Flushing to the Meatpacking District to partake in this seminal cultural experience. (A hint I ignored because I can think of few activities less palatable than a contemporary art field trip with my mother.)

In other news, while Norah Simmons was hothouse-blooming into an art phenom, the verifiers established that this OG fan of a target, whom we only ever knew by his profile handle, Charretter, was in fact a synth, a freakily smart one. And what I've been pondering for the past few weeks, since *Norah Simmons: Refracted Selves* opened to record attendance rates, is whether all of this is:

Coincidence: the synth recommending an artist who shortly afterward blows up.

Prescience: the algorithm that powers the synth detecting patterns within the informational quagmire of the Internet that foreshadow Simmons's imminent popularity.

Or, perhaps, control: the person in charge of the algorithm deciding to back this specific artist, and using the synths to secure Simmons's success.

Lucinda Clay originally developed Soulmate's synths as a way to overcome the lying limitation, which has always been the matching industry's hairiest bugbear. For as long as matchmakers are predicting compatibility based on data that their users provide, and those users aren't being fully honest with or about themselves, matching will never be the guarantee of happiness that so many people wish it can be. (And outfits like Veracity continue to get plenty of business.) Lucinda's solution: embed synths on Soulmate's platform that were capable of influencing the humans they interacted with into conforming to Soulmate's compatibility predictions, through a seemingly benign proffering of opinions and suggestions. Gradually, invisibly change people into behaving, into believing, as they should—as they claim to others, and perhaps also to themselves, they do. Maybe in another spin of the multiverse Lucinda would've gotten a Nobel. In our world, she was a tech zealot with an extremely wonky moral compass.

But as if that wasn't creepy enough, Polaris Capital, the private equity firm that owns Soulmate, got wind of the synths and saw more lucrative, and far-reaching, use cases for them. Why limit the synths to making uninspired conversation with singletons online, laboring to reshape individual by flawed individual, when they could reshape, potentially, everything? Whether one artist becomes a cultural touchstone and another falls into the void of obscurity, whether one start-up's clever, frivolous app goes viral and another's is never downloaded by more than ten people, whether one politician wins their race and another loses: these are all the outcomes of people's choices. Which means that if you can determine what choices enough people will make . . .

"—the glasses is a reference to Clark Kent/Superman?"

"It's re*frac*tion, not re*flec*tion—"

Surely, though, Polaris couldn't have marshaled the power of the synths in the past several months to effectively anoint Norah Simmons as the artist of our overcrowded zeitgeist. Bellwether synths—the name I came up with for the synths with the capacity to influence, which I'm hoping to wear down Becks and Squirrel into using as well—emerged on Soulmate only last summer, starting with Charretter; and as of December, Polaris was still trying to wrest control of the synth program from Lucinda. Also, the verifiers have been monitoring the profiles on Soulmate that we know are or suspect to be bellwethers, and we've seen no indications of them advocating for particular agendas; any suggestions they make in a conversation with a user appear responsive to what that user has said.

I'm reminding myself of all this right now, and yet my disquiet only heavies as I'm sucked deeper into the shrimp pond, until it starts to feel like I'm sinking as well.

"I love the aqueous sentiment of the *Jordan* pictures—"

"Can you watch where you're going?"

The barricade of bodies before me shifts and loosens. I get a glimpse of colors, the corner of a frame. It feels like being offered one piece of a puzzle. I squirm closer, until I'm right up against an older couple who have anchored themselves in front of this artwork with the majesty of a pair of ocean liners.

"The effect remarkably approximates synesthesia," I hear the man say. "I can taste the solitude."

"Cilantro," agrees the woman.

After a moment he says, "Almonds. Bitter almonds."

"Everything tastes like almonds to you," she says as they set sail, ever so unhurriedly, for the next portrait. If we were in a murder mystery, cyanide poisoning for sure; I would be the tertiary character who unwittingly provides the crucial clue to solve the crime.

As soon as there's space I step up. The photograph before me is of a light-skinned Black woman who sits on a picnic table against a generic backdrop of grass and trees. She looks to be in her early to mid-twenties, with shoulder-length braids and a sturdy, athletic frame. The placard beneath reads: KELSEY #5. Simmons works in series; I remember reading that somewhere. She conducts a photo shoot with the subject, selects one of the portraits as her base, and then alters it. The original isn't shown, so the viewer doesn't know what has been changed, only that something has.

"—showing how unknowable we all are—"

"Hey, it's you."

"Do you think this could revive NFTs?"

I guess I'm not sensitive enough for the synesthesia, but I do understand what the couple meant by solitude. There's something about the way the subject is looking—not looking at the camera, the impermeability of her smile. I wonder if *Kelsey #0* vibes the same, or if Norah Simmons was able, somehow, to introduce that specific sentiment into the picture I'm staring at now.

"Jiayi, right?"

I turn—did someone say . . . ?—and jump backward, only to be bounced into place again by the flesh wall pulsing behind me.

"Sorry!" says Amalia Suarez, sounding amused rather than apologetic. "Didn't mean to scare you. We met at that Somnang screening last month."

"I remember," I say. "Laundry room. Furry hat." I muster the focus to stop reciting irrelevant details. "What . . . are you doing here?"

She tips her chin at *Kelsey #5*. "Looking at art."

"Right." I swivel to face the wall. There's a protocol to follow in the event a verifier comes face-to-face with a target. I don't exactly know what it is, because I skimmed over that part of the policy during my orientation—the odds of such an occurrence seemed exceedingly low, and anyway, what did it matter since the target would have no idea who I was?

"What do you think?"

I say, most banally, "This looks like something you'd put on a matching profile."

She smiles at me. "It does, no?"

"What about you?"

She turns back to the portrait, quirks her mouth. This girl has the longest eyelashes. "I think the artist is challenging our understanding of what it means to be a person."

She says that—and again I'm thinking about those damn synths. Whether the bellwethers could really be responsible for this frenzy of appreciation around us. The power that Polaris would have to manipulate all kinds of outcomes—financial, political, social—by deploying them as an invisible, insidious army of tastemakers. What a two-and-a-half-person operation can possibly do about any of this, especially when one person thinks *nothing* and the half doesn't seem to care.

Amalia side-glances at me; I must have exceeded the appropriate response time. "You may be challenging my understanding of what the artist meant," I say.

"You have heard of this theory that there's no such thing as a coherent self, because our brains are always changing? We're not the same person we were a week ago or a day ago or even a minute ago."

"So then . . . we've never met before."

She laughs. "Not the person you are now and the person I am

now. Norah Simmons's pictures, they make that point, no? Each of these Kelseys, maybe they are different people."

"How does memory come into this?"

"Hmm," she says. "Say more."

"The idea of who you are is built on what you remember of your experiences. The person I am now remembers meeting you then."

"It's true," she says. "I don't know what that means."

Before I can ask what *she* means by that, she offers up a shrug and another one of those easy, expansive smiles. "Anyway, just my random theory. You are here with your girlfriend?"

At first I think she's using the term platonically, the way some straight women do, and then I remember: my fictional better half. "No. She, ah, hates crowds. I came with friends." I look about like invoking them might cause Max and Benny to pop out of the multitude. "What about you? You came with Mason?"

Oh shit—Mason. *That's* why the protocol matters. Because meeting the target may also mean meeting the person who hired you to spy on said target, and god only knows how the client will react. I could totally see Mason "I'm So Smooth" Perry trying something dumb, like joking in front of Amalia about how he and I have a secret.

"You know Mason?" says Amalia.

My heart feels like the puck in that strongman game at funfairs where players take turns hammering a lever to see how high it will rise, each time more aggressively than the last. "You mentioned his name." Didn't she?

"I guess I must have." Her frown eases. "Good memory."

"How he went all the way to that dessert place in Sunset Park. It left an impression." Specifically, as something most unlikely for Mason Perry to do, given that the entire time I was observing Amalia he didn't once make it into Brooklyn to hang out with her. The closest he got was Governors Island, which they visited one weekend; whenever they spent the night together, it was at his place in Gramercy.

And maybe he didn't. Maybe Amalia lied about that, just as she lied about him having watched all the Somnang Files movies. Maybe the boyfriend she's been talking up is the one she wishes she had, not the one she settled for.

And maybe, as in definitely, none of that has anything to do with me.

Amalia is saying that she's here on her own. "Mason has to work this weekend, poor boy. I'll see him later tonight." She pauses. "If you were also by yourself, I was going to say we should get a drink, or something."

We both turn back to the wall. In the time we've been talking, we've drifted to one side, and it's *Kelsey #4* who's looking at us now. Same picnic table, same sun-glossed park setting, but this Kelsey is staring at the camera like it's a task she can't wait to get over with.

"I really enjoyed meeting you," adds Amalia. "Not only because you helped my argument about Liên and the Dream being different people."

And we walk out of this insufferably crowded room and into a bar down the street, a place with a low decibel level and flattering lighting and a robust selection of pale ales, where we can sit in a corner and talk to each other like we really did just meet by chance, two blank balls that bounced against each other once and then again in the humongous Powerball lottery of people that's New York, and the person I am right now gets to meet Amalia Suarez again, truly, for the first time.

My pocket buzzes and, thank god, calls a time-out to that fantasy. "Me too," I say. "Meeting you. But, yeah, I should go find my friends. We have a reservation at a raw food place, and there's a rumor we might have to grow the food ourselves before we can eat it, so we need to get a head start."

Amalia laughs. "You're funny."

"I've been told it's a defense mechanism." What did I just—? "Anyway, I'll see you around."

As I'm turning, she touches my forearm. "Hey. My friend has a show next month and I'm helping her promote it. Is it okay if I send you the information? It's really, really good. Kind of weird—I don't want to mislead you—but good."

"Sure," I say. "I like weird." So not true: I'm always making fun of the Bushwick art shows that Max drags me to for being too avant-garde.

We look at each other. She smiles. "So then . . . you want me to text you? Email? Send you a postcard?"

Right. "Email works." Except not my personal, which has my name in it, and not my work, either. Luckily, I do have a third account. "It's *hapjackflappiness* at gmail. Like, *flapjack* and *happiness*, but with the first letters switched." As I'm explaining, it's becoming clear to me what a fake-sounding email address this is; and from the way Amalia's smile has receded, I suspect she thinks so, too.

"I'm not trying to ghost you," I say. "That's really my email." Albeit one I've long forgotten the password for. The last time I used it was in an attempt to find out if the Romantick, an online group of never-matchers that Sarah Reaves had been in contact with, had any intel on what she had been investigating when she died, and that was a complete fail.

She touches me on the arm again, a beat longer. "Don't worry, I believe you."

Is it possible—is Amalia Suarez—is she flirting with me?

I say, "I really have to go."

She gives me a thumbs-up. "I'll email you!"

I get a safe distance and then peek behind me. Amalia hasn't moved from her pole position in front of *Kelsey #4*. She's the only person who doesn't have their phone out for pictures, who's just gazing straight ahead of her, looking.

As I take the stairs down I check my phone. I'm expecting an update from Max, but instead it's a text from an unknown number, a California area code.

> Hi Claudia—This is Jessie. Sorry for
> bothering you, but could we talk? I'm
> worried about Charles.

III.

I COME INTO THE OFFICE on Monday to see Squirrel ensconced in my chair, squinting at my monitor screen.

"You could at least have asked," I say. "'Claudia, would you mind if I destroyed any illusion you might have of privacy on your computer?'"

"When did you last update Gatekeeper?"

I've never heard of that program. "Recently."

He snorts. "I thought you were supposed to be a good liar."

"And I think you just insulted me twice in the same sentence."

"I'm a coder. Nested functions, baby."

"Every time I'm sure you can't possibly get any nerdier . . ."

Squirrel pushes against the edge of my desk and wheels backward across the hardwood floor. As always he's dressed as if he came from the gym—a windbreaker and sweatpants, the clothes too large for his small frame—although I know by now that he abhors exercise. His Orioles baseball cap is pulled low across his forehead, his dark hair tufting out beneath its edges. He says,

"This nerd just saved your laptop from imminent self-destruction, so you're welcome."

"Thank you," I say, feeling marginally contrite. "Is that what you came in for?"

"Course not." He jerks his head in the direction of Becks's closed door. "There was a threat of violence."

The door opens and Becks steps out like that's her cue. "I meant to your woodcutter," she says to Squirrel.

"His weapon of choice is the axe. *Axes*, plural. That doesn't make him a fucking woodcutter. He's a disgraced noble from the Wayfarer family."

I say, "Did we just slip into a Tolkien fanfic discussion forum?"

"Kyrik is my avatar in *Ashes of Empire*," says Squirrel.

I blink at Becks. "And you play that game, too?"

She grimaces like I've wronged her by even posing the question. "I have a contact."

"Level forty-six," says Squirrel, such depths of longing and envy in his voice that I want to hug him and tell him it's okay.

"Forty-eight, now."

"God*damn*."

My pulse notches up as I follow Squirrel into Komla's office. Ahead of us, Becks marches to the window ledge that runs along the far wall and then turns around. Squirrel pushes himself up to sit on the now-empty desk. I stand in the middle of the room so I can face them both. "Is this something about the synths?" Not only that—something big. Becks wouldn't have summoned Squirrel otherwise, and Squirrel wouldn't have agreed to show up.

Becks grimaces. "Pradeep Mehta died last week."

I look from her to Squirrel. He's staring out the windows like he isn't part of this conversation. "Who?" I ask.

"Our February sixth two p.m. intake. He ranted about his ex stealing his profile. We kicked him out."

The injured deer, I find myself thinking, even before his face clarifies in my mind, and then the memory of him walking out of the room after we told him there was nothing we could do.

"How?"

Becks holds my gaze as she says, "Bicycle crash."

For an instant I feel myself falling again, that whole-body help-lessness as gravity has its way with you. My last bike accident took place right below where we're standing now, on the street outside Veracity—and, it turned out, wasn't an accident.

"What happened?" I ask.

An early-morning ride in Fort Washington Park, black ice on the bike path, skidding and hitting his head on the asphalt. No one came across his body until hours later, a function of the wretched weather conditions that day and how isolated that sec-tion of the path was.

I say, "But you don't think that's what really happened."

Becks tilts her head.

"You said *crash*. Not *accident*."

She nods. Then she says, her tone considering, "If someone broke up with me, and my goal was to fuck with them, I can think of a hundred more effective ways than a copy-paste job on their dating profile."

"I would hack into their online accounts and start posting weird shit."

She turns to Squirrel. "Thank you for that useless contribu-tion."

I say, "Pradeep was really affected by it. Maybe that's why his ex did that. He knew it would trigger something for Pradeep."

"Maybe." Becks glances back at me and then away again. "I don't know if you remember, but I told him to report this to Let's Meet."

"Yes. It didn't seem like he was going to, though."

"The Silent G profile has been taken down."

A minor surprise, like an aftershock from the news of Pradeep's death: I'd been sure he didn't want Let's Meet involved. "Okay. I guess he did after all. Or the ex-boyfriend got tired of being an ass and deleted it. What does this have to do with how he died?"

"It does if Let's Meet built Silent G in the first place."

"You think . . ." I can feel the room warping around me from the weight of Becks's statement, into a world where murder is no longer a plot device in mystery novels or a crime rate that New York City mayoral candidates bang the podium about. No: not again. "You mean, if Silent G was a synth? And so, when Pradeep contacted the company about it . . ."

Becks says a second time, more slowly, "Maybe."

"But all he would've done was lodge a complaint that someone else was using his information to create a fake profile. It would've been clear that he knew nothing about the synths."

"Would it? He practically had a panic attack in our office talking about the profile. Who knows what the fuck he said to Let's Meet to try to get them to remove it. He could've told them one of their employees was responsible. Threatened to file a lawsuit. Exaggerated the situation so Let's Meet would take it more seriously—and then they did."

I don't know: my intuition is insisting that Pradeep wanted as few people as possible to know about the fake profile and what he believed to be the cause of it. "Did our filter flag Silent G as a synth?"

"No, but that doesn't mean shit. Let's Meet could be swarming with these types of synths and we would have no idea."

"Our filter can't pick them up?" I ask Squirrel. "Like, not at all?" We track synth activity on the Big Three matchmakers—Soulmate, Partnered Up, and Let's Meet—using a filter that Komla and Squirrel developed to identify such profiles, leveraging Komla's inside knowledge of early versions of Soulmate's synths. The filter's accuracy has been declining, especially for bellwethers—as Squirrel put it, they are becoming too humanlike for the filter to distinguish from actual humans. I know Squirrel has been tweaking his program, though, trying various ways to refine it; and surely *decline* can't have turned to *obsolescence* in such a short time.

Squirrel tilts the bill of his baseball cap up and then tugs it back down. "Because it was never designed to," he says. "The filter searches for composites. That's the Soulmate approach. If Soulmate wants a synth that passes as a, I don't know, thirty-year-old Irish Catholic male, it takes its blank slate program and feeds in all the aggregated data it has from the Irish Catholic males in their late twenties and early thirties who are on the Soulmate platform. Eventually that program figures out how a thirty-year-old Irish Catholic male is likely to behave, what he'll do and say, and it's off to the races."

Now I get it. "But Silent G isn't a composite. It's a replica of an actual person."

"Exactly," says Becks. "An extra-special kind of problematic. Let's Meet isn't just systematically putting synths out there that deceive their subscribers. They're co-opting their subscribers' own data in order to create their synths—and that's something they absolutely cannot have those subscribers find out about."

I say, "*If* that is what Let's Meet is doing. Why would they, when it's riskier and they already have the composite synths?"

"Because their composites aren't very good. Soulmate is the only matchmaker that's been able to come up with synths like Charretter."

"Bellwethers."

"An arguably inaccurate application of the word, but—fine. The synths that Let's Meet and Partnered Up are putting out are stuck in how-to-be-human kindergarten. I could see Let's Meet deciding to give up on the composite approach and trying something new. Especially now that . . ." Becks shakes her head, a terse motion. "Now that, apparently, Soulmate's synths are out of commission."

"I want to tell her!" says Squirrel, over my somewhat squawky and entirely uncreative "What?"

"For the love of god, more coherently this time."

"February fourteenth," he says, with the solemnity of a World War II documentary narrator. "Every active synth on Soulmate went dark. Since then, no hits with the filter. Not a single one."

I look from him to Becks. "Someone hacked them?"

She's staring off into the space above my shoulder, eyes narrowed and mouth pursed. "Seems like it."

Squirrel says, "Someone being Komla."

The news is at once startling—and not. I think again, as I have any number of times over the past three months, of the conversation Komla had with Lucinda Clay in a bid to obtain a confession from her, and how she asked him for help in stopping Polaris from taking control of Soulmate's synth program. "Are we sure?"

"That's why he chose that date. He loves those kinds of gestures."

"Because it's . . . Valentine's Day?"

"Because that's when he started Veracity." Becks's gaze drifts around the room like it's come unmoored. "He brought us all in here and he told us this would be like nothing else we'd ever done. Should have asked for some fucking details."

I can picture it so clearly. Komla in his armchair, Becks by the windows, Squirrel up on the desk. The gray glow of the winter sky, the heat cranked to broil the way Komla likes it. That scene in a story when the team is assembled and the adventures can commence. I wish I could have been there as well, at the beginning of things.

Becks pushes herself away from the ledge that she's been leaning against. "And he didn't do it by himself."

At the very end of Komla's exchange with Lucinda, he said a couple of things to her that the other verifiers weren't able to hear—and that did make me wonder. I knew he still loved her. "We don't know that for sure," I say, but something twists in my stomach, a fish too slippery to be caught.

"I mean," says Squirrel, "Komla is mad-scientist level, but he's been out of Soulmate for years by this point. He would've needed inside help. Or a SWAT team of hackers, and if he'd recruited one I would have heard something."

"It's also been months since he went to the cops with the recording—since he said he would, anyway—and there have been absolutely zero updates on the investigation," says Becks. "He fucking did it. He let Lucinda Clay escape."

Soulmate neutralized. Lucinda at large. Pradeep dead. Let's Meet maybe resorting to using its customers' most personal data to build a new kind of synth. In a murder mystery, getting dodgeballed with these revelations in a single, breathless scene would be proof to me of either authorial laziness or a fatally flawed sense of pacing. Which would still be better than what's happening here, where Becks and Squirrel have known everything all along and are only now deciding to clue me in because, guess what, another potential murder. They found out about Soulmate's synth failure almost a month ago, for god's sake. And they must have been monitoring for news on Pradeep, or they would never have heard of his apparent bike accident. Why didn't Becks tell me?

Squirrel says, "Either way, taking out Soulmate's synths like that is badass."

"It's shortsighted and irresponsible," says Becks. "It slows Soulmate down, true. But that also creates an opportunity for the other matchmakers to get ahead—which will mean multiple types of synths out there, developed using methods we have no insights into, that we won't know how to keep track of. It's already happening. Let's Meet effectively cloning its subscribers for synths?

And we can't even confirm that, since finding a way to identify these synths is beyond you."

"I'm making headway. It's programming, not magic. Not that you'd know the difference."

"What I know is our existing filter wasn't picking up half of the Soulmate profiles that the St. Elmo intel said were synths—"

"A third! Jesus."

"—and we have nothing at all to help with the clone synths. Weren't you always whining about how Komla was holding you back? Now that he's left, it's clear it was the other way around."

I glance at Squirrel, startled: He thought that about Komla?

"You want to do this?" Squirrel hops off the desk. "Really? Because you're the one who fucked up big-time here. That dude came to us, and you pushed him into Let's Meet's arms. Plus you didn't cache the dupe profile and now it's gone. If you had any, *any*—self-respect—you would have quit after you let Faras—"

She says, a gate slamming down after its trip wire has been set off, "Don't."

Squirrel's mouth hinges shut and then opens again like a faulty nutcracker. I realize I'm talking only when I hear myself say, "Let's find the ex."

They both turn to me like I've caught them loading rocket launchers into the back of a truck headed for the North Korean border. More things they haven't told me. Becks briefly closes her eyes. When she speaks, it's with her usual brusqueness. "What for?"

"Pradeep thought he was behind the Silent G profile. Shouldn't the first step be to check whether that could be true? *Our* first step?"

In lieu of any sign of contrition for having shut me out until now, she says, sounding like a babysitter who not-so-secretly dislikes children, "It's not him."

"You're sure of that. The way you were sure that there was no evidence Sarah Reaves was murdered."

Her gaze sharpens into something distinctly skewer-like. "Do you even remember his name?"

Crap. "It will come to me." Probably not, but it will be in Becks's notes; she types up an unnecessarily detailed summary after every client intake meeting and saves it on our shared drive.

"Matthew Espersen." She closes her eyes again. "Fine. Let's rule him out and move on."

Or rule him in, and case closed. No new murder to solve or matchmaker scheme to unravel. My six-months-prior self would have been disappointed. Now, I'm crossing my fingers and toes that's all it is, a creatively vindictive former boyfriend and a bike accident. Since solving the death of Sarah Reaves, I no longer think of murder as a puzzle, an exercise in cleverness. It's a sinkhole, and anyone close enough gets dragged in as well.

"I'll send around his visual ID," says Becks. "It's shitty, but it'll narrow down the search."

Squirrel mutters at the wall, "I can run that through Match Insights."

"We have a picture of Matthew Espersen?" I ask.

"I took a picture of the picture Pradeep showed us," says Becks.

"That was . . . devious."

She walks out without replying.

I've arranged to get a drink with Jessie this evening and hear her out on Charles, which means I need to leave the office by five thirty. Which in turn means that at two minutes past five thirty I'm knocking on Becks's door.

I endure a silence the length of two back-to-back YouTube ads before I hear: "Come in."

She's standing in a corner pulling on her coat. "You're heading out already?" I say—she's typically around until after six.

"Dinner plans. You have five minutes."

So much for hoping to toe-dip my way into this ice bath. "Why didn't you let me know that you were tracking Pradeep Mehta?"

Her hands rest on the scarf that's hanging from the wall hook for a microsecond. Then she's lifted it up and begun looping it around her neck. "I wasn't tracking him. I just told Squirrel to set up an alert for any news about him."

"Because you suspected that Let's Meet was behind his fake pro-file! Why didn't you tell me any of this?"

She walks over to her desk, picks up the mystifyingly large bag she carries everywhere, and turns to face me. Her chin lifts as she says, "I don't know if I can trust you."

I feel myself flinch, and I hate that I do, almost as much as I hate what I say next: "How can you say that?" Not the question, but my voice: how imminently breakable it sounds.

Her gaze slants away from me. "If I had told you," she says, a new quietness in her tone, "that I thought Silent G might be a synth built from Pradeep's data, what would you have done?"

"I don't know. I wasn't given the option to make that decision."

"You would've sprinted out there to try to figure out if Let's Meet was really behind Silent G and why they chose Pradeep if so. Made any number of bad decisions. Become invested in the problems Pradeep was obviously mishandling when it was none of our god-damn business. Possibly drawn Let's Meet's attention along the way."

I'm so indignant at these entirely hypothetical accusations that my reply is a tad sputtery, which, while undignified, is still prefer-able to sounding like a kid who can't get a turn on the swings. "I would have done none of those things. You're assuming the worst of me and using that as an excuse to shut me out."

"I'm not assuming. You've been ranting about how we need to quote-unquote *stop the synths* ever since the gala dinner."

"Polaris wants to use them to take over the world!"

She flicks her hair back over her shoulder, her trademark tic of annoyance. "You're overly dramatic, reckless, and foolish."

"And *you're* arrogant and condescending and—"

I stop. Both because Becks appears ready to swing her bag at my head and because I can't help thinking that the flush of pink in her cheeks—from outrage, no doubt—is making her look very radiant right now.

"And?" she says.

I take a long step back. The smell of the perfume she always wears, smoky-sweet and complex, stays with me. "And we're partners now," I say. "Maybe you disagreed with Komla's decision to make the three of us co-owners of Veracity, but he did, and we are. Which means we tell each other what's going on and decide what to do together."

A pinging sound issues from the recesses of her bag, as if signaling the end of a bout. We both look down at it.

"I don't have time for this," says Becks. "I have to go."

In the doorway, she glances back at me over her shoulder. "For the record," she says, "I do disagree with Komla's decision."

IV.

THE BAR WHERE JESSIE PROPOSED we meet is in Kips Bay, one of those nondescript parts of Manhattan where everything is dull colors and chain stores and blocks of identical-looking apartment buildings. I charge inside and over to the table in the corner where Jessie is sitting, scrolling on her phone and sipping from an almost-empty wineglass.

"I'm so sorry," I say. I should probably offer some explanation or excuse for why I'm so late. "I was stuck in a meeting." The memory of my exchange with Becks, which I was obsessively replaying as I sped up First Avenue heedless of road etiquette or traffic lights, pushes its way back to the front row of my mind. "An infuriating one."

Jessie gets up from her chair. "It's totally fine. Thank you for coming to my area." She hesitates. "Would you . . . prefer we go somewhere else?"

I glance around. The bar, like the neighborhood, feels like a generic execution of its concept: indifferent lighting, functional furniture, TV screen displaying some miscellaneous sporting event. It seems as reasonable a location as any other to have this conversation, though, especially when it's three-quarters empty.

"I didn't remember until after I suggested this place . . . Charles told me he doesn't drink, because of your father. I don't know if . . ."

I look back at Jessie: *Ah.* One of the footnotes in the sorry legacy of the absconded Lin patriarch. "Oh, I do. I probably shouldn't, huh."

Her forehead pleats up.

"Not copiously or anything. Just to make sure I never remember what I did the night before."

She says, "Should we go get bubble tea instead?"

I can't tell if she is joking or realizes that I am. My brother, like Coraline, tends to date a recurring type of person—in his case, women who are agreeable to the point of abnegating their personality. Maybe it's a reaction to all the opinionated women in his own family. I've met Jessie a handful of times by now, and if you asked me to describe her in three words, they would all be thesaurus entries for *nice*.

"Does decent bubble tea exist in Kips Bay?"

"There's a place a few blocks from my apartment. Charles likes it."

"He has low standards," I say, and then realize how that sounds. "For bubble tea, I mean. Exceedingly high standards for everything else."

Jessie says, "Charles does ask a lot of his Nespresso machine."

Probably joking. I say, "Let's stay, if you're fine with it? I love my bubble tea, but a beverage that can chemically improve my mood would be great right now."

I come back with my beer—Jessie declines a second round—and sit down across from her. "So. My brother."

"Your brother." She says that like she's setting down a weight she's been carrying, knowing she'll have to pick it up again soon. "When did you last see him? Lunar New Year?"

"Yes. We missed you, by the way."

"I was at my aunt's place in Massachusetts."

"Definitely the better choice."

The way she pauses makes me think that Charles might have neglected to tell her how our reunion dinner went down. Then she says, "How did he seem? Charles?"

"The usual." To be honest, I have zero recollection of what my brother was like that night. I was too distracted by Richard's presence (and Chinese-language fluency), Coraline's agitation, the Damoclean sword of our mother's displeasure shining right above our heads. Charles felt like the one person I could afford not to pay attention to.

"He was originally thinking of skipping that dinner."

The meaning of what she's saying flits about us like a moth that's just out of my reach. "As in," I say, "not joining us? He said that to you? Like, expressly?"

She nods.

I sit back. Would this have been his version of my sister's *fuck you*, not showing up at all?

"He had something due at the end of the week. I had to convince him that spending three hours with his mother and sisters wasn't going to ruin him."

Now I remember my brother thumbing away on his phone, and how he'd stepped out mid-meal to take that call. It feels like free-falling into a foam pit of relief: of course. "He's always been like that about work," I say.

"Why do you think that is?"

I smile. "That's a very teacherly sort of question."

Jessie smiles back at me, in a way that makes clear she's not going to let me avoid an answer.

I say, "He wants to be rich, I guess."

Her mouth thins out. "Do you really believe that?"

Is this what she's like in the classroom? I may have underestimated Jessie Shen. "I mean," I say, "I'm sure that's part of it. He wants . . . a certain kind of life. VIP job title. Summer home upstate. Private schools for the kids. Luxury vacations. That whole *look at me I've made it* package."

She says, softly, "It seems like he does."

It's not as if I don't know why. Charles wants everything we never had, growing up in a dingy apartment in Jackson Heights with a single mother who was perpetually short on funds and long on anger. And I hate that he does, because what does that mean for everything we did have? Our childhood was more than the sodden fodder of immigrant deprivation. It was round-robin *xiang qi* games where Charles would ask me if I was sure about my move while Coraline would stay quiet and then checkmate me with excessive glee. Instant-mix pancake dinners on the nights our mother was working late, rides on the F train from Roosevelt Avenue through the tumultuous belly of Manhattan all the way to Coney Island and back. *Wushu* lessons from Uncle Benson, who claimed to have been a stunt double for Jackie Chan back when, according to him, Hong Kong movies were legendary (and who, thinking about it now, must have tolerated us only because he had a crush on our mother). The elaborate mysteries that Charles would stage on my birthdays for me to solve. All the best parts of growing up for me that apparently don't mean anything to my brother.

"Do you remember Charles's ex-colleague . . . Cameron Keller?"

Hearing that name, and said by Jessie, of all people—it's a jolt, like I've grazed up against an electric fence. "Um. Sounds familiar?"

Jessie pinches the stem of her wineglass with her fingers and begins turning it, around and around. "Charles was talking about him on Christmas Eve, how he had suddenly passed away."

Right: I'd forgotten that Jessie joined our family that evening. "Yes," I say. "A heart attack or something like that."

"A cardiac arrest." She sounds apologetic about correcting me. "People who knew him think it was from overwork. He'd just moved over from Precision to one of the big matchmakers, a more senior role than before . . . he must have been dealing with a lot."

All of which I know from having researched Cameron's career trajectory, but it seems odd that Jessie would as well, unless—"Did Charles bring him up again to you? After Christmas?"

"The last time I saw him. You know he took over one of Cameron's matters. It's the main reason he's so busy."

"What did he say?"

"Something about how Cameron handled the project, especially right before he handed it over. Charles felt it could have been better." Now she sounds apologetic about vicariously, and posthumously, badmouthing Cameron.

Charles said as much to me the one time I managed to talk to him about the work he was doing for the matchmakers. That was before I knew about the synths or who Cameron Keller was, and it sounded like a case of outgoing employee syndrome. Considering it now, I wonder. Was there any chance that Cameron's sloppiness could have been intentional? And if so, why?

"I'm not saying the same thing will happen to Charles," says Jessie.

I blink at her. "What same thing?"

"A cardiac arrest, or anything so drastic. But he can't keep working like that. It's unsustainable."

I say, automatically, my mind preoccupied with these new questions around Cameron Keller, "Charles will be fine. He's very sturdy."

She looks at me like I'm one of her students who's just told her Hamlet is the prince of England. "Don't you think everyone thought that about Cameron? That he would be fine, he was used to long hours and unreasonable expectations?"

I take an abashed glug of my beer.

"Claudia, if Cameron did die because he was pushing himself too hard, it wasn't because of his new job. He was at that company for only a few months. What killed him was a path that he began going down while he was still at Precision, or maybe even before that, until he got to the point where he couldn't step off." Jessie pauses. "Do you understand what I'm saying?"

The question, and her earnest yet exasperated tone, triggers all my squirmy-student reflexes. "I do," I say, "I was just . . ."

And then I do really understand, and it feels like something knocking out the floor of my stomach. My working theory has always been that Lucinda Clay found out Cameron was snitching on her, sending details about Soulmate's synth program to Sarah Reaves, and so she duly offed them both before they could expose her. But—as Jessie just said—Cameron could have started down that path prior to joining Soulmate. Precision is the go-to consulting firm for the matching industry. Its website and press releases list a whole bunch of projects that it's completed for various matchmaker clients, both the Big Three and the boutiques, as well as ancillaries, the industry's term for companies that provide matching-related services to consumers and businesses. I don't see the matchmakers letting Precision in on the synths—it would be way too risky to trust an external contractor with that kind of information. But they could still be leveraging Precision's skills and expertise on synth-related initiatives that they've disguised as, say, projects around improving data collection or matching algorithm accuracy. The fact that Precision was part of Sarah Reaves's investigation shows she thought that was, at the very least, a possibility.

And what I can see is Cameron Keller as a clever, curious employee becoming suspicious of what the true purpose of these highly confidential matchmaker projects might be. Learning that the long hours and unreasonable expectations he was subjected to were in aid of large-scale deception and fraud. Realizing, maybe, how far the dangers of this technology could spread, like a haze swathing all types of online forums. Deciding to try to stop it.

What if Lucinda hadn't killed Cameron to stop him from interfering with her plans—what if, dear god, someone else at the matchmakers had, because of what Cameron had done while he was still at Precision? Or perhaps Cameron hadn't done anything at all, not at that point. What if he was killed simply because he had uncovered the truth about the synths? If Becks is right that Let's Meet would kill Pradeep Mehta for knowing that his data had been used to create a duplicate profile, then we have to assume that Let's Meet—or another one of the Big Three with as much to hide—would have done the same to Cameron. In which case, anyone who's taken over Cameron's work at Precision, who's now in a position to find out the same things Cameron found out— they could be in danger. The surprise-cardiac-arrest, fatal-bike-accident type of danger.

"I don't mean to scare you."

Jessie is watching me with that pleated concern. "No, no," I say, even though I feel like the girl in a horror movie who's about to open the door to an empty room when she starts hearing freaky noises on the other side. "Thank you. For . . . bringing this up. I'll talk to Charles."

Her face eases. "You know your brother much better than I do, obviously. Maybe I'm overreacting; I hope I am. I just think someone who cares about him should see what's going on."

If she didn't wince right then, as if she had spoken without thinking, I probably wouldn't have noticed. I give it a beat and then say, "You mean, someone *else* who cares about him? Because you do, right?"

After a moment she says, "I do. But . . ."

"Is it because he works too hard?" I ask, a whole other kind of panic swirling up inside me. "He can change that."

"It's not . . ." She picks up her empty wineglass as if hoping for a magical refill and then sets it down. "Charles took me to Mexico over the new year. He planned out everything, and—it was really sweet of him. The whole time we were there, though, he was working. Calls every day. Documents he had to look at and comment on. We would go out for dinner and then he'd get back on his computer."

"Did you tell him—"

Jessie gives a slight shake of her head and I shut up. "I wasn't upset about that," she says. "He has a demanding job and his career means a lot to him. But I saw how he always said yes. Whatever his clients wanted. The more extreme the ask, the more eager he was to agree, because no one else would."

Her pedagogical intuitions must tell her that I'm clueless about what the moral of this story is meant to be, because she says, "What you said, about how Charles is so committed to his work because it affords him the kind of life he wants? I think it's more than that. I think it's important to Charles to feel like he's needed, and that's what his job at Precision gives him. He can make himself indispensable."

I don't say anything, because I'm remembering a conversation my brother and I had, months ago now, as he was driving me home from Flushing. He had had to cancel plans with Jessie so the two of us could endure yet another emotionally fraught dinner with our mother, and he told me it bothered him that Jessie never seemed to mind, that she never wanted him to go to any trouble for her. What did he say? *It makes me feel like she doesn't need me.* At the time, I interpreted it as standard-issue relationship anxiety talk. Especially because I realized, listening to him, how much Jessie meant to him.

Jessie says, like she's peeking through a window into my memory, "I sense that he's hoping for me to need him in a way that . . . I don't. And I don't think I ever will. It's not that I don't care about him; I wouldn't have reached out to you otherwise. But, I don't know, maybe I'm too pragmatic." Her smile flickers in and then out again. "Or someone else might say, afraid."

"Charles," I say, "*he* really cares. About you. Like, really."

She bows her head. "I know."

My panic is settling into a sustained chill. "You've already made up your mind. That's why you reached out to me." I was wrong, earlier. Jessie isn't planning to pick up my brother's weight again.

This time she doesn't wince. "Would you feel all right not mentioning this to him for the time being?"

"You're asking me to keep the fact that you're dumping my brother from him?"

"Until I can find a better time to talk to him about it. He's under a lot of stress right now, and I don't want this to become one more thing he has to deal with. Emotionally, I mean. I was planning to wait until things had calmed down with his project; I think he has a deadline coming up in May." She adds, with her wry, flickery smile, "I was definitely not anticipating that our conversation would go in this direction."

Despite myself I say, "You're so considerate."

"If what I'm asking makes you uncomfortable," she says, "never mind."

I shake my head. "I'm not breaking up with him for you by proxy." Just thinking about how Charles will react makes me feel as if there's a bruise being pressed into the depths of my chest. I can picture him pushing his glasses up his nose, blinking too vigorously, saying he understands, and all the while splintering up inside like a ship being dashed against the rocks until it's a jumble of debris. "Anyway," I say, forcing a flippancy into my tone, "I have a lot of practice in keeping things from him."

"So I've heard."

Jessie says that with her usual demureness, an allusion to how I secretly quit my previous job as proofreading minion at an investment firm, which Charles got way more bothered about than necessary. I find myself wishing that I'd gotten to know her a little better before she decided to exit stage left on the Lin family. I say, "Charles told me he talked to you about my leaving Aurum Financial and you helped him see things from my perspective. I should have said this earlier, but thanks for doing that."

"He meant well. He has your best interests at heart."

"Yeah," I say. "My brother is very sure that he knows exactly what's best for me."

"How's your new job going?"

I run a finger through the condensation that has beaded on the sides of my glass. "It's going." I think of Becks's final statement, how she nocked it like an arrow and loosed it into the center of her target: *For the record, I do disagree with Komla's decision.* "I, um, got a promotion recently, sort of."

"Congratulations."

"It feels like a lot sometimes," I say. "And my colleagues, I don't know if . . . if they think I deserve it."

"Do you think you do?"

I hesitate. "I don't know that, either."

She nods. "Would you like to hear my thoughts, or should I just listen?"

"That's . . . such a refreshing question." And the antithesis of my family's approach, which would be to force-feed me their advice like I was a stubborn goose refusing to accept my fate as foie gras. "I would love to hear your thoughts."

"I have no idea what your job is like and how good you are at it, so I can't say if you deserve the promotion. At the very least, though, you deserve the chance to find out if you do."

And that chance—perhaps it's whether I'm able to figure out what happened to Cameron Keller. Although trying to prove myself at Veracity is suddenly feeling less important, if my alternate theory is correct and Cameron became aware of the synths because of his work at Precision—and was killed for it. If *that's* what happened, then what I have to figure out is whether the project that Cameron handed over to Charles—which Jessie is already convinced could destroy my brother, even without factoring in a corporate conspiracy to control the hearts and minds of the online public—contains anything that the matchmakers need to keep a secret.

We head out of the bar together. On the sidewalk, Jessie says, "Before I forget, Charles said that Symposium is also one of your favorite bands?"

I'm so braced for further unwelcome information that I hear *Charles* and my brain stalls before starting up again. "Oh," I say. "Yes. I love them."

"I have an extra ticket to their New York concert, if you want it."

Now I remember that Jessie is a Symposium fan as well. "Thanks," I say. "I'm all set." This is the group's first tour in two years, to promote their new album, *Chrysalis*, and I was able to purchase my tickets right after they were released for sale through assertive browser refreshing. I hesitate. "Is this because . . . Was that ticket for . . ."

She says, and I can't tell if I'm projecting the wistfulness into her voice, "It wouldn't have been his thing anyway."

As I walk to the sign pole where I parked my bicycle, I pull on my hat and tie the earflaps together in the inevitably futile effort to block out the wind, and think about deaths, plural. Cameron Keller. Pradeep Mehta. Accidental, or not.

The headlights of a passing car wash my surroundings white. As the darkness closes in again, I suddenly have the sense of someone watching me. I look around. There's only a solo pedestrian, heading in the opposite direction, and, on the other side of the street, a delivery guy getting on his e-bike. I listen to him humming away, and something else that Becks said comes to me, not from this afternoon but during another, earlier disagreement: *Not in whatever implausible, histrionic way you're imagining.* And here I go, imagining that I'm being tailed. I wish she weren't right all the time.

V.

I ASK SQUIRREL to send me the news reports about Pradeep's death. There's a short piece on an Upper Manhattan community news site about a fatal bicycle accident in Fort Washington Park. The deceased is identified as Pradeep Mehta, thirty-two years old, leasing manager at Faraday Realty, living in Midtown Manhattan, originally from Gujarat, India. A post on the *Bike New York* blog contains the same information, along with the additional detail that Pradeep was a volunteer for the Five Boro Bike Tour event the past two years running; also, a note on the importance of wearing a helmet for cycling safety.

The third link I click on launches a webpage epileptic with ads for cars, cruises, and (I'm guessing based on the video) old-people medications. In the midst of this grand display of e-capitalism, there's a foreign-language headline and a photograph of Pradeep's face beneath it. The script is curling and elegant; it makes me think of a series of stylized dance poses. Google, anticipating my needs as usual, asks if I would like to translate this page from Gujarati to English. Yes please.

The translation is serviceable but stilted, which makes me feel a touch better about the near-term threat of humankind's subjugation by AI. *Former youth cricket champion for Gujarat's new American has his life ended in cycling accident.* I scroll on, past Pradeep's picture, and start reading. There's a familiar, maudlin whiff to the prose: so young, how tragic, everything he had yet to do. And, because I'm a bigger sap than a springtime maple tree in Quebec, it's clogging up my emotional sinuses. I met Pradeep only that one time, but I feel like I knew him in a way most people didn't. He let us get close. Not because he wanted to, but because he needed our help—and we weren't able to give it to him.

The article is from what looks like a Gujarat online newspaper, filed under the local section. I learn that Pradeep was from a town called Prantij, that he was the second of four children and the only son, that he was vice captain of the Gujarat under-nineteen cricket team, that he studied electrical engineering at Gujarat Technological University, that he was to be married in May—

Hold up.

I read the relevant sentence again, about how Pradeep and Heema Kothari, a twenty-eight-year-old interior designer, were introduced by their parents last December, when Pradeep was back in India.

The implications of that one fact settle on everything I already know and now I can see what was previously invisible, like fluorescence glimmering under UV light.

The way Pradeep said to us: *You don't understand. I can't have that profile out there like that.* And: *He knows. That's why he's doing this.*

How he broke up with Matthew Espersen right before his most recent trip to India.

The dating profile of him that I found through Match Insights—he had switched from Let's Meet to Partnered Up a few days after he came to see us—last active the morning he died: looking for men between the ages of twenty-six and forty.

I shove myself back from my desk and stand up. I feel all buzzy, like someone has taken a jackhammer to my insides. I put on my coat, check that I have my phone and my keys, and leave.

Outside, there's a papery quality to the late-morning light. I get on my bike, ride on the sidewalk—bad, I know, but cobblestones— to the intersection, then turn left and coast down Greenwich. The street is busy with nannies pushing strollers, blonde women in leggings who look like they're continually heading to or from exercise classes, and a first round of lunchgoers revolving out of all the office buildings in the neighborhood.

I haven't fully decided where I'm going until I turn onto the Hudson River bicycle path and pedal north. Overhead the sky is a fleecy gray. On my right the traffic is thick on the West Side Highway; on my left, the painstakingly maintained walkways and piers of Hudson River Park.

I've never told my mother that I'm gay. In high school, I was in semi-denial. College was in rural Vermont, far enough away that I felt no need to inform her about anything I was doing while I was there, including the conclusions I reached after I kissed a girl and felt like I was seeing the world in color for the very first time. When I moved back to New York after graduation, I didn't intend for that to change. My mother specializes in leveraging her children's vulnerabilities, and I had no desire to expose yet another aspect of myself to her censure. But then she started her *let me find you a nice Chinese boy, stat* campaign, and what had originally been a simple plan of omission snarled into one of ongoing deflection. So last Christmas I came out to her—or I would have, if I hadn't been too much of a wuss. (And, really, how could I have a conversation with my mother about sexuality when we fast-forward through make-out scenes in the shows we watch together?) Instead I asked her to stop trying to matchmake me, and, astoundingly, she might have gotten what I meant. At least, in the three months since, she hasn't once brought up the topic of my romantic life, or utter lack thereof.

And maybe that purgatory isn't such a bad place for us to stay, because even in a reality where I was dating someone, I'd have absolutely no desire to put her in a situation where my mother could have at her.

The thing is, though, if my mother had lost it and declared that my wanting to be with another woman was unacceptable, that I was an abhorrence, that she would disown me—any of the things a small, shrinking part of me did believe she would say—I would just have walked away from her. From Charles and Coraline as well, if I had to. I'm not sure what that shows about me. That I'm a selfish, ungrateful brat, thinking only of my own happiness, ignoring the values and expectations of my family. That I've been brainwashed by the American mantra of individual liberty above all else. That, unlike Pradeep Mehta, I feel I have a choice.

———————

I've ridden up through Fort Washington Park a bunch of times, to the Cloisters and back, but this is the first time I've registered how secluded the route can be. Stretches of the path are hemmed in by trees, still scraggly at this time of year, although there are a few optimistic winks of white and green. Even when my surroundings open up to patchy brown grass and picnic tables and the constant rush of water, I hardly see anyone. A couple of dog walkers, a jogger, a man pushing a shopping cart that has been meticulously packed, like a space optimization exercise, with plastic bags of assorted shapes and sizes. I know that during the summer the park is a popular site for barbecues and birthday parties, but on this chilly weekday in March, it feels like it shouldn't even be part of the city, it's so empty.

The *Bike New York* blog post included a photograph of the area where the crash occurred, and it's easy to recognize when I get there: for several hundred feet, the bicycle route runs parallel to a set of railroad tracks, separated by a high metal fence. I prop my bike against the fence and survey the scene. On the opposite side of the path from the tracks, a tangly line of shrubbery establishes a natural wall between the bike path and the footpaths on the other side. Generally I'm all for sparing bikers from the fatuousness of pedestrians, but right now I can't help thinking that if Pradeep's crash had occurred farther south on the Hudson River Greenway, where it's more populated, or north, once cyclists have to share the path with walkers and runners again, or pretty much at any point except where it did, he would have been found sooner. Potentially soon enough to save his life.

Inspector Yuan is a big fan of feeling out the energy of a place where a death occurred, even if the reason for doing so is inconsistently explained across the novels. Sometimes the violence of a murder inflicts a psychic scar on the site of the crime; other times it's the murder victim's spirit, unable to let go. Either way, the energy here vibes no different from anywhere else to me. Subdued, I guess, because of how quiet it is, and how still, in a way that feels, *creepy* would be an overstatement, but—

The patch of sunlight I'm standing in chooses this moment to fade out, leaving me with goosebumpy forearms. Right, let's get on with this.

First I take enough pictures of the location for a wedding photography recon. Then I swing myself back on my bike and ride up and down this length of the path, trying to pay attention to the feel of the asphalt under my wheels. Pradeep Mehta was an experienced cyclist. The only circumstances under which I could see him skidding was if he was executing a tight-enough turn—and the path here is ruler straight—or he got jolted off-balance somehow.

After several times going back and forth like I've become

trapped in an existential loop, I settle on . . . maybe. The road is definitely overdue for a resurfacing. Some of these cracks have attained chasm-like dimensions; there's one particularly treacherous-looking pothole that Pradeep could have swerved to avoid and lost control of his bike on the ice.

"Watch it, asshole!"

I look over my shoulder: a cyclist is coming at me, swooping over the slight downward incline that the path provides when heading from the south. Time does that selective slowing thing so my brain has the opportunity to foghorn, *Imminent disaster!* but my body isn't able to do anything to avert it.

The man cuts to my left—much closer than necessary—and zooms on past me. I have the minor satisfaction of watching him bounce right into the mega-pothole and out again. "You're the asshole!" I call after him.

Good grief, Claudia. A preschooler would have done better.

Although, to be fair, I'm parked right in the middle of the path like an oblivious tourist on a Citi Bike.

The clattering of the guy's bicycle hushes away, and— Is that the sound of someone laughing?

Okay, *that* is creepy.

The entire ten-mile slog back to Tribeca, the wind slicing at me sideways from the water, I hear that laughter, and think of ghosts.

VI.

SQUIRREL SETS UP a new folder on our shared drive and drops into it over a hundred dating profiles that his search program pulled using the image we have of Matthew Espersen. He obviously didn't review them first—or, giving him the benefit of the doubt, has a mild case of prosopagnosia—because a dozen or so of these are men (or, in a few cases, women) who look nothing like Matthew. Of the remainder, I'm able to eliminate over half based on details in their profiles that conflict with what Pradeep told us. That leaves me with nineteen could-bes. I message each of them from a shell account: Hi Matthew—this is a friend of Pradeep's. I have important news about him. Please text me at (xxx) xxx-xxxx.

When I update Becks, she says, "Let's see if any of them even turn out to be him."

She tells me that, on her part, she's been unable to find any information on Matthew Espersen. "The right Matthew Espersen—there's a gastroenterologist in Copenhagen and an English retiree who posts gardening videos. It's not just social media, like Pradeep said. There are no real estate records, no entries in any of the people-finder directories that we know of, nothing."

I say, "That sounds kind of like us."

One thing that baffled me when I joined Veracity was how nothing seemed to exist online about the company or its employees. Now I know that's thanks to Squirrel's ongoing efforts—he has several programs dedicated to scouring the Internet and sending automated requests to any websites or platforms that have collected our details asking to be removed from their records, complete with citations to data privacy regulations and a note on the prospect of legal action.

"Yes," says Becks. "This man is actively trying to keep his data off the Internet."

Well, he does work in tech, and for a matchmaker. He probably knows better than most the risks of hanging his personal information out to dry in the cyber-ether.

Becks has started bashing away at her keyboard again, so I say, "I'll let you know if we get any promising responses," and turn to go.

"Hold on."

I pivot back around on that same foot until I'm facing her again. She's scowling at me. I try to think if I could have done anything new to piss her off. No overdue case-summary memos. Nothing exciting happening with any of my active verifications. I guess I haven't been updating the shared calendar with the dates and times of my observations, but that's something I've never done, so it's not really fair for her to start bitching at me for it now—

"What we talked about on Monday. In my office."

Ah. That.

Becks stands up and steps out from behind her desk. She starts saying something, then stops. "Are you even listening?"

"What?" I say. "No. I mean, yes. I'm just . . . Did you actually say I was right? I didn't hallucinate that?"

"I did. Say that."

I'm silent, because brain-exploding emoji.

"We *are* partners now." She speaks like her toenails are being pliered off one by one. "In indulging our clients' paranoid fears. In monitoring the matchmakers. And in deciding what to do about the synths."

"In everything," I agree. "Professionally, I mean."

"But that goes both ways. No more running off behind my back to investigate suspicious deaths or make contact with targets."

A tiny frog jumps in my chest at the reference to Amalia Suarez. "That only happened once. Both of those things." Bumping into Amalia again at the Whitney surely doesn't count. Plus, it wasn't a big deal. Mason wasn't with her, I didn't divulge anything except uninspired art criticism, she still knows nothing about the truth.

Giving her my email address . . . well, she hasn't contacted me.

"One mistake can be enough," says Becks. She crosses her arms like she's bracing herself. "Look at Pradeep Mehta."

"We don't know yet that Pradeep's death wasn't an accident," I say.

She says, more to herself than to me, "I never seriously considered that something would happen."

"And maybe nothing did."

Something wavers in her face, like a candle flame left unprotected in a draft, and the fact that I can even pick up on it tells me how perturbed she must be. I find myself moving closer, wishing there was something I could do to reassure her. "Even if it wasn't an accident, that's not on you."

She shakes her head. I touch her shoulder.

"Hey," I say.

She drops her arms, dislodging my hand. "Of course it's on me." The exasperation in her voice is as sudden and impenetrable as the forest of brambles that twists up out of the ground in a fairy tale the instant anyone dares approach. "If Let's Meet killed Pradeep Mehta, it's because of what I told him to do."

"What we told him to do, then," I say. "But—"

"Don't you have an observation to get to?"

That's not until the afternoon, but I say, "Right. Okay."

When I close the door behind me she still hasn't moved from where she's standing in the center of the room.

VII.

WITHIN FORTY-EIGHT HOURS, three of my Matthew hopefuls have messaged the phone number I provided.

The first sends a plethora of dick pics, which I promptly delete while reflecting on how glad I am that I'm gay. The second says he has no idea who Pradeep Mehta is, but he also loves queer rom-coms and Lindy Hop—interests I listed in my shell profile—and would I want to grab a drink sometime?

And the third: Why do you know Pradeep?

I see the message in the morning, when my alarm drags me into semi-wakefulness and I roll over and pick up my phone. How to respond?

He came to us for help. I can meet you and tell you more. I read that through, then add: To confirm that you're Matthew, can you tell me what your and Pradeep's last names are?

The text was sent at 3:01 a.m., so I'm not expecting a reply until later in the day. But I check my phone anyway, after I've brushed my teeth and washed my face and changed, and there are two new messages.

How about tomorrow?

Mehta. I prefer not to give you my last name if you don't know it already. I can tell you it starts with E.

———————————

I try to sound like I fully expected my plan would work when I tell Becks and Squirrel that I've found Matthew Espersen. We're gathered in Komla's office again. "I'll suggest someplace public," I say. I've already decided where: In *Inspector Yuan and the Vengeful Huntsman*, the inspector brings the suspect to the farmhouse where he and his sister grew up. The man, overwhelmed by his memories, is tricked into admitting that he lied about not seeing his sister the night she died. "Like the High Line."

Becks's mouth twists into that familiar pretzel of disapproval. "Squirrel and I will listen in," she says. "And I'll be in the vicinity. Who knows how the hell he'll react when you tell him Pradeep is dead."

I say, "I put the phone number into Finders Keepers, but nothing shows up."

"If he's too paranoid to let Google know where he works, he's definitely too paranoid to leave his GPS function on. Have you been able to verify that he's actually employed at Let's Meet?"

I nod. "I used the dentist trick." It's something we use to check if a target is really employed where they say they are, on the rare occasions we aren't able to find any backup evidence online. We call the company, say that we're from the target's dental office and sorting through some insurance paperwork, and ask if we can just confirm that this is the correct number for the target. (As Komla said once: *Invoke the specter of health insurance in America and no one will think to question you.*) Sometimes an overachieving receptionist will ask questions, but in this case the woman simply said, "Well, he's showing up in my Outlook so I guess he works here."

Squirrel says, "Was it necessary to drag me all the way here for this?"

"Probably not," says Becks, "if we could be sure that while you're sitting in Red Hook you're paying attention to this discussion and not streaming on Twitch."

"My fans demand content."

"Also, I wanted you to look me in the eye and tell me that you're making progress with Operation Pour-over."

"Pour-over" refers to our ongoing monitoring of the synths put out by the Big Three—to the extent our much-maligned filter is able to catch them. The introduction of code names for our synth-related endeavors is one of my proudest contributions to Veracity. When I first proposed it, Becks went into conniptions— "Veracity is not an arena to play out your Walter Mitty fantasies, goddammit"—but Squirrel thought it'd be fun, as I knew he would, and the member vote was two to an extremely cranky one. Democracy in action! And, I'll give this to Becks—she's been strict about using the code names since the policy went into effect, albeit with an entirely superfluous eye roll each time, like right now.

Squirrel twists his baseball cap a full 360 degrees around his head before he says, "I had to take a break. It was stifling me." His nose twitches, which I can recognize by now as a sign of excitement. "I'm working on something much more fun right now."

"*I'll* stifle you. If it's the fucking hot-air balloons again—"

"Even more brilliant. Co-opting what should."

He looks at us like he's waiting for us to fall at his feet and declare him a genius. I say, "What should . . . what?"

"For someone who works at a tech start-up," says Becks, "you are willfully uninformed about developments in technology."

I want to object to her description of Veracity—we are, obviously, a detective agency—but now isn't the time to engage in an existential debate. I settle for: "I'm not the one who reads dead-tree books."

"That," she says, "is an aesthetic choice."

Squirrel says, "WhatShould is an AI chatbot for ethical questions. You have a dilemma, you ask it what you should do, it gives you advice based on the major theories of moral philosophy. Stanford launched a prototype last month."

"Stanford is behind it?" says Becks. "I didn't realize that. The computer science department?"

"And philosophy. Run out of the Katrakis lab."

"How does that work?" I ask. "Wouldn't you get different answers depending on which theory you apply?"

"Who cares?" says Squirrel. "It's all BS. What people want is to be able to share what's bothering them and get a response that makes them feel like they were heard—but with no judgment. That's what WhatShould really gives them. It doesn't understand what you're asking. It just goes through its dataset of philosophical texts, finds what matches best with your question, and spews that out. The user feels comfortable being completely honest. And that gives us a way to find out what's on someone's mind."

I realize: "From the questions they ask."

He points a finger at me like a game show host psyched to start giving away prizes. "Exactly. It's like your search history but more incriminating. I've been lying to the person I'm dating about x, y, or z—what should I do?"

Becks says, "And how are you going to get a particular target's questions from WhatShould?"

"There are ways."

"You haven't figured it out."

"I'm troubleshooting right now. It's just a matter of finding the most elegant solution."

I say, "Do you guys think . . . Doesn't something like that seem a bit too . . . invasive?"

Becks shifts against the window ledge. Squirrel says, "What are you talking about? Our entire business is invasive."

Which doesn't exactly make me feel any more sanguine. "To a certain extent. But, as you said—someone tells WhatShould certain things about themselves precisely because it's a computer program that doesn't understand the meaning of what the person is saying. We're taking advantage of that."

"It's not like no human ever looks at that data. The Katrakis lab collects everything to use in their research."

"But not on the individual level."

"So they say."

"Well, they shouldn't, either."

Becks says to me, "It's a tool. Like any other. There will be situations where its use could be warranted."

"I don't know," I say. Where people go, what they do, what they say about themselves and to each other—the things we currently track are, at least, happening in the shared world that all of us inhabit. What Squirrel is talking about feels like spying on a person's inner world, the concerns and questions that they express only because they know no one else is listening. Surely Veracity should leave that unbreached, especially when we have so little that is truly private these days.

After a moment she says, "Anyway, all of this is theoretical until Squirrel can show us something we can actually use for our verifications."

Squirrel holds out his index finger and thumb a quarter of an inch apart. "This close."

"And get your ass back to work on Pour-over. Not having a filter for the clones is just embarrassing at this point."

"There's still the possibility that Silent G isn't a synth," I say. "Matthew—"

"That possibility is lower than climate change turning out to be a hoax," says Becks, "and after tomorrow we'll stop wasting our time on Matthew Espersen."

"We're not wasting our time."

Her eyebrows lift. I should probably have caveated that statement, but I'm too annoyed by her certainty that—as always—I have no idea what the hell I'm doing. Sure, as far as revenge tactics go, creating a fake dating profile of your ex-boyfriend is an unusual one. But it *was* effective, in Pradeep's case. I remember his anxiety squeezing the air out of the room like a giant inflatable; and I understand, now, his fear of having that profile active on Let's Meet's platform, something he couldn't control. He must have seen it as a threat by Matthew: *Look at what else I could tell the world about who you really are.* Which is the other issue I have with Becks's assumptions. Given how Pradeep wanted to keep his sexuality hidden, would he really have reached out to Let's Meet about Silent G, knowing he would have to explain the profile, Matthew, the breakup, all of that, to a series of strangers?

Becks says, "And if we are?"

"I'll buy you dinner," I say.

Her expression goes still in a different way from the resting bitch face that I've become accustomed to.

"I mean," I say, "unless, if you think, that would be a further waste of our time."

"I . . ." she says. "Don't. Think it would be."

The sound of her voice bounces into my ear and then onward to my brain, and suddenly I feel all sparkly inside, like there's a fireworks display going off under my skin. I say, "But that goes both ways."

The edges of her mouth turn up, and—did a dimple ever-so-

fleetingly indent her cheek? Immediately I find myself compelled
to try to coax it forth again.

Squirrel says, "I want a free dinner, too."

We both look over at him. "Once you get us that filter," says
Becks.

"What? That's, like, boss-level difficulty."

"It's also your job. I don't know why the fuck we have to bribe
you with food to do it." She steps away from the ledge. "You'll set
things up with Matthew Espersen?" she says to me.

"I'll text him after this," I say. "And whoever's right gets to
pick the restaurant."

"In that case," she says, "I'll send you my list."

VIII.

I HAVEN'T BEEN UP on the High Line recently, and now I remember why: the tourists, filing along the repurposed railway spur like pilgrims with selfie sticks. I squeeze myself onto the end of a bench by the Gansevoort Street entrance, next to a ruddy mountain range of a family in matching I ♥ NY sweatshirts who, if I had to guess, are not loving being either here or in shoulder-to-shoulder proximity to one another. There's such a pathos to people who are miserable on vacation, the effort they've put into leaving where they are for this other place precisely because it's supposed to make them happy. I guess I should be glad my family was too poor for us to ever go anywhere farther than Rockaway Beach.

I'm looking around, ostentatiously holding open a paperback copy of *The Quiet American*—Becks's, excavated from a pile in her office, and the book I told Matthew Espersen he could identify me by—when I see him. He's on the other side of the walkway, against the railing, watching me in a way that might be creepy if I wasn't all psyched that he's actually shown up. I recognize him at once, even bulked up in winter clothes and with a knit cap pulled over his scalp. Maybe it's how he holds himself, which is just as I imagined he would: apart, as if he's superimposed on this scene, someone who could fade away and leave everything unchanged.

I jump up and cross over to where he's standing, photobombing a couple in my haste. "Matthew E.," I say.

He's not a tall man—measuring up from my own height of five-four, I'd say he has three inches on me, max—but he's mastered the art of making me feel like he's looking down the blade of his nose at me. His expression, at once remote and calculative, does not change. "And you are?"

"Claudia."

"All right," he says. "Claudia. Tell me more."

I think of all the bereaved Inspector Yuan has had to notify throughout his illustrious career, that long-suffering parade of husbands and wives and concubines, parents and children and siblings and cousins, teachers and disciples and friends. It never seems to trouble him, the fact that he's drawing the uncrossable line between their before and after: the world is fine; the world has come apart. If Matthew is still in love with Pradeep—

Matthew, his voice sharp: "What is it?"

"Pradeep passed away." I sound panicked, as if I just found out. "Last month."

Matthew closes his eyes. Something tidal washes over his face, wiping it empty. I look away, at the tourists walking back and forth before us, and the bright blue sky domed overhead.

"What happened?" he says.

"It was a bike accident," I say, and describe the context.

When I finish he says, slowly, "And they're sure. That it was accidental?"

My mind spins off like a dreidel hurled into motion with more enthusiasm than skill: Is he asking about murder?—does he have his own suspicions about Let's Meet?—is there some *other* reason Pradeep could have been killed?

Then the somewhat less sinister, and rather more plausible, alternative occurs to me.

I ask, "What else do you think it could have been?"

He sighs. "Can we walk?"

We join the northbound lane of pedestrians. It's not so crowded as to be uncivilized, but there's definitely both an upper and a lower speed threshold in effect. At this time of year, the park is a palette of brown and green and gray, feathery grasses and branches like spindles.

"Pradeep and I used to come to the High Line a lot," says Matthew.

"Did you?"

"It's where we had our first date." There's no sentiment in his voice: this is a relating of an incidental fact.

We walk past a little amphitheater with glass windows that look out on Tenth Avenue. A scattering of people are sitting on the wooden steps, staring out at the glitter of traffic like they're watching a really suspenseful movie.

"The last time we were here," says Matthew, "we ran into someone he knew. From work. Pradeep introduced me as his friend."

"He wasn't out at work?"

His mouth curls. "Pradeep wasn't out anywhere."

"That must have been hard," I say.

He says, like I haven't spoken, "You said in your message that he came to you for help. Help with what?"

You. "He was on a matchmaker, and he saw that someone had set up a fake profile using his information. He wanted us to get it taken down."

Matthew is silent. We enter a more enclosed part of the trail, trees and shrubs pressing in around and above, and switch to walking in single file. Beneath our feet the steel line of the old railway track leads us on, on, on. I'm reminded of the stretch of the Fort Washington Park bike path where Pradeep crashed.

Matthew's voice, behind me: "I'm not sure I understand. You work for the matchmaker?"

"No. I think Pradeep was just trying everything he could think of."

"Which one was it? Which matchmaker?"

I wait until the trail widens and we are side by side again. "Let's Meet."

Matthew stops walking. I hear an exasperated huff right before someone pushes between us—a middle-aged woman, frizzy hair and pointy elbows, exercise tights. She has the temerity to glare back over her shoulder as she brisk-walks onward, when the real questionable act is trying to get in your cardio on the High Line.

"Let's move out of the way," I say.

We step off to the side, onto a small rectangular lawn that sits like a carpet in front of another set of big wooden steps. Matthew says, "Pradeep thought I was behind it?"

"Why do you say that?"

"I work for Let's Meet. I'm guessing Pradeep told you that. Just as he told you about me, because otherwise I don't see how you would know, and he wouldn't have done that unless he believed it was relevant to that fake profile."

This man thinks like a detective. Here goes. "And . . . *were* you behind it?"

He does the look-down-the-nose thing at me again. "I don't owe you an answer."

"You don't. But aren't you curious about how all this is connected: Pradeep, the profile, my . . . organization?" If he thinks like a detective, he'll want to know.

"I see," he says. "You want to trade information."

I wait.

"All right."

The indifference in his tone rolls toward my conviction, threatening to capsize it like a shoddy kayak: he's agreeing because he knows he has nothing to give up. I feel, even more acutely than before, the weight of the plastic disc sitting in the inner pocket of my jacket; Squirrel rigged me up with a listening device adapted from a baby monitor, leading to predictably snide commentary from Becks. They're both tuned in to this exchange, and I bet they're thinking the same thing I am: I got it wrong.

Matthew says, "You can start."

We sit down on the steps, and I give him the two lines on Veracity that Becks and I agreed on: how we're an agency that verifies people's online-dating personas, and Pradeep came to us because a prior client led him to think we could help with his situation.

"But you couldn't," he says.

He sounds like he means it as a clarification, but my insides twist like an especially dirty dishcloth being wrung out. "No," I say. "We did suggest he contact Let's Meet directly and ask them to remove the profile."

"That would have done nothing."

"The profile is gone now. I checked after we heard about Pradeep's death."

His eyebrows lift. "I suppose if he included enough lawsuit-related key words, his form submission would have been routed to a human instead of a mailbox that no one checks."

And people wonder why America is such a litigious society. "Or," I say, "the person who put it up decided to take it down."

I try to look at him meaningfully, which leaves me feeling a bit cross-eyed.

"I had nothing to do with that profile," he says. "Why would I do something bizarre like that?"

"Because you were upset about Pradeep breaking up with you."

He stares at me for a beat too long. Then he says, "If that's what Pradeep told you, it's false. I was the one who broke up with him."

"I guess sometimes things get a bit messy toward the end," I say, as if my own experience isn't entirely breakup adjacent, consisting of inept hints to the girls I've been hooking up with that we should stay friends, or, even lamer yet, just ghosting them to avoid the awkwardness, like one of the douchebag targets I verify. "It can be hard to tell who technically broke up with who."

"No," says Matthew. "It was very clear. I told Pradeep I couldn't be with him anymore, not the way things were."

"And how . . . were things?"

I half expect him to refuse to answer. Instead he sighs, as he did earlier, and says, "I'll give you an example. We never came back to the High Line after the time we ran into that person Pradeep knew, because Pradeep was too afraid we would see her again."

He turns to face the lawn that we're sitting at the edge of, across which a gender-indeterminate toddler is staggering with the epic tenacity of Amundsen toward the South Pole while their mother films them and coos encouragement. "Pradeep had a real life and a fantasy life. The fantasy was what he had with me. What was real was everything else. His family in India, his friends, his job. His cricket club. That was more real than I was."

"Maybe both lives were equally real to him," I say. "And both meant as much."

I intend that as a comfort, but Matthew reacts as if I've said something repugnant. "It was never real. How could it have been real when he had to hide it from everyone? Pradeep—he was weak. Too weak to fight for what he really wanted; too weak to accept that and let go of it." His gaze cuts over to me. "You said he was on Let's Meet. He was matching with men, wasn't he?"

I don't have to say anything. Matthew exhales and looks away again. "That's why I asked if his death was definitely an accident.

The position he was in was . . . untenable. If he had decided to give up, on everything . . ." His voice sinks, as if he's drifting away from me. "I wouldn't be surprised."

"He slipped on ice. It doesn't sound intentional."

"I suppose it doesn't make a difference. Whatever it is, he's gone."

We sit in the hollow of that statement. The toddler has plunked themselves down on the grass, expedition abandoned. I feel the same way—I believe what Matthew is saying, that Silent G has nothing to do with him. There's nothing vindictive or conflicted in his manner, and his account of his and Pradeep's relationship is consistent with what I've discovered about Pradeep. He left Pradeep because Pradeep couldn't give him what he wanted; he had no reason to pull a stunt like Silent G.

I glance over. Matthew's profile reminds me of a promontory, the type star-crossed lovers would hurl themselves from. He's staring at a fixed point somewhere above the heads of all the people thronging past us. If I sidled away right now, I don't think he would object, or even notice.

Except . . . I will not let Matthew Espersen be a waste of time, dammit. And he doesn't have to be. He's a Let's Meet insider—he has access to the company's systems, and he's familiar with its tech. Plus, he cared for Pradeep. He would be motivated to find out the truth about Pradeep's fake profile, about the circumstances of Pradeep's death.

First, though, I would have to share with him a teeny bit more about what Veracity is up to, which Becks and I most definitely did not agree on. But, I mean, she has to afford me leeway to improvise, right?

"Are you thinking the same goes for Pradeep's duplicate profile?" I ask. "That it doesn't make a difference now?"

Matthew's shoulders twitch like he's a voice-activated android. "What I think," he says, "is that it never made a difference. Anything you put online can get taken and used by someone else. If you can't deal with that, keep the information to yourself."

"But who would want to take Pradeep's information like that and use it to create a second matching profile? For what purpose?"

He shakes his head. "I'm guessing," he says, like he's being drawn in despite himself, "that Pradeep went on Let's Meet after we broke up. I hope so, anyway. That was in December. And he came to you in . . ."

"The beginning of February."

"Which means Pradeep's profile was up for only two months when that happened. Maybe he met someone and it went badly, or he attracted the wrong person's attention." Matthew shakes his head again. "Who knows? People are strange."

Amen to that. "We think the question of who's responsible for Pradeep's duplicate profile, and what they wanted to do with it, could be really important. Pradeep believed that person was you. That's why I contacted you—to try to find out whether he could have been right."

"He wasn't," says Matthew, distantly, like he's thinking of a hundred other things Pradeep wasn't right about. "But if that's the story you would like to tell, you're welcome to it."

"No," I say. "I believe you. Actually, that's the problem."

My phone buzzes in my pocket: text received.

He turns to look at me. "What do you mean?"

"We have two theories about this duplicate profile. One is that you put it up." Another buzz. "The other . . . is that someone working on behalf of Let's Meet did it."

There's a faint rippling across his face, like I've reached out and touched a finger to a secluded surface of water. "Why would Let's Meet do that?"

A promising response: he doesn't sound like he considers the idea to be self-evidently absurd. "We know that Let's Meet has been trying to develop artificially intelligent profiles that can pass as human on their platform. Pradeep's duplicate could be an example of that."

Buzz—buzz—pause—*buzz*. I briefly consider that Becks is resorting to some version of Morse code and then decide she's just getting exponentially agitated.

"Profiles that they're generating from their customers' personal data?" says Matthew, like he read that a while ago on Wikipedia. "That's a serious allegation."

"As you said, anything you put online can get taken and used by someone else."

"Do you have any evidence?"

"We're in the process of gathering it." My phone feels like it's transmogrified into a swarm of bees. Better finish this up before Becks stampedes in and hauls me away. "We could use your help, given your role at Let's Meet."

"When you say *we* . . ."

"My agency," I say. "In addition to the verifying people stuff, we also do, uh, this." In the extremely remote event that I get to recruit another volunteer, I'll need a snappier pitch.

He says, "You're asking me to inform on my employer."

"Solely to establish if they're doing anything illegal." I consider floating the possibility of Pradeep's murder as well. But we have no proof, as of now; I should spare Matthew from that terrible doubt. "Don't you want to find out what Pradeep's duplicate profile is really about? Whether Let's Meet was misusing his information?"

Matthew Espersen gazes at me. His eyes are small and deep-set, light brown, considering. From his readiness to entertain what I've been saying to the militancy with which he guards his own data, I'd bet he has his concerns around all the private information that the average networked person is firehosing out into the public world, how it's being recorded and collected, who might be in a position to take advantage of that. I'm about to try appealing to his civic duty when he asks, "Are you a romantic?"

I blink at him. "That's a bit of a personal question."

He shrugs. "It's also a key part of everything we're talking about."

I suppose that's one way of looking at it. In my pocket, my phone has stilled. I'm renewedly aware of Becks listening, probably preparing to scoff.

"Hopeless," I say.

His expression ripples again, more deeply this time, something submerged starting to rise before sinking back down. "I see."

I say, meaning it as a joke, "Was that the right answer?"

After a moment he says, "Yes. Thank you." He takes a breath. "What's the handle of the duplicate profile?"

I get the sense he had been about to say something else and changed his mind. This line of questioning is encouraging, though. "Silent G. And Pradeep's was—"

"That's Deep?"

There's a rueful lift in Matthew's voice. I nod.

"All right," he says. "I'll see what I can find for both profiles."

This feels more gratifying than rescuing an Ultimate game in the final seconds of play with a desperate, charmed fling of the Frisbee into the end zone. I so want to high-five someone right now. "Awesome!" I say. "I mean, sounds good. Um, in terms of letting us know what you find—"

He stands. "We should keep moving. We can discuss what the safest methods of information exchange would be."

As I get up as well, I decide I was wrong. Matthew Espersen doesn't think like a detective. He thinks like a spy.

IX.

I EXIT THE STAIRWELL into the third-floor lobby to the sight of Becks marching back and forth on the other side of Veracity's doors, wearing her fury like a fashion statement. It looks like she might have been doing that for a while, and also like this might be a case of time letting a wound go gangrenous rather than healing.

She yanks one of the doors wide. "And what the fuck was that?"

I want to ask her what *that* she's referring to, in retaliation for all the occasions she's berated me for my millennial sloppiness with language—especially rich for somebody in her thirties, which means she's one of us no matter how much she's in denial about it—but then she might implode and take me with her. "Let's talk inside?" I say.

She shifts back just enough for me to enter and close the door behind me. I say, "We didn't get the chance to discuss it beforehand, but—"

"We discussed it. You find out whether Matthew Espersen had

anything to do with Silent G, you say goodbye. The end. You don't confide in some guy you met ten minutes ago about the synths. Jesus Christ. Why stop there? You should have shouted it out to everyone walking by on the High Line."

"Matthew isn't some guy. He's—"

"He's some guy who works for Let's Meet."

"Exactly! He—"

"He could go in to work tomorrow and tell his buddy that he heard something crazy about how their company is building bots based on customer data. Or get it into his head that he should talk to compliance, just in case. He could leak what you told him in fifty different ways, and I guarantee you it will reach the people at Let's Meet who are behind the synths."

"I don't think Matthew Espersen is the type to—"

"You have no fucking clue what type of person he is."

"Can you—for the love of god—stop interrupting me?"

Becks's eyes go bulgy for an instant, which would actually be entertaining in a less stressful situation. Then she flicks her hand at me like a lord allowing their peasant to beg pardon for this year's atrocious harvest instead of presumptively having them dragged out back and flogged.

"We need someone on the inside," I say. "Like St. Elmo was, for Soulmate. Even more so here. We're starting from zero with these clone synths. We don't know how to identify them or how many of them there are. We don't know if they've reached bellwether level or aren't that sophisticated yet. We don't know how Let's Meet plans to use them. Any intel we can get on any of those questions is important."

Becks opens her mouth.

"Hold on—just, one more thing—Matthew is the perfect asset. He's in IT, which means his job is officially to poke around in all the places that Let's Meet stores its information. He's already

attuned to the dangers of how much data we put out about ourselves online. His connection to Pradeep means he'll be invested
in finding out the truth about Silent G."

I stop, but only because I'm winded from having gotten all of
that out in one breath.

"Can I speak?" says Becks. "Or do I need the conch?"

The idea of what Becks would be like in a *Lord of the Flies* situation is terrifying. "Go," I say. "Please."

"When did you decide to switch genres?"

"What?"

"Listen to yourself. Asset? Intel? Next you'll be asking Squirrel
to build you an exploding Fitbit."

Once she says that: yes. (Did I really use the term *asset*? I blame
the Somnang films.) We're out of classic murder mystery territory now, with its roll call of suspects and motives, the clues that,
when properly arranged, allow for only one irrefutable conclusion,
the relentless drive toward revelation and the restoration of moral
order. This is the pea-souper of the espionage narrative: double
agents, secretive organizations, ongoing machinations for influence and control. Where an untoward death isn't a rift in the social
fabric that must be mended but a move on a game board that may
be rewarded; and so you compromise your way to victory, hoping
it will all have been worthwhile in the end.

"You're right," I say.

"Of course I'm right."

"Can Squirrel really do that?"

"He can't even build a bookshelf from Ikea."

Disappointing, even if I wouldn't actually have wanted an
exploding anything—knowing me, I would end up setting it off
by accident during the brunch rush at Groucho's.

"Tell Matthew Espersen you came to your senses and you're
calling off the spy games."

"What's the alternative?" I ask. "We wait for Squirrel to build a semi-accurate filter that can pick up on the clones? How long is that going to take?"

I feel bad discrediting Squirrel like that, but it's true—without Matthew, we're stalled for now. Becks makes a small, disgruntled noise, which I interpret as an admission that I've made a valid point.

I say, "We can't pass up this opportunity."

Now she says, "That's what this person is to you? An opportunity?"

I shake my head. Learning to handle the guilt trip was a prerequisite for survival in the Lin household, and on that front, Becks has nothing on my mother. "His willingness to help is an opportunity. A great one."

"Sarah Reaves must have thought the same about the opportunity she had. An insider with plenty of information on Soulmate's development of synth profiles. How could she have passed it up?"

This time I have to glance away. "You're right." Again—which is what makes working with her both aggravating and satisfying. I was too focused on convincing Matthew; I didn't let myself think through the potential consequences for him. If Let's Meet did engineer Pradeep's death after all, when he went to them with the news of Silent G, they would totally do the same to Matthew if they caught him snooping around trying to find out more about that very profile. "I have to let Matthew know about the potential danger. He might change his mind."

"Even if he doesn't," says Becks, "if something happens to him, we'll be responsible. Can you handle that?"

I find myself thinking about all the ways the various local providers of information and shelter to Somnang in his missions across Southeast Asia end up ruined: livelihoods destroyed, promises of passage to England revoked or conveniently forgotten, family members kidnapped, shunned by their communities, tortured, killed, or all of the above. If the lesson of murder mysteries

is to cultivate a healthy suspicion of your interpersonal relationships, the lesson of spy thrillers is probably to stay well away
from espionage unless you're an upper-class British or American
citizen with the political wherewithal to ensure your government
will extract you, eventually, from whatever death trap they order
you into.

"I don't know," I admit. "But I don't think that means we
should take the choice away from him."

"You're saying that because you've never had to be responsible."

I say, irked by her readiness to swat aside my opinions, "I'm
saying that because I believe it. Just like I believe we can't step
aside now and let the matchmakers keep going with the synths.
Those things could reshape our society, and no one even knows
they exist!" I'm about to bring up Norah Simmons as a potential
example, but the recollection of everything Becks doesn't know
about Encounter Number Two with Amalia Suarez stops me. "If
players like Polaris get their way, they'll be controlling what we
want, what we think—everything."

"I was monitoring the synths before you even joined Veracity,"
says Becks. "I'm aware."

"Yes, and aren't you the one who told me that we have to stay
in until it's cleaned up?"

"That was when . . ."

Her gaze angles away. When what? When we thought we
were dealing with an isolated death, a single adversary, a case we
could see all the corners of? When Komla was still around to provide expertise and direction? Or even—when I wasn't part of the
decision-making?

Before I can ask, she says, "Do you really think you can go
up against the biggest corporations in the matching industry and
win?"

"I do! It's asymmetrical warfare." Also gleaned from the Somnang Files: the Dream haunting Saigon, working her way down

the list of Western diplomats she has been instructed to kill; the Viet Cong setting their ambushes and then ghosting back into their tunnels, aware that if they could blow up enough truckloads of American soldiers everyone would go home. "We're not trying to destroy the matchmakers. We're just getting them to give up on the synths. I'm sure there are ways we can do that. Some sort of public exposé, once we have enough information on what they're doing—"

"The sort Sarah Reaves had in mind before she was murdered for it?"

"I mean, we would be more careful." I add, because I can tell Becks is winding up to lob another softball of snideness at me, "Or, with Let's Meet, we could work with Matthew to sabotage their synth project. His usefulness isn't limited to providing information."

She sighs. "And the problem with bringing him in isn't limited to the risk to him. There are risks to us as well. We have no idea how credible he is. Or trustworthy. He could be feeding us a load of bullshit, or turn around and sell us out to Let's Meet."

"So we'll test him out for now and limit what we tell him. He doesn't even know Veracity's name. Even if he wanted to, he couldn't give Let's Meet anything."

I watch an opaque calculation clicking across her face. Finally she says, "No. He'll be less inclined to help us if we appear to be holding back ourselves. We'll just give him inaccurate information about who we are."

"As in, lie to him? Our own agent?"

"Of course. We have no certainty that he's really acting as our agent."

That sounds like the kind of thinking Niccolò Machiavelli would have approved of, and also like Becks is saying–not saying we can go ahead with Matthew Espersen, so I'm not going to quibble. "Okay."

She narrows her eyes at me. "This doesn't mean I've conceded that we aren't wasting our time."

"Not yet!" I say.

My mood for the rest of the afternoon is chirpier than a crew of parakeets, and it's hard to say which excites me more: landing a bona fide informant at Let's Meet, or the prospect of Becks treating me to pancakes at Groucho's.

X.

THE MORNING AFTER my conversation with Jessie, I texted Charles to say we should catch up and suggested Sunday night takeout at his place in Long Island City—a plan, I figured, that required minimal exertion on his part. It took him three days to respond with *Too busy right now*, and in that prolonged silence my paranoia started breeding like bedbugs in a Times Square movie theater. All those possible nexuses between Cameron Keller's murder and Cameron's work at Precision, Cameron's work and my brother, my brother and information on the synths that someone would kill to safeguard: an entire Venn diagram of machinations and danger. I even spot-checked Charles's presence on Finders Keepers and was inordinately reassured to see him show up at Precision's offices in Hudson Yards.

Since then, we've been going back and forth at a speed more appropriate, on his part, for the Pony Express than cell tower transmission. I'll suggest a date, he'll give me some variation of *That won't work*. Finally, much as I hate to, I play my trump.

> I need to talk to you about something.
> I need some help.

This time he texts back within the hour: About what?

Can I drop by your apartment tomorrow night? After I make the request, I type as a follow-up: Promise not to take up more than 30 minutes of your precious time. Too snide? He'd probably find it odd if I wasn't. I tap SEND.

> You can have as much time as you
> need. 8 pm okay?

Well, now I feel like an ingrate.

Charles answers the door dressed like he teleported in from the office right before I rang the doorbell, and also—

"Wow, *Dà gē*," I say, "you look like a jaundiced panda."

He grimaces at me as he unlassos his tie. "Can I kick you out right now?"

I trail after him into his studio. His laptop is in its docking station on his desk, and both monitors are lit up. My brother's home work setup is superior to my work-work one. I say, "I'm not sure if you've already eaten, but I picked up some *lu rou fan*."

I cross the room to place the plastic bag on his kitchen island, which positions me at an angle where I'm able to see what's on the monitors. On the left, an email inbox; on the right, a website.

"Oh," he says, like he's forgotten that food is a thing. "I'm okay. Thanks. Go ahead if you're hungry."

The end of his statement is punctuated by an electronic chime, and at the same time I see a chat box pop up on one of the computer screens. My brother takes his phone out of his pocket. "I have to talk to someone," he says. "Shouldn't take more than fifteen minutes."

This might be easier than I expected. "No problem."

He glances up at me. "Uh . . ."

I say, as if I haven't noticed, "So hungry." I lift one of the bowls out of the bag and then pause. "Do you want me to step out?"

Charles shakes his head. "You eat. I'll just go into the bathroom."

I nod and mouth, *You're the best*, as he puts the phone to his ear. "Fred," he says. "I thought you wanted . . ."

He closes the bathroom door behind him and the edges of his voice blur away. I slide in my socked feet across the floor to his desk. The chat message, at the bottom right corner of the screen, is from a Frederic Toum: Call me ASAP. Based on the thumbnail photo next to his name, he looks like the sort of guy who would interact with the world via directives, although I should give him a break since I wouldn't have had this opportunity otherwise.

I shift my attention from the chat box to the rest of the screen. This website has a lot going on. A banner image of the Manhattan skyline stretches across the top like a low-budget tourist brochure. There's a column of icons on the left-hand side of the page and a news feed running down the middle. The most recent headlines:

Welcome Jim O'Grady—Analyst, NY
9,421 Trees Still Needed for Completion of Plant-a-Tree
      Initiative. Act Now!
Denver Office Renovations to Commence 04/01

Ah.

I check the URL to make sure—oh yes. I'm looking at Precision's corporate intranet.

My brother's voice is a low, placatory blur. I type *Cameron Keller* into the search bar at the top right corner of the page and press ENTER.

The page reloads with a total of 264 results. PowerPoint presentations. Excel spreadsheets. PDFs. Word documents. There's no preview or summary of what the items contain, only the file title, the name of the creator, the date the file was uploaded to the system, and when it was last updated. I scroll until I see a file that has Cameron J. Keller named as creator and click on it.

Access Denied: Contact the file administrator to request access.

I backspace and take a closer look at the file details. *Project Ulysses 1st interim report*, PDF, uploaded in January last year and most recently updated just two weeks ago.

The next item I try, again with Cameron listed as the creator, gets me the same *Access Denied* message. Same with the third and fourth.

Finally I click on a file that has a different creator. This time it obligingly opens up into an Excel document, rows and rows of information in the tiniest font. After some squinting I deduce (aided by the file's title: *STG Matters+Pipeline 9-Month Summary*) that this is a project tracker of sorts for Precision's social-tech group, which I know Charles is part of. I do a search for Cameron Keller within the spreadsheet and he comes up as responsible for five projects: Bahamas II, Mykonos, Phuket, Santorini V, Tahiti. Either Precision has a very specific code names policy or the people who work there are desperate to go on vacation.

When I return to the main search results page, I see that the file was last updated over a year ago, in February. Which makes sense: it would be a historic document, given that Cameron left Precision last March and would have handed off his matters to other employees in the group. Including Charles.

I straighten up from my increasingly arthritic hunch over the keyboard. All these file titles and code names, the intermittent sounds of Charles's voice behind that bathroom door—my mind is feeling a bit like an under-oxygenated aquarium teeming with colorful, distractible fish. Think, Claudia. Ninety percent of desktop verification work is understanding what information would prove or disprove the point you're seeking to verify, and how to convince Google to serve it up to you—or, here, Precision's less-than-cooperative search engine. I have the names of the projects that Cameron was working on; I know Charles took one of them over. What I need to find out is which project that is and whether it's related to the synths.

Then it comes to me. In *Bearers of Gifts*, Somnang's mission is to identify and infiltrate a radical student group suspected of plotting a large-scale attack on the eve of Malaysia's federal elections. His only lead is the corpse of a young man known to have been a member, and a key found on his person. With the help of a local locksmith—who, surprise surprise, is killed a few scenes later—Somnang realizes that the key is for one of the student activity rooms on the University of Malaya's campus. He then checks the room's booking records to determine which organizations had access during the relevant times and cross-references that information against the deceased's extracurricular affiliations—in a meta flourish, the group in question turns out to be masquerading as an esoteric film appreciation society. (Because this is the Somnang Files, as atmospheric yet ultimately unsatisfying as a Murakami story, those kids prove incapable of plotting anything other than a scathing critique of Western cinema.)

I haven't been able to open any of the Cameron files I tried because they're linked to matters that Charles isn't a part of, and I'm logged in to Charles's account. But one of the five beach holiday destinations that I saw in the spreadsheet must be the project that Charles is beavering away at—and so I should be able to look at the files that Cameron created for it. I just need to search for Cameron Keller's name combined with each of those projects in turn, and see which project allows me access to Cameron's files.

Bahamas II: *Access Denied.*
Mykonos: *Access Denied.*
Phuket: *Access Denied.*
Santorini V: *Access Denied.*

Of course it would be the last one that I try. I key in *Tahiti Cameron Keller* and start scrolling through the hits.

"Claw? What are you doing?"

My heart leaps like someone in a movie who is trying to escape their pursuers by vaulting from the roof of one building to the next but fails to clear the distance and plummets fifty flights screaming in terror. I force myself to wait a second before I look up. Charles stands in the half-open doorway of the bathroom, holding his phone like he was in the midst of checking messages when he noticed where I was.

From his position, he can't see what I'm looking at. He's exhausted and preoccupied. And . . . he trusts me. Those three facts twist together into a rope that I can grab on to and use to pull myself up to safety.

"I'm checking the weather." That's the voice of someone with nothing to hide. Isn't it? "It's supposed to rain later tonight, so I want to make sure I get home before it starts."

"If it's raining, you're not biking."

I slide the mouse cursor up to the URL box so I can switch to the Weather Channel website—and then back down again, to hover over the file name *Relevance Factors Prelim Ranking*. So close! "Ideally not." *Click.* "That's why I'm checking."

Access Denied: Contact the file administrator to request access.

What?

Charles pads over. "What happened to your phone?"

I shut down the browser altogether. He asks this like he expects me to have dropped it in the river while I was cycling over the Queensboro Bridge to get here; all I have to do is play into his notions of me as the hapless baby sister. "Dying. I forgot to charge it last night."

My brother doesn't even look at the monitors when he reaches the desk. He pulls open a drawer and removes a neatly coiled USB cable. "Here. Charger's next to my bed. There should be a free port."

As I take the cable from him, I glance at the other screen, on which his email inbox is displayed. Almost every one of his messages is marked with a little flag in a range of colors, and so what stands out is the email halfway down the index that has no flag at all, like a spy who's looking a touch too nondescript.

>   *Withers, Rae*
>   *Re: re: Tahiti—next steps*

I plug in my phone and then join him at the kitchen island. The oily, pungent aroma of *lu rou fan* thickens between us, and suddenly I feel faintly sick.

"So," says my brother. "What did you want to talk about?"

Why Cameron's files for a project that you're leading are locked away from you. What does this mean? I'm aware I should be relieved—if Charles can't view the work that Cameron has done, that lessens the chances of him stumbling upon some fatal secret—but I'm not. If anything, my unease is compacting into something smaller and denser, sinking deeper, becoming even harder to dislodge.

"Claudia?"

My brother is squinting at me like he isn't sure if he should be concerned or annoyed. I rouse myself: there's still part two of my plan. "Don't freak out," I say, and that's as much to myself as to him.

"Oh god," he says. "Did you lose your job again?"

"I didn't lose my job at Aurum, I left. And that's not it."

"You're being evicted."

"What? Why would you think that?"

"Because your building is in violation of a hundred different housing regulations."

"That's why the rent is so affordable."

"You got into a bike—"

"There's this girl."

The look on my brother's face, like I said I saw a tarantula creep inside his sleeve—I almost ask to borrow his phone so I can take a photo. "I met her online," I say. "She seems really cool, but at the same time, you know, it's like I know so little about her."

I came out to my siblings through a message I sent to the Three Cs the sheepish yet self-satisfied morning after I'd hooked up with my TA from Romanticism and Anti-Romanticism. Coraline's reply was instantaneous: OMG I thought you were asexual! Charles didn't respond, which niggled at me more than I wanted to admit, like a pebble in my shoe I just couldn't shake out, but the next time we saw each other he said to me, "I kind of wondered if you might be, uh, gay." It was the week of Thanksgiving; I'd taken the bus down to Port Authority, where he had picked me up, and we were driving to our mother's apartment. I was so consternated that I was having a face-to-face conversation with my brother about my sexual orientation that I said, "Hope you don't mind." I'd meant to be flippant, but after I spoke I wondered: *Did* he mind? And if so, what would I do? "Of course not," he said. He sounded upset that I might think he did. "It's all cool." Then he turned up the music and we listened to his whiny alt-rock playlist without speaking for the remaining hour of the drive.

"Do you think," says Charles, "Coraline might be a better person to talk to about . . . this kind of thing?"

"Being into cute girls?"

He adjusts his glasses. "Right. Yeah. True."

"Plus, I want some of your intel. From the matchmakers."

"What are you talking about?"

"Your big project at work is about improving the data you get on subscribers. So . . . what's important here? What should I be trying to find out about her to have a better idea of who she is?"

The way he looks at me right then—I don't understand it, but I feel my chest clotting in apprehension. When he speaks, his tone is impatient. "What you're asking makes no sense."

"Wow," I say. "Harsh."

He lowers his gaze to his phone, placed facedown on the counter before us. "You want to know what this one person is like," he says. "That doesn't matter to the matchmakers. It doesn't matter to them what anyone is like, as long as they can predict how well that person will match with another person."

"But they need to know who those two people are in order to predict that."

"They need data about those two people. Micro-level data that's specific to the person and macro-level data about their demographic. Once the matchmakers have enough of that, they can build models and look for patterns. They don't have to understand why those patterns are the way they are. Only what outcomes they point to."

"So a computer program can tell who we should date, and . . . it's not even about who we or the other person are?"

"Why not?" he says. "There's consistent research showing that most of the things people do are driven by their subconscious. The reason that they give for their actions is just their brain post hoc rationalizing. If that's correct, then this question of who someone is, in the way we currently think of it, becomes meaningless. It doesn't help us get to the right answers."

"And you believe that?" I ask.

"It doesn't matter what I believe."

His tone sounds like he was aiming for levity but lacked the jet fuel to get off the ground. He must hear it, too, because he says, "You should get home before it's too late." He pauses, and I wait for him to offer to give me a lift the way he always does, even though I always say no. "Take all the *lu rou fan* with you. I'm really not hungry."

What the hell is going on with Charles? This isn't just over-work; he has been overworked since his freshman year at Harvard. In fact, the more burdened he is, the livelier he gets, like a masochistic camel. He's one of those people who loves to complain about how busy they are—and now, thinking about what Jessie said, this seems like another symptom of her diagnosis: how my brother has to feel needed.

Shit. Jessie. Did she move up her breakup timeline? Maybe she didn't even intend to, but then in a conversation with Charles everything ended up unraveling, the way one loose thread can snag on a nail and destroy the entire sweater.

I slide off my seat like I'm readying to leave. Next to me, my brother remains sagged on his barstool like a stuffed animal carnival prize that its winner couldn't wait to discard. "By the way," I say, "I met up with Jessie last week."

At the sound of Jessie's name his head turns, a slow, bemused motion. "How did that happen?"

For a moment, I wonder. But my brother isn't disingenuous in this manner—if Jessie had left him, he wouldn't be acting as if matters were status quo. I say, "She wanted to talk to me about how you're working too hard."

"Oh." His gaze slides away again, something too tiring to hold. "That. Yeah."

"Judging from how I could stash a corpse in one of those bags under your eyes, she has a point." When did all my metaphors become so macabre? I hope it doesn't indicate anything unhealthy about my state of mind.

"I'll be fine. She's overreacting."

Because I'm the type of person who takes my life cues from literature, when I unexpectedly found myself in the romance business, I decided to reread the rom-com that started it all: *Pride and Prejudice*. That expanded into a larger Jane Austen appreciation project, and I'm currently midway through *Emma*, the key takeaway of which is not to try matchmaking . . . but. What if there's something I can say, or do, that might affect what will happen between Jessie and Charles?

I say, "It's also because she wants to spend more time with you."

He stares down at the counter like he's trying to drill a hole through the marble with his gaze. "How do you know that?"

"She told me about how you were working throughout your Mexico trip."

He winces. "I know. I had to, though. No one else could do it." He pauses. "And I didn't think she minded."

"Because she's too nice and she gets that your career is important to you. Which is exactly why she'll never say to you that she wants you to work less so she can see you more." Ironically, it's my favorite line from *Emma* that's inspiring me here: *If I loved you less, I might be able to talk about it more.* "That's what she's after, though."

Charles doesn't say anything, but I can see the idea winding the scenic, sleep-deprived route through his brain: that Jessie does need him, more than she appears to. If he can believe that, maybe he'll stop asking it of her, and then, maybe, that can lead Jessie to change her mind.

I go over to where my phone is charging on his bedside table. "I mean," I say, "that's why she reached out to me."

"Or she's just gotten it into her head that I'll end up like Cam Keller."

I fumble as I unplug the phone and it thuds onto the floor, startlingly loud in the sealed quiet of the room. "Sorry, downstairs neighbor," I say. "Who?"

"Jessie didn't talk about him?" Charles's tone is hard-edged, as if he suspects the two of us of some sort of collusion against him, which I suppose wouldn't be unwarranted. "The guy from my firm who passed away last year, how that shows something bad will happen to me if I don't ease up on work?"

At least now I don't have to shoehorn Cameron Keller into this discussion. "I guess she mentioned him." I crouch down to pick up my phone. "He was—"

"Cam didn't die from overwork."

So glad my face is hidden from my brother right now, because I can feel it doing all sorts of twitchy things. How would someone who has *not* reached that very same conclusion react? "How do you know?"

"I saw what he was like at Precision. He didn't come in on the weekends. He never volunteered for Asia matters because of the time difference. He left early for his tennis games." Charles speaks like a kamikaze pilot opining on those weaker-willed aviators who would prefer to remain alive. "He didn't turn into a totally different person when he joined Soulmate. Most people here think it was suicide. He was in his apartment by himself when he died. I heard something about drugs."

Just like Sarah Reaves. Something hums within me at that thought, like a string being plucked. I turn around. Charles is sitting sideways on his stool at the island, staring ahead of him.

He says, "Maybe he went to Soulmate and tried to get away with the same shit that he did at Precision, and it backfired on him. Or there was something else going on in his life. Who knows."

It's oddly disconcerting, hearing my brother swear; he's usually careful to keep it G-rated in my presence, never mind that I'm going on twenty-six years old and inured to profanity from my years in a cobwebby corner of the New York City public school system. I ask, "What did he get away with at Precision?"

"I don't know if he did this on other projects, but the one

I took over from him—it was a disaster. Holes in the datasets. Nothing updated, half the documents that were supposed to be in our system missing. Even the contact information for the client was wrong. I wasted my first three months trying to figure out what was really going on and falling further behind." He pauses. "And Cam knew all that, obviously, when he recommended me as replacement lead. We did the handover and he straight-out lied about what information there was, what he'd told the client, ten different things. And then he smiled and said, *Good luck*, and left me to drown."

Cameron Keller asked for Charles to be responsible for the project? That fact pins me in place, like a butterfly to a corkboard of uncertainty, of sudden strange dread. "He told you that? About wanting you to be his replacement?"

"He must have figured that, out of all the VPs in the group, I wouldn't say anything about how he mishandled the project," says my brother, and I realize that he's answering a different question, not the one I asked but the one he's been asking himself. "Just put my head down and clean up after him. And he was right. That was exactly what I did."

XI.

I CAN'T TELL IF THE TEMPERATURE has actually dropped or it's just how I'm feeling after the conversation with Charles, but when I step out of my brother's apartment building, the cold rushes at me like an assailant. My bike is locked to a signpost across the street. As I quickstep over I reach into my jacket pocket for my keys and take out my phone instead.

She picks up on the second ring. "What is it?"

"It's Claudia," I say.

"I know. That's what phone contact lists are for."

That familiar snark is actually calming right now. "Can I . . . Can we talk? Like, in person?"

Nothing.

"I know it's late—"

"Where are you right now?"

"Long Island City. I'm happy to come to wherever you are." Fingers crossed that it doesn't require climbing more than one bridge.

"You're on your bike?"

"I am, but it's fine."

"Tell me that again when you've bought a helmet. I can be there in twenty-five. Find a place where we can have a private conversation and text me the address."

I walk the couple of blocks over to Vernon Boulevard, a highlight of every LIC condo developer's sales pitch. I pass a few bars that are more crowded than I would like and a restaurant with soft-lit, date-night vibes. Finally I go into an empty bubble tea store manned by two Asian girls who look about fourteen years old and are both leaning against the back counter, entranced by their phones. It's mainly a take-out operation, but there are a few sets of tables and chairs along the window.

Becks marches in five minutes early. She has her work coat on, but she's switched out her tailored pants and ankle boots from earlier for sneakers and a pair of extremely flattering joggers. Her hair is up in a high ponytail. She puts her bag down in the chair across from me and turns to survey the menu on the wall.

After I've recovered from the shock of seeing Becks in athleisure, I say, "We can go somewhere else if you'd like."

She waves a hand. "This is fine. They have what I always get. I'll order for us. What do you want?"

Becks has a go-to bubble tea drink? "The mango sago coconut slushie," I say. "With an added topping of pearls."

Her nose crinkles. "Is that necessary?"

"You can never have too many chewy things in a drink."

When she comes back from the counter, Becks drags a third chair over to our table and sits down kitty-corner from me. Her foot nudges mine, and we both tuck our ankles beneath our chairs.

"What happened?" she says.

"I was visiting my brother," I say. "You know he works at Precision Consulting and took over one of Cameron Keller's projects for the matchmakers."

She watches me, waiting for me to continue.

I tell her, first, about trying to open one of the files that Cameron created for Project Tahiti and failing. "Which is . . . wrong. Charles is the project lead now. Why wouldn't he have access to his own project's files?"

"Are you sure that's the one he took over from Cameron?"

I nod. "I saw an email in his inbox about that project."

One of the girls at the counter calls Becks's name. I push my chair back. "I'll get it."

The color of Becks's drink is the default bubble tea beige, giving nothing away. Like the woman herself. I pass it to her and sit down, scooting my chair forward. Our feet touch again. I'm about to shift away when I realize, with a tiny lurch like I've tripped and I'm falling, that Becks is staying right where she is.

I open my mouth to continue with Cameron Keller and find myself asking instead, "You came from the gym?"

She leans back in her chair. The press of her foot against mine remains, like she's cruising down an empty freeway on a bright blue morning, looking forward to wherever she's going but in no hurry to get there. "Muay Thai."

That's at once surprising and not: I can totally see Becks spending her after-work hours kickboxing the stuffing out of a punching bag. "How long have you been doing that for?"

"Twenty-four years."

"What? How old are you?" I wince. "Sorry. That bounced off the inside of my skull and out of my mouth."

"Thirty-six," she says. "I don't get why people are coy about age. It is what it is."

Eleven years older than me, then. That's . . . a lot. Not that the difference in our ages has anything to do with anything. "You must be really good."

Beneath the table her foot withdraws. She says, "It could just have been an error in Precision's system. That file being blocked."

Something she doesn't want to talk about: got it. "Or it's so sensitive that even project team members can't look at it."

"If that was the case, whoever wants the file restricted would have made sure it didn't come up in any search results in the first place."

Probably true. Which, again, should be a relief, in terms of implications for Charles, but isn't.

Becks takes a long pull at her straw. I watch a convoy of boba glide up to and between her lips, and decide it would be safer to direct my gaze elsewhere.

"There's more. Isn't there?"

I look back at her. Charles's expression when I brought up the matchmakers and his project, the exhaustion in his voice. Not asking if I would like a ride home. How he placed his phone facedown on the counter, not faceup, and didn't check it at all. The smallest details, but.

"We've been assuming that Lucinda killed Cameron because he leaked Soulmate's synth program to Sarah," I say. "But that's not the only possibility. He could have been killed because of something he did, or learned, while he was still at Precision." It feels like turning a page and seeing the answer to the question I was reading about: now I understand why the similarities between Cameron's and Sarah's deaths matter. "And I don't believe Lucinda is the murderer."

I tell Becks what Charles said about how Cameron died. "It's too much like what happened to Sarah. Alone in their home. Some kind of overdose. We'll have to confirm when we get the autopsy report, but if my brother was correct, then it wasn't Lucinda. She's too smart to kill two people in the same way and within such a short period of time."

"Or too arrogant to imagine that she could get caught."

I met Lucinda Clay only once, at a charity gala where she was receiving an award and we were trying to nab her for Sarah

Reaves's murder, but there was nothing of arrogance in her manner. Confidence, yes, and conviction. If she had perceived Cameron as an obstacle, she would have removed him as efficiently as clipping a hangnail—and ensured no one noticed any parallels to a recent, equally sudden, equally unexpected demise. "It's a Murder Mystery 101 mistake. She wouldn't get tripped up like that."

Becks looks at me like I should be expelled from the table for invoking the murder mystery as a source of authority, but she says, "What makes you think there could be a Precision angle?"

I lay out that theory: the matchmakers are using Precision to help with their development of the synths, Cameron found out, someone at the matchmakers realized this and decided to remove a potential threat. "If that's true," I say, "this Project Tahiti could be one of those projects that the matchmakers are presenting as something benign but is really designed to help them improve the synths. What I've heard from Charles is that it's about trying to improve the compatibility algorithm by getting better step two data."

"Specifically step two?"

"I think so." Information about how a person acts and behaves, as opposed to step one data, which is what a person says about themselves.

"That's a novel approach. The matchmakers love to talk about step two data and all the incredible insights they could derive from it, but when you look at what they're actually coming up with, it's embarrassingly obvious. Joe likes to date women who keep pet raccoons and women who only wear stripes, so let's find him the social misfit who does both. That's always been the problem with step two data, drawing the connection between behavior and meaning. If your brother's client is seriously exploring this, either they've figured out something no one else has or they're desperate."

"Or," I say, "it's a cover. The more data the matchmakers have about how subscribers are behaving, the more effectively they can use the bellwethers to alter those behaviors. Maybe that's the real reason this client is asking Precision to work on collecting accurate step two data."

Becks's eyebrows settle into that familiar *V*. I wait for her to tell me exactly why I'm wrong, that there's no way the project I've just described could have any tie-in to the synths.

"And if it is," she says, "then your brother could be in the same position that Cameron was in."

A dark, viscous dread is oozing up from someplace deep within me. "I . . . That's what I'm afraid of."

Her expression turns inward: I can see her assessing the situation, considering potential options. I find myself wishing I could pull her aura of competence over me like a blanket and take a nap.

I say, "Charles told me that Cameron left the project in a really bad state. He could just have been checked out by that point . . . or he could have done it intentionally, to slow down progress on the synths." I pause. "And apparently Cameron recommended my brother as his replacement. Charles thinks it's because Cameron knew he wouldn't call out what Cameron had done, just focus on getting things back on track."

"And therefore the client wouldn't realize Cameron had effectively been trying to undermine the project," says Becks, "assuming that was what he'd been doing."

"Assuming," I say.

"Although, if your line of reasoning about who killed Cameron is correct, then the client *did* realize."

My insides are starting to feel like the site of an especially toxic oil spill. "Right."

"Any idea who this client is?"

"Not really. Charles has been annoyingly conscientious about

not letting anything slip. It sounds like they want to keep everything more confidential than a government mutant eugenics program, and my brother is big on following orders."

"Is he? Too bad that doesn't run in the family."

"Well, that's why he's the boring one," I say—and, in this case,
thank god Charles isn't the type to raise pesky questions about
why, and whether, and what for. To himself or to others. "It must
be one of the Big Three, though. Who else?"

Becks says, quietly, "That's the question." She tilts her head
at me. "Have you seen anything to make you think your brother
might suspect this Project Tahiti isn't what he's been told it is? Or
that he's aware of the synths?"

I hesitate. "Not from what he's said."

"But from something else?"

"He was . . ." How to describe it, this sense of wrongness that I
had when I was with him earlier? "There was something off about
him tonight. Maybe it was work stress, or, I know there's some
stuff going on with his girlfriend. But he wasn't himself." That
statement sounds absurd once I hear it aloud: How could Charles
be anything but himself?

After a moment, Becks says, "Is there someone he would confide in?"

"Not really. I spoke to his girlfriend last week, and he told her
even less than he told me."

"What about some*thing*?"

"Like . . . a journal?" I ask, confused. "Charles would be the last
person to keep one. He's not very self-reflective."

She sighs. "WhatShould."

Like your search history, but more incriminating. For a moment
I see Charles peering down at his phone, thumbs moving, eyes
hidden by the reflections of the screen in his glasses. "Squirrel said
that wasn't ready yet."

"It will be if we light a fire under his ass. He's been spending eighteen hours a day in *Ashes of Empire* trying to find an enchanted sword or some shit like that."

Which Becks knows, presumably, thanks to her *Ashes of Empire* champion acquaintance: I wonder who that is. "Isn't WhatShould going to be an exceptional-circumstances sort of thing?"

She raises an eyebrow. "This doesn't qualify?"

"I don't know," I say, like I did when Becks said that WhatShould was just a tool, no different from any other, but this time what I'm not sure of is whether I can spy on my brother like that. Lurking in his mind, waiting for him to expose what he's truly thinking and feeling—not only about Project Tahiti and his work at Precision, but everything else as well. Jessie. Our family. Some tender, conflicted part of himself that I have no idea about. Maybe, in some ways, the closer you are to someone, the harder it is to learn more about them.

Becks nods like she expected my response. "Sleep on it."

"Okay."

"But you should start tracking him on Finders Keepers."

"You really think—"

"Just in case."

I exhale, too shakily for my taste, like I'm peering over the edge of a roof. "I was hoping that when I told you all of this you would say I was being overly dramatic again. I was counting on it, actually. For once."

"You probably are," she says, as if she didn't see the need to state something so obvious. "But right now we don't have enough information to confirm that. And we know what people working for the matchmakers can do. Have done. Also . . . this is someone you care about. So. We take it seriously."

Before I can say anything, she reaches for her bag and stands up. "Let's get out of here," she says. "Those girls need to go home and pack their lunch boxes for school tomorrow."

XII.

MATTHEW IS SITTING on the steps facing the lawn that we walked to the last time we spoke. This time around the High Line is almost deserted. It's been raining on and off since midmorning, and the sky is as sullen as a misunderstood teenager. If I had some way of contacting him I would probably have rescheduled, but he made it clear that going forward our only communications would be in person, to avoid the risk of any messages being tracked or intercepted. I guess this is the way people used to do things in ancient times: you arranged beforehand on a time and location to meet, and then . . . you did.

He stands as we approach, hands in the pockets of his windbreaker. His gaze twitches from me to Becks and back again.

"Any issues with your commute?" he asks me.

"None," I say. "You?"

He shakes his head.

Becks says, "Is this supposed to be code for *I wasn't followed here* or some shit like that?"

"Um, this is Becks," I say. "We work together." And of the three of us, ironically, she's the one who would be pegged as the spy by any passerby possessing the faintest familiarity with Hollywood tropes, in her camel trench coat and boots, hood up to cover her hair from the drizzle, the top half of her face enciphered behind oversize sunglasses. Matthew has his anchorite thing going. I'm in my usual hoodie and jeans, and at this point in the day my sneakers have turned into mini-marshes that I feel like I'm sinking deeper into with every step.

Matthew and Becks stare at each other like they're engaging in a psychic wrestling match. This is going to be fun.

"Have you found anything on the Silent G profile?" I ask.

He turns back at me. "In a sense. I've found nothing at all. There's no record of that profile or handle in the system. Which may mean something."

"It could mean we're mistaken," says Becks. "Or just fucking with you."

Matthew says, still to me, "After I tried searching for Silent G, I went through Pradeep's match history. He had set his preferences to receive one match a day. I pulled his matches for January and February, until the date he took down his profile. There's nothing for January thirty-first."

I say, "Because that day his match was Silent G. Let's Meet deleted that record."

"Possibly."

"Or there was a glitch and he didn't get a match that day," says Becks.

"Possible as well." Matthew pauses. "I also checked to see if anyone with admin privileges had accessed Pradeep's archived account information in the recent past. There had been a log-in on the sixteenth of February. The ID was tagged to a group, not an individual, so I don't know who it was."

This is all fitting with our theory that Pradeep submitted a complaint about Silent G to Let's Meet, which alerted them that he was aware of his clone profile and led them to remove all traces of it. "What about Pradeep's complaint to Let's Meet?" I ask. "Were you able to find that?"

"No," he says. "But I would expect that if someone was deleting information relating to Silent G, they would have deleted that, too."

"The group tag," says Becks. "Is that normal?"

"It happens sometimes. With consultants, mainly, or temp staff."

"Which group was it?"

"It's called the Chemistry Lab. First time I'd heard of it. It's a subgroup, technically—it sits within Data Strategy. As far as I can tell it collects and analyzes data on so-called successful matches, to try to get insights on why they worked. Something the new head of DS came up with."

"So-called?"

"The whole thing is BS."

"That's a surprising position to take," she says, "for a person who works at a matchmaker."

"In a war," says Matthew, "the safest place can be by your enemy's side."

Now why does that sound familiar?

Becks says, "You think we're in a war?"

He tilts his head back in a doomed effort to look down his nose at her. "Don't you?"

"I'll put this out there right now. It fucking annoys me when people answer questions with questions."

"Hmm. I get the impression that a lot of things fucking annoy you."

I cough. "Swallowed wrong," I say to no one in particular.

Beside me, Becks takes her phone out of her pocket. Matthew

steps back like she's produced a baby cobra. "No phones." He looks at me. "Didn't you tell her?"

She raises her eyebrows at him. "I was just going to see who this new head of Data Strategy is."

"His name is Ed Cannon. You can do your research after we're done here."

There's a coolness to the way Matthew says the name that makes me ask, "What do you think of him?"

"He's useless," says Matthew. "Which could be worse. He could be competent, or brilliant. At least this way he's not dangerous."

I glance at Becks. She tips her chin at me: *Go ahead.*

"Speaking of danger," I say, and note to self that I really should work on my segues, "you should know . . ."

"Finding out certain things could be dangerous?" Matthew's smile wisps into place and then away again. I think of the smoke curling up from the firefly glow of Somnang's cigarette into the humid, verdant Saigon night. *In a war, the safest place can be by your enemy's side.* Now I remember: Liên Duong says that to Somnang the second time they meet, as they're leaving the room after a morass of a strategy discussion between the South Vietnamese leadership and the Western powers. Not surprising that Matthew would be familiar with those old-school spy films. I should ask him if he has a theory about the Dream's true identity.

"Yes," says Becks. "And not because you could get fired, or blacklisted, or sued for everything you own, or even go to prison. All that, yes. But also." She takes a breath, and I know, suddenly, that she's going to talk about Pradeep, our suspicions about his murder.

"One of our other sources," I say—since we're faking Matthew out about Veracity, might as well make us sound more impressive than we actually are—"at a different matchmaker." Becks is looking at me, but she doesn't say anything, so I keep going. "He was providing us with information on the matchmaker's synths—that's what we're calling these bots that can interact with subscribers in a convincingly human manner. He passed away suddenly. Officially, due to a health issue." Somehow I manage to make it sound as if poor Cameron Keller committed a faux pas, dying like that.

Matthew's expression remains impassive. "It's not just Let's Meet that's doing this, then." A slight shake of his head, at himself rather than us. "No, of course not."

"If you want to think about it, whether you want to continue—"

"No need."

Becks says, like it's a fault, "You're very calm about this."

"I was in a car accident once," says Matthew. "I thought I was going to die. It changed the way . . . It made me realize that life and death are both states of being, and they can coexist. We are all in the process of dying." He pauses, and I wonder if he's thinking of Pradeep—another accident, a reminder of how close death always is. Then he says, "In any case, I won't be caught."

"No one ever thinks they will," says Becks.

"I'm just doing my job. It's part of the IT function to check that every group's files are being properly backed up. I'll start that process for DS tomorrow."

"If you find something, though, you still have to get it to us."

"How I do that will depend on what I find."

"Mm," says Becks, in the truncated way she does when she recognizes that someone else is right but doesn't want to acknowledge it. "How long will you need?"

"Give me the rest of the week," says Matthew. "We can meet next Monday. A different spot on the High Line, and at a different time. No patterns. We should come up with a protocol for what to do if one party doesn't show up."

Becks says, "Why don't we consult an *Espionage for Dummies* handbook while we're at it?"

"You're the ones who have just told me that I'm at risk of being murdered for what I'm planning to do. It seems reasonable to take a few precautions."

I say, "That's a fair point?"

Becks mutters, just loud enough for me to hear, "Fucking regret this already."

———————

We take the stairs at West Twentieth down to the street. As we walk to the subway, Becks says, "Why didn't you want me to tell him that we think Let's Meet was behind Pradeep's death?"

I don't answer right away, because—it was for her, in a sense. I know how she feels responsible, and I kind of worry that the more we talk about this the more weight it will assume. But I'm not sure how to express that without sounding presumptuous or weird, so I just say, "We don't have any real evidence."

"That's never stopped you before."

"Maybe you're rubbing off on me."

She makes a scoffy sound in the back of her throat that's more attractive than it has any right to be. "If that were true, we wouldn't have spent twenty minutes in the rain being lectured by a paranoid Luddite about spy protocol."

"Come on," I say. "You have to agree that was useful."

"There's something off about that man—beyond all the things I just identified."

I glance at her, but between the sunglasses and the hood, all I can see is the imperious line of her nose. "What do you mean?"

"The car accident he was talking about."

"He did get a bit Zen Buddhist there, but I don't—"

"He was hiding something."

I look at her again. "About being in an accident?"

"The circumstances of it, maybe. He didn't want us to know what really happened."

"Wait," I say. "He volunteered that information."

"That doesn't make it accurate."

"But if he wanted to hide something, he wouldn't have brought it up in the first place. It's not even related to anything we're doing with him."

"Don't get defensive."

"Defensive? I'm not. Why would I be defensive about Matthew Espersen's accident? I'm just pointing out that what you're saying makes no sense."

"You recruited this asset. You're his handler. It's natural that you want him to be clean."

I stop at the top of the stairs descending into the drippy pit of the Fourteenth Street station, because when did Becks start speaking like she's in a John le Carré novel? Below us I can hear the low, torturous screech of a train arriving.

Becks removes her sunglasses and clicks the temples closed with one deft motion of her hand. "What?" she says. "I'm aware of spy tropes." She takes one step down, and now we're at eye level. "The second you trust someone, that's when they betray you."

XIII.

I SPEND A COUPLE of days compiling a dossier on Edmund H. Cannon, head of Data Strategy at Let's Meet, a task I grab on to as a distraction from Charles. I even labor over formatting, which I've always regarded as the hobgoblin of anal-retentive minds. (Needless to say, every single document Becks produces is formatted like an exhibit of *The Chicago Manual of Style*.)

Ed, the name he goes by, is new to the matching industry, at least based on his LinkedIn résumé and the several corporate bios available online that are all composed from the same set of mix-and-match details. Prior to Let's Meet, he spent the entirety of his career at two evocatively named companies, Lumina and Maverick, in each case ascending a stepladder of increasingly important-sounding roles—most recently, as president of content at Maverick Development Division.

It takes me a few tries to find the right Lumina and Maverick, in part because I'm not expecting . . . video games? Lumina turns out to be a small game developer that released a hit RPG several years ago and was promptly ingested by Sony. Maverick is one step down the supply chain. It's a midsize game publisher, and its in-house development studio, Maverick Development Division, accounts for about half of the games that the company puts out. A specific type of video game, too—MaDD, as the studio is commonly referred to, specializes in zombie apocalypse first-person shooter games, a series called *World's End*. You'd think that's a one-and-done concept with niche appeal, but so far MaDD has launched half a dozen titles—zombies on the moon, zombies in the Vatican, zombies taking over the White House—and each has been more successful than the last. The next time I see Benny, which hopefully will be later rather than sooner, I'll have to tell him to include zombie apocalypse violence in his idea of our zeitgeist.

So. Why would someone abandon a career dreaming up ways for zombies to take over the world so he can head up a Big Three matchmaker's data projects, and why would that matchmaker want him to do so in the first place?

I glean a potential explanation to the first part of that mystery in *The New York Times*'s Vows section. The article is from eighteen months ago and opens with a silent retreat in the mountains of northern Thailand, where Ed Cannon finds himself immediately drawn to the attractive, copper-haired woman sitting across the hall from him in their twelve-hour meditation sessions. She turns out to be Mandy Fisch, the owner of a chain of so-called fitness labs in the Bay Area that—according to the BetterYou website—help their clients achieve their goals through customized programs based on the comprehensive collection and in-depth analysis of their health data.

Ed and Mandy speak for the first time a week later, after the retreat has concluded, as their shuttle pulls out of the compound. They share their stories of what brought them there. Ed's best friend passed away recently, which occasioned some questioning around his own life choices; he has become plagued (his word) by the fear that developing new zombie apocalypse scenarios is too trivial. Mandy has had to come to terms with some health issues of her own. They discuss their vulnerabilities, exposed by their week of silence like corpses floating to the water's surface as they decompose. The shuttle arrives at Chiang Mai International Airport, and they both reschedule their flights. They spend the next month traveling around Southeast Asia, swimming beneath waterfalls, trekking in rain forests, sampling different colors of curry. When they return to the States, Ed quits Maverick and relocates from Seattle to Palo Alto to be with Mandy. He originally intends to help Mandy run and expand her business, but is recruited by Let's Meet for a senior management position. He will start his new job after his and Mandy's honeymoon in Croatia, splitting his time between California and New York.

I click through the *Times*'s slideshow of the Cannon-Fisch wedding pictures. Mandy looks like you'd expect a successful entrepreneur in the fitness industry to, toned and tanned, a slightly aggressive smile. Ed, on the other hand, surprises me with his unprepossessing appearance. He stands slightly stooped and his hair is thinning, and in all the photos he appears perplexed by the festivities being conducted for and around him.

Since becoming head of Data Strategy last year, he hasn't said much in public forums. All I can find is an interview with the Amherst College alumni magazine, where he was asked about his surprising move from gaming to dating. I include his response to that question in my notes:

> *Is it surprising? When I look at matching, I see the gamification of dating. You win when you find the person you're most compatible with. The dates you go on are like stages you clear to get closer to that end goal. The way I think about it, I'm helping Let's Meet to build a better game for daters.*

I'm proud of the games I created for Maverick. Our goal was
always to provide players with the best gaming experience pos-
sible. We succeeded because we understood what players truly
wanted and gave it to them. Same thing here. My task is to
understand what people who are looking for love want, and
give it to them.

———————

When Becks, Squirrel, and I gather for our now semi-regular
meetings in Komla's office, I ask Squirrel if he's familiar with any
of MaDD's games.

"I scored a decathlon hit in *World's End: McMurdo*," he says.

"Oh, let me guess," I say. "You killed ten zombies using methods derived from the ten events of the decathlon?"

"It's—"

"Irrelevant," says Becks. "And that guess makes no sense.
What, you hurdle them to death?" She leans back against
the window ledge and crosses her arms. "Let's Meet made an
interesting hire there. Someone with no background in either
matching or data analytics—officially, anyway—to run data
strategy for the third-largest matchmaker in the business. Also
a one-eighty from the previous DS head, Solomon Grand, who's
been in the industry his whole career. Maybe whatever he was
doing wasn't working, and Let's Meet felt they needed something different to try to keep up with Soulmate and Partnered
Up."

"What if Ed Cannon is a front?" I say. "He doesn't know how
things work in the matching industry. He won't know if the company is doing something sketchy with its customers' data. And if
things do blow up, Let's Meet can pin the blame on him."

She nods. "Also possible. Although if we assume what Matthew told us is true, then it was an employee from the Chemistry Lab who accessed the Silent G profile, and Cannon who started the Chemistry Lab."

Squirrel says, "Hang on. You've got it all wrong."

"Doubtful," says Becks, "but you get the benefit for sixty seconds."

"You don't *kill* zombies. They aren't alive. The correct term is *pulp*. Some people use *exterminate*, but that's just dumb. You waste so much time getting those extra three syllables out."

"Thirty seconds."

"Thirty-seven. Also, I fucking can't stand it when people who've never played a video game assume it's mindless because pulping zombies is a part of it."

"I can't tell," says Becks, "are you refuting my point or advancing it?"

"*McMurdo*'s so full of mind, it's like sudoku on acid. You have to figure out who sabotaged the station and why. You need weapons and tools, and those are hidden all over the station. There's this scientist you have to save. Okay, you don't have to, but you open up a really cool storyline if you do."

I say, "Why don't we play this game together?"

"No," says Becks.

"Yes!" says Squirrel.

"Squirrel's view is that *World's End: McMurdo* is a complex, challenging endeavor." I glance at him; he pops a thumbs-up. "Your view is that it's inane and a waste of time. The best way to reconcile those views is for us to all experience the game together."

"What's *your* view?" says Becks.

That in order to understand Ed Cannon, and what he might have to offer Let's Meet, we have to understand his work. As the inspector put it in *Inspector Yuan and the Penitent Courtesan*, to know what a seamstress is thinking, dress up in the robes that she has stitched. To know what a game developer is thinking—

"My view," I say, "is that I can pulp more zombies than you can."

Her eyebrows spring up like a catch has been released.

"We'll see about that," she says.

XIV.

ANOTHER GRIPE about working in Tribeca: a lack of diversity, specifically in terms of cheap, tasty lunch options. Usually I take advantage of the observations to pick up something from whatever neighborhood I'm in, as guided by the wisdom of the r/FoodNYC subreddit, but I have none scheduled for this week—we're still in our post-Valentine's, pre-warm-weather fallow period—which is how I find myself at the halal food truck on Chambers Street for the third day in a row. I should ask them to consider starting a loyalty program.

While waiting for my order, I take out my phone to check on my brother's whereabouts. Since I've started monitoring him, all he's done is zip-line between Precision and his apartment like the rest of the city is nothing more than rain forest canopy. I'd wondered if he would work out of the client's premises, as he sometimes does—which would provide a clue to just who this client is—but so far, no. He hasn't spent any time with Jessie, either. I didn't feel comfortable tracking her as well, but what I did was add her number as an affiliate of Charles's on Finders Keepers and set up a notification for whenever both numbers were in the same location.

I've just opened the app when a banner slides down from the top of my screen. Incoming call: *Dà gē*. My phone vibrates in my hand, and for an instant I feel like it's coming from within me, an alarm tremoring deep beneath my skin. Something is wrong—Charles wouldn't be calling me like this, in the middle of the workday, otherwise.

"Hello?" I say. "Charles?"

A beat, and then: "Hey." Another beat. "You okay?"

The only emotion I can pick out in my brother's voice is a mild bemusement, like a breeze ruffling over flatland. I hope I didn't sound too agitated. "Yes. Just . . . surprised that you're calling."

"Thought I'd try to catch you at lunch. I should've called earlier, but . . . a lot going on. You have a few minutes?"

On the other side of the food truck window, the man picks up an industrial-size bottle of hot sauce. I wave frantically at him. "No!"

"Um, okay—"

"No, no," I say. "I was just averting a hot sauce disaster." I mouth *thanks* as the vendor hands me my box of uncontaminated lamb on rice and then jump back on the sidewalk to avoid being bowled over by a group of high school kids shoving and laughing at each other as they pass. Living in New York really does require constant vigilance. "What is it?"

"When you came over that night."

Charles pauses, the way you do when you're about to say something you would rather not, and my heart somersaults up into my throat. He's found out about my Cameron Keller searches. Of course he would have; all he had to do was look at his search history. "Uh-huh?"

"I only realized after you left. How we ended up talking about the matchmakers, and that ex-colleague of mine, and what he did, and all of that."

I'm such an idiot. What am I going to say? There's no semi-legitimate reason for me to be sifting through Precision files on his work laptop.

"And so we didn't get to finish discussing what you should do."

What I do say, like a faulty echo: "What . . . I should do?"

"About the girl you're seeing."

"Girl I'm seeing? Have you forgotten who I am?"

"Did it not work out? Already? With the girl you said you met online?"

So this is why MI6 subjects Somnang to all those simulated interrogations before each mission—to ensure his cover story doesn't pop out of place like a dislocated rib at the first application of pressure. "That girl," I say. "Gotcha. I wouldn't call that situation *seeing*. We've only been on a couple of dates."

"How did they go?"

Ah, so this is what the call is about: Charles feels bad for monopolizing our prior conversation when, as far as he's concerned, it was supposed to be about my romantic conundrums. Excellent! I can feel my own guilt dissipate like a flock of pigeons taking off once all the breadcrumbs are gone. "Not too bad," I say.

"What you were saying—about getting to know her. You feel like that's happening?"

I start walking, to the street corner and then right onto Greenwich, back toward the office. "I know a bit more about her now," I say, "but that's not the same thing."

"No," says my brother, like he would have thought such insight was beyond me. "I guess not."

"And there's always that worry that maybe they're just lying to you."

"Sure: the lying limitation. Although that applies to everyone, not only the people you match with."

My guilt alights again, a flappy, feathery commotion. "Wow," I say. "That's pretty cynical."

"It's true. Like how you lied about the job thing, right?"

He says it matter-of-factly, without accusation, but I can't help but wonder if he's bringing this up . . . why? To chastise me; or to signal that he suspects, or knows, there's more that I'm keeping from him? I say, "Are you pulling a Mom?"

"What?"

"Trying to guilt me like that."

After a moment he says, "That wasn't what . . . I get it. Sometimes you don't want everyone to know what's going on. It doesn't mean anything."

He stops, and I feel the same unease that I did when I was in his apartment, like a stone embedded behind my sternum, chafing with every breath. I say, turning on snarky-little-sister mode, "Since when did you magically become so understanding?"

I sound annoying even to myself, but all Charles says is "What's her name?"

"Who?" I say.

"The girl you're not seeing."

"Um—Rebecca."

Was that an example of my unconscious flexing? If so, it needs to stop now.

"Which matchmaker are you using?" he asks.

"Let's Meet," I say, since that's the one that has me all hot and bothered these days.

"Huh."

My conspiracy antenna perks up. "What?"

"You didn't go for a boutique? I thought you'd find the Big Three, I don't know, too mainstream."

Crap: true. If I were in fact to try matching, which looks ever less likely the more I learn about the matchmakers, I would end up on some defiantly esoteric platform for bike commuters who enjoy reading murder mysteries. "Max set up my profile," I say. "It was a surprise. And he put all that effort in—I felt bad not at least giving it a try."

"What was your comp score?"

"Hmm," I say. "Solid C-plus."

"Are you doing this on purpose?"

My heart rate ticks up. "What are you talking about?"

"To try to prove the algorithm wrong, or something like that."

"Oh," I say. "No. I just . . . I find her really attractive. I kind of wish I didn't."

"Okay," says Charles, like he's wondering, yet again, how I turned out so strange. "How do you think she feels about you?"

"Sometimes it seems like she thinks I'm funny, and other times it seems like I exasperate the hell out of her."

My brother laughs. "Basically, she has you all figured out."

"Not helpful."

"Sorry. I'm not exactly a champion at dating."

"What are you talking about? You landed Jessie. I know I used to say she was boring, but she's actually really cool."

"She is," he says, such fondness velveting his voice that I want to put him on hold so I can call Jessie right now and beg her to reconsider. "I have to go. I just wanted to touch base. About your situation. It's . . . good. That you're giving this a try."

"Matching?"

"Or just, you know, going out there and meeting people. Seeing if there's someone you want to be with. It's an important part of things."

We hang up and I stare down at my phone screen. My *brother* has opinions on my dearth of a love life?

"Halal truck again?"

I jump. "How do you do that?"

Becks glides into step next to me. "Make unerringly correct deductions?"

This is the first time I'm seeing her today, and I have to pause to appreciate how fine she looks in her oversize sweater and black jeans. "I was thinking sneak up on people like a ninja. But, okay, this"—I lift my plastic container—"too."

"That and the taco stand are the only places you get lunch at when you're in Tribeca, and tacos are in the other direction."

I'm unduly flustered by the thought of Becks observing my lunch habits, and so I blurt out, like I'm a character in a textbook exercise illustrating the fallacy of the non sequitur: "I was just talking to my brother."

Her head turns, barely. "And?"

"I think . . . we should try WhatShould."

This time I can feel her staring at me. "You sound extremely unsure."

We reach our building. Becks swipes on her phone to unlock the door and we enter.

"I am," I say. "I have no desire to go poking around in my brother's head."

We get into the elevator and ride up to the third floor. When we step out, Becks says, "Sometimes we do something because the alternatives are worse."

I follow her into the office. Worse . . . like not knowing what is troubling Charles, and worrying. His obvious unhappiness when we were at his apartment, the weirdness about Cameron Keller, what he just said about not wanting everyone to know what was going on—

Becks turns around and I walk right into her. She catches me, one hand on each of my arms: prepared as always. She looks down into my face. Her eyes are intent, like she's searching for something, and all of a sudden I can feel my heart like a bird crashing around in an atrium.

"Do you want me to do it?" she asks.

"Do . . ." Jesus Christ, why do I sound like I just dashed up a mountain? ". . . what?"

"Monitor what your brother says. On WhatShould. If that would make it easier."

Right. The matter at hand. Or hands, because Becks still hasn't let go and her touch is very gradually scorching through my sleeves. "No," I say. "I mean, thanks, but . . ." Charles might ask something that reveals the constitutionally maladjusted nature of our family, and I don't want her perception of me, already unflattering as it is, to change because of that. "He's my responsibility."

She drops her arms. Neither of us steps back. "All right," she says. "I'll get Squirrel to come in next week and give us a demo."

XV.

"I THINK THEY built a tomb," says Matthew.

Becks says, "What's in it?"

I crane myself out over the railing in a bid to make eye contact with her, rendered challenging both by Matthew standing between us and the wind fluttering her hair like a bright scrim across her face. "He said *tomb*."

"I heard. For the love of god, can you not constantly be contorting yourself into a position of imminent danger?"

I straighten back up. "Should we be a bit more troubled by this?"

"It's obviously some imprecise term of art." She says to Matthew, "What, a drive or a folder that other people in the organization can't open?"

"Can't even see," he says. "It's buried. It doesn't show up for anyone who hasn't been given permission."

"Then how do you know it's there?"

"Each group at Let's Meet gets a shared drive for its files. The

Data Strategy drive uses up two hundred and forty-one gigabytes. I added up the sizes of all the files in the drive and it only came to two hundred and thirty-eight."

"Nice!" I say. "The twenty-first-century version of the detective discovering the false wall by measuring the dimensions of the room."

"Does that happen in detective stories?" says Matthew.

"Do not get her started," says Becks. "These tombs. How common are they?"

"Hard to say. The only people who know about a specific tomb are the IT rep who sets it up and the project members who can access it."

"Surely someone in the organization must be keeping track."

"Guess so. Above my pay grade. Tombs are supposed to be used only for projects designated at the highest level of confidentiality."

"All right," I say. "So now we have to . . . raid the tomb? Did I get the terminology right?"

Matthew says, "Two members of the Chemistry Lab are due for laptop upgrades. They'll have to log in to their new machines so I can configure them. The process typically takes three to four hours. While I'm doing that . . . I'll see what shows up on their version of the drive."

Becks says, "This Chemistry Lab. How many people does it have?"

"Eight—no, seven."

"All hired by Ed Cannon after he joined?"

"I'll have to check. He might have moved a couple over from other parts of DS."

"What else makes up Data Strategy?"

Matthew is able to speak to this only in the most general of terms: there's a division focused on improving the quality of the data that Let's Meet collects, although he doesn't know in what respects, and another division looking at options for data monetization, although he's unable to give us specific examples. Those divisions were set up by Ed Cannon's predecessor; Matthew hasn't noticed any changes since Cannon took over.

While Becks continues to interrogate him, with rapidly diminishing marginal returns, I contemplate the literally and metaphorically edgy facade of the condominium jutting up less than three feet from the railing where we're standing, on one of the little overlooks that pockets the Twenties stretch of the High Line. The mystery to me here is what type of person would care to pay a heart-palpitatingly high premium to live with a perpetual tourist parade outside their floor-to-ceiling windows.

I hear Becks say, "Do you really not know something as basic as reporting lines?"

Intervention time. "Matthew, did someone leave the Chemistry Lab recently?"

He turns to me with the haste of someone shutting the door on a large, angry dog. "Yes. Very recently. How did you know?"

"The way you corrected yourself just now. It sounded like there used to be eight people at the Chemistry Lab, and now there are only seven." I figured I'd save the question: one thing I've learned about working with Becks is that it's useful to have tools for diverting the track that a conversation is on before it screeches off a cliff.

"IT keeps a list of what equipment all employees have and when they're scheduled for upgrades. There were eight names for Chem Lab. Three marked as having pending laptop upgrades. I emailed all three to set that up. One of the emails bounced. I forwarded that email to HR, and they told me the individual was no longer with the company."

This time it's Becks who steps away from the railing to look at me behind the back of Matthew's head, and I know what she's thinking as if she beamed it right into my mind. I ask Matthew, "How up to date is that equipment list?"

"It's automatically refreshed at the end of each month," says Matthew. "So he was still in the system as an employee as of one and a half weeks ago."

Becks says, "What's his name? What do you know about him?"

"Rodrigo Santos. There's no record of previous equipment upgrades for him, which means he joined within the last twelve months."

"Can you get us his phone number?"

Matthew pauses. "Do you think it's a good idea to talk to him? He could still be in touch with people at Let's Meet. It might get back to them that someone is asking questions about Chem Lab."

I say, "What if you did some recon when you meet with those other employees to swap their machines? You could say that you thought you were giving Rodrigo Santos a new laptop as well, ask them what happened to him. People like gossiping about that kind of thing." I'm fully invested in the ongoing soap opera featuring the children's watch company where Max works, and I'll never meet any of those people.

A longer pause. Then he says, like I've suggested he give pole dancing a try, "I'm not good at that kind of talk."

"Doesn't matter," says Becks. "No one expects IT to have social skills."

Now I wish I had thought to prepare more than one deflection question. "Anyway . . ." I say. What's something else I can ask about? "Why do you think Ed Cannon is useless?"

"You looked him up?" says Matthew.

"Yes."

"Then it's obvious why. He's the least qualified person in his own group. He knows nothing about the matching industry. One of his VPs had to tell him about the lying limitation, explain how to account for it in step one data sets."

I say, "What about the idea that matching has made dating feel more like a game? And so an Ed Cannon can help Let's Meet turn its platform into a better game than what Soulmate or Partnered Up can offer."

"I'm sure that was management's rationale. He used data analytics to develop games everyone wants to play, so let's give him Let's Meet's customer data and see if he can do the same for us."

"In what sense?" says Becks. "Data on how people date is very different from data on how they kill zombies. It better be, or we're looking at a whole different set of problems."

"But the purpose of the analysis is the same: to predict what players want so you can give it to them."

Which is more or less what Ed Cannon himself said in that interview—and, come to think of it, is also a way to describe what Lucinda Clay hoped to accomplish with the synths. I ask, "How do video games do that?"

"Everything a player does in a game is a machine-readable output. Whether they go left or right. Speed up or slow down. Save the princess or kill her. If the publisher is able to capture and analyze all of that data, it can learn a lot of things. What a player will choose in a given situation. What they like or dislike about a game. Aggregate the outputs from a large enough number of players and the trends will become apparent. Maverick is a leader in this area."

Becks says, "Why are you so well-informed about this? If video games collect even a fraction of the data about their players that you say they do, I don't see you going anywhere near them."

"No. It's one more way to be surveilled."

"Then?"

Matthew's mouth opens and closes once before he says, "Pradeep did." He sounds both like he's grateful for the excuse to say the name, to invoke Pradeep one more time, and like it's being fish-hooked out of him. "He played all the Maverick games. He was the one who first told me about Maverick's use of data analytics to calibrate its games."

The same way Pradeep believed in using data to calibrate his own life. "I remember," I say, "when we met Pradeep, he was talking about his physio KPIs—"

Matthew says, louder, "And Cannon wasn't even the quant guy at Maverick. He had a partner who did the actual data work; he just took the outputs and applied them to the games."

And now I remember, as well, that the tracker Pradeep was using had been a gift from Matthew. I guess he doesn't want to be reminded of that.

"Cannon knew enough to start this Chemistry Lab," says Becks.

"Just because they don't want the rest of the organization to know what they're working on doesn't mean it's of any value." Matthew drops his hands from the railing. "Finding someone to be with isn't about racking up points to get the highest score. Sometimes I think that's the worst thing that matching has done to us. Making us believe we can't be happy until we do."

XVI.

"YOUR BROTHER?" says Squirrel. "Awesome. I need a test case. The way the user's inputs show up on our server is all wacky."

Becks says, before I can, "Her brother is not your fucking lab rat. This has to fully work before we can apply it to anyone."

"Of course it works." Squirrel gestures at the wall screen, which is currently projecting what's on his laptop. "This is the mirror portal I created to the WhatShould program. Looks exactly the same as the official log-in page. If you access WhatShould through this portal, your conversation will be tagged by your username, email, and IP address, and a copy will be stored on a server that I've set up to hold this information."

As he speaks he keys in his name and an email address I haven't seen before, and clicks GO. A new webpage loads, a chat window with a single message.

> Hello, Squirrel. What's on your mind today?

Squirrel types his question on his laptop; I watch it appear across the wall.

> What should I do if a member
> of my party on an AoE quest
> is a selfish bastard who never
> shares his bounty with the others?

Are you referring to Ashes of
Empire, the multiplayer fantasy
action role-playing game?

> Yep

Humans have a tendency to inflate
their own contributions while
diminishing the contributions of
others. As an initial step, you should
consider whether you share your own
bounty and to what degree. Perhaps
this party member is responding to
what he perceives to be your less-
than-ideal behavior . . .

Becks says, drawing my attention from the rest of the response, "This chatbot is an insufferable ass."

"Doesn't stop people from using it," says Squirrel. "Like I said, it's not the advice they're after. They just want to talk. You should see some of the crazy shit that gets fed into WhatShould."

"How are you able to see that?" I ask.

His gaze shifts back to his laptop. "Someone on the Stanford team showed it to me."

Across the table, Becks's expression doesn't change—if she

didn't already know this, she isn't surprised. I say, "You're getting information about WhatShould directly from Stanford? Is that how you set up the mirror site?"

"This," he says, pointing at the wall again, "is the product of genius. Mine. Knowing how Stanford collects their data from WhatShould streamlined one or two basic things, but that was it. I would've come up with the exact same solution."

"Still," I say. "If that person shared with you . . . unless . . . do they know what we're planning to do with WhatShould?"

He stares at me. Then he starts laughing, which always makes him sound like he has a fatal case of the hiccups. "If she did, I'd be in a black site right now. She'd have hacked into the CIA's database and put me at the top of their people-to-torture list."

I look at Becks again: still completely unimpressed. I say, "But then maybe we shouldn't be doing this with their program—or, at least, we should think about it a bit more."

"She's not going to find out."

"You just said she could hack into the CIA."

"So can I. Not that hard."

"Right. Okay, setting that aside, it feels . . ." I almost say *unethical*, but that seems like too much judgment, especially with WhatShould's sanctimonious presence glowing down at us. "Potentially problematic. If she trusted you, and—"

"If she's stupid enough to trust me, then she deserves whatever the hell she gets. Anyway, this is nothing compared to what she did. Less than nothing. She should be grateful."

Now Becks says, "Squirrel has some issues that he's never going to work through, both on the institutional and individual level."

Squirrel scowls at his laptop screen, his shoulders ramparted around his ears.

"Can I enlighten Claudia?"

"Whatever," he mutters.

"The person Squirrel is referring to is Geraldine Napier. She and Squirrel were college classmates. At Stanford, in fact."

"Until she manipulated me into dropping out."

"They had an idea for a video game. Squirrel took a year off so he could focus on developing it and never went back."

"She knew from the start that it would go nowhere. The whole thing was a ploy to get me out of the way."

"Out of the way of what?"

"The Fenwick Prize."

"Awarded to the graduating senior in the computer science department with the best thesis," says Becks.

I say, carefully, "Causing you to drop out of college feels like a convoluted approach to winning a department prize."

"Gerri Napier is a psycho. If you talked to her for two minutes you would get it."

"But, after all that, you've stayed in touch?"

Becks says, "That's on Geraldine's part. The last time she reached out—before now—was to let him know that she was back at Stanford as a postdoc."

"She's obsessed with me," says Squirrel.

From the sound of it, any obsession might well be mutual. Now I recall the exchange Becks and Squirrel had when Squirrel first raised the idea of WhatShould to us and mentioned that it was a Stanford initiative. "She's a postdoc at the lab that's developing WhatShould? The one that sounds like a Greek dessert?"

Becks says, "*Katrakis* sounds nothing like *kataifi*."

"My memory works by food associations." I say to Squirrel, "So Geraldine was the one who told you about WhatShould and how it works and what data it gets. Why?"

Squirrel snorts. "She asked if I was interested in collaborating with her on it. What the fuck?"

That does seem a tad tone-deaf. "And you said no."

"I sent her a virus."

"God," says Becks, "you are such a man-child."

"We are using this shitty bot," says Squirrel. "The only thing it's good for is getting people to confess their secrets."

I imagine the tower of Jeremy Bentham's panopticon, Charles locked away within its circular depths, wholly exposed. If he never finds out what I did and we're able to determine whether he knows, or suspects, anything about the synths—those ends justify these means. Don't they?

Becks looks over at me, eyebrows slightly raised.

"I'll get Charles to sign up," I say.

———————————

I've just powered off my laptop for the day when Becks walks up to my desk. I say, "I'm still working on it."

She frowns. "On what?"

"How I can introduce WhatShould to my brother."

"All right."

From her tone, I can tell that wasn't why she came over. I wait, but she just stands there, hands in her pockets, squinting at me. I get up from my chair. "Was there . . . ?"

"Are you free for dinner?"

An excitement unfurls within me like one of those bud-to-flower time-lapse videos. "Oh," I say. "Right. That."

"I doubt you'll ever send me your restaurant list, so I made a preemptive reservation at Daizen in the West Village. Do you like Japanese?"

I'm about to joke that somehow, even though I've won the bet, we're ending up at the restaurant of her choice—not that I mind; if she'd proposed McDonald's I would've been into it—when my short-term memory reactivates and I remember that I'm already late to meet Maddie and Julia. "I can't tonight," I say. "I'm going to a concert."

Becks blinks like she's vestigially shocked that I have after-work plans. "Okay," she says. "Some other time."

She turns and it feels like she's taking something away with her. Before I can let myself think this through I say, "I can get an extra ticket. Would you like to come?"

XVII.

WHEN WE SHOW UP at Rocaille, the bar in the East Village where Maddie, Julia, and I like to do our concert pregaming, Julia literally-as-in-literally spits whatever she was swilling around in her mouth back into her cocktail glass.

"Okay," she says, "when you said you were bringing someone, I did not—"

Maddie gets up from the table, stepping in front of Julia as she does so. "I'm Maddie," she says to Becks. "And this is Julia. We went to high school with Claudia." Thank god I have one friend who wasn't raised by wolves.

"Becks," says Becks. The lighting in this place is a murky sort of blue that always makes me feel like I'm a bottom-feeder in an aquarium, but it seems like she's smiling as she says that, the way normal people do when they're introduced to other people at gatherings. Hard to tell when I'm trying to look at her without looking like I'm looking at her.

She adds, "Do both of you love this band as much as Claudia does?"

"No one loves Symposium as much as Claudia does," says Julia. "When Claudia loves something, she goes all in."

"Is that so?" says Becks.

Maddie says, "They're a fun band to watch live."

It feels dangerous to leave Becks with Julia, even with Maddie running interference, but at the same time a threshold level of inebriation may be necessary for navigating the rest of this evening. "I'm getting a drink," I say. "Anything, anyone?"

"Let me get it," says Becks. "What do you want?"

Julia doesn't even let Becks make it halfway across the room before she says, much too loudly, "So *that's* your Blonde Assassin."

I say, "Is that a TV show?"

"She doesn't seem that scary."

I glance behind me. The bar counter is its usual jostly scene, but Becks has succeeded at both shouldering her way to the front and getting the attention of the bartender. That, at least, isn't surprising. "Maybe she's off duty tonight."

Maddie says, "How did this happen?"

"That's a good question. She was supposed to buy me dinner, but—"

"Wait, like a date?" says Julia.

"Volume control, please!"

"Sorry. It's crazy loud in here. There's no way she can hear us."

"Not a date. We had a bet about . . . the outcome of something at work."

"Isn't that just a pretext for a date?"

"Shh," says Maddie. "She's coming back."

From Rocaille we head over to Drake Hall, a few blocks north. The opening band is a brother-and-sister duo from Edinburgh with charming accents and pensive, folksy melodies. They play for an hour and then the lights come up again. Becks gets us all another round of beers. When I try to protest, she says, "Price of admission." In a social setting, she's quieter than I would have expected. She speaks when one of my friends asks her a question, but otherwise she's listening to Maddie and Julia and me be inane around one another the way we have been since we met in eighth grade. (Thanks to Maddie I learn that Becks has been in New York for sixteen years and lives in the area around Lincoln Center. Thanks to Julia I learn that she has two tattoos, which thoroughly distracts me from whatever we go on to talk about next because I'm speculating about what, and where, they might be.) Then again, I would never have expected her to be standing here in the first place, on the sticky floor of a concert venue that should have been condemned last century, so I guess it's anything goes for what might happen from here on out.

It's almost midnight when Symposium comes on, and the audience is delirious with fatigue and impatience. Three chords into "Bestiality," a rollicking song making fun of the Greek gods' penchant for turning into animals and mating with humans, and everyone starts screaming. From there the band hopscotches through their latest album, *Chrysalis*, occasionally detouring into *Kleos* and *Nostos* territory for favorites like "108" and "Men Are Swine." Cellos and French horns are brought out for "A Thousand Ships." Midway through the set the lead singer, Hollis Gentle, tells us about how he rode a Citi Bike over the Brooklyn Bridge yesterday, nearly killing multiple pedestrians, and only realized afterward that there was a separate bike path: "That's why everyone was looking at me like I was the jackass. I was!" It's all exactly what I need right now, a mobbed dance floor in a pocket of the universe that's plexiglassed away from all manner of suspicious deaths and synth conspiracies and family dysfunction. I can't tell if that's in part despite, or possibly because of, Becks's presence, and at some point it no longer matters.

For their third and final encore, Symposium gives us an acoustic version of "The Boy in the Borrowed Armor." That song has always been one of my top three: it's about Patroclus donning Achilles's armor to fight on the battlefield at Troy, and also about a high school boy in love with his best friend. This rendition, slowed down and sparse, a melancholy sweetness, destroys me. I'm still in a daze of vicarious wistfulness when the lights brighten and the cheering of the audience begins, finally, to subside.

A touch on my shoulder, and Becks saying into my ear, "Let's start moving before everyone else does."

She takes my arm—it feels almost proprietary, and also familiar—and tows me along after her. One of Becks's superpowers is identifying where a gap in a crowd is about to emerge and positioning us to take advantage of it; I remember this now from the charity gala we gate-crashed in December. The closer we get to the exit, the squeezier things become. Finally she says, like she's trying out the Bene Gesserit Voice, "Coming through," and people actually scoot aside enough for us to champagne-cork out into the cold relief of the night.

We station ourselves a few feet away from the open doors. Becks says, "I don't see your friends."

"Let me text them," I say. "They're probably still trapped inside. I've never gotten out of a concert this quickly before."

I let Maddie and Julia know where we're waiting. When I look up from my phone Becks is leaning against the wall next to me, arms crossed, scanning the street like she's ready for the inevitable ambush. I have that feeling of realizing deep into a dream that you're dreaming, and then having to forge on with an acute awareness of how fantastical everything is. Becks's hair tucked behind the curve of her ear, the knife's edge of her jawline, her skin glowing pale under the lights of the concert hall awning. Sharp lines and softness. Something shivers through me.

An aftereffect of too many Symposium ballads. I clear my throat and say, "That was the best one of their shows I've been to yet. I'm really glad you were there."

Her head turns.

"So you could experience it, I mean."

She rocks herself away from the wall to face me, eyebrows V-ing together. She slides her hands into the pockets of her coat, as if checking herself from what she wants to do. "This would be a terrible idea," she says. "Wouldn't it?"

I've never seen her eyes this dark. Maybe it's because we've never stood outside on the street at two a.m., and so close, closer than the other day in the office, closer than two people with a professional relationship have any right to be standing, so close I can see the faintest constellation of freckles across her nose and cheeks. Not at all as close as I want to be.

"What would?" I ask, and what I hear in my voice is *Who cares?*—and from the quick intake of her breath, an assessment in her gaze that makes me feel suddenly, feverishly unsteady, I know Becks hears it as well.

"Oh my god, that was incredible!"

Julia bounces up beside us like she's commandeered an invisible pogo stick. She sings the first two lines of "Bestiality," atrociously, waving her arms in the air. "I saw you dancing," she says to Becks. "Don't deny it."

Maddie comes up on my other side. She glances at me and then says, "Julia, want to share a car to Brooklyn?"

"Impossible," says Becks. "I don't dance."

"What? Let's go get food. The pierogi place on Saint Mark's."

Becks says, "I'll head home. Nice meeting you both." Her gaze grazes mine. "Thanks for the ticket." She's already speedwalking away as she says, "See you tomorrow."

XVIII.

I DON'T IN FACT SEE BECKS the next day. By the time I sub-
due the evil progeny of alcohol and dehydration that annexed my
skull overnight, a feat that requires my entire remaining supply of
expired Advil, and then drag my contrite self over the Brooklyn
Bridge and into Veracity, she's left for her afternoon observation.

I slouch at my desk and slog my way through an essay advocating for universal basic income by a blogger known as the Socialist
Wonk, who I have determined is my new target, Chris Reichert.
Another project that Squirrel has been spending time on, in lieu
of developing a clone filter, is a program that can pick out unique
markers in a person's writing style and then search the Internet
for instances of that style. This allows us to find out what else our
targets may have been posting online beyond the accounts and
handles we're aware of. So far, it seems what this program excels
at is identifying plagiarism in everything that people write, from
matching profiles to Tripadvisor reviews—which is why we're
calling it To Catch a Plagiarist, or TCAP—but now and then it

turns up something more interesting. Like Chris Reichert's blog, discontinued four years ago now. I've been going through the entries, which expound on topics like immigration (vital) to climate change (real) to tax rates (way too low), and any one of them would have gotten him excommunicated from both the Heritage Foundation, where he is a fellow, and Meet Conservative, the boutique where he matched with our client. At first I thought TCAP made a mistake, but I was able to match enough references in the blog to facts I knew about Reichert—the rescue dog he adopted, a surgery he had (cue indignant piece on health care reform), mentions of an upbringing in suburban Maryland—to feel relatively confident that it's the same person. What could have happened to him in the last four years to flip his entire suite of political, social, and economic views inside out like an attempt to reuse one's final pair of underwear? Or is he faking it now, and if so, why?

My phone, lying next to my keyboard, lights up, and I grab at it with an urgency that would be unseemly were there anyone around to notice. Becks hasn't contacted me at all today, which is unprecedented—she's typically haranguing me on at least two separate communication channels about all the things I haven't done or she's certain I'll forget to do. Is it because of last night?—of course it's because of last night. What does it mean?—what do I want it to mean? My insides feel like a two-in-one soft-serve swirl of hope and foreboding.

The message is a notification from Venmo—I have an incoming payment from Becks R. Comment: *Symposium ticket.*

The soft-serve melts into something gloopy and indefinable. I reject the payment and turn my phone facedown.

The remainder of the day is even more unproductive than what preceded it; my big accomplishment is saving a new Word document as Chris Reichert's as-yet-unpopulated diligence report. I check my phone again right before I leave. Nothing further from Becks, which, whatever. But in my hapjackflappiness account is an email from amsuarezrivera@gmail.com, with the subject line *Any second thoughts on e-bikes yet?*

I read it while taking the stairs down to the first floor. Amalia's note is as friendly as it's brief. She hopes I've been going on fun bike rides and asks if I'd be up for accompanying her to her friend's show in Williamsburg, opening at the start of next month. I tap the link at the bottom of her email and skim the show description: a reimagining of Emma Woodhouse as 3M-M@, a know-it-all romantic compatibility algorithm in android form that's purchased by a Mars colony to match up its inhabitants.

I step out of the building, still perusing my phone, and get beeped at by a delivery e-bike guy who, firstly, shouldn't be swerving around at such speed on the sidewalk, and, secondly, shouldn't be on said sidewalk at all. I almost hit REPLY right then to share those thoughts on e-bikes with Amalia, but that would just be compounding the mistake I made of giving her my email address.

I slide my phone into my pocket and cross the street, looking both ways in the event of more errant e-bikes. Going to that play with her—a whole other magnitude of mistake. Obviously.

XIX.

MY PHONE STARTS QUACKING as I'm heading out of my apartment to bike to an observation on the Upper East Side. At first I assume it's some kind of weather alert—all my cycling has made me obsessed with monitoring wind speed and precipitation—and then I see the calendar reminder: *Mom Birthday*.

I check the Three Cs and then the family chat group that we use for organizing our gatherings, with our mother forwarding the occasional Chinese government propaganda video. Nothing. Have I had a birthday alarm set for the wrong date all these years? That might still be marginally better than the alternative.

I text Coraline: Is today Mom's birthday?

I can see that she reads my message almost right away, but she doesn't say anything until midafternoon, which feels like some kind of power move. It's funny. Of the three of us, Coraline's relationship with our mother is the most fraught, and at the same time, in many ways, the two of them are also the most similar. Or—perhaps that's why. I should give up trying to divine the

reasons for my family's dysfunctional dynamics. Too many possibilities.

When she eventually deigns to respond, all she says is Yup.

> Why didn't anyone say anything?
> When are we celebrating?

> What's that supposed to mean?

I don't know

I mean that means I don't know

Could she still be pissed about how the reunion dinner went
down? That was so many layers of winter clothing ago. I type,
Too short notice to do it today. I'll suggest tomorrow? That work for
you? Coraline's schedule is the one we always have to plan around,
since she needs to be triple-booked in order to feel like she's not
missing out.

Oh I'm not joining so you can do
whatever

I sigh at the screen. Definitely still pissed.

> Why not?

I have more important things to do

When I call her, she picks up right away. "Guess where I am!"
I almost open up Finders Keepers, but that would be cheating.

I listen: cars passing, a truck backing up, some sort of construction, background chatter. Also, church bells? "Outside MoMA . . . waiting for Richard?"

"Wow. That's, like, creepy. How did you know?"

Score! "I can read minds."

"How? Can you teach me?"

"Cor, if I could read minds, I would rule the world." I take a breath: time for the Sherlock spiel. "It was a combination of things. Your office is in Columbus Circle and you're out at lunchtime, so you can't be too far away. The people around you sound like they're speaking in foreign languages—international tourists. You think I would be surprised, which means this isn't a place you typically go. I heard bells ringing, and Saint Patrick's Cathedral is a few blocks away." I pause. "Also, MoMA has a new show on contemporary East Asian art, which seems like something Richard might be interested in seeing." I've become well-acquainted with MoMA's exhibition calendar. The museum is a popular early-date spot for many of our clients, especially on pay-what-you-wish Fridays.

Coraline says, sounding disappointed, "So it was a lucky guess."

"Deduction is *not* . . . never mind." If she's supposed to be meeting Richard, I may not have more than a few minutes. "So, Mom's birthday dinner—"

"I've started meditating."

Sometimes talking to Coraline is like trying to play Whac-A-Mole. "That sounds like a good thing."

"It's the best thing ever! Richard made me try it after dumpster fire *tuan yuan fan* and I was sure it would be a waste of time, but it actually works."

Of course Mr. I Wish I Were Chinese got my sister into meditation. "Works . . . how?"

"It's helping me let go of wanting Mom to apologize for all the fucked-up shit she did. Abandoning me and Charles in Taiwan. Using us as an excuse for every single fucking thing. Why she stayed with Dad, why we were so poor, why she had to work her shitty jobs instead of becoming the next big I-don't-know-what—like that would've ever happened. Threatening to leave. With you, obviously."

What she's saying wraps around me like an ambush of poison ivy, an insatiable itching sensation that spreads and spreads until I would have to rip my skin off in order for it to still. I can't stand it when my sister does this. In part because my preferred approach to our childhood is to keep those memories stacked up in the storeroom of my mind, door triple-locked and all the keys thrown away; and in part because I know that, of the three of us, I lucked out. How our mother is with me has always been different from how she is with Charles and Coraline. It's not simply that she was mean to me and meaner to them while we were growing up. Living with our mother was like standing beneath a perpetually overcast sky, but from where I was, every now and then I would be able to see a glimmer of blue—how she would brush my hair into place with her fingers, or smile at what I said like it was the cleverest thing she had ever heard—and so I knew that the sun was there, just hidden behind the clouds. My siblings never saw that. To them, she was only opaque.

Coraline is recounting the time in junior high when our mother packed Coraline's belongings into a suitcase and left it outside our apartment, and refused to let her enter until the next morning, after my sister declared she would rather go look for our father than continue to live with our mother. Once she's done, I say, "But if you've let go"—notwithstanding how readily and indignantly she just recited those grievances—"then . . . things are okay, right?"

My sister doesn't say anything.

"You shouldn't miss Mom's birthday. She would want you to be there."

"So she can gloat to the mah-jongg aunties about how much her three children love and respect her—which, what a joke, when she spent fifteen years telling us she wished we'd never been born."

It's true that our mother treats one-upping her friends as a competitive hobby, but I do think she will be hurt if Coraline is a no-show for her birthday celebration. Also that such hurt will immediately scab over into irascibility and spitefulness, and the resultant evening will make our Lunar New Year dinner seem like the stuff immigrant-family sitcoms are made of. I say, "I don't think you're being fair to Mom."

"Are you fucking kidding me? You get to tell me what's not fair?"

"I just meant—"

"That's so typical. Just thinking about how it is for you, when you know—you *know*—you have it better than the rest of us."

God, that again. "And *you* know that's not my fault. It wasn't like I chose to stay in New York with Mom—or that she even wanted me to. If our grandparents had space for baby Lin number three, she would've dropped me off the first chance she got."

If not for the ongoing blare of New York street noise, I'd think that we had been disconnected.

"Coraline?"

"It is." My sister sounds calm, suddenly, as if she spent the space of that silence lighting a joint and puffing herself to a higher place. "You don't see it, but I do now."

"What is?"

"It is your fault, too. You're in a position of privilege. You could talk to our mother about the way she's treated me and Charles—like, really talk to her. But you won't, because things are fine for you. You're complacent in this situation."

I've never heard Coraline use this kind of language before, about our family relationships or anything else, and it's oddly upsetting. "*Complicit*," I say. "I think you might be trying to say *complicit*."

She says, so, so calm, "You know what I'm saying. Oh—Richard is here. I have to go." And then, like a courtesy reminder, "I'm not going to talk to you for a while. I don't know how long."

"Coraline, don't be like—"

I can't tell if she heard me before she hung up.

My Mandarin vocabulary these days is limited to a running list of dumpling and noodle varieties—more impressive than it may seem: there are a lot of nuances—but there was a while when I lived in that language. This was before Charles and Coraline came over from Taiwan, so it was just me with my parents and a conveyor belt of babysitters, all of whom I called *ā yí*.

The heavy shelling between my parents hadn't yet commenced in earnest, but now and then there would be a scream-a-lot-and-break-things fest that would culminate in one of them tirading out of the apartment. When it was my father—it was usually my father—my mother would come look for me afterward. She knew my hiding places: closet, bathroom, under the bed. She would coax or carry me out, make me a snack, fuss over me. And she would talk to me.

Of course she wasn't really talking to *me*. As an audience I was the equivalent of a potted plant or a barely toilet-trained puppy. But I understood more Mandarin than I spoke, and also more than I let on. Maybe it was a form of survival. Now I have no idea what the words are for any of the things she said, but I remember their weight. I can still feel it when I think about it, like a rope tied around my waist dragging me right to the bottom of the ocean. Even then it was clear to me how sad she was, this person I loved most in the world.

I'm not sure when all that meaning flattened into nothing but sound for me, a small light in my mind going dark. Definitely by the time my siblings got here: Coraline likes to bring up how shocked she was that I couldn't understand the most basic phrases. (Also how weird it was that I absolutely hated the game of hide-and-seek.) Maybe that was also a form of survival.

———————

That evening, I call my mother. "Happy birthday, Mom."

"Don't remind me," she says, but I can tell she's pleased.

We talk about how her day was. When Charles got out of business school and started his job at Precision, he told our mother that if she wanted to stop working he would support her. She took him up on that offer, in part, I suspect, so everyone would know what a filial son she had raised. Since then she's lived as a lady of leisure, Flushing-style: dim sum, mah-jongg, esoteric classes at the community center, petty feuds with her neighbors. The one exception is taking care of inventory at her friend's Chinese-language bookstore in downtown Flushing, which she continues to do so she can ensure access to the latest Inspector Yuan mysteries.

After I've commiserated with her about Apartment 4J's atrocious hallway trash chute etiquette, I say, "I was checking with Charles and Coraline. They're both really busy right now, so we thought we would celebrate in a couple of weeks?" That's usually the amount of time it takes for one of Coraline's huffs to dissipate, and I'll add in some buffer for ingratiating myself with her before broaching this birthday celebration topic again.

"You mean next month?" says my mother, like we're talking about some hypothetical event that may or may not occur.

"It's a bit further out than usual, but—"

"When?"

"I don't know, the first weekend of May?" In the silence, I know that I've sprung her trap, even if I can't tell yet whether the floor will cave beneath me or I'll get stung to death by a nest of scorpions. I say, "Do you already have plans for that weekend?"

"I may be in hospital."

What? "The hospital?"

"I'm going to the heart doctor that Friday. If he decides to do tests, then I will have to go into the hospital."

Now I remember: for the past several months, my mother has been complaining about how her heart will sometimes feel fluttery when she's climbing stairs or walking too briskly. "I'm glad you're finally getting that checked out."

"I told all of you in our chat. But I know my health problems aren't your priority."

"Of course they are. I thought the appointment was later in May, that's all. Um, do you . . . Would you like someone to go with you to this doctor?" Coraline sometimes accompanies our mother to medical appointments, but since that's not an option right now, I guess I should offer and cross my fingers that she says no.

"Cora will go with me."

"She said she would?"

My mother pauses. "She will when I ask her."

So much for the brief, glorious hope that Coraline might have finished letting go and started picking up again in the half a day since I spoke to her. "Okay. She may not reply right away. Because, you know, of how busy she is."

"I can count on her, not like you."

I hear Coraline saying, *Complacent*, and why did I have to correct her when she was right, it wasn't as if I didn't know what she meant, and then I'm saying, "Mom, it would mean a lot to Coraline if you apologized. About—"

"Do you have children?"

That shuts me up.

"How can you even say that," says my mother. "The parent gives the child everything. Gives up everything. What do they have to say sorry for?"

She sighs, the heaviness of a theater curtain falling. "I could have left you."

Even now I think I can hear the regret in her voice that she didn't, that she made the decision to stay.

XX.

The Three Cs
Dà gē, Coraline, Me

Me: What do you both think about celebrating Mom's birthday on the first weekend of May?
9:47 AM, 04/17/20xx

Me: Hello?
8:04 PM, 04/17/20xx

Dà gē: Okay.
2:48 AM, 04/18/20xx

Dà gē: If Mom's okay.
2:49 AM, 04/18/20xx

Me: She is! I'll make the reservation. Golden Phoenix, 4 people? I'm assuming we'll spare the SOs. If any of that's not correct, let me know by end-today.
7:29 AM, 04/18/20xx

Me: Given resounding silence, I went ahead. We're confirmed for that Saturday at 6 pm.
3:15 PM, 04/19/20xx

Me: Also, has either of you heard of WhatShould? My friend is 1000% convinced that it's going to be the next big thing in social tech.
7:53 PM, 04/19/20xx

Dà gē: What friend is this?
11:22 PM, 04/19/20xx

Me: Someone from Margrave. Now at a Stanford AI lab.
11:27 PM, 04/19/20xx

Dà gē: The next big thing isn't going to come out of academia.
11:30 PM, 04/19/20xx

Me: Unlike the Internet?
11:31 PM, 04/19/20xx

Me: Anyway, it's really cool. It's a web chatbot, so you don't need to

download a separate app or anything. If you have like an ethical dilemma or you're not sure what you should do about something, you tell them your situation and they'll basically give you advice based on their review of all the major theories of moral philosophy. According to my friend it doesn't actually understand what you're asking, the way a person would. It comes up with its responses based on looking for patterns in its dataset and presenting you with the best match.
11:32 PM, 04/19/20xx

Me: It's nice too that you know it's a bot, not like one of those programs that pretends to be human.
11:35 PM, 04/19/20xx

Me: https://www.what-should.com
11:36 PM, 04/19/20xx

Coraline: *Message Deleted*
10:40 AM, 04/20/20xx

Coraline: *Message Deleted*
10:42 AM, 04/20/20xx

Coraline has left The Three Cs

XXI.

THE NEXT TIME I meet Matthew, he asks, "Where's your chaper-one?"

"She's indisposed," I say, a term that could also be applied to my current relations with Becks. She's actually more polite to me now than she has ever been before, in a distant, careful way, which only gives me the eerie sensation that she's been body-snatched. It's clear she's decided that the entire night of the concert was a terrible idea—and, I mean, she's right. Even if we weren't run-ning Veracity together and trying to thwart the matchmakers, and all of that, Becks Rittel would never just be a hookup. The opportunities for me to mess up would be infinite, and the odds that I would about the same. So semi-polite coworker status quo is . . . for the best. (Which doesn't stop me from playing out, now and then, what might have happened that night in an alternate timeline. What her skin would have felt like, and her mouth, and whether we would have gone back to one of our places, and, and, and.)

Matthew tucks the rolled-up magazine he's holding into one of his numerous windbreaker pockets and begins walking north on the High Line, toward the blue gleam of The Standard elevated above us, twin facades of windows, too many of them with curtains open. I add, as I fall in next to him, "And she's not my chaperone."

We walk beneath the hotel, through the covered passage that runs between Fourteenth and Fifteenth Streets. Large photographic portraits mounted on easels line both walls: one of the High Line's periodic art installations. I'm reminded of Norah Simmons, although here the pictures are all of different people, head-and-shoulders shots against blurred backgrounds—and then, once I angle closer, I realize these aren't photographs at all, but insanely realistic paintings. The little placard accompanying each picture includes a QR code that passersby can scan to learn more. Matthew is a foot or so ahead, having neither shown the slightest interest in the art nor given me the courtesy of waiting for me. I quickly take out my phone and scan the code for the portrait I'm standing next to.

I catch up with Matthew as we emerge back into the pale afternoon. "Did you find out what's in the tomb?" I ask.

He tilts his head from side to side. "They have different permissions."

It's funny how sometimes people conduct a conversation like their brain is a fishbowl and whoever they're talking to can follow their thought-guppies shimmying around in the water. I say, "Do you mean . . . the two people with the laptop upgrades? You saw different things on their drives?"

"They were all raw packages, but of different IDs. Twenty on Zaki's drive; fifteen on Minerva's."

I stop walking, because trying to decipher what Matthew is saying while multitasking is beyond me. "Okay. Packages. IDs. What are those?"

Matthew blinks at me. "Sorry. That's how Let's Meet refers

to subscriber information. *ID* just means a subscriber, because everyone gets an ID number when they create an account. *Package* is everything that Let's Meet has on an ID. Although these were raw—no analysis, just the data Let's Meet has collected. What the ID puts on their compatibility questionnaires. What's on their dating profile. What's on any other online profiles they've linked to their dating profile. Their activity history and patterns. Who they search for, who they message, what they're saying on the platform chat app, all of that."

I say, "Both step one and step two data. But why would that be hidden away from everyone else at Let's Meet? It's information that's basic to the matching business."

"Exactly. It shouldn't be hidden. And it isn't. I only had time to go through two of the packages, but I didn't see anything nonstandard. It's what Let's Meet collects on every person who sets up a profile. That same information is available in other parts of Let's Meet's system."

"Do you have the profile handles associated with those packages?"

He looks at me. "Why?"

"We can pull up their profiles and activity on our end, and see if anything seems noteworthy. One possibility is that these are synths, like Silent G, which would explain why the Chemistry Lab wants to hide all evidence relating to them." I add, because I've been treating these sessions with Matthew as opportunities for wish fulfillment, "We have a filter that can screen for that, to an almost-perfect level of accuracy."

"You have access to Let's Meet's subscriber database."

It's not a question, and he doesn't sound surprised. "We have proprietary methods of obtaining relevant information," I say, which is the officially sanctioned response, even if I feel like an ass whenever I have to resort to it. According to Becks it's because I don't speak with enough conviction.

He nods, as if acknowledging what that really means: *Stop probing.* "I'll pass you the list the next time we meet."

"Thanks," I say. "And those names you mentioned just now, Zaki and Minerva—those are the Chem Lab employees you gave the new laptops to? Did you find out anything about them?"

"Like what?"

"I don't know. What they're doing at the Chemistry Lab. How long they've been there, whether they like it . . ."

Matthew says, a touch stiffly, "I was only supposed to ask about Rodrigo Santos."

"Yes," I say. "Of course. I just thought . . . maybe you'd be curious."

After a moment he says, "They're both data analysts. That's what their job titles say, at least." A beat, then: "Zaki is looking for a new apartment. I overheard him on the phone." Another beat. "Minerva goes by Minnie."

"That's telling."

He looks at me as if he thinks I'm making fun of him.

"Really. If I were named after a Roman goddess, I wouldn't ask people to call me by the name of a cartoon mouse instead."

His laugh sounds like a concession I've surprised out of him. We start walking again. We pass a guy sprawled out on one of the wooden deck chairs, holding a tattered edition of *Middlemarch* propped upright on his chest. I feel that minor sense of kinship I always do when I encounter, out in the wild, someone reading a book I myself have read and feel deeply about.

I hear Matthew say, "Maybe it's to help manage expectations."

"Do you ever go by Matt?"

His stride stutters and he falls a step behind before drawing up beside me again. *That's* telling, even if I have no clue of what. I keep my gaze ahead, like I haven't noticed.

"No." His voice sounds the same, dry and uninflected. "I dislike the sound of it."

My question was a casual one, but perhaps I should try to follow up. "It sounds more infor—"

"She was a bit upset about Rodrigo's departure. Minnie."

Does he have some sort of negative association with that name? Anyway, what he's saying now is more relevant. "How so?" I ask.

"That he didn't let her know he was leaving."

"They were friendly?"

"I guess so," says Matthew, as if he finds the notion of getting along with your coworkers mildly mystifying.

"What about Zaki?"

"He said he guessed Rodrigo found something else. Specifically: something else easier."

Easier being a euphemism for *not ethically and legally hazardous?* "What tone of voice did he say that in?"

"Tone of voice?"

"You know. Dismissive, like he thought Rodrigo wasn't smart enough for the work, or envious, like he also wanted to do something else, or . . . or jokey, or . . . anything else."

"I didn't notice."

We walk by the Tenth Avenue overlook, and my gaze follows the cars as they accelerate through a yellow light. I say, "What if Rodrigo learned something about the Chemistry Lab that upset him so much he felt like he had to quit? Or, if it was something he wasn't supposed to know—what if he was fired?"

"Here."

When I turn back to him, Matthew is pointing that magazine he's been carrying around at me like a baton. I take it and unroll it: last week's edition of *The New Yorker*. The address label has been torn off.

"There's an interesting article on opioid addiction treatments," he says. "Page twenty-two."

We step to the side and I open the magazine. The sticky note in the center of page 22 looks like a bright, tiny artwork within a very wide frame. A phone number and an address in sloppy but legible ballpoint blue.

"Looking forward to yesterday's news," I say, which is what Somnang says when he picks up his copy of *Le Monde* from the newsstand outside Hotel le Royal in Phnom Penh, one of the city's hubs of covert communication between MI6 and its spies.

Matthew says, with more amusement in his voice than I've ever heard, "Is that supposed to be a British accent?"

"It might have detoured to Queens." I roll the magazine back up. "Busy this weekend?"—which, according to the code we've devised, is a proposal to meet next Wednesday, at three p.m.

"Same as last week."

I leave first, walking back south to the Seventeenth Street stairs. I feel almost like I'm cheating on the murder mystery, but I have to say, these spy shenanigans are pretty fun.

XXII.

THE DOOR TO BECKS'S OFFICE is always closed. When I first started working at Veracity, going in there to talk to her felt like entering a dragon's lair, hoping that whatever information I'd managed to procure about a target would be enough of an offering to avoid the scorch of her disdain. (Inevitably, no.) I got over that after the first few months. Now, though, the prospect of closing myself in that room with her feels dangerous again, albeit in a whole other kind of way.

So I sit down at my desk eight feet away and write her an email summarizing my meeting with Matthew.

I send that off, pick up the copy of *The New Yorker* from my desk, and flip to its table of contents. Coraline's douchebag ex was a writer who, if he were a character in a murder mystery, would slaughter a path to appearing in the Fiction section of this magazine. Since he isn't, he settled for writing about my sister's traumatic childhood, without her knowledge or her permission, and got that story published in a prestigious literary journal that no one who hadn't been through an MFA program would ever have heard of. Before I found out what Lionel was really like, we were friendly, and he would complain to me about the writers *The New Yorker* did choose to publish ("One of the Jonathans *again*. Give new voices a chance!"). I wonder who it'll be this time.

It feels almost like my thinking of Lionel is why I'm seeing his name, rearranged from the letters of whichever other writer's name should truly belong there.

Lionel Timbers   57   "The Capote Syndrome"

I turn to that page. My hands are trembling ever so slightly, which I'll blame on over-caffeination.

I take in the full-page graphic of a man looking at a woman looking at a framed photograph of a family, of which two of the three children are drawn only in outline, like unfinished sketches. The first line of the story, opposite: "Fourteen months after I met her, I stole Caroline's life."

"You're fucking kidding me!" I say. "You shameless bastard!"

"Is this week's Shouts and Murmurs really that bad?"

I jolt—I'd totally forgotten that I'm in the office, that I'm holding on to this *New Yorker* because it's a vehicle to convey a secret message, that synths might be taking over the world. I spin my chair around to see Becks standing just outside the doorway of her office, coat on and bag on her shoulder. Her gaze flicks from my face to the magazine in my hands and back again.

When I don't say anything, she says, "So you think Rodrigo Santos left Let's Meet because of something he found out. Such as?"

I put down the magazine. This aspect of my life, I can do. "Plenty of options. That his company is building these synths. Or that it's using customer data to do so. Or, maybe, what Let's Meet is planning to do with the synths."

"Or what it did to Pradeep Mehta."

How could I have forgotten about the Pradeep angle? "It's possible. If he learned that someone at Let's Meet was ready to kill for this project, he might decide it was safest to get out of the way."

She gestures at my phone, lying on my desk. "Where does Finders Keepers say he is right now?"

———————

One of the ancillary skills that working at Veracity has helped me to cultivate is the ability to identify semi-comfortable, not-overtly-filthy surfaces on New York City streets where I can park my butt while on observations. The stretch of Dean Street between Vanderbilt and Carlton Avenues, where Rodrigo Santos's gym is located in between two anonymous, shuttered storefronts, poses a challenge. No benches or railings around, no furniture discarded at the curb, no traffic barriers. There's a row of front stoops farther down, closer to Vanderbilt, but they're all gated. Across the street, a jungle gym of scaffolding, and behind that the plywood walls of a construction site—yet another luxury condo development, judging from the glowingly aspirational picture on the WORK IN PROGRESS: RESIDENTIAL sign.

I get here before Becks does, feeling smug about how—yet again!—the bicycle proves to be the superior mode of transport, and plonk myself on a standpipe that extrudes from the wall two buildings away from Primal Fit. While waiting for her, I pull up Lionel's story and read it. The unnamed narrator is a writer who struggles, most earnestly, with his decision to write fiction that's based on his Chinese American girlfriend's personal history. It's an apologia for what he did to Coraline—to our entire family, really—and not, ultimately, in the sense of an apology. He recognizes the betrayal, but at the same time, the artist has a responsibility to illuminate the world in which we live. Oh, the burden!

Becks arrives as the narrator is going on yet another walk along the Williamsburg waterfront and thinking about what Truman Capote would have done. I stand up and slide my phone into my pocket. "Rodrigo's still in the gym," I say.

She nods. "According to the schedule, there's a so-called Combat Cardio class going on until seven thirty."

That explains it—when I first arrived and slow-rolled past on my bike, I saw a group of people on dojo-style mats bashing away at strike pads while the instructor paced around them. Even through the glass I could hear the satanic rasping of a heavy metal soundtrack. I meant to check Primal Fit's website to see what that was about, but then when I took out my phone, all I could think of was Lionel's god-awful story.

Becks leans one shoulder against the wall. "Let's wait here until that travesty is over. Few things upset me more than watching uncoordinated beginners trying to learn improper striking techniques."

This is the first time since our impromptu bubble tea excursion that she's referenced, however indirectly, her confrontational hobby, and it emboldens me to ask, "Why Muay Thai?"

After a moment she says, "It's vicious."

"You're . . . into that?"

"I used to be." She sighs, the softest sound. "It's vicious, but it's also clean. Not like so many other things. It's you and whoever you're fighting, and you both know what you're in there for. What you're trying to do to each other."

I say, "Based on a YouTube video I watched titled '10 INSANE Muay Thai Knockouts!,' I can't disagree. Especially with the vicious part."

The edge of her mouth lifts and then straightens out again.

She's watching me in the intent way she has, and it's making everything else around me go a bit blurry, as if nothing's quite as real as her gaze, the tinge of pink in her cheeks, the hollow at the base of her neck. Remember: terrible idea. Terrible idea—

She says, "What were you reading in *The New Yorker*?"

Well. She could not have more effectively quashed that little mutiny of desire. "I . . ." I stop, because I've never talked to anyone about what Lionel did. The whole thing felt so squalid—that he would take advantage of Coraline in such an intimate, insidious way; that the prolific disaster of my family gave him the opportunity to do so; that this was yet another Asian victimization narrative. I just wanted to pretend it never happened.

Becks draws back, and the shadows slide over her face like a mask. "If it's none of my business, then say that."

"The fiction piece," I say, like a confession. "It was by someone I know. About someone else I know. Who doesn't know."

"That they were being written about?"

"I should have told her." My excuse to myself was that Coraline would have been even more upset about the breakup than she already was, but really, I didn't say anything because it was easier not to.

"You knew about the story?"

"Not this one. But he wrote an earlier story, about the same person, and—it was dumb of me. I thought that story would vanish down the great sinkhole of unread literary fiction, and instead it launched his fucking career." Just saying it makes me feel like I'm being stung by a fire ant colony of outrage. That my family drama turns out to be the gift that keeps on giving to Lionel "What Would Capote Do?" Timbers—

A woman's voice, behind me, just loud enough for me to make out the words: "Oh my god, that was a killer class."

I turn. Two women are heading in our direction. Even if they weren't dressed like Lululemon brand ambassadors, I could have guessed that they were coming from Primal Fit from the palpable air of post-workout smugness. "Crap," I say. "Is it seven thirty?"

"I *know*. That last thing he made us do, the alternating kicks? My legs were *burning* by the end of it."

Becks already has her phone out. "Almost seven forty-five." She pauses. "He's still inside."

"Is he a new instructor? I don't think I've seen him before."

"He's been subbing for Lennie for the last two weeks. I like his style, but he's super intense. After the last class, I couldn't raise my arms above my head for days."

The women are past us now, continuing to one-up each other as to their self-inflicted injuries. I can see the door to Primal Fit swinging open and shut, more people exiting in ones and twos and stumbling away. None of them Rodrigo Santos, though—Finders Keepers continues to show him as remaining on the premises.

Finally Becks says, "Let's make sure he survived that killer class."

The only person visible through Primal Fit's glass storefront is the guy I'd pegged earlier as the instructor, pushing a flat mop across the mats. He's in his late twenties, with heavy brows and mountain-man facial hair. Dark green tattoos coil the lengths of both forearms, which are just as muscled as you would expect from a super-intense Combat Cardio instructor.

When Becks pulls open the door, the same dense, furious music from earlier gnashes out at us. She mutters something I can't make out but is no doubt inordinately rude. I follow her in and past the reception counter—unattended—to the edge of the mats, where the striking pads have been haphazardly piled. Now I can see that there's a weight training area in the back, racks of dumbbells and kettlebells and also larger, more complicated-looking equipment; it's empty. Despite the AC the air feels damp, probably from all the recent vigorous sweating that occurred on-site.

The man looks up. "Sorry," he says. "Gym is closed."

"At seven fifty on a Monday in New York?" says Becks. "That's outrageous."

"Just for this week. We have reduced hours because we're short-staffed."

"Also, can you turn off that noise before our eardrums explode?"

He hesitates, then sets down the mop handle. Becks is going to have no difficulty breaking him down.

He takes his phone from his pocket and taps the screen, silencing the current song mid-snarl. He says, "If you want to sign up for a membership, you can—"

"We're looking for Rodrigo Santos."

His forehead puckers up. "What for?"

Did Becks have to say that like she's collecting on a kidney? "We heard his classes were really good," I say. "We were wondering if he does personal training as well."

"Oh." He smiles: a quick, pleased showing of teeth amid all that beard. "I'm Rodrigo. Who referred you?"

"Diana. She said you were a *killer* instructor."

He squints at me, then says, an apology, "I'm bad with names. But glad she enjoys my classes. I do try to make them as challenging as I can. Haven't actually killed anyone yet, though."

I glance at Becks. She's staring at Rodrigo, perhaps considering the same question I am: Would he be so flippant if he was aware of an actual murder?

"What are your personal training goals?" he asks, looking between us. "Individually and as a couple?"

I can feel every ounce of blood flooding up to the surface of my skin like firefighters in an embarrassment emergency. "We're—"

"Not." Becks's tone creates a tundra microclimate in the gym without at all affecting my personally overheated situation. She adds, dropping the temperature by a further ten degrees, "A couple."

"Ah—right. Okay." He chuckles. "Oops!"

I say, in a bid to rev this conversation out of the ditch of awkwardness that it's steered itself into, "So, um, what's the craziest personal training goal you've heard?"

Rodrigo nods like a relieved bobblehead. "Good question. I wouldn't say craziest, because that can sound a bit judgmental. You know, everyone's goals are valid. How about . . . unique? I have a client who wants to run a hundred-mile self-transcendence race."

Becks says, "That's objectively crazy."

"It's ambitious, for sure. But I'll get him there. He's only been training with me for a month, so we're still in the process of building up his health and fitness dataset. Once we have enough to go on, I can start analyzing the input to understand how to best achieve his goal."

How often does a random question generated out of agita yield potential mystery-solution returns? Hopefully Becks thinks I orchestrated this. "So," I say, "if I were to sign on as a client . . . what would happen? What would we do?"

"Happy to talk through that. I'd start out with having you fill out questionnaires on your diet and exercise regimens, what you want to accomplish from the personal training. The quality of that data won't be the best—people aren't good at self-reporting, for all kinds of reasons—but it will give me enough to put together an initial program for you. And then, from that point, I can help you monitor your metrics more accurately, and we can track your progress toward your stated goals—which could also change along the way. It can take a while to figure out what kind of active lifestyle you want and can maintain."

"Monitor how?" says Becks.

"Through a combination of wearables and apps," says Rodrigo. "I always recommend the Triple-Helix. The range of metrics it can track, the precision, the automatic cloud backup. If you're looking for something more affordable, HealthHack is the best alternative.

The important thing is to collect quality data, and over a long enough period of time, so you can identify the patterns. X causes Y and so on. Once you have that, you know what to adjust for better results. You can optimize your workout program to get to the outcomes that you want."

And Drill Sergeant Rodrigo meets Data Nerd Rodrigo, here in the land of the physio quants. Perhaps this is why he left Let's Meet, so he could focus on the type of data analytics that he truly enjoys.

"That," says Becks, "is the worst spiel I've heard in a long time. X doesn't cause Y. A hundred different variables cause Y. Even if you can see what the pattern is—and let's face it, you probably can't—you won't have the first idea how to change it."

"Not if you have to manually adjust each variable and wait to see what the effect is," he agrees. "But you don't have to. Triple-Helix has an incredible simulation function, if you know how to use it. It can take all the data it has on its wearer and build what's called a 'digital twin.' Essentially an AI that responds as the wearer would respond, in the areas where the AI has sufficient data. The twin tests out different exercise programs on behalf of my client—which happens on a highly accelerated timeline, since everything is simulated—and my client gets to go with the program that's best suited for him."

"An overpriced watch can do all that?"

"The Triple-Helix has more computing power than the rockets NASA sent to the moon. All our smartphones do. Wild, isn't it? We're walking around with supercomputers in our pockets. Most people have no idea what their devices are capable of. Like that digital twin. None of my clients even know how it works."

"But you do," says Becks.

"I have a background in data science. And I had some experience developing digital twins at my previous job. Much more complex ones—compared to that, what I'm doing now feels easy."

The light bulb blazes on so brightly that I can see all the cob-webs in the corners of my mind. "What were the twins at your other job used for?" I ask.

He shrugs. "I left before the twinning was complete."

Becks says, "No one bothered to tell you why you were build-ing those incredibly complex twins?"

"I mean," says Rodrigo, "there were all kinds of use cases. We were more focused on whether what we were doing—whether it could even be done. The project was an extremely challenging one. For example, it involved interaction."

"It's true," I say, "interacting with your coworkers can be extremely challenging sometimes."

He says, all earnest, "Between twins, I mean. Having two twins, from two different sources, in the same sim. That makes predicting outcomes exponentially more complicated, because how one twin behaves will affect the other twin. The dynamic is continually evolving. In some ways, it's like trying to develop an NPC with no parameters."

Becks says, before I can ask if *NPC* stands for *not politically correct*: "Except your non-player characters . . . are replicas of players. Effectively. In order for your twins to achieve any kind of accu-racy, you'd need a shitload of personal information from the people they're based on, wouldn't you?"

Rodrigo blinks like he's just noticed that the purportedly local train he got on is running express and he's halfway to Coney Island. "Depends on how it's being done, I guess," he says. "But that's not an issue with these Triple-Helix models I'm talking about. All you're feeding in are your health and exercise stats, and you decide what you want to provide, obviously." He looks at me. "Did I . . . answer your question? If it's something you'd be interested in, we could try a trial month."

Becks lets Rodrigo talk about his rates for all of ten seconds before she tells him we'll be in touch once we decide on our per-

sonal training goals—separately—and then shoves me out the
door. "Let's walk," she says.

We head west on Dean, away from the lights and the noise of
Vanderbilt. The night flattens everything into shapes and shadows: the trees on the sidewalk, the half-hexagonal facades of the
brownstones, the other pedestrians ahead of us. Becks waits until
we've crossed the intersection to say, "What do you think?"

I say, slowly, still lining up in my mind the different pieces of
what we know and what we've been learning, trying to see which
edges fit, "From what Rodrigo said, the function of the digital
twin is to predict what its source human would do in a given
situation, by running a simulation of that situation and looking at
what the outcome is."

Becks says, "And, by running enough simulations, identifying
the best outcome. Whatever the hell *best* means."

"Which is what the matchmakers are looking for. To be able
to predict the outcome of matching any two subscribers together.
Maybe that's why Let's Meet is taking the clone approach to the
synths. They're not putting synths out there to try to influence
people. With the digital twins, they don't need that."

"No. If they can predict what people will do, they can simply
position themselves to take advantage of it."

"And if they're able to build the right digital twins, then . . .
they could start predicting things with larger consequences. Like
what actions a politician or a CEO, or anyone in an important
position, could take."

She shakes her head. "Not just that. They could ensure that
person took the actions they wanted. They would know which
conditions would lead to which outcome. So—arrange for the
right set of conditions, and the outcome will follow."

We stop talking, as if we've mutually agreed that this conversation has become too depressing. I kind of want to make a com-

ment about taking over the world, but I suspect Becks would not appreciate that right now—or ever.

We walk by a fenced-in Astroturf field, floodlit white and green. There's a co-ed soccer game in progress. A girl runs after the ball, her dark curly hair swinging in a ponytail, and for an instant I panic that it's Amalia Suarez. I decided not to reply to her email, period, so she would think I'd given her a fake address and leave me alone. If she sees me now, and Becks finally finds out—not only about the Whitney run-in but the show invite as well—

"I should get back to my bike," I say, just as the girl spins around and reveals herself to be, after all, a stranger.

As we move away from the field, the darkness folds back in around us. I say, "Although, based on what happened with Pradeep and Silent G, Let's Meet still has some way to go to predicting compatibility."

"What do you mean?"

"That hundred percent match. Silent G basically predicted that Pradeep's perfect match was, in effect, himself."

We walk back past Primal Fit, which is now closed, its enthusiastically graffitied metal shutters rolled down, and stop in front of the sign pole where I've parked my bike. I take out my keys.

Becks says, "Or it was an accurate prediction. Just useless."

"That . . . our best match is ourselves?"

"That the optimal result is to be alone."

"Wow," I say. "What a soul-crushing conclusion."

"Is it?" In the darkness Becks's face is a cubist portrait, oranges and purples and grays, a strange, forbidding beauty. "Do you want to be with someone?"

I'm still corralling my thoughts, which reacted to that question by bleating off in a hundred different directions like a distressed flock of sheep, when she adds, even more tetchily than usual, "I mean the general *you*. Obviously."

I unlock my bike and snap the U-lock into its holder. "Presumably most people do. That's why the matchmakers have so many subscribers."

"They want to be with the idea of someone. Once they get close enough to see who the other person really is, things fall apart."

The second half of that line from the Yeats poem comes to me: *the centre cannot hold.* "If you really believe that," I say, "why did you become a verifier?" It's always puzzled me. Being a verifier feels like a gig that someone designed after touring the inside of my brain—detective stories, Jane Austen, cycling around New York, comfort-casual attire, quadruple-check!—and that was even before we leveled up into solving murders and uncovering conspiracies. But: Becks Rittel. It feels like she should be the CEO of a Fortune 500 company, or a professional poker player, or, yes, an assassin for hire. Not sifting through the detritus of New Yorkers' love lives.

She looks at me as if she's evaluating why I would want to know. "Komla asked."

And that, apparently, was enough. The puzzle within the puzzle: Komla and Becks's relationship. When I first joined Veracity, I spent a while trying to confirm my suspicion that the two of them had developed their own silent, coded language. Eventually I decided it was just a mind meld. A client would walk in and start talking, they would glance at each other, and by the end of the meeting they would be agreed on whether the verifiers could take on the case and how to proceed if so.

Then Sarah Reaves walked in with her secret, and by the time we figured out what it was, and who had killed her to keep it hidden, it seemed like maybe none of us—myself, Squirrel, even Becks—really knew Komla after all. There's so much I've wanted to ask Becks since the night of the gala dinner where we set up a murderer to confess her crime and made it impossible for Veracity to continue as it had been. How she feels about Komla having left us, having lied. What they were to each other, and whether there's any of that left at all. If she thinks he might ever come back.

But the closest I can get, brushing up against the barbed-wire borders of her reticence, is what I ask now: "How did you and Komla meet?"

I'm prepared for her to shut me down, but she slips her hands into her pockets and rocks back on one heel and says, "I married his cousin."

The word *married* swallows me up. I have a vision of Becks in white lace, sunlit, getting ready to pledge herself to someone else. Possibly even smiling.

"You're," I say, and this feeling of desolation is truly confounding. "Married?"

Her mouth twists. "Is that so unbelievable?"

"Not, I don't mean, that anyone would marry you"—although that, too, totally—"but . . ." Have I been deluding myself all this while? The way she looks at me, and what she said after the concert, and how what she wanted—what we both wanted—ionized the air between us. I couldn't have made all of that up. Could I?

"It was for his green card." Becks says that like I've been teleprompting my thought process across my forehead.

"Oh." That sounded way too relieved. "I see." Doing the math: Veracity has been around for more than two years, and you need to be married for only two years in order for the foreign spouse to receive permanent resident status. (Something I know thanks to a recent case where the target neglected to tell our client that he agreed to a green-card marriage scheme in exchange for getting his student loans paid off.) "So. Ah. Are you still? Married?"

"Widowed."

This is like opening up a set of exploding *matryoshka* dolls. I say, automatically, "I'm sorry," and then wish I'd been able to offer something less trite.

A single-shoulder shrug. "It was a long time ago."

Her gaze tilts past me. I wonder if she's thinking of him, her husband, and also what she was like then, how different she might have been. I hold on to my handlebars and look away as well. Across the road, someone is leaning against a stretch of scaffolding, staring down at the tiny glow of their phone screen in their hand. They've positioned themselves just beyond the diffuse radius of the nearest streetlight, the way I would if I were on an observation.

Huh.

I glance around. Becks and I are the only two people on the block right now. Just ahead of us is the Primal Fit storefront, which this person would have a clear view of from where they're standing. Were they here when I first arrived?

Even if Rodrigo left Let's Meet for benignly personal reasons, maybe the company thought it would be prudent to keep a watch on him, given the top secret nature of what he was working on.

On the other side of the street, the person—their hood is up, I can't see anything of their face or hair—pockets their phone and begins to walk away, moving farther from us.

Or I'm being paranoid, especially after the Amalia Suarez scare.

"Never tell him this, but I think Squirrel might have a point."

I turn back to Becks. "That might be the most shocking thing yet you've said tonight."

She says, "Rodrigo brought up NPCs in the context of talking about the digital twins he was working on while at the Chemistry Lab. Plus we already know that Ed Cannon, who started the Chemistry Lab, came over from gaming. In fact, that's why Let's Meet wanted him to head DS, because of his experience developing video games."

I say, "You think that might carry over into developing the synths?"

"It's something we should look into. And the logical starting point is the games that Cannon himself built." She sighs. "We're going to have to kill those fucking zombies, aren't we."

XXIII.

MY RESOLVE TO GET HOME and springboard into the deep end of Google's nine hundred million results on digital-twin technology dies a sheepish, squirmy death on the stairs between the second- and third-floor landings. I hoist my bike higher on my shoulder and keep climbing. I'll start that research tomorrow.

I open the front door to the sight of Max sprawled on the couch, comic books sheafed across the coffee table, and every single working light in the apartment on. "Hey!" I say. "Are you home for tonight?"

"Yep," he says. "I texted you to see if you wanted to get takeout from Ginza."

"Do I ever. I ran out of all my office snacks this afternoon, so I've been thinking about food since four." I close the door behind me. "Is Benny joining us?"

"He's visiting his brother in Austin until Tuesday."

Wow: I can't remember the last time I had Max to myself. "Cool!" I say. "That he's close to his brother, I mean."

Twenty minutes later we're slurping up our bowls of miso ramen. I decide not to comment on the *chashu* add-on to Max's order; I guess he hasn't reconciled himself to full-time veganism. "I saw this when I was on the High Line earlier," I say, taking out my phone and sliding it across the table. "Have you heard anything about it?"

He peers down at the screen. It's the website linked to the QR code I scanned this morning, when Matthew and I walked by that art installation, and displays an image of the portrait that I saw: a middle-aged woman with her hair tucked away beneath a patterned headscarf, olive complexion, a severity to her features that seems more like default than choice. Leila S., *the Troupe.* Below, there's a brief paragraph on the exhibition, *Seen/Unseen*, which comprises eighteen artworks that *interrogate our perceptions and conceptions of the people around us*, and another on the Troupe, the group behind it. The Troupe is described as an international hyperrealist art collective committed to deconstructing reality through the simulation of it, which confuses me thoroughly and is perhaps the goal.

"No," says Max. "I haven't heard of the Troupe, either. I could never be part of a collective like that. I need personal recognition for what I do."

"The pieces made me think of Norah Simmons."

He swipes at the screen and the picture changes to a different portrait. "I can see why. They're both questioning authenticity. With Simmons it's emotional authenticity—like, what are her subjects really feeling? These portraits . . . maybe they're about existential authenticity? We don't know whether they're of real or imaginary people, which then makes us think about how that would change our viewing experience. If it does." He swipes again. "Love the colors."

"*Existential authenticity*," I say. "I nominate that for pretentious term of the night."

"You're the one who brought up contemporary art."

"Speaking of, have you reached out to any of the galleries on Becks's list?"

Max has met Becks once—in our apartment, in fact, under both complicated circumstances and the Max Teffler original artwork that hangs on our living room wall. Perhaps the most unexpected outcome of their encounter was that, after she had reamed Max out for his stereotypically millennial lack of fortitude, Becks emailed him the names and contact details of people she knew at several art galleries. That was back in December, and I've been waiting for an update from Max ever since.

He pushes my phone back over to me. "A few," he says. "Speaking of, how's Becks doing?"

I get that Max is as sensitive as a sanatorium patient about his art, but it stings to know he doesn't feel like he can talk about it with me. I shrug. "As per usual," I say, and I think of her telling me about Komla's cousin, the planes of her face in the dark. Every time I begin to imagine that I have a sense of who Becks Rittel is—how she likes her coffee, the different ways she wears her hair, what authors she rereads, her penchant for organized violence— I learn something new that reminds me: not at all. "Spiky as a sea urchin."

"You know, they're also creamy and explosively delicious. Inside."

I choke on a gob of seaweed that I didn't notice in my broth. When I finally cough up the morsel of death—no thanks to Max: my lousy best friend doesn't even offer to perform the Heimlich, not that I would trust him to—he says, "You want to, don't you?"

"I have no idea what you're talking about."

"Fine. I am talking about you wanting to go down on your extremely hot and equally intimidating—"

"Stop! Too much."

"Are you a Victorian spinster or a twenty-first-century lesbian?"

"Both? You know I can't handle talking about sex. Repressed Asian upbringing, blah, blah, blah." Growing up I never saw my parents once touch each other—in affection, that is—and the entire topic of sexuality was treated in my household like the Gobi Desert, a distant, deadly place that we had heard existed but would never visit and so was not worth mentioning. Charles gets all blushy as well whenever things turn too explicit; Coraline, unfortunately, has no issues oversharing.

"Is it because she's your boss? That makes it even hotter."

"I don't report to her anymore. We had a bit of a reorg." I swirl my chopsticks around in the bowl to see if I've missed any noodle strands. "Nothing's going to happen. It would be too . . . and in any case, I'm allergic to *uni*."

Max frowns. "I think this metaphor has officially gotten away from us."

I stand up and carry my bowl over to the sink. "We can admire it as it gallops off into the distance."

"I'm just watching out for you. I mean, you don't want to be alone forever."

He says that like I'd be living with a disfiguring skin rash. I say, "Good to know. I'll make a note."

"It can feel scary to go online and put yourself out there like that, but—"

"There's nothing scary about it. I just don't want to do it. And even if I did, I can't because of my job." As a verifier, we're not supposed to be matching, to avoid the risk that a target or a client comes across our profile. I've told my friends that the matchmaker research start-up they think I work for strongly encourages us not to maintain active matching profiles; Max reacted like a gun nut who'd been informed the government was coming for his AR-15s.

"Do you think that's why you took that job in the first place?"

"What are you talking about?"

"So you'd have a reason to stay offline."

I rinse out the bowl, open the cabinet under the sink, and chuck it into our plastics recycling bin, which should have been emptied several yogurt containers ago but I really cannot be bothered to do that right now. "I took the job," I say, "because if I had to double-check the links in one more report on the health of the global semiconductor sector, I would have started to question my existential authenticity."

He says, with a little chuckle, "Sure you did."

When I turn around, he's on his phone. I move past him into the living room and drop down onto the couch. Max likes to harass me now and then about not dating—his reasoning, which is sweet if unfounded in truth, is that I'm doing the queer women of New York a disservice by keeping myself off the market—but never quite so smugly. Four months with Benny and he's more insufferable than Mr. Collins at Hunsford.

Okay—stop. Max is happy, in a way he hasn't been before, and I'm happy for him. I am! Just, also, annoyed.

"Are you doing anything for the rest of the night?" I say. "Want to watch a movie?"

I look over to see him texting, his smile like a secret pressed into the corners of his mouth. After a few seconds he says, without looking up, "What?"

"Movie? You can pick."

"I'm FaceTiming with Benny at nine."

"After?"

"We'll be a while."

The smirky way he says that makes clear why; I appreciate him sparing my repressed sensibilities. I say, "It's almost like you guys will be separated for four years and not four days."

Max doesn't seem to register my facetiousness, which is just as well. "I miss him already," he says. "Oh—I've got to go get ready."

He gets up from the table and heads down the hallway, leaving his bowl—and box of uneaten gyoza, and utensils, and can of soda— where they are.

I take a long shower and read some Inspector Yuan, and get into bed once I've confirmed that I can't hear any noises from Max's room; our walls are thinner than models during Fashion Week. I'm exhausted, but my mind feels like a snorkeler paddling about in warm, dark waters, unwilling or unable to dip too far beneath. Finally, I pick up my phone—guess I'll be learning about digital twins tonight after all.

The concept has been around for a while. Build a computational replica of a physical object or system, integrate the two through an ongoing flow of data, and you can leverage that digital model to help you detect issues with or predict outcomes for the original asset. NASA relies on digital twins to test space capsules; manufacturers to monitor their production lines and machine performance in real time.

As far as creating digital twins of humans, there's a fair amount of chatter in areas like health care and sports performance and product design. The workout program use case that Rodrigo told us about comes up a few times. Triple-Helix is the unquestioned leader in that field, and I'm diverted into reading about how accurate its predictions are, how easy its dashboard interface is to use, and how various fitness bloggers' physiques and life outlooks have been transformed. Also how your data is more secure than the nuclear codes, with access limited to a fixed number of trusted devices designated by the user—a measure put in place after a breach that leaked subscribers' triglyceride levels all over the Internet.

Not surprisingly, nothing even remotely related to the types of digital twins that a matchmaker might be interested in. All the applications being discussed involve the collection of bodily data:

heart rate and blood oxygen level, biomechanical attributes and eye movements, sensory inputs. To build a twin that could predict who someone should fall in love with, what kind of data would you need?

I think of the packages that Matthew saw on the Chem Lab employees' drives. I'd assumed they were synth data, but perhaps that information belongs to actual subscribers—and it's what Let's Meet is using to build the twins.

I'm making a note on my phone when the email notification banner slides across the top of the screen.

> **Amalia Suarez**
> **Re: Any second thoughts on e-bikes yet?**
> This reminded me (haha) of what we talked
>   about in the Whitney:

The rest of the message is cut off. I open up the email. It's a link to a paper in a scientific journal titled, rather dauntingly, "Antero-grade Amnesia and the Understanding of the Self: Reviewing the Case of Patient H.M."

Who *is* this girl, late-night-reading *Journal of Cognitive Psychology* articles and sending them to people she bumps into at art shows?

Not too hard to find out. Hit REPLY, thank her for both this intellectual stimulation and the earlier cultural invitation, say that if the latter is still open then I'd love to go. At least I can be fairly confident that Amalia Suarez is harboring neither a deceased spouse nor a quarter-century history of recreational combat experience that she doesn't like to discuss.

I need to go to sleep before my thoughts become stranded in truly hazardous terrain. I download a PDF of the article: Hopefully it will be a soporific? I don't make it past the first page.

XXIV.

I'VE JUST GOTTEN IN the next morning when Becks stops by my desk. "You have ten minutes?"

Of course, she catches me mid-mega-yawn. "Sure," I say when I've regained control of my facial muscles. "Can I get some tea while we talk? I haven't had the chance to caffeinate yet."

We go into the pantry, and I open the cabinet to survey the possibilities. Komla was a tea connoisseur, and he kept us well stocked with a half dozen varieties that he would order from some fancy tea company in London. Fortuitously, that supply contract provided for automatic renewal—as we discovered during the year-end audit that Becks insisted we conduct, an experience of unique misery—and so I continue to be the beneficiary of his excellent taste in *Camellia sinensis*.

"Is this about the digital twins?" I say. "I did some research last night."

"Finish making your tea. You're an inferior multitasker."

After I've put down my mug to let the tea steep, I turn to face her. She's leaning against the sink across the aisle from me, arms folded, looking faintly miffed as usual. She says, "I read Lionel Timbers's stories."

So that's why she waited until I was done preparing my tea; I would have spilled boiling water all over myself otherwise. I want to say she should have asked me first, but that would sound so silly—she has the right to read whatever the hell Lionel has written, even if it's essentially a recounting of my family's tribulations. Which she now knows all about, and no doubt has judged me three times over for. The thing is, Lionel did succeed in portraying what it meant to grow up like we did. The incessant, chafing anxiety of poverty. How cruel our mother could be, how strong she had to be. How her children understood too little and too much at the same time. The story feels true, the way good art does, and that's probably the worst of it.

"Why?" I ask, unsure of what I'm feeling except that it's all coiled together in my chest and rather unpleasant.

"To see if there was something I could do."

The coil loosens and expands into something else altogether, even more startling, equally disorienting. "Oh," I say.

"After I read them," she says, "I ran both stories through TCAP. I got the results this morning."

I'm still parsing the fact that Becks did all this for me, in the twelve hours we've been apart, and it takes a moment to register what she's referring to. Our plagiarism program. "What do they show?"

The set of her features relaxes into a small, self-satisfied smile. "There was a story published in another literary journal nine months before Lionel's story came out in *Zinc Cabin*. Different subject matter, but there are enough similar turns of phrase—a few practically identical—to make a credible case that he copied that other author's work."

Even after everything, it turns out I can still be disappointed in Lionel. "I can't believe he would have," I say.

"If he would steal for his content, it's not surprising that he would steal for his style," she says. "The question is what you want to do about it. If it were me, I'd publicly humiliate him and make sure he never publishes another fucking thing."

I could have done that to Lionel at one point, back when I found out about the *Zinc Cabin* story. I chose not to—and, I realize, I still don't regret it. The true loss was the person Coraline believed him to be, and there was no reclaiming that.

Becks says, a sigh in her voice, "You're not going to."

"Probably not." This certainly gives me negotiating leverage with him, though, once I decide on what I want to ask for.

She steps away from the counter. "You're a soft touch. And your tea is getting cold. I'll send you the TCAP results."

"Becks," I say, "thank you. You didn't have to . . ."

She makes a shruggy sort of motion. "I also considered finding him and breaking a couple of his ribs, but that would've involved more logistics. Still a backup option, though."

She walks off, and I'm left wondering just how serious she is.

XXV.

I SIT DOWN next to Matthew as he's unwrapping his sandwich. "What did you get?"

"Ham and cheese." He elbow-points at the paper bag on the seat between us. "There's one for you, too."

"You brought me food?" I say. "You've just made it onto my favorite-people list."

"In case you're hungry later this afternoon, when you're back at the office."

Ah. Just as well—if sandwiches were mysteries, the ham and cheese would be the butler-did-it outcome. I take the bag. "Thanks."

Inspector Yuan believes that what a person eats, and how, can provide insights into their temperament and character. If so, Matthew Espersen is both unadventurous and strategic. I watch him maneuver to maintain a consistent filling-to-bread ratio as I recount the conversation with Rodrigo Santos and our new digital-twin theory. "If we're correct, then maybe the packages on those Chem Lab employees' drives are subscriber data after all, to be used to create those subscribers' twins. The reason they're hidden isn't because the content itself is problematic. It's what Let's Meet is planning to do with them."

I wait while he literally and metaphorically digests. "If so," he says eventually, "then Minnie and Zaki should have had more on their drives. Draft versions of the twins, or test simulations. Something other than just the packages."

"Unless different people are responsible for different parts of the twinning process. Maybe the two of them just deal with the data gathering, and then they hand that off to someone else in Chem Lab. Can you find out what's in the other employees' tombs?"

"It will take some time. The next round of hardware upgrades is in the fall."

"Fall?" I say. "These twins will be running for Congress by then. Can't you . . . ?" I wave my hand.

"Simply hack into their accounts and extract all the highly incriminating information without them knowing?"

"Exactly!"

"That's one of the reasons I stay away from contemporary spy fiction. Their reliance on the superhacker as the solution to all problems is both lazy and completely unrealistic."

"One hundred percent with you," I say, "although here it would have been convenient. Okay. Is there any way to do the upgrade earlier?"

"I would need to get the new laptops first. The next delivery isn't until September."

"What about the laptop that was meant for Rodrigo Santos?" I ask. "Do you still have it?"

He dabs at his mouth. "That's true. I could use that. That's only one upgrade, though."

I grimace. "I know. I hate the one-chance-to-get-it-right scenarios. They make my palms sweaty. Who are our contenders?"

I must admit I'm not expecting much, given Matthew's apparent DMZ approach to intra-office relations, but he tells me about each of the five remaining Chem Lab members like he's swallowed a fact sheet. Nick Gianduci: data scientist and team lead, part of Data Strategy since the group was set up thirteen years ago, previously running DS's quality assurance division before Ed Cannon transferred him to the Chemistry Lab. Greg Colson: statistician, hired by the prior head of DS four years ago. Miles Fontaine: software engineer, hired by Cannon eighteen months ago, previously at Sony Interactive Entertainment. Hailey Park: software engineer, hired by Cannon seventeen months ago, previously at a digital media agency called Unbrand. Jake Neuberger: data scientist, hired by Cannon twelve months ago, previously at Walmart.

"Walmart has data scientists?"

"Walmart collects two-point-five petabytes of unstructured data from one million customers every hour."

"It's funny how we come up with these words to represent sets of numbers that are way too vast for our brains to comprehend. What's *petabyte*, a squijillion?"

"Too much," says Matthew. "It's too much fucking data."

"Who would you pick?"

"Gianduci." He prods a renegade sliver of ham back into place between the two halves of his baguette. "He's the safest bet. He's in charge. Whatever this is—digital twins, or something else—he has to know what's going on."

"Yes and no," I say. "He's in charge of the Chemistry Lab. But that's Ed Cannon's initiative, and this Gianduja guy reports to him."

"Are you suggesting . . . Cannon himself, then?"

"Also yes and no." I'm increasingly convinced that Ed Cannon joined Let's Meet to help the company develop these digital twins and whatever simulations the twins are to be run through: a game more challenging than anything he's had the opportunity to create before. But that also means we can't risk him getting suspicious now, before we've amassed our evidence and confirmed our theory.

He sighs. "Then— What?"

"We should go for whoever on the team Ed Cannon would assign the function of actually building the twins. Taking a subscriber package and turning that data into a synth designed to run in multiple simulations. It's not something Let's Meet was doing before, so he would have had to hire for it. And, given the similarities to game character design as well as his own experience, I'm guessing he recruited within the video game industry."

"So not Gianduci or Colson, since they were around before Cannon. And not Park or Neuberger, either—they didn't come from video games." He pauses. "Fontaine. That's who you would go with?"

"Yes," I say. "And I suspect it's not a coincidence that he was at Sony before he went over to Let's Meet. Ed Cannon worked for an indie game developer called Lumina for a long time. He only left to join Maverick when Sony bought Lumina."

"All right." I can't tell if Matthew is impressed or skeptical, or doesn't really care. Then he says, "So that was Pradeep's digital twin. The synth profile that matched with him."

"We think so."

He puts down the remainder of his sandwich and starts wrapping it back up in its foil packaging, all five bites' worth of it. Frugal as well, which fits with what I've observed about him—I've only ever seen him in the same windbreaker and pair of running shoes; and while he's careful not to reveal any personal information, we have shared before our views on all the luxury condos we pass on our High Line jaunts, and we're in violent agreement about the foolishness of paying a premium to live in Manhattan or the trendier parts of Brooklyn.

"I wonder," he says now. "If the twin could have shown Pradeep what his life would be like, based on his choices . . . whether he would have changed his mind."

———————

Back at Veracity, I extract the Saran-wrapped sheet of notepaper that Matthew folded in between two slices of cheese. I'm glad he chose a dryer sandwich than the banh mi that Somnang had to disassemble in *A Gentleman's Game*.

Matthew wrote down the profile handles from Minnie's drive on one side of the paper and the handles from Zaki's drive on the other. I open Match Insights and search for Saunderstan, the first handle on the Minnie side. Thirty-seven years old, nonbinary, arts administrator, lives in Hamilton Heights. Match Insights is set up to store user activity for the past six months, and there isn't much of it. Alex (the name Saunderstan signs off with in their messages) logs in once a week, clicks through a few profiles, rarely contacts anyone. Their own profile provides only enough for the flattest of representations, like those paintings of medieval saints before linear perspective was discovered. They do link to an external social media account, but that turns out to be for a role-playing community set in a fantasy world with a convoluted origin story.

The next few handles I search for are only incrementally more forthcoming. Weird. If my theory is correct, and the Chemistry Lab is collecting the information of bona fide subscribers in order to build digital twins, why choose this set of individuals? Logically, it should have gone for the high-activity, high-disclosure users, people who would provide the maximum amount of data about themselves. Unless I'm wrong, and these handles *are* twins after all? In which case, the sources that these twins are based on should have their own profiles up on Let's Meet.

I send the list on to Becks and Squirrel, letting them know my findings so far, and ask Squirrel to check if, for any one of these handles, there's a second profile up on Let's Meet with the same information.

The rest of the afternoon is spent working on a diligence report for a client who's coming in next week to receive her interim update. During her intake session, Ana Vitale told us that she wanted the target verified because she had never matched so highly with anyone before. "We've been dating for almost six months," she said, "and things are fine. As in, just fine. If we really were a ninety-three percent match, wouldn't things be more, like, amazing?"

"Some people just have limited emotional depths," said Becks; she's especially brutal to clients who treat our meetings like opportunities for free therapy.

Ana shook her head with such vigor I feared her lightning-bolt earrings would fly off and blind one of us. "Not me. I feel things strongly. Very strongly."

"So what you're saying is . . ." I said, and then strategically paused so she could enlighten us.

"Maybe he lied about himself, and we've been matched up incorrectly."

I asked, "Have there been any indications of potential dishonesty? Inconsistencies in things he's said, evasiveness on any particular topics?"

"Nothing comes to mind right now. But, you know, those things can be hard to tell. That's why I came to a professional."

I would have liked to point out the other possibility: that Soulmate's compatibility algorithm might simply not be all that great, especially now that Soulmate no longer has its synths to help obtain additional intel on subscribers. But one of Veracity's rules is that we don't get into our own views of the matchmakers, which after all are shaped by the secrets we know about them. And, recalling that conversation now, it's clear Ana believed in Soulmate's ability to predict her happiness, more than her own.

Our clients generally do. They want a professional to tell them whom they should be with, just as they want a professional to tell them if that match is lying. The Big Three's bet is that as long as they can give people what they want, no one will bother about how it's done or consider what it might cost. If the matchmakers are right, that might be the scariest part of it all.

XXVI.

THE HOUSE BEFORE ME looks like it was teleported out of the suburbs, dipped in a vat of mustard yellow paint, and set down in Red Hook just a few blocks from the water. Empty lots on both sides; across the street, a Pentecostal church with an august Romanesque facade and a shopping cart piled with junk listing against its wire fence. I check the address Squirrel gave me: Can this be it?

Then I see Becks, standing on the curb with her arms crossed, looking rather like a sculpture titled *Severity*. I guess so. I lock my bike to a pole that hosted a sign once upon a time and join her. "This is nice!" I say, and then hope I didn't sound too obviously surprised.

"From the outside," she says.

The door is unlocked and creaks open like a masterful horror-movie sound effect. We walk into a large living room that looks like a showcase of furniture salvaged from sidewalks all across Brooklyn: wingback chairs, dorm-room futons, Shaker-style cabinets. A vivid green menagerie of potted plants hangs from the ceiling along the row of windows.

"What are you doing here?"

Squirrel stands at the banister midway up the staircase that leads to the second floor. This is the first time I've seen him sans baseball cap, and it's amazing how much of a difference hair can make: his is a giant puffball and makes it impossible for me to take him seriously.

"Zombies," says Becks.

"That's today? Shit. I haven't finished setting up."

He turns and dashes up the stairs, disappearing from view. She glares after him, then crosses the living room to follow.

When we get to the second floor, she heads down the hallway like she knows exactly where she wants to go. "You've been here before?" I ask.

"A few times. When he was in his *hikikomori* phase."

I'm still processing her reference to the Japanese phenomenon of severe social withdrawal, and its application to Squirrel, when she stops at the last door on the left. She raps on it once. "We're coming in."

What's inside looks a bit like a call center that happens to be located in a cave. Two rows of cubicles that run along opposite walls, panoramic computer screens, blackout curtains, the odor of what I'm able to identify, from a childhood spent subsisting on the junkiest of foods, as sour-cream-and-onion potato chips. The only light in the room comes from the couple of monitors that are on, a pale somnambulant glow. Squirrel is seated at one of them, baseball cap donned. He says, without turning around, "Set up your avatar first."

Becks and I each take one of the cubicles with a lit screen, which displays a character dashboard. The interface is relatively easy to understand. Your character works at McMurdo Station, the largest U.S. science facility in the Antarctic; you get to select your occupation, which gives you a particular configuration of strengths and weaknesses. I go through the choices. Mechanical engineer: good with tools, can fix machinery. That seems useful. Line cook: good with knives, can build fires. Hmm, also useful.

"Done?" asks Squirrel.

"Um, almost," I say. I click to the next occupation. Zoologist—why not?

Once we've finalized our avatars, Squirrel talks us through the multiplayer version of *World's End: McMurdo*. "We'll each start out in a different area of the station, so the first thing we have to do is find each other."

Becks says, like it's an imposition, "We're playing as a team?"

"We have to," says Squirrel. "If we play competitive, I'll annihilate both of you."

"And doesn't it make sense?" I say. "I mean, we *are* a team."

Squirrel designates a meeting place—the Crary Lab: "centrally located and the core pod has some useful shit"—and instructs on zombie-pulping essentials. "Go for the head. Blast it off if you have a weapon that can do that; otherwise, try to do as much damage to the nasal cavities as you can. They go primarily by smell, so if they can't smell you—or you don't smell human—they won't attack."

"Sounds good, but how do we actually do any of that?" I ask. "I mean, using game commands and stuff."

"You'll figure it out. It's intuitive."

I'm about to protest—the only thing that feels intuitive to me is throwing the keyboard at the screen—but Becks cuts in: "How do we win?"

"There are a few ways. We can escape from the station, which is lame and what you would do if I wasn't around. We can stop the zombie outbreak: pulp all the existing zombies, defeat the boss who's behind the whole thing. Or we can take over the station and become leader of the zombies."

"I thought the zombies want to kill us," I say.

"More like they're just following their zombie nature. And not all of them are adversarial like that. There are two kinds of zombies. One kind wants to turn humans into zombies. The other kind wants to turn themselves into humans."

I ask, "Can they?"

"No," says Squirrel. "The closest they can get is to find a human and follow them. It becomes fucking sad if you think about it too much." He turns away from us to face his screen. "Let's start already."

At his direction, I put on the goggles and headphones that are sitting on my cubicle desk. The former reminds me of high school science lab, but with a heavier feel and a more comfortable fit. The latter, once clamped into place, turns the inside of my head into a sterile white space. I lean forward in my chair and click the pulsing → icon on my screen.

I was half expecting to feel like I'd be watching a National Geographic documentary, albeit one populated by legions of reanimated corpses, but instead this looks like what you'd get if Monet set up his easel on McMurdo Sound for the Antarctic summer. Everything is color and light and texture and shape: the patterning of ice across the dark soil, the movement of water, the geometries of buildings, the bright sky. Sound effects, on the other hand—highly realistic. I wake up outdoors, in the station's harbor, the wind battering at my eardrums. Beneath that, I can make out the ongoing crescendo and crash of the waves against the shore downslope from me. When I start walking, it almost feels like I'm sensing rather than hearing the rhythm of my soles across the soil.

The first time a zombie comes for me, lurching around the corner of a warehouse, I yelp in a most embarrassing manner. Renewed appreciation for both MaDD's decision not to go for photorealism—an impressionistic depiction of exposed intestines is about all my wimpy self can take—and the headphones' phenomenal noise-cancellation properties. After some panicked clicking around I hit it in the rotting face with the baseball bat that's the only object resembling a weapon I've been able to find. Okay, how did I do that?

By the time I find my way to the Crary Lab, I'm down to a fingernail's width of life force. Becks's and Squirrel's avatars are waiting for me in the entry corridor, on either side of a display case of a stuffed penguin. They both look dispiritingly robust. A number of zombies are lined up against the wall behind Squirrel; these must be the nonhomicidal ones.

I hear Squirrel's voice in my ear: "You really let them chew on you, huh?"

"Fighting zombies is not at all intuitive!" I say. "Also, why didn't you tell us we can talk to each other? I could have called for help five maulings ago."

"Only when our avatars are within earshot."

Becks says, "I picked up a first aid kit somewhere. Can that do anything?"

Squirrel says, "I'll apply it. I'm a medic, so if it comes from me she'll get an extra boost."

"Good. I need to free up space in my inventory."

The overhead lights spasm on and off as we walk single file down the hallway; it sounds like an invisible series of moths are being electrocuted. Squirrel guides us into what looks like an empty office. His zombie retinue—I count six, all in various stages of decrepitude—shuffles in after him. I ask, "How do you get the zombies to join you?"

"And what do they do besides crowd you and drop body parts on the floor?" says Becks.

"You have to train them. At first they just mimic you. After a while, though, they'll start to act on their own, based on what they think—"

There's a scrabbling sound at the door, right before it swings

open and zombies start piling in. I'm still reaching for my baseball
bat when Becks's avatar shoots the ones in front with a futuristic-
looking rifle that I could've sworn she wasn't carrying until now.
They collapse, limbs continuing to paddle.

"Wow," I say. "You're really good at this zombie-pulping
thing."

Another set of zombies clambers over their fallen comrades to
enter. Becks steps between them and me. In between impeccably
accurate head shots, she says, "I have a nickname to live up to,
apparently."

My avatar clutches her useless bat while my corporeal self
cringes at the increasingly splattery screen. How would Becks
know—gah, when we were at Rocaille with my friends, before the
concert. She must have overheard Julia after all. I try to recall how
the rest of that conversation went, and if anything too incriminating was uttered, but all I remember are Julia's and Maddie's lifted
voices, my glimpse of Becks leaning against the bar counter, a
dense foliage of noise.

"That's nothing," says Squirrel. "Watch this."

His avatar sprints toward the doorway, one hand reaching over
his shoulder to unsheathe what I now realize is a gigantic sword
strapped across his back. He runs up the slope of fallen undead and
leaps into a somersault. The blade flashes like an arc of lightning,
and he dispatches the last of our zombie attackers, their heads
bouncing onto the floor.

I say, "I would applaud if I knew how to."

Becks says, "Why the hell is there a Kurosawa film prop in a
U.S. research station?"

While Squirrel applies the first aid kit to my injuries, his zombies undertake cleanup, moving the corpses from the doorway to
a corner of the room. Two of the zombies also station themselves
outside the door, presumably to watch for new threats. "Are your
zombies acting on their own initiative?" I ask.

"Sort of," he says. "They're doing what they think I want them to."

"How do they determine that?"

"Combination of watching what I do and getting feedback. Like now."

The zombies, task complete, are now standing in front of the desk, side by side. Squirrel's avatar goes over and pats each of them on the shoulder. "This lets them know they got it right, basically," he says. "Okay, let's make a quick stop at the aquarium. There's a really gross sea creature I want to show you."

Becks says, "Does that even have anything to do with the game?"

"We're *in* the game. Everything we do has to do with the game."

I'm ambushed not long thereafter by a zombie hiding in the microscope room of the biology pod, where we've gone to look for penguin cell samples that, according to Squirrel, will provide a vital clue to who's behind this current infestation of the undead. Squirrel's zombies drag my assailant off me, but not before it gnaws off a chunk of my face. My entire screen goes a filmy red— I guess an attack like that is fatal. I'm a touch relieved.

I remove my gaming accoutrements and turn around. Squirrel has paused the game on his screen; he's facing me, headphones around his neck and goggles pushed up on his forehead. "You couldn't have kept yourself alive until after you analyzed the samples? That's the only thing the zoologist is good for."

Becks stands up from her cubicle. "Give her a break. This is her first time playing the game. I was sure she wouldn't even make it to Crary."

I say, "I thought you hadn't played *McMurdo* before, either."

"Just to prepare for today."

"Wasn't the point of today for us to try out the game?"

"I hate doing anything badly." She steps out into the center of the room. "That was a surprise."

"I was right, wasn't I?" says Squirrel. "*McMurdo* is awesome."

"The game itself was exactly the kind of tiresomely violent escapism I thought it would be. But, from our discussion with Rodrigo Santos, I expected more from the NPCs."

"The zombies?" I say.

"I met a few humans. They were extremely unimpressive. Barely interactive."

Squirrel says, "That's because the MaDD games are about the zombie action. Any humans that show up are just there to be rescued or to give you stuff. There's no point in developing them beyond that."

She says, as she opens the door, "Fine. Then what do these video games have to do with what Let's Meet is doing?"

She leaves. The door gapes behind her, the light from the hallway filtering the room in a grayish hue that's not too different from the zombies' skin tone. Squirrel says to me, "Was she expecting us to answer that?"

I sigh. "I wish I could."

When we go back downstairs, Becks is standing in the living room with a gigantic white guy who's holding a watering can in one hand and a pair of shears in the other. He says to Squirrel, "You didn't tell me Veracity was going to be in the house. We could have baked a cake."

"Marsh," says Becks, indicating me, "this is Claudia. She joined us last summer." To me: "Squirrel's housemate. Patron saint of horticulture and patience."

He raises his watering can in greeting. "How's it going so far?"

"Good," I say, fascinated by the mathematically spherical quality of this man's face. "There's always something new to learn, like the most efficient way to kill—I mean, pulp—zombies."

"Which one did you all play?"

"*McMurdo*," says Squirrel, "and they totally failed to appreciate it."

"Come on," Marsh says to me and Becks, like we've personally let him down. "The receptive zombie? That's one of the most incredible ideas to come out of shooter games in the past five years. Any kind of game, period. It subverts the traditional role, and notions, of the zombie in the video game. It highlights the struggle we all face between who we used to be and who we are now. How a part of us wants to go back, and we fucking can't, and another part of us wants to destroy that past self. And by making the receptives an extension of the player, the game both leverages on and calls out the player's narcissism. The zombies are us, man. The zombies are us."

Squirrel says, "Okay, that's pretentious bullshit, and not why *McMurdo* is a great game."

The zombies are us: that does sound profound. Although maybe it's simply the certitude with which he speaks, because what does that even mean?

And then I realize. What it *could* mean.

"That's what the zombies are. Literally." I turn to Becks. "As in figuratively. Or—trying to be us. Or not trying, but . . ."

I stop, because Marsh is looking at me with a keen, kindly interest.

"Marsh knows," says Becks. "About the synths, and the digital twins, and all that. Squirrel blabs."

"Only when we get tired of arguing about politics," says Squirrel.

Marsh says, "And I'm entirely trustworthy."

He speaks like he's reassuring me, and it occurs to me that these three people know one another in a way that's inaccessible to me, a shared past in which I didn't exist. Among us, I'm really the one standing on the outskirts of this circle. I push that thought aside and say, "Matthew—our source at Let's Meet—said that game makers try to predict what their players want by looking at the data of what they're doing in the game."

"Hmm," says Becks, like she's reluctant to acknowledge that anything Matthew Espersen said might be of value.

"MaDD's receptive zombies . . . it feels like a way of doing that in real time. The game is using the receptives to test out its predictions of what a player wants."

"Hmm"—a longer, considering sound.

"Other games only provide data on what the player actually does. The receptives are a mechanism for getting data beyond that. What the player would do. Over time, how the player thinks."

"That's true," says Marsh. "Now and then one of my receptives does something and it's exactly what I wanted."

Squirrel says, like he's one-upping his housemate, "Sometimes I didn't even know I wanted it to happen until they did it."

Becks says to me, "That's not a setup Cannon could implement at Let's Meet."

"No," I admit. "Having zombie NPCs follow Let's Meet subscribers around to gather information on them wouldn't work."

"I agree it's related, though. We just have to figure out how."

Marsh is inspecting one of his hanging baskets of ferns, finger lifting up a frond like it's a songbird. "I hope the twins never find out," he says.

"Find out what?" says Becks.

"That they aren't really the people they were programmed to predict."

"Marsh—these things are a bunch of commands and data. They aren't alive."

He moves his hand away and the frond droops after it. "They believe they are. They experience everything their source humans do and respond as they do. At a certain point, don't you think they might as well be?"

PART THREE

PART THREE

I.

**Things I might ask the real WhatShould if Squirrel
hadn't convinced me that his nemesis, Geraldine Napier,
set up the program for her own nefarious purposes**

1. What should I do if I think my best friend's boyfriend is
   not right for him because this boyfriend is self-absorbed,
   possessive, obnoxious, and overall not a nice person? I've
   considered at length the prospect that I might just be
   jealous, and I don't think so but obviously can't be
   100 percent positive.

2. What should I do if my sister and I argued and now
   she's ignoring me, and I think she has a point but I
   don't want to apologize because (*i*) she'll make a big deal
   out of it and it will be emotionally exhausting, and
   (*ii*) I have this fear that is probably paranoia that instead

of making a big deal out of it she won't accept the
apology at all and that will be even worse?

3. What should I do if a former client of my company
   (who doesn't know I work there) has asked me to
   hang out, but company policy expressly forbids
   any contact? She's really fun and interesting, and I
   would love for us to be friends. Wouldn't it be a
   shame to just let someone like that pass out of my
   life, especially when I can get judgy about other
   people (see question 1)? It's possible I'm also feeling this
   way because I've gotten a not-completely-platonic vibe
   from her, which is (*i*) exciting, as I find her very cute
   myself, but simultaneously (*ii*) perplexing, as I know
   she's in an exclusive relationship. Which in turn
   makes me more curious about her, which I'm aware
   is a dreadful reason to do something I'm not
   supposed to do.

4. Do other people ask such rambly questions?

11.

SPRING IN NEW YORK always feels overrated to me. It's wet and skittish and unpredictable. There's a mushiness in the ground, a clinginess to the air. The best part is those few weeks when the city just explodes with pink and white flowers, a fleeting, extravagant beauty. Cycling down some of the streets in Brooklyn can make me feel like I've joined a fairy-tale procession, passing beneath fragrant canopies and over carpets of petals. All that is always offset, though, by the ordeal that I know will follow.

"Are you sick?"

I honk into a take-out napkin—luckily I've accumulated a stack on my desk. "Just allergies."

Becks takes two steps back, her gaze narrowing like a polygraph android scanning for indicia of lying. "Are you sure?" she says. "I don't want you spreading disease in here."

I blow my nose again, more vigorously. "As long as we stay six feet apart, you should be fine."

It comes out sounding weirdly like a challenge. I ball up the napkin and toss it into the wastepaper basket so I'll have an excuse to break eye contact.

"I meant for the clients. I can handle your germs."

Which also sounds, kind of, like a challenge.

"Although," she adds, "maybe it wouldn't be a bad idea if you infected some of them. Fewer idiots to deal with."

The online-dating populace doesn't agree with my assessment of spring—after the post–Valentine's Day lull of the past two months, our intake numbers have begun ticking up again. There's a different vibe to these new clients. They aren't fretting about having someone suitable to present at holiday parties or family gatherings, and I don't sense the same lonesomeness I sometimes did during our winter intake sessions. The clients who show up at Veracity now are assured and optimistic. More than one, upon hearing about their match's duplicity, has thanked us and said they would probably continue seeing the person anyway, prompting Becks to ask why the hell they bothered with a verification in the first place. "It's like getting a health checkup," said Jason Wiseman, whose match was living with her parents in Jersey City instead of in the Financial District with roommates like she'd told him. "This kind of stuff, it's good to know. But finding out that my cholesterol is on the high side isn't going to stop me from enjoying, I don't know, oysters. Things are a lot of fun with Kylie right now. I want to let this play out."

That afternoon, when I come back from an observation with an eggplant parm sub and more take-out napkins, there's a box of Kleenex on my desk. The next time Becks marches out of her office, I say, "I've never used three-ply tissue before. I'm not sure I can go back."

"It helps to muffle the noise," she says. "I can hear you from inside. It was driving me insane."

"Well, thanks."

She's halfway across the room when she stops and turns around. "There's more in the bathroom cabinet."

——————————

Cameron Keller's autopsy report, which the City of San Francisco finally sends to us after I'd forgotten I even requested it in the first place, doesn't clarify anything except my existing theory that Lucinda Clay wasn't responsible.

According to the medical examiner, the cause of Cameron's death was a fatal arrhythmia induced by the chemical conflagration in his system at the time. I google my way through the toxicology section. In addition to alcohol and cocaine, cetirizine (prescription allergy medication), metandienone (a steroid popular for athletic performance enhancement) and multiple types of benzodiazepines (prescription antianxiety medications) were all found in Cameron's blood samples. I text the list to my biochemist friend Caleb and ask him which of these drugs increases the risk of sudden cardiac death.

This is how you're killing your victim now? he replies.

Caleb believes, because I told him so at some point during my Sarah Reaves investigation, that I'm writing a murder mystery.

Second victim.

Isn't that pretty similar to the way you killed the first one? That was a medication overdose, right? You don't think that makes the M.O. too obvious?

Exactly! Which is why the second crime must have been committed by someone else.

Ooh I like that. Maybe that can
be a red herring for the detective—
they assume at first it's the same
murderer because it's the same M.O.

What? No. My detective is smarter
than that.

Readers like that, though. Figuring out
who did it before the detective does.

Do they? I'd be annoyed if the detective in the book I was reading was a twit. I'll think about it. Anyway, my question . . .

Right, sorry. Definitely cocaine
+ alcohol. How much detail
do you need?

Why not. Give it all to me.

Fifteen minutes later, Caleb is offering to draw me the chemical structure of cocaethylene, an active metabolite that's produced
when cocaine and ethanol are both present in the bloodstream
through a process called "transesterification," which sounds like
what an evil mage in an epic fantasy novel might do to his ene-
mies.

This is already super helpful. So
the combination of alcohol and
cocaine is primarily what
causes the cardiac issues?

Yep. The other stuff . . . metandienone
also increases the risk, because it's an

AAS and the anabolic effect on the
metabolism of nitrogen causes muscle
hypertrophy. But the interaction of
cocaine and alcohol, in large enough
quantities, is enough to kill someone.

You should think about writing
a chemistry PhD student into
your mystery for your detective to
consult. A brilliant, devastatingly
handsome 27 year old male.

                              I'll call him Kaleb.

When I go over the findings from Cameron's autopsy with Becks the next day, she says, "You clearly have a theory. What is it?"

"I think the killer is someone who knew Cameron relatively well," I say. "They knew that Cameron used cocaine; maybe they also knew he was taking steroids. They arranged to meet at Cameron's apartment, did some coke with him, encouraged him to drink more than was safe. Maybe they even brought the coke and told Cameron it was less pure than it really was so he would take more of it."

"Or he went overboard by himself and died due to his own poor choices."

"You don't really think that."

"It's a factual possibility that we can't rule out at this stage."

"Either way, the first step is figuring out who the people in

Cameron's life were: who he worked with, who he saw socially, who he would invite over to his place."

"We," says Becks, "and specifically you, are doing none of that."

"Then how are we going to rule out the possibility that his death was an accident?"

She flicks her hair back over her shoulder. "Even if it wasn't, what happened to Cameron Keller isn't our responsibility. He was someone we didn't know who died three thousand miles away. The only reason you followed up on it was his connection to Soulmate's synth project—and that project has stopped. Which means, from our perspective, that the matter is closed."

I almost let it go, because I wish it could be that easy. "It's not," I say. "We don't know if Cameron was killed because of his connection to Soulmate or to Precision. And if it was Precision, something he did, or learned, while he was there, then . . ."

Becks is quiet. Then she says, "Any updates with respect to your brother?"

"No. His activity is the same on Finders Keepers, and he still hasn't said anything to WhatShould." My spiel on the Three Cs worked, sort of: Charles created an account the next day, although he has yet to do anything with it. I knew that if I told him someone who sounded semi-legit—in other words, not me—viewed WhatShould as an important social-tech development, FOMO would compel him to check it out. He provided an email address I didn't recognize, but his username, Wallpath, was our childhood code word for when our mother was in a foul mood, which meant it etched itself into the Most Frequently Invoked Terms in the Lin Household list.

"Which isn't a bad thing," says Becks.

"No."

"The most straightforward explanation would be that there's no issue."

We both say, at the same time, "Occam's razor."

Becks smiles, a twist of wistfulness to her lips that makes me want to move closer; that was one of Komla's favorite references. "You continue to watch your brother, and if anything changes we'll discuss. Cameron Keller . . ." She pauses. "We're not going to be able to meaningfully investigate from here. And it's not like we can press pause on everything else and go off to California for two weeks."

"I guess not," I say, and close the door that had swung open in my mind to reveal a vision of me and Becks toiling up one of those insanely steep San Francisco streets, pastel-pretty, pointy-roofed row houses lining both sides, on our way to solve Cameron's murder.

"There's . . . a person in SF. I can ask her to try looking into this for us." Becks speaks like she's already having preemptive qualms about what she's saying. "She's helped us previously."

I blink. "With other murder investigations?"

"As hard as it may be for you to fathom, Veracity was once a murder-free environment. We had to track someone down."

"A target? I thought we didn't go beyond the tristate area."

"Jesus Christ, it doesn't matter. I'll talk to Jodie, and if she turns up anything interesting I'll let you know. Now can we go over the talking points for Tony Masajo?"

I almost say that if it really doesn't matter, she might as well tell me, but working with Becks is an ongoing lesson in picking your battles, and her agreeing to keep Cameron Keller's case open feels like enough of a win for now.

Plus, I completely forgot that Tony Masajo is coming in this afternoon for his final debrief.

"I'm starving," I say. "Let me go grab something to eat first."

From the look she gives me, I know she knows I haven't drafted those talking points. But all she says is "Fine. We'll do it after lunch then."

III.

THE BUNKER SITS between two apartment buildings on Metropolitan Avenue like a toy block that a child wedged in there and forgot about. Its door is propped open, and a quartet of people stand outside chatting loudly, a display of asymmetrical hairstyles and artistic tattoos and overall off-kilter cool. The conversation, which I've been eavesdropping on for the past twelve minutes, ping-pongs from a postmortem of last weekend's party to what summer concerts they're most excited for to whether the perpetual two-hour wait for some pizza place on Leonard is deserved.

This was a dumb idea. I should leave. For that matter, I should never have—

"Sorry I'm late!"

Amalia Suarez strides down the sidewalk looking even prettier than I recalled, her smile wide and her hair gloriously unruly. The patchwork sweater she's wearing would pair nicely with Joseph's Technicolor dreamcoat. When she reaches me, she gives me a quick one-armed hug like we're meeting up for our weekly lunch engagement; she's carrying her folded e-scooter in her other hand. "My boss's classic move," she says. "Schedule a meeting at six to go over something I sent him weeks ago."

She's so at ease that I find myself saying, in the role it feels like I'm supposed to be, "I hope it was to tell you that he had never seen a finer piece of work."

"I wish. We have different points of view on this issue, so we keep trying to convince each other. And, so far, both failing." As we move toward the entrance of the Bunker, she says, "But I am going to stop talking about work. How are you? This weather is amazing, no?"

"To be honest," I say, "I can't wait for all the flowers to die. My allergies are destroying me."

Inside, the ceiling feels even lower than the exterior would have indicated, although I do like the exposed brick walls. The theater's lobby consists of a guy standing at a folding table. Amalia shows him our tickets on her phone, he hands us xeroxed single-sheet programs, and we duck through a curtain into the seating area. Six rows of chairs arranged on a set of plywood steps, spaced to create an aisle in the middle. Around a third of the seats are occupied.

Amalia, to my mild consternation, goes for the front-and-center seats right on the line of duct tape on the floor that marks off the stage. As I sit down next to her, I say, "There's no chance of audience participation, is there?"

"Only the part in Act Two where they pull people onstage to talk about their matching experience." She laughs. "Your face!"

"If that actually happens, I'm volunteering you and leaving."

"I'm kidding. Although you don't think that would be interesting?" She glances over her shoulder and then leans toward me, angling her head so that her words form as the gentlest of breaths against my ear: "I'd love to hear what some of the people here have to say. Especially the couples."

I almost shift away—not because the closeness isn't welcome, but because it is, a prolonged fluttering beneath my skin, as delightful as it's unnerving. Let's face it. That's why I'm here, trapped in what feels like the kind of shelter you'd build for a real-life zombie apocalypse, braced to watch an experimental theater troupe have at Jane Austen's masterpiece. For the third chance to be in Amalia Suarez's company, and to try to glean—in a situation where I'm neither hired to spy on her nor ambushed by her unanticipated appearance—what she really wants from me.

Instead I ask, "What would *you* say?"

She draws back to look at me as if I've gone off script—and she likes it. She says, smiling, "I don't really believe in it."

"In matching? But you—"

"Welcome to the Bunker! A couple of quick reminders . . ." It's the guy from the lobby, now standing at the front of the stage, close enough for me to nudge him with my foot. Could he be the only person who works here? I sit back in my seat and listen to him preemptively shame us about cell phone usage. I've got to be more careful; I can't believe I almost let on that I know Amalia is online—or was, anyway, until she met Mason.

And speaking of Mason. What did Amalia tell him about tonight?

As the lights dim, I feel her lean in again. Her shoulder presses against mine; I whiff the scent of her hair, a floral freshness. "To be continued," she murmurs.

The upside about going into something with zero expectations is that they can be exceeded. My acquaintance with New York theater is limited to a handful of school excursions to Broadway musicals; I don't count the time Charles brought me and Coraline to see *Death of a Salesman*, after his AP English teacher pronounced the play essential for understanding the American dream, because all three of us fell asleep. What *3M-M@* lacks in elaborate set designs and energetic, synchronized dances, it makes up for—at least for me—with some engrossing ideas. It's clear Amalia's friend, who wrote and directed the play and also stars as the titular matchmaker in a metallic full-body leotard and matching face paint, both appreciates her source work and wants to move beyond it. The novel's disjuncture between Emma Woodhouse's perspective and what the people around her really want is explained here as the algorithm's innate inability to logically process human irrationality. 3M-M@ goes about matching the singletons in Highbury Settlement on the basis of compatibility of values, interests, and life plans, only to receive feedback from George Knightley, the colony's agriculturalist, that people aren't happy. "That is inaccurate," says 3M-M@. "They are. This is what they want. Them not being able to see that doesn't make it less true."

I'm expecting the play to end the way the original does, with the algorithm chastised and the human characters free to form their own alliances. It's a genuine shock when the colonists vote to listen to 3M-M@ because, as Unitarian minister Filipe Aldoño puts it, "It knows better." Those who disagree, including Frank Chao and Jane Fairfax, are asked to leave. The lights fade on a silent scene of the remaining colonists gathering before the android, who begins to separate them out into pairs.

After curtain call, the actors come back out onstage to mingle with their friends, who turn out to compose just about the entire audience. Amalia and I have to wait, like third-tier nobles at a coronation, to congratulate her friend Sophia. When we're up, Amalia hugs her friend and declares that she was phenomenal. "This is Jiayi," she says, turning to me. "We met at a Somners of Gotham screening."

I was wondering how I'd be introduced. I say, "That was great. Especially the ending, how it subverts the resolution of the novel."

Sophia beams at me. She's still in face paint and costume, so the effect is slightly manic. "Thank you so much for coming!" Her smile sharpens as she adds, "Although . . . I don't know if I agree with you. Maybe the play just ended at an earlier point than the book did."

"What do you mean *maybe*?" says Amalia. "You wrote the thing."

"The work takes on a life of its own! Many lives. Each person who experiences it has their own interpretation."

I ask Sophia, "Does that mean you're working on a sequel?"

"Sort of," she says. "Thematically related. The premise of this one is that a computer programmer creates his perfect date."

"Oh," I say. "Is it based on that Greek myth?"

"Exactly."

"Which myth?" asks Amalia.

"Pygmalion and Galatea," says Sophia. "Guy carves a statue that he falls in love with, and then it comes to life. I always thought he sounded like a real creep. In my play, things don't turn out so well for him."

We relinquish Sophia to her next set of admirers and exit the theater. "Want to grab something to eat?" asks Amalia. "One of my top three Thai restaurants is right around here."

A mini-cacophony starts up in my head: a voice that sounds a little like Becks telling me not to even think about it, another that's all Max going on about how I won't say yes because I'm scared, a third asking don't I want to find out what Amalia meant when she said she didn't really believe in matching?

"No pressure. I know it's a weeknight."

I briefly wonder how disappointed she'll be if I decline, and then I'm saying, "I love Thai."

She smiles like she's won a prize. "It's a five-minute walk. Do you want to leave your bike or bring it along?"

"How do you know I rode here?"

It's a throwaway question, but for the first time this evening I sense that I've discomfited her. "You rode to the *Gentleman's Game* screening," she says finally. "I remember thinking, *If she's biking around in February, she's the type who bikes everywhere.*"

Something swoops in my stomach—that she noticed and thought about it, about me. "You were right," I say, which doesn't answer her question. "Um, let me unlock my bike."

By the time we reach Sawadee Thai, Amalia has loosened back into her former liveliness. I recognize the restaurant from her Instagram posts, a narrow, unfussy space with framed portraits of the Thai royal family and a curtain to separate the dining area from the kitchen, behind which I catch glimpses of a matriarch doing battle with a flaming wok. We sit down at the last available table, squeezed in between a pair of white women with hard-edged eastern European accents and an older Asian man whose forehead is popping with sweat as he consumes a gigantic bowl of soup noodles. I order pad thai, as I always do at a new Thai restaurant; Amalia orders a curry with three chili signs, leading me to view her with renewed respect.

We hand over the menus, and Amalia says, like no time at all has passed since we last spoke about this, "Why did you sound so surprised when I said I don't really believe in matching?"

"I guess I assumed that's how you met your boyfriend," I say.

That word, the meaning it contains, sits on the table like a box that neither of us want to open but know we should, just in case there's a time bomb inside. It's hard to tell with women sometimes, and so my default is to presume platonic intentions unless expressly told—or shown—otherwise, but this whole evening has felt sort of maybe just a tad like a date. Which is neither good nor bad. Just . . . how it feels.

"It was," says Amalia. She lowers her gaze: those eyelashes! When she looks up again, there's an impishness to her expression. "Maybe that's why."

I laugh before it occurs to me that maybe I shouldn't. "Does that mean . . . ?"

She shrugs. "We broke up."

"Sorry to hear that."

The insincerity of the statement leaks into my voice like paint fumes through a closed door. Amalia says, "I'm not. We had some fun, but . . ." She shrugs again. "It happened not long after I ran into you at the Whitney."

I think of her first email to me, sent the day after the Symposium concert. Had she stopped dating Mason Perry by then—and was that why she wrote to me?

"What about you?" she asks.

"What about me?"

"How did you meet your girlfriend?"

Why would Amalia think— Oh, right, because I said so. Of all the things to come back and bite me. "Same. We matched."

"So it's worked out for you then."

She's watching me through her lashes, and suddenly I want so badly to stop lying. "Not really," I say. "We're not together anymore."

Her voice is soft: "What happened?"

Gah: even in order to stop lying I first need to lie more. "Nothing really happened." What are the reasons that couples break up? "We just didn't want the same things."

Our food arrives right then, thankfully. "This looks amazing!" I say to my glistening tangle of noodles, glad I can be sincere this time.

For the rest of our meal I work like an overzealous barista at keeping the conversation frothy. We exchange restaurant recommendations and New York apartment horror stories. I find out again that she's originally from Mexico City and moved to Los Angeles when she was in high school. (I ask what she misses most about L.A. "Driving," she says.) I learn for the first time that she's also one of three siblings, the sister in between two brothers. She asks me about growing up in Jackson Heights, and I give her the Disney Channel version that everyone but my closest friends hears, in which our mother's threats involved making us memorize all 101 verses of the *San Zi Jing* instead of abandoning us. We discuss the distinctions between the detective novel and the spy novel, and agree that genre fiction is underrated.

It's only when the bill comes that I remember: "How much do I owe you for the ticket?"

Amalia waves my question away. "I invited you. It's on me."

"What?" I say. "Only if you let me get dinner."

She gives me one of those through-the-lashes looks, then smiles. "Deal."

When we step outside, the street is a velvety hush. I breathe in the chill of the air and feel bracingly alive. "Which way are you heading?" I ask.

She points. "I'm farther north in Greenpoint."

I say, like this is a fact I vaguely recall, "I thought you lived somewhere else in Brooklyn."

"I just moved. My lease was up and the landlord wanted to raise the rent by some insane amount. You?"

"Gowanus." I find myself pointing as well, in a random direction, since I don't actually know where we are.

"I guess this is good night, then."

"Um," I say, "well, thanks for the invite." Smooth, Claudia. I add, "I had a lovely time."

Amalia reaches out and touches my arm, like she did at the museum, except now her fingers slide down my skin, lighting sparks all along the way, and curl around my wrist. Something opens inside me, the desire that's been waiting all evening spilling out. She says, "Me too."

Her mouth is soft and warm and full, and she kisses like I might have expected, not that I've spent any time thinking about Amalia Suarez's kissing style. Confident, playful. Her tongue probes my lips: *Yes?*—*yes.* We're just about the same height, which I always like, hip bones and chests and shoulders lining up nicely. I step in closer and her breath quickens as she does the same. Ready for more, if I am.

When we finally lean away from each other, she's smiling at me, and I almost ask if she'd like to go back to her place, which, after all, is now conveniently close by. I'm not sure what stops me— I'm pretty sure she would, and boy, do I want to right now. But instead I say, "Do you want to do this again soon?"

"This?" she says, index finger ticking between her chest and mine. "Or"—she lifts her arm to encompass the restaurant behind me, the silent street, the sky above—"this?"

"Both?"

She laughs. "Yes."

While I unlock my bike, she unfolds her scooter like a magician restoring a familiar to its true form and squeezes out onto the road between two tightly parked cars. She turns to look back at me. "Next time, you decide the activity."

"It's not going to be as cultured, unless I come across a kefir-making class."

"I don't mind," she says, in a way that makes me seriously reconsider not just beelining to her apartment right now.

I wait for her taillight to blink around the corner before I take out my phone so I can check Google Maps and figure out where the hell I am. Well. Not such a dumb idea after all.

IV.

MY MEETINGS with Matthew Espersen shift indoors after the time we meet on the High Line and my sinuses self-destruct.

At first we try going to a coffee shop nearby in the Meatpacking District, one of those single-origin, custom-brew places. It's clogged with tourist overflow, and we end up at a table next to a voluble group of Italians who keeps encroaching on our space and then apologizing most charmingly. Matthew is supposed to be telling me about a presentation that the Chemistry Lab division gave to the larger Data Strategy group—the cover story about its work, how it's been assessing what types of data would be most relevant to improving Let's Meet's comp-score accuracy and comparing that with the data Let's Meet actually collects about its users—but he keeps stopping at the end of each sentence and staring off in the direction of the door. It reminds me of when I get caught in the rain while biking, and the whole time I'm out what keeps me going is the eventuality of returning home and changing out of my supremely squelchy underwear.

As we're leaving, I say, "That was really crowded. Do you want to meet somewhere else next time?"

He says, quietly, "All right."

We step out onto the sidewalk. Matthew stares over my shoulder, blinking as if in thought. I wait for him to suggest an alternative venue.

Instead he says, "Sometimes tight spaces can be a bit difficult for me."

There's a patina of embarrassment in his tone, and so I say, "I feel the same way. All those people." I don't, in fact—shrimp ponds masquerading as art shows aside, or Times Square on New Year's Eve. I'd prefer not to have to stand in line for twenty minutes to buy an overpriced cup of tea, but I've always enjoyed being surrounded by other people, watching them and imagining what their lives could be like, the private wealth of their thoughts and joys and preoccupations.

"It's not that." Matthew's voice is so low I can barely hear him. "When I was in that crash, I was trapped in the car until the ambulance came. It took a while, and being in there with . . . with everything smashed to hell, not able to get the seat belt off or open the door or even move . . . That was the worst part. Once I realized I was still alive. Having to sit there with what I had done."

Komla sabotaging my bike to scare me off investigating Sarah Reaves's death would top my list of memorable traffic injuries, but the most dramatic one occurred years ago, when I slammed into a car door that opened suddenly on me and ricocheted off my bike and across the asphalt. At least it was a classy dooring—it occurred in Soho, the car was a Peugeot, and the couple who emerged from it looked like minor Scandinavian royalty en route to an embassy ball. The woman was freaking out, which amused me, sort of, given how I was the one with the skin of both my forearms flayed off. That and some cage-fight-worthy bruising were the extent of my wounds, but for the next few weeks I would get random heart palpitations when I cycled past parked cars. To be in the kind of accident where death stops in front of you, considers, decides: *Not yet*. Did that have anything to do with Matthew moving to New York? You could spend a lifetime here and never have to drive.

"Were you badly injured?" I ask.

"Nothing permanent."

"How did it happen?"

"Skidded off the road. It was late. I was tired." He clears his throat and says, louder now, "Ironically, the biggest seat belt manufacturer in the Midwest was headquartered in our town. Haines Safety Systems. It was their hundredth anniversary that year."

"Well, it's not technically ironic, since the seat belt did save you." I intend to say that in a *look on the bright side (considering)!* way, but of course I sound like an insufferable literary pedant.

He looks at me, then away again. "Yes. It did."

"I just meant, it's a common misconception of what irony means. In Jane Austen's novels—" Stop talking, Claudia. "Sorry."

"It's fine."

We stand like that for a while, side by side, facing the street. A man in a suit whizzes by, the psychedelic Vroom logo gleaming down the stem of his e-scooter. I've been seeing a lot of those logos lately, blurring past me on the sidewalks and in the bike lanes, although maybe I just notice them now because of Amalia. From that thought of her, my mind hopscotches back to the evening we spent together: her voice in my ear as we sat next to each other in the theater, her fingers running down my arm. The way she said, *Next time*.

"You're very easy to talk to."

I glance over. Matthew's head is tipped slightly back: he's gazing at the segment of the High Line that's visible from where we are, steel beams and feathery grass suspended in the air between the buildings on both sides of the street.

"It's the petite, soft-spoken Asian female effect," I say. "Tricks people into thinking we're good listeners."

He continues to watch the people promenading back and forth above us. "I'll have to be more careful," he says. "Can't have you finding out all my secrets."

———————

It's Becks who suggests the Rubin Museum of Art as an alternative meeting spot with Matthew, a few blocks east of where he and I have been meeting on the High Line. "I did an observation there recently," she says. "The place was so calming it made me irritable."

So I use our corporate account to purchase an annual membership to the Rubin, which allows the member and one guest free entry, and Matthew and I discuss espionage techniques while we wander through dim-lit galleries educating ourselves on Tantric Buddhism. I tell him about how Chinese revolutionaries plotting the overthrow of the Yuan Dynasty smuggled messages in mooncakes. "It's too bad we don't have anyone to send secret messages to. Baking mooncakes is beyond me, but I could probably manage muffins."

"They could be used as a signal for a dead drop," says Matthew, "if we ever needed to perform one."

"I have the perfect spot," I say. "There's a community garden in Gowanus that hardly anyone ever visits, and it has a platform that's raised a couple of inches off the ground. You could hide something beneath it and no one would notice. I used to think about it in terms of a place to stash a murder weapon, but it would work for a handoff as well . . . provided we do it between May and October, because the garden is closed the rest of the year."

We now know what's in Miles Fontaine's tomb. Sort of. Matthew carried out the laptop upgrade and, while he was logged in as Miles, saw eight files on Miles's hidden drive. Unfortunately, we don't know what those files *are*. Matthew didn't recognize the file type—he told me they were all in some .alt format—and he was unable to open the files, which required a program that wasn't installed on the computer. He tried looking at the source code, but it wasn't a language he had seen before.

When I updated Becks and Squirrel, Squirrel assured us that if we could get him that code, he would be able to figure it out. "How?" said Becks. "You just admitted"—following targeted questioning by her—"you have no fucking idea what an .alt file is."

"Doesn't matter," he said. "I'm gifted."

"Also," I said, "we kind of have no other options."

I go back to Matthew to ask if he could make a copy of the source code and pass it to us. "We have people who'll be able to understand it," I say, having decided that I'll take Squirrel's claim at face value.

He nods. "Once I saw what it was, I knew I would need more time. I left out part of the upgrade. That way I'll have an excuse to get his computer back for a couple of hours."

"Nice!" I say.

"*Bearers of Gifts*. It's what Somnang does when he delivers the fax machine to the British embassy in Kuala Lumpur." He adds, "Although I dislike being perceived as incompetent."

"It leads people to underestimate you."

"I dislike that as well."

The plan I propose, having just read two John le Carré novels back-to-back that utilize a version of this technique, several generations of technology ago, is that we give Matthew a burner phone to take pictures of the source code, which he can then pass back to us.

He shakes his head. "I'll get my own burner."

"You still don't trust us?"

I'm surprised by how disappointed I sound. I guess I've gotten used to thinking of Matthew as being on our team, part of this make-it-up-as-we-go mission to find out what the matchmakers want to do with the synths and prevent anything too dastardly. Plus—turns out I like the guy. He takes seriously the idea that there's another world shifting beneath the one we all see, and that it might be possible to change it.

He turns his gaze to the beatific gleam of the Buddha figurine that we are standing in front of. "It's not that I don't . . . But there's so much you haven't told me. Like what you're doing about the other matchmaker that's also developing synths." He glances at me. "That's Soulmate, isn't it? It has to be—they're the most powerful of the Big Three. And is it just them? If Soulmate is doing this, Partnered Up won't be far behind. Let's Meet's twins are only a small piece of what we have to deal with."

Can't really argue there. Trying to stop the synths, one matchmaker scheme at a time, is an asymmetrical war that *isn't* in our favor—eventually, we'll need to come up with an overarching plan. But for now, learning what we can about Let's Meet's digital-twin project is important. Not only because Let's Meet is building a different type of synth from what we've seen before, but also because the possibility remains that someone there killed Pradeep Mehta when he revealed that he knew about his duplicate profile.

Matthew continues: "Or maybe the problem . . . it's even bigger than the synths. Maybe it's the very nature of the matchmakers. They're trying to quantify what's unquantifiable and destroying it as a result."

"Do you really think so?" I ask, taken aback—that's kind of an extreme position to take, even for a matching skeptic. Especially when: "Don't you use them?"

He says, like I've pointed out a weakness, "That doesn't mean I want to."

I hear a shuffle of footsteps behind us and glance around. Two older women enter the gallery. They stop in front of a painting a few feet away, a large, intricate geometry of a mandala. They're standing close to each other, but with a reserve that makes me think they might be on an early date. I wonder if they matched, and if so on what platform. What would it be like, at that age, to begin to open yourself up to a stranger? It makes me think about how my mother has never dated, since my father left—at least, not that I know of.

"Anyway, it makes sense for me to get the burner. It saves us one additional step."

I turn back to Matthew. Squirrel isn't going to like this; he's finicky about the tech he uses.

"It goes both ways," he says. "Do you trust me?"

V.

"ABSOLUTELY NOT," says Becks.

"Come on," I say. "Without him, we would have no idea what Let's Meet is doing."

"With him, everything we know is what he's told us. The Chemistry Lab. These packages. The files that are of some type that no one has ever heard of before. The idea of the digital twins."

"Rodrigo Santos was the one who first brought up the twins."

"And who pointed us to Rodrigo Santos?"

I laugh. "Even if Matthew had enlisted Rodrigo in a campaign to deceive us, I think he was too scared of you to have lied about anything."

Becks regards me, something unfathomable in her expression.

"I meant that in a positive way," I say. "Being scary is an asset. In interrogations and stuff like that."

She sniffs. "That session with Rodrigo was a goddamn sharing circle."

"What about the list of profile handles? Matthew delivered on that."

"He could have randomly pulled them off Let's Meet's platform."

I take a step back from her desk. "Do you seriously think he's been making all of this up?"

"No. A man like that doesn't have the creativity."

"Then why don't you trust him?"

She flicks her hair back. "This is because you recruited him."

"It truly isn't," I say. "He's given us no reason to doubt him."

Again she looks at me in that odd, appraising way. This time I say, "What?"

"Nothing," she says, followed immediately by: "You've been in a . . . perky mood lately."

"Have I?"

"You aren't even annoyed about my insinuation that you can't be objective when it comes to Matthew."

"Doesn't seem worth getting annoyed about."

"You certainly did the last time I made that point."

"Endorphins? I've been playing really well at Ultimate." Which is true, if not really responsible for the buoyancy I've been feeling since that date-in-all-but-name with Amalia, especially whenever I think about seeing her again. Maybe this dating thing has its merits after all.

"You're not plotting something, are you?" says Becks. "Some ill-conceived side mission against the synths that will blow up in all our faces."

I smile at her. "Are you sure you want to be inspiring me?"

She glares back. Then she says, "What do you know about Matthew's car accident?"

No idea where this conversational switchback is headed, but I'm glad to move on from the reasons for my current state of mind—even aside from the ex-target complications, the thought of Becks finding out about Amalia makes me uneasy. "I've told you everything he told me," I say. "He was driving late at night and skidded off the road. No lasting injuries, but it sounds like the car was all smashed up, and now he doesn't really like being in confined spaces."

"Was he alone?"

What kind of question is that? "Yes." Except—did Matthew ever actually say that to me? "I think so," I amend. "He's never mentioned anyone else being in the car with him."

"There was," says Becks. "The boy who was driving."

She sits back in her chair and watches with obvious enjoyment as I try to hinge my lower jaw back into place. "Matthew wasn't driving?" I say. "But then— Wait. How do you know this?"

"The *Mansfield Herald*. Local newspaper of Mansfield, Nebraska."

"I still don't . . . ." Then I realize: a parenthesis in the email I wrote to her summarizing Matthew's accident. "Haines Safety Systems."

Becks nods.

"You found out where Haines was headquartered, so you knew where the accident had taken place. And you knew when, because it was the year of the company's hundredth anniversary."

"I realize it's a murder mystery trope, but it's really not necessary to explain my deduction process back to me."

"Sorry," I say. "I'm just impressed." And a tad put-out: Why didn't I come up with that? Because it never occurred to me to cross-check Matthew's story. "What did the paper say?"

"Two high school seniors were involved in a car accident. The driver was someone called Drew Wilkins. Matthew was in the passenger seat. Otherwise, what happened sounds consistent with what Matthew told you. It was late at night, the car went off the road, the emergency responders had to cut them out of the wreck. Matthew just erased Drew from the narrative."

"What happened to him?" I ask, although I suspect I already know.

"Broke his neck."

I think of what Matthew said about irony, and me, oh god, correcting him. "That could be why. It was too hard for Matthew to talk about him."

Becks moves aside the copy of *The Waves* that's sitting on her desk and picks up the sheaf of papers underneath. She holds them out to me. "Here are the articles. Two on the accident itself, an obituary of Drew Wilkins, a separate story about his nascent-to-the-point-of-nonexistent baseball career, two *how is the community coping with this tragedy?* pieces filled with the most banal of quotes. Obviously, nothing newsworthy going on in Mansfield. Just as well, because the writing is embarrassingly bad."

The top sheet is a black-and-white printout of a page from a physical newspaper, a portion of it. The headline reads "Local Teens in Fatal Car Crash." The photograph below looks almost abstract, the wreckage a blurry blackness defined by the negative space of ground and sky around it, merging into whatever it was that it hit. I flip through the next few sheets. They're all similar, and evoke a memory of the first time I tried to feed a reel of microfilm into one of the readers in the Margrave library and jammed up the machine. "This is from microfilm." Which makes sense—Matthew is thirty-seven, so the accident must have been around two decades ago. The online archives of a small town's newspaper wouldn't have gone that far back. "You got this from the New York Public Library?"

Becks pauses in a way that, if it were anyone else, I would classify as hesitation. "The library in Mansfield."

I look down at the papers in my hand. "You went to *Nebraska* for this? When?"

"Of course not." Again that pause, a beat longer this time. "I called in a favor."

"From someone in Nebraska?" That feels almost more implausible—how many people are there even in Nebraska?

"Within reasonable driving distance. Relatively speaking."

"Who?"

"Doesn't matter. They got us the information."

I almost let it go, because I'm curious to start reading these articles, but Becks's use of *us* holds me back, like the gentle press of a hand on top of mine. "It does matter. This is verifier work, which means we're in it together."

The clean lines of her eyebrows slant downward. "Fine," she says. "It was my brother."

This is so unexpected that all I can say is "You have a brother?"

"Not so uncommon."

Her tone makes it sound like she would prefer if it were. I remember the odd exchange we had on the first day of Lunar New Year, when she came into the office and seemed disgruntled to see me there, said that thing about her family being a pain in the ass, and walked right out again. The explanation seems clear now, like I've wiped the condensation off a windowpane: she had arranged for someone to meet her there because she thought I was out that day, and so when I showed up, she had to change her plans. And— I'm suddenly sure of it—that person was someone from her family.

"What did you tell him about why you wanted to find out about this?" I ask.

"Nothing. It's none of his business. I knew he would do it because he hates the fact that he owes me." She stops. "If there's nothing further to discuss, we both need to prep for the one p.m. intake."

I get all the way to the door and then turn around. *"Relatively speaking?"*

She doesn't look up from her screen, but I catch her mouth twitch right before she says, "For the fucking love of god."

VI.

THE WINDOWS OF Great Wall Books are covered with ads for
health supplements, tours to China, and a dance performance
involving the large-scale twirling of silk ribbons. Lanterns hang
from the store's marquee, large red globes with gold tassels—
based on how battered they are, they may have been part of the
opening day decor.

Inside, cardboard boxes and wooden bookcases form a maze of
narrow aisles, within which a few customers are wandering, a mix
of elderly men and mothers with young, squeaky children. I'm
momentarily mesmerized by a poster pasted to the side of a book-
case (CHART OF THE FOOT REFLECTIVE ZONES HEALTH THERAPY)
that illustrates, in colorful, psychedelic glory, what organs of the
body the different regions of the feet correspond to. Then I sight
my mother, sitting behind the checkout counter to the left of the
entrance.

I go over. She continues writing on her legal pad, a steady, absorbed scratching back and forth across the page. Books are scattered around her, some open, others closed. While I wait for her to notice me, I take in the Chinese landscape painting on the wall above her head, its stylized mountains and smudges of mist, and the cyclopean eye of the security camera nestled in the corner formed by the wall and the ceiling above the door. This place is like a one-stop shop of Chinese cultural stereotypes.

Finally I give up. "Hi, Mom."

The nib of her pen indents into the paper. She raises her head, slowly, as if she's pulling against a weight that wants to keep her submerged. I smile and wave.

"Claudia." She says that like it's a spell to make me disappear. When I don't, she continues: "How do you know I am here?"

"I went by your apartment first. When you weren't there, I figured I'd try the bookstore." At least, that's what I would have done if I didn't have Finders Keepers to make the process more efficient.

"You didn't tell me you are coming."

"I thought I'd surprise you?"

The truth, of which we are both aware, is that if I had let her know I wanted to visit, she would have arranged to be occupied throughout the weekend. My mother holds on to a grudge like a winning lottery ticket, something to safeguard until it can be exchanged for a payout. I would have waited even longer to present my unfilial presence to her—and possibly just left it for the next nonoptional Lin family event—but that exchange with Becks about her brother stayed with me. I guess it felt like both a cautionary tale and a reminder that I have no excuse not to try harder when my mother lives across a polluted river and not half the country. (More's the pity.)

"This is not a good time. I am working."

"I won't stay long," I say, in lieu of noting that I was getting a distinct *Waiting for Godot* vibe while standing here. "I just wanted to say hi and give you this."

My mother is a staunch believer in the ascendancy of Chinese gastronomy, along with all other aspects of Chinese civilization, but she does acknowledge that when it comes to pastries, the French can do some pretty special things with flour and butter. I introduced her to almond croissants a few years back, which has benefited us both. She's discovered a new favorite food, and I have an easy means of bribing myself back into her favor.

She takes the paper bag I placed on the counter and opens it. "So unhealthy," she says, peering inside.

"You can share them with your mah-jongg group."

"What? No. They're so small."

She triple-folds the top of the bag and stashes it behind the counter. "Have you eaten? The *zha jiang mian* at the noodle shop nearby is not bad."

"I'm good, thanks."

"Only the *zha jiang mian*. Don't get anything else there."

I indicate the pad in front of her. "What are you writing?"

She glances down at it like she's never seen it before. "A letter."

"To who?"

"You don't know them."

I've always wondered if my mother keeps in touch with anyone from Taiwan. Her parents passed away while I was in middle school, first my grandmother and then my grandfather a few years later. I remember Coraline's tidal sobbing when she heard about our grandmother, and our mother grabbing her shoulders and shaking her, shouting at her in Mandarin. Our mother flew to Taiwan for the first funeral, and the whole two weeks she was away we were terrified she wouldn't return. That was her last visit to Taiwan. She has two older brothers, and enough aunts, uncles, and cousins to establish a martial arts sect; she has never talked about any of them, but Coraline told me. (There was also a younger sister who died of some illness very early on—again, from Coraline.) And she must have had friends—from childhood, school, work.

She came here when she was twenty-six. I'm turning twenty-six in July. The idea of putting away my entire life up until this point and never touching it again seems impossible. I mean, who would I even be?

"Did you lose your job?"

I blink at my mother. "No," I say. "Why would you think that?"

"I heard that the economy is doing badly. Companies letting go of workers. The ones at the bottom always get fired first."

If that's the case—and I must confess my brain shuts off whenever I'm listening to NPR and they start on a story that references financial statistics—it doesn't seem to have dampened people's willingness to pay for nonessential services like running checks on their online dates.

"Also," says my mother, "you used to complain about your job all the time, and now you never talk about it."

I've thought before that my mother would make a decent verifier: she's observant, suspicious as hell, and very into finding out about other people's relationships. "I guess I've made my peace with it." I pick up one of the books lying on the counter. The title is inscribed in a sweeping font, next to a graphic of a mask and a dagger. "Is this a new Inspector Yuan mystery?"

"Different series, but with some of the same people. What do you call that?"

"A spin-off?"

"That sounds wrong. The detective in this one is Bai Junjie, the spy in *Yuan lei zhi . . .*"

That's about all I understand of the title my mother is referring to, but I do recognize the name. Spymaster Bai: the head of the Wanli emperor's spy service, part of the Ming Dynasty Chronicles' recurring cast, and possibly best described as Inspector Yuan's frenemy. The two of them are constantly sniping at each other when they meet at court; he's shameless about claiming credit for the results of the inspector's sleuthing. At the same time, he has provided Inspector Yuan with invaluable intel on a number of occasions, and in *Inspector Yuan and the Forgotten Bride*, he actually goes to Inspector Yuan for help when a secret that he has kept hidden for half his life is in danger of being revealed. I find him to be a fascinating character, in part because he defies the moral clarity of the Inspector Yuan universe.

"What do you think of it?" I ask. "No spoilers, please."

"Lousy," my mother pronounces, and goes on to tell me why in a manner that completely disregards my request. Operation Distraction successful.

It's only on my ride back to Gowanus, as I'm pedaling south along the Williamsburg waterfront, right after the tin-ceilinged bars and doggie bakeries cede to blocks of old-world apartment buildings and parked school buses with Hebrew lettering along their sides, that I realize: she was the one who distracted me.

VII.

THE BOOK THAT Matthew Espersen hands me is an old, yellowed copy of *Stamboul Train*, and although I'm aware of what it contains, I'm still momentarily surprised by its weight.

"I'm looking forward to reading this," I say. In fact I gave up on it years ago; Graham Greene's extremely unenlightened portrayal of the lesbian character infuriated me too much.

"There's something else," says Matthew. "I found a new program on Miles's computer. It was installed three days after his upgrade."

My residual annoyance at *Stamboul Train* subsides. "For the .alt files!"

"Yes. This time I was able to open the files."

"And?"

"They look like dashboards. Unclear what they were measuring, or recording."

"Did they look anything like the dashboard in the Triple-Helix app?"

A vertical line folds itself into place between his eyebrows. "I'm not familiar with Triple-Helix. What is that?"

"It's a fitness smartwatch. Rodrigo Santos told us about it. It can build a digital twin of its user for purposes of coming up with the ideal workout program. You access the twin through a dashboard where you can edit what user data is being fed to the twin and run simulations. Maybe the .alt files are similar dashboards for Let's Meet's twins."

"Maybe." He gestures at the book in my hand. "You can see for yourself."

There's a shortness to his manner; I hope I wasn't coming across as mansplainy. "And what about the program itself?" I ask. "Did you learn anything there?"

"It's an application for creating these dashboards," he says, "customized for Let's Meet—it pulls data directly from their systems. I included some pictures of the interface."

In turn, I update Matthew on our review of the profile handles he gave me. Squirrel didn't find duplicate profiles for any of those handles, indicating that the handles do belong to actual subscribers who are being used as sources for the digital twins—which resurfaces the question of why the Chemistry Lab would select these individuals. "You'd think they would go for the users on their platform who make available the most information, so they have more to work with."

Matthew says, "Then there has to be some other channel of information they've set up for those users beyond what you see."

I wonder if he's thinking of Pradeep, because I sure am. Pradeep Mehta was example numero uno of a subscriber who hid important parts of who he was from everyone—including, I'm guessing, himself. He barricaded his romantic desires and relationships away from what Matthew referred to, with enough acidity to spawn a colony of peptic ulcers, as Pradeep's *real life*; he would have been very careful about what he shared with Let's Meet or with people he met on the platform. So how did Let's Meet obtain enough data about Pradeep to build Silent G? The matchmaker must be leveraging in some way on MaDD's data collection techniques, as we discussed at Squirrel's place after our *McMurdo* session. It's too coincidental otherwise: the hiring of Ed Cannon, Rodrigo Santos's references to video games being used as a framework for the twins—

—and Pradeep being a player of Maverick's games.

"Could it be the zombies themselves?" I say.

To his credit, Matthew actually seems to be making an effort to understand my question before giving up and saying, "What are you talking about?"

"Do you know if Pradeep played *World's End: McMurdo*? Or any of the other *World's End* games? They're a series of zombie apocalypse shooter games by MaDD, Maverick's in-house game studio."

"He did," says Matthew. "How is that related?"

I tell him about playing *McMurdo* and our theory on the purpose of the receptive zombies. "We thought Let's Meet was trying to apply what MaDD is doing in the matching context. But that's probably too advanced for Let's Meet at this stage. From what Rodrigo Santos said, the Chemistry Lab is still developing its digital-twin technology. For that, data from a limited number of subscribers is sufficient. Maybe the data that the Chemistry Lab is using to build this initial set of twins *is* MaDD's player data."

"That Ed Cannon took with him when he left Maverick."

"Yes."

"It's a better explanation for why Let's Meet hired him than anything else I've heard," says Matthew. "It wasn't for expertise he didn't have. It was for what he could steal."

"If we're right, then that's what the subscribers on your list have in common. They're *World's End* players." I look down at the book in my hand. "And, hopefully, the .alt files are their twins."

"If they are, what then?"

"We'll have to be able to prove it. Depending on what these dashboards look like, maybe we can match them to specific subscribers. That would show how Let's Meet is using subscriber data to create fake profiles."

"That's not enough. Fake profiles are everywhere. What matters is what these twins can do and what they can be used for. If Let's Meet is successful, nothing that we think or feel will truly be ours again."

Who let whom in on this synth conspiracy in the first place? "I know," I say. "But proving that will take more than screenshots. That's why our tech experts are looking at the source code."

"Say we have the proof. A digital twin linked to a human person, able to predict how that person would act. What would you do with it?"

"Well, at that time, we would . . . decide. On next steps."

"The first time we spoke, you said you would stop the synths."

"That does sound like the kind of reckless, declarative thing I would say," I agree.

"I would like," says Matthew, "to be a part of that."

There's a formality in the way he speaks, as if he's presenting himself at the entrance of a private club. "You are." I hold up *Stamboul Train*. "We learned about the digital twins because of you."

"I don't mean as an information source. I mean, to be part of your movement."

What is Matthew Espersen saying—he wants to become a verifier? "I wouldn't really call us a *movement*," I say. "More like . . . a group of engaged citizens?"

"What are you planning? I can help."

"We're considering a few options," I say, all of which so far feature only in my mind.

When I don't say anything further, he says, "You don't trust me after all?"

The *Mansfield Herald* presented a straightforward story: a traffic accident, the loss of a small town's high school baseball star. Which was why it took me a while to notice the patches of fog in the facts of what happened, like the strategic dousing of torches in *Inspector Yuan and the Jade Dragon* that allowed for the rebellious prince to be assassinated the night he was carried into the Forbidden City in his palanquin.

One of the articles had interviewed a bunch of teachers and students from Mansfield Central High. They spoke almost exclusively about Drew, who sounded like the golden retriever of the high school dog run: sweet, friendly, effortlessly athletic, universally liked. Matthew got one mention, sort of: "According to Jeanne Schmitt, the school's guidance counselor, both boys were headed to Florida State University in the fall, Drew on a full baseball scholarship. 'Matt was a good kid,' Schmitt said. 'He cared about other people. Like Drew.'"

Otherwise, Matthew Espersen might not have existed in the universe of Mansfield Central High, or Drew Wilkins, at all. It seemed equally striking that none of the interviewees described them as friends and, at the same time, that no one speculated on why they had been in the car together in the first place. Perhaps the reporter hadn't thought it appropriate to ask. But her writing on the crash itself hadn't raised that point, either—I'd checked the bylines, and everything in the packet Becks handed me had been written by the same person, a Jemma Milkbank. Nor had she addressed other pertinent questions, such as where the boys had been coming from at four a.m., or what they might have been doing prior, or even what might have caused the crash, speeding or intoxication or fatigue or anything else. The only quote from the county sheriff throughout all of this: *This is a truly devastating tragedy.* From Jemma Milkbank's coverage of the funeral service, it appeared that the pastor omitted all reference to the accident itself, instead speaking of Drew *leaving us* like the kid had been the one worthy soul snatched away in the Rapture while everyone else had to stay behind. The overall effect felt like Shirley Jackson crossed with *Murder on the Orient Express*: creepy town collectively decides to impose alternate narrative on problematic events.

I should ask Matthew right now why he led me to believe that he had been alone in his accident—because he did, even if I couldn't bring myself to say so to Becks. Except then he would know that we verified him, and we all know *trust, but verify* is an oxymoron.

"It's not that," I say. "It's . . . the way we operate."

"I could get you Fontaine's .alt files. Actual copies."

"What? How? Wait— Are you a superhacker after all?"

He says, firmly, "No. But Miles Fontaine likes to save his work locally, on his hard drive. And I still have his old laptop."

"Amazing," I say. "Thank goodness for poor cybersecurity habits."

"Unfortunately it doesn't include Pygmalion. He must have deleted it before he handed in the device."

"Pygmalion?" I ask. Has Matthew unilaterally decided to start employing new code words? I wouldn't put it past him, although in this context I have no idea what George Bernard Shaw's play is meant to refer to.

"That's what the program for the .alt files is called."

Now I remember, from talking to Amalia's friend Sophia. The original myth, the sculptor whose creation came to life. I say, "We'll find another way to open the files."

"I'll do it if you let me in."

I look at Matthew, his all-weather pallor. I have a hard time picturing him either in Tallahassee or at one of the biggest party schools in the nation. "Why?" I say. "Why do you want to join us?"

He answers like the question is a test to determine if he will be permitted to step through the doors or if they will swing shut in his face. "There are two reasons that people use matchmakers. Some of them think there's a way to guarantee happiness. With enough information, you can find the correct answer. I never thought that. But what I do think, and I'm sure I'm not the only one, is that I don't really have a choice. If everyone else is online, then I have to be as well. As long as the matchmakers continue operating like they are now, that won't change."

Spread out across the wall behind him, tiny yogic adepts twist themselves into poses that make my joints ache in sympathy. We're in a room showcasing full-scale photographic reproductions of murals from a temple in Lhasa—a superior view, according to the exhibition description at the entrance, than would actually be possible if visiting the temple.

I say, "What do you mean, *operating like they are now?*"

"I want to help with the larger cause," he says. "Putting an end to all of it."

And that's when I realize who Matthew believes we really are.

VIII.

SINCE HIS DECLARATION of universal source code mastery, Squirrel has been turning Komla's office into a computational ecosystem. CPU towers with innards exposed, mega-size monitor screens, laptops of varying sizes, mysterious miscellaneous components, wires and tubes of different colors and thicknesses writhing in all directions. Whatever he's up to, he must be doing it overnight. I still don't see him while I'm here, and no equipment seems to get delivered to the office, but each time I peek inside what I've started calling the Nest, it's in greater disarray than the last.

Then, one morning, Komla's door opens and Squirrel bounds out in a manner more reminiscent of his namesake than I've witnessed before. "I've solved it," he announces, over what sounds like a dedicated Bitcoin-mining enterprise whirring out of the doorway at us.

I'm shuffling back from the pantry with my mug of tea—as

usual, overambitious in filling it up—and I almost slosh it all over myself. "Have you been here all night?"

He ignores me and goes to bongo-drum on Becks's door until she flings it open and tells him to lean out a window so she can shove him.

"Later," he says. "First we have to appreciate my genius."

When we enter the Nest, I decide that the answer to my question is most likely yes, based on the energy bar wrappers crinkled across the floor and the coat in the corner that's been folded into what looks like a makeshift pillow. Also the Gatorade bottle on the window ledge filled with a liquid of a turmeric-yellow hue unlike any Gatorade flavor I've ever encountered.

Squirrel directs us to the four screens that he has set up on the desk, angled to form half of an octagon. The two on the left are dense with programming code. The two on the right each feature an image of an .alt file dashboard, part of the set of photographs on Matthew's burner phone. Becks, Squirrel, and I looked through those images when I first got the phone from Matthew. Matthew had taken pictures of eight different dashboards, each labeled with a person's name and containing the same categories of data. There was a list titled *Data Inflows*, which we guessed referred to the information that was being fed to the twin; a list titled *Data Outflows*, which we guessed referred to simulations that had been run using the twin; and a number of other lists with titles—*Experience Level* or *Reliability Potential*, for example—which we had no decent guesses for. All of this, of course, assuming that the dashboards were in fact digital twins of Let's Meet subscribers.

"They're using Reflect," says Squirrel.

Becks says, "How much did you take?" She looks down at the surface of the desk, which is textured with crumbs. "You didn't do it *here*, did you?"

"Just enough to open up my mind."

Belatedly I realize what Becks and Squirrel are talking about—

and, also, that whatever drug he's on could account for this unchar-
acteristic peppiness.

"Doesn't seem to have changed anything. You're still talking
gibberish."

I say, "Reflecting what?"

"What?" says Squirrel.

"You said, the code . . ."

"Reflect. Yes. Close enough to Cinderella and J-square for me
to pick it up in twenty-four hours."

Becks says, "Does any of this mean you can confirm that these
dashboards are proof that Let's Meet is developing digital twins?"

Squirrel says, "Is that what we're doing?"

"That's the first step," I say. "Understanding how Let's Meet is
coming up with these synths and what it wants to use them for."

"If Let's Meet is using Reflect to write the .alt files, then yeah,
it's probably digital twins. It's a great language for that. A lot of
flexibility for specifying inputs and outputs. Allows for validation. Sure. Digital twins."

"Probably," says Becks, "as in *look at me pulling this out of my ass*,
is not confirmation."

"How do you expect me to confirm anything when I'm working with fucking screenshots? I'm a genius, not a miracle worker."

I say, "So if you could look at the actual .alt files . . . ?"

Becks turns to me. "Matthew Espersen can get us the files?
Then why the hell are we messing around with these pictures?"

It's been three days since Matthew passed me the burner phone
and said he wanted to be a part of whatever we were planning, and
I'm still going back and forth on whether my theory is inspired or
insane. Time to find out what someone else thinks.

I explain what Matthew told me about Miles Fontaine's hard
drive. "He says he'll give it to us," I say, "if we . . . let him in."

"Let him in *where*?" says Becks.

I wave at the room around us. "Here."

She says, like Matthew is volunteering for latrine duty, "He wants to be a verifier?"

"Sort of. I think he thinks we're someone else."

"Who?"

"Um, the Romantick?"

Her expression would seem to indicate: *insane*. "You think Matthew Espersen thinks we're a bunch of nutjobs flapping our hands about how the evil compatibility algorithms will destroy humanity."

I used to share Becks's uncharitable view of the Romantick. From its mission statement to the campaigns it tries to organize— lobbying for matchmakers to be banned, staging protests outside the Big Three's corporate locations—to the mini screeds that its members enjoy posting, the group seems duct-taped together by historical failure to find love through matching and a readiness to attribute all of America's problems to the prevalence of the matchmakers. When I was looking into Sarah Reaves's death, though, I saw that her files included entries from the Romantick blog—and once I set aside the hyperbole and dubious grammar, what it was actually accusing the matchmakers of wasn't all that outlandish. "The Romantick flagged the issue of synth profiles," I say.

"And the issue of matching technology being introduced by extraterrestrials as an interplanetary guerrilla tactic."

Some accusations, anyway. "The very first time Matthew and I met," I say, "he asked if I was a romantic. I thought he meant, you know, philosophically. It didn't even occur to me that he might be familiar with the Romantick. But . . . he's said a number of things along the way, which make sense if he thought he was talking to someone from that group. Like what he said to you about us being in a war. And he said once that maybe the problem wasn't the synths but the matchmakers themselves. At our last meeting, he referred to us as a movement. He said he wanted to help with the larger cause. It all fits with how the Romantick portrays itself."

"This dude needs a hobby," says Squirrel.

"I can't stand movements," says Becks. "They're so fucking self-righteous."

"In Matthew's defense," I say, "he probably thinks we're something we're not because we set out to make him think that. I've been telling him all kinds of untrue things about what Veracity can do. And I'm not saying this just because I recruited him."

Becks says, "When are you meeting him to get that hard drive?"

"Next week. He said he would need a few days to get a replacement hard drive and swap it for Miles's drive."

"So what are you going to tell him then?"

"He's helping us," I say, "because he believes we belong to the Romantick. And we need that help."

She watches me.

"I'm not going to lie. I'm just not going to clarify. For the moment."

There's another reason I don't want to tell Matthew he's mistaken—not yet—but I don't mention it because she'll scoff. Somewhere, somehow, Matthew became convinced that the Romantick was an organization worth committing corporate espionage for, and I want to find out why.

"That won't be enough," says Becks. "He said he wants you to let him in. You'll have to give him something more."

"Tell him we're going to take over the synths."

Becks and I turn to Squirrel like uncoordinated partners in a dance: me all at once, her like she's pushing through water.

I ask, "Can we do that?" If so—we could program them to announce to the world what they really are. Let's Meet would go down like an exploding blimp; the other matchmakers would be frightened away from continuing their own efforts. Plus, the irony of the matchmakers being betrayed by their own creations is appealing. Very O. Henry.

Becks says, "We can't do that."

"Someone's controlling the synths. Might as well be us."

"That is a singularly useless statement."

"Let me dumb it down for you," says Squirrel. "Who's controlling the synths right now?"

"Are you fucking serious?"

I say, quickly, "Let's Meet." I can tell from his expression that's not the answer he's looking for. "The Chemistry Lab? Ed Cannon?" Still no. "Is this a trick question?"

He sighs. "Even easier. Who controls the *twins*? Ultimately."

"Who . . . Oh," I say. "Do you mean . . . the subscribers who the twins are based on?"

He points a finger at me. "Ding! The beauty of the twin approach, for the matchmaker, is that it already has the data it needs to create the synth. Everything is transmitted over from the subscriber."

Becks says, "If Claudia's right about Cannon using MaDD's game data to build the twins, Let's Meet clearly doesn't have what it needs. It's stealing information from zombies."

"I mean more broadly. The zombie data is a data flow from the human source to the twin. So is the data from the source's online profiles. Their activity. Everything about the source that can be measured can be turned into a data flow to the twin. That Triple-Helix watch or wristband or whatever it is that we looked at. If Let's Meet can find a way to steal the data that thing collects as well, and integrate it into the model, then we're talking a whole different level of predictiveness."

Squirrel sounds elated by the prospect, rather than dismayed. I ask, "And how does all of this help us control the twins?"

"The twin is connected to its source via those data flows, right? That's how it's programmed. It behaves according to whatever inputs it's receiving from the subscriber. Which means the person who controls those inputs also controls the twin. Let's Meet can turn its system into the Iron Fortress; it'll still need to get data on the subscriber in order for the twin to continue functioning. And your average consumer wanders around the Internet holding up a sign that spells out where they live, what times they're out of the house, and where they hide their spare key."

"So what you're proposing," says Becks, "is that we quote *take over the synths* unquote by sabotaging one poor schmuck's dating profile at a time. When will we be done, you think, a hundred years later?"

"That's the amateur solution. What *I* would do is target the connections rather than the input. Cut them off, so the twin becomes static. Or—wait for this—connect all the twins to the same set of data. Can you imagine? Let's Meet would go apeshit."

"Which would require breaking into the Iron Fortress after all."

"We don't know if their system *is* like Ferantia. That was just an example."

"Because we don't know anything about their system, period."

"We will once you give me something more than a few pictures of a third-tier character dashboard."

I say, "Is this Iron Fortress . . . another *Ashes of Empire* reference?"

Becks looks at me. "Well, you certainly can't give Matthew any idea of the truth now, or he'll catch on that trying to join us is the dumbest thing he could do."

IX.

I'M SO PREOCCUPIED with Matthew and the Romantick and getting our hands on the .alt files—and, fine, ideas for a low-key yet
engaging outing that I could propose to Amalia as a follow-up to
theater-and-Thai night—that I lapse on checking in on Charles for
a few days. Maybe I've also managed to convince myself that whatever was troubling my brother has since been resolved. After all, it's
been more than a month of monitoring, and still no cry of distress
to WhatShould, no changes to the grim rhythm of his routine. No
communication on the family chat group or the Three Cs, either,
but that's not unusual when he's tunneling toward a work deadline.

What disabuses me of that hopeful notion is the notification
I get, which I'd set up back when I first started tracking Charles
on Finders Keepers, of an overlap: Charles's and Jessie's phones
registering as being in the same location. At first I'm glad that
he's finally spending some time with Jessie. Then I consider the
fact that it's three o'clock on a Wednesday afternoon and they're at
a café on the Upper East Side. The school where Jessie teaches is

in the neighborhood, so they must be meeting right after she got off work. But why would they arrange to get coffee near her work-place, like business acquaintances, instead of doing something more suitable for two people who've been dating for more than a year? Of course, once I think that, I'm afraid I know. I've seen variations on this theme in a few of my cases—a semi-impromptu meetup in a coffee shop, a park, the MoMA lobby, Penn Station—and it's never been an occasion for joy. At least Jessie will be kind.

The overlap lasts for forty-five minutes, and after that things get weird, because instead of returning to work, my brother heads out to . . . Brooklyn? I watch him stop-start his way down the FDR and onto the Williamsburg Bridge, until I have to put away my phone to attend a final debrief where I'm supposed to be pre-senting our findings to the client. I spectacularly botch that—after the second time I say, "I'm not sure where I was going with that, but, well, anyway," Becks takes over, glaring at me like she would love to toss me out of my seat with the power of her mind.

At the end of the debrief, Becks shows our client out. When she returns to the conference room, she says, "That was a display of utter fucking incompetence."

"My brother," I say. "I think something might have happened. Is happening."

Her anger falls away like a cloak she's let drop to the ground, and she's all composed attentiveness. "Like what?"

I tell Becks about Charles's meeting with Jessie and show her his current location on Finders Keepers. He's on the Belt Park-way now, curving along the New York Bay, tracing the southwest perimeter of Brooklyn. "He's been driving around for more than an hour."

She pulls out the chair next to mine and sits down. "Do you think this is his car?"

"It must be. When he first started moving I assumed he was in a cab, but . . . it doesn't look like he has any actual destination."

"That would mean he drove to meet his maybe-now-ex-girlfriend."

"Yes," I say. "Which makes zero sense. He would have had to drive from LIC to Hudson Yards, and then over to the east side—"

"Or he didn't go in to work."

That never even occurred to me: if one of Ed Cannon's apocalypse scenarios ever came to pass, Charles would battle through the undead hordes to get to the office. I tap the app's historical activity icon; the map changes to show us Charles's past locations on an hourly basis. Becks is right—he drove from his apartment in Long Island City to the Upper East Side, and prior to that he was at home. I scroll all the way back; Finders Keepers can record up to twenty-four hours of activity. At this time yesterday, he was again passing through Bay Ridge, on the Belt Parkway, heading east. I say, "Did he take a few days off to sit in New York traffic and contribute to carbon emissions?"

Becks says, "Would your brother be listed in Precision's people directory?"

"I . . . guess so. I've never looked him up, but he should be."

She reaches across the table to pull her laptop in front of her. "Let's see," she says as she types. "God, what a poorly designed website."

While she searches, I replay Charles's drive from yesterday at accelerated speed. He followed the Belt Parkway all the way into Queens, then turned left onto the Van Wyck Expressway. North through Jamaica, then Kew Gardens. Past Flushing Meadows—

"Do you have his work email?" says Becks.

My brother is scrupulous about not leveraging company resources for personal use, but I'm able to find it from, of all things, the email he sent to his business-school buddy to help me get a job at Aurum Financial, which he bcc'd me on. I forward the address to Becks.

"It bounced," she says. "He's not in the directory, either."

I lean in to look at her computer screen. *Message undeliverable. User does not exist.* "He quit Precision." It's the only logical explanation for his behavior, and at the same time mystifying. "I can't believe he didn't tell us."

Perhaps it's seeing that Aurum email again, from so long ago, but now I'm remembering my phone conversation with Charles, how he said that I had lied about my own job. That hadn't been about me at all; he'd been thinking of himself. *Sometimes you don't want everyone to know what's going on.* I say, "Could it have been because of the synths? He found out the truth about Project Tahiti and decided he didn't want to be a part of it." But even as I'm speaking, I realize I can't believe that. My brother's career matters too much to him. He would find ways of reconciling himself to what the matchmakers are doing, like he does for every situation he finds himself in. Maybe he said as much to me, when I was in his apartment and we were talking about the matchmakers' ability to predict compatibility: *It doesn't matter what I believe.*

Becks closes her laptop, a slow, deliberate motion. "I think you should talk to him."

That evening, my brother drives deep into the Bronx before turning back toward Long Island City. I call him during the ten or so minutes that he stops at a gas station in Parkchester. The line rings over to voicemail. I end the call and text him: Da ge, can you call me please? Need to talk to you. It's past ten p.m. by the time he gets home, and he doesn't call me back.

X.

I FIND JEMMA MILKBANK through her Facebook page, where she has amassed quite a following for her gluten-free baking videos. (I watch one, provocatively titled "The best sticky buns you've ever had!" While I remain skeptical, I'll concede that there's a beautiful glisten to them.) She lives in Kansas City now. She describes herself on Facebook as being passionate about celiac research, school reform, and the Monarchs. There's no indication she has, or has ever had, a career in journalism. I feel confident I have the right person only after I see her post about returning to Mansfield to give a talk at the library about the history of Haines Safety Systems.

I send her a message saying that I'm doing research on how small-town local newspapers have evolved in the past two decades, the *Mansfield Herald* is one of the papers I'm profiling, and I would love to chat with her about her experience as a reporter there during that time frame. In a P.S., I note that I'm a big fan of her recipes, in particular the sticky buns.

She responds the next day and suggests a Zoom call.

The person who shows up on my screen feels like the bad-cop version of the cheery, plumpish, maternal woman I watched stirring caramel glaze as she expounded on the sin of microwaving butter. She says, right away, "You said you were doing research. What is it for?"

I think of Norah Simmons's photographs: Jemma #1 versus Jemma #2. "A journalism class," I say. "Thank you for agreeing to speak with me." I have a more extensive explanation prepared, if she asks, but one of Inspector Yuan's maxims is that the more a man has to say, the more he has to hide.

"Why the *Mansfield Herald*?"

"I have a friend who's originally from Mansfield. He suggested the *Herald*."

"From Mansfield," says Jemma. "And . . . why me?"

She's looking at me like she thinks she already knows the answer. Is it possible? I say, "Also because of that friend. He gave me your name. He's Matthew Espersen."

Something strobes across her face, two different colors overlapping to create a third. Surprise, but also recognition. "Matt Espersen," she says. "Wow. I wouldn't have thought . . ."

When she doesn't continue, I ask, "You remember him?"

"Of course." Her voice is soft—tender, even. Jemma #3. "What did he say? About how he knows me?"

"You were the reporter who covered a car accident that he was in."

"I was. The poor kid." After a moment, she says, "He must be, what, almost forty now. Not a kid anymore. I hope he's doing well."

"Well enough." This next part makes me feel like I'm climbing into a weasel costume and zipping it up, but I need to know if we can trust Matthew. "He's never fully gotten over Drew's death."

Jemma nods: no surprise this time. "It was a horrible thing to happen. Such a horrible thing."

I say, hoping the fallibilities of both ego and memory will make her receptive to this statement, "He asked me to tell you that he appreciated what you did for him."

"What I did," she says, as if she still thinks about it from time to time, and whether she should have done something else. She sits back in her chair. "It sounds like . . . you and Matt, you're close?"

"We are," I say: the way two people trying to stop a match-maker AI conspiracy are close.

"Did he . . ." A slight shake of her head. "What exactly did Matt tell you? About the accident?"

It always feels a bit like trying to dance blindfolded when I let my intuition lead. "He was in love with Drew."

She sighs; I see rather than hear it.

"And the community . . . disapproved."

Jemma squints at me, and the floor I thought I'd landed on swings open. But then she says, "I can see why he thought that. People didn't realize, though. Drew was on good terms with everybody, and Matt, of course he would want to hang out with the most popular kid in school. There was a teacher—or maybe she was some other kind of staff—it might have crossed her mind. But I doubt she would even have mentioned it to anyone. Especially with what else was going on."

That *what else*: that must be what Jemma Milkbank and Sheriff Langston and Pastor Franklin and the rest of Mansfield decided they would look away from when Drew Wilkins died. Something to do with the circumstances of the accident, I'm guessing, which accounts for all the caginess there. But there's no need for me to delve any further; I've gotten the confirmation I was hoping for.

On the screen, Jemma leans forward. "Could you tell Matt . . ." I can see her selecting and discarding words, wanting to make sure what she says is right. "Tell him I'm glad to hear from him. And I still remember Drew the same way he does."

After Jemma and I hang up, I spin myself around in my chair and think about Matthew Espersen, eighteen years old, waking up in a hospital and learning that the boy he loves is dead. A hole the size of the universe. Maybe the only way to survive that was to refuse to see it: if Drew Wilkins didn't exist, then he couldn't be lost.

I shuffle through the *Herald* articles until I find the one with Drew's and Matthew's photos, reproduced from their high school yearbook. Matthew is unrecognizable to me, which has as much to do with the low quality of the resolution as how his face hasn't yet been pared into the spare, angular features that I've become familiar with. I hold up the page in one hand and, with the other, I pull up on my desk monitor the meta-picture of Matthew that Becks took months ago when Pradeep Mehta showed it to us on his phone. I start to zoom in on Matthew's face—past Pradeep's forearm, past the frame of the phone—and then stop. I zoom back out again. The black watch strap around Pradeep's wrist, the three silvery lines twining together that, I now know, are the Triple-Helix logo. And what did Pradeep say?

He gave me this.

That watch: it had been Matthew's gift to Pradeep.

To help monitor my physio KPIs.

But, when Matthew and I spoke, he said he had never heard of Triple-Helix.

If Matthew had helped Pradeep set up his Triple-Helix account as well, then he would know how to access the information stored within it. Pradeep's bike rides, for instance. He would have been able to familiarize himself with the patterns of when Pradeep rode and what routes he took. Combine that knowledge with the ability to pinpoint where Pradeep was in real time based on the location of his device, and—

"No," I say. It sounds like a wish, the sort you make knowing there's no way it can come true.

I realize I'm still holding the article and put it back down on the desk, next to the piece with the large photograph of the crash site: "Local Teens in Fatal Car Crash." The longer I stare at that picture, the more it assumes a Rorschach quality. You could see whatever you wanted to see in those shapes. Car, road, trees. Accident. Suicide. Or . . . something else.

What if that had been Jemma's *what else*? A suspicion that the car crash might not have been completely accidental, and a staunch, concerted repudiation of that suspicion. I go through the articles again, this time looking for references to the sheriff. There it is: *Sheriff Paul Langston, who is Matt's maternal uncle.*

Perhaps the Espersens were a powerful family. Perhaps Matt was so young and had come so close to dying himself. Perhaps no one could bear to consider what it would mean if Drew's death had been anything other than mischance. So the town stayed silent, and twenty years later another person Matthew Espersen is in love with dies: another empty road, another sudden, unfortunate death, too early in the morning.

XI.

SQUIRREL IS SQUATTING on the seat of Komla's chair, bobbing his head and performing an urgent percussion piece that involves the keyboard, the mouse, and an occasional feral grunt. In the implacable glow of his screens, he resembles a Morlock plotting the overthrow of the entire Eloi race.

I sidle into his view, in front of the desk, and wave at him over his monitor-wall.

He tugs off his headphones. An instrumental sweetness rises from the squishy depths of the twin earpieces. Is that . . . anime music?

"Knock before you come in."

"I did."

"And wait for me to say you can enter. What if I'd been doing something you shouldn't have seen? You could have been scarred for life."

"Let's not go there," I say. "Can I pull up the blinds? And maybe crack open a window?"

As I do so, I tell him what I've discovered about Matthew Espersen. He doesn't pause in his activities, but when I'm done he says, "I always knew there was something wrong with that guy."

"You've never met him."

"Don't have to. Anyone so ready to help us must have problems."

I say, "I was thinking . . . we assumed that Pradeep told Let's Meet about Silent G, which was why the profile was taken down. Is there any way we can check that?"

Squirrel scratches at his chin, which is beginning to take on a wispy texture. "He would have done it through Let's Meet's feedback portal. That's the only way the company lets users communicate with them. So . . . you could check the portal archives, I guess."

I gaze at him as beseechingly as I can, which is especially hard with Squirrel because he seems to equate eye contact with disease transmission. I'm starting to feel cross-eyed by the time he says, "Sometimes it sucks being the only smart person in this place."

"You are. And we really appreciate you."

"But I want to finish this"—he juts his chin at the screen directly in front of him—"first."

"Squirrel," I say, "if my theory is correct, then . . . Matthew killed Pradeep." I haven't said this aloud until now, and I can feel the air coagulating around me, the possibility now out in the world like a spirit twisting itself through a crack in reality. "I think it's important to confirm this as soon as possible."

"Fine," he says, the way you do when you've stopped paying attention to what the other person is saying and you just want them to go away.

"How long will you need, two hours? I can come back then."

That gets me both eye contact and attention, of the bulgingly outraged variety. "Start the stopwatch on your phone."

He hunches forward and starts blizzarding away on his key-

board. I move around the desk so I can stand behind him and see
what's on the quartet of screens. A CGI still of a forest clearing:
a medieval Mr. Universe, one axe in each hand, faces off against
what looks like a dun-colored, demonic Big Bird. User dashboards
from different programs—I recognize one of the .alt file pictures,
as well as the Triple-Helix interface and Squirrel's game character
dashboard from *McMurdo*. Multiple windows of code, white text
on black.

"Time."

I glance down at my phone and realize I forgot to tap START.
"Ah . . . five minutes?"

"Damn, I'm good." He rocks back and his chair glides away
from the desk. I perambulate him forward again. "Okay, let's see
what we've got."

We both look at the rightmost screen, which displays a spreadsheet of what appear to be user handles and time stamps, along
with other configurations of numbers and letters that are indecipherable to me. According to Squirrel, this is Let's Meet's log of
subscriber feedback submissions for the months of February and
March. He runs a search for Pradeep's handle: nothing.

"Could Let's Meet have deleted it?" I ask.

"They could have deleted the form. But the system also regis-
ters the process of submission itself—the account it comes from,
time and date—and to go in and erase that would be a lot harder."

I gaze at the rows upon rows of data. How to prove that something *didn't* happen? "Not impossible, though."

Squirrel shrugs. "We done here?"

Maybe I should see instead about proving that something did.
"Can we get into Pradeep's Triple-Helix account?"

"Do we have to? Exercise is fucking boring."

"I think Matthew knew about Pradeep's bike route beforehand,
because Pradeep used Triple-Helix to map and save his routes;
and he was able to track Pradeep on the morning of the crash

through Triple-Helix's geolocation function. Step one is seeing if Pradeep's account has all this information in the first place. Step two is checking if the account has authorized access for multiple devices. If Matthew was secretly logging in to Pradeep's account, he had to be doing so from his own device, which means he had to add it as a trusted device."

"Even if there is one, it's not going to be labeled with Matthew Espersen's name, not unless he's a complete moron. Is that step three, hoping he's a complete moron?"

"Step three," I say, "is confirming if we already have the device Matthew was using to log in to Pradeep's account."

I pause, as detective-novel etiquette dictates you should before presenting your brilliant inference to the soon-to-be-stunned audience.

"What, you mean the burner phone he gave you?"

I blink at Squirrel, who has opened up a new window on his center-right screen and is filling it with text. "You figured that out, too?"

"What else could it be?" He swivels his focus to the right-most screen; the spreadsheet is replaced with Triple-Helix's member log-in page. "Although it might not be the same phone. He could've dumped the phone right after he killed Pradeep, then bought another one to take those pictures."

"He could have," I say. "But I think he might have considered that a waste."

Eight minutes later—officially timed—we're in Pradeep's Triple-Helix account, in what Squirrel calls "ninja mode." I navigate us over to Pradeep's workout history and specify in the viewing options that I only want to look at *Bike Rides*. (Other categories: *Cricket Practice, Cricket Games, Strength Training, Miscellaneous*.) Squirrel is appalled. "Fifty kilometers—what's that, thirty miles? In a day? He must have been faking it."

The most recent entry was on the day of Pradeep's death and is saved as *Draft*. When I click on it, I see that the watch mapped Pradeep's route from his home in Midtown up to the site of the crash. *Start Time: 6:41 a.m. End Time: 7:25 a.m. Distance: 13.21 km.* Graphs display metrics like incline, heart rate, and speed throughout the ride.

I go back and take a look at his rides in the weeks prior. Every Tuesday, Wednesday, and Thursday morning, starting between 6:30 and 6:45 a.m., ending between 8:25 and 8:50 a.m. Always the same route: along the Hudson River bike path past the Cloisters, turning off on Dyckman Street, zigzagging to Broadway, following that road north over the Harlem River to Van Cortlandt Park, and then all the way back down again. Here and there, he would include brief notes on specific rides, mainly to explain anomalies in his performance. *Detour bcos construction @ km 8–10 and 20–22. Flat @ km 12. Weaker than usual—bcos poor sleep?* And, for Tuesday, before his final, fatal ride the next morning, he noted, *Helmet strap broke @ km 19.* If Pradeep had wanted Matthew to ambush him, he couldn't have been more helpful.

Squirrel, sounding dangerously querulous: "How much longer is this going to take?"

"Almost done. Where's the burner phone?"

"It's either in that box or *that* box," he says, pointing at two different corners of the room. "Or I left it in Red Hook."

Thankfully I find the phone at the bottom of the second box, albeit not so thankfully underneath a wadded T-shirt that is more BO than cloth at this point. I bring it back to Squirrel, and he plugs it into a box on Komla's desk that's in turn plugged, via a Rapunzel braid of wires, into one of the towers on the floor. He installs the Triple-Helix app on the phone, opens it, enters Pradeep's log-in information, taps SIGN IN.

An icon appears in the center of the screen, what looks like a DNA structure but comprising three strands instead of two. I watch over Squirrel's shoulder as it twists in place. "It wouldn't take this long, would it? If the phone could—"

The log-in page and the icon vanish, replaced by the same *Welcome, Pradeep* that's at the top of Pradeep's Triple-Helix account homepage being displayed on the monitor screen.

"Stet that," I mumble. Really: Matthew Espersen? He's our conduit to the Chemistry Lab and its digital-twin project. A fellow believer in the possibility of reforming the matchmakers. The person I share my amateur spy ideas with. Above all, he loved Pradeep—I could tell from the way he spoke about him. Why would he do this terrible thing?

Unless, of course, that's why. Maybe Pradeep was telling the truth after all when he said he had been the one to break up with Matthew.

"The cheap bastard," says Squirrel.

I say, "This shows Matthew had the means to kill Pradeep. We still have to establish that he actually did." And if we can do so . . . that would mean Let's Meet had nothing to do with Pradeep Mehta's death. Which would mean, in turn, that what happened to Pradeep wasn't the verifiers' fault. Us telling him to submit a complaint to Let's Meet didn't change anything. He never contacted Let's Meet, and the company never knew that he found out about his digital twin.

"We have to let Becks know about this," I say. "She should be back from her observation soon."

While I've been absorbed in my deductive process, Squirrel has returned to his Axeman vs. Evil Big Bird battle. He says, as his avatar winds up for an axe throw: "She'll be happy. She never trusted him." The monster hops out of the way and the axe arcs past it, spinning so rapidly it looks like a large silver circle. Squirrel adds, "Can't stand how she's always right."

I sigh. "Me neither."

Except—Becks isn't *always* right. She was the one who proposed that someone at Let's Meet had killed Pradeep; and when we discussed it, Squirrel called her out on what sounded like another mistake she had made, back before I joined.

I wait for Evil Big Bird to unfurl its wings and swoop at Squirrel's avatar to say, "What about Faras, though?"

"Yeah, she fucked that one up," he says to the screen. Axeman is hacking away at his opponent, pushing it back—Squirrel's headphones, still hanging around his neck, emit a series of muffled, furious screeches.

"Who is he? Faras?"

Axeman finally lands a blow, slashing through one of Evil Big Bird's wings. Major ickiness ensues. "The third man."

I consider whether Squirrel could be making some sort of analogy to Harry Lime—black-market dealer? faked his own death?—and decide no. "Third of what?"

"Verifiers."

Becks and Squirrel let me in on Veracity's origin story after they accepted that I wasn't going away despite rescinded employment, bicycle sabotage, personal injury, and potential criminal charges. I can be as tenacious as a barnacle sometimes, and about as bright. What they said then was that Komla had brought in the two of them to help him. They never said, though, that there had been no one else.

"What happened to him?" I ask.

Squirrel's hand, reaching for his mini–Death Star of a mouse, spasms in place before he grabs it. "Couldn't handle it."

I step away; I've probably exhausted enough goodwill to troubleshoot a dozen laptops. Then I remember how pissed Becks was when she learned I had been in contact with Amalia Suarez, and the word she used: *dangerous*. "Did he try to . . . interfere with our clients' relationships?"

"Fuck!"

I take another step back, equally startled by Squirrel's exclamation and how he's begun jabbing the same combination of keys on his keyboard over and over again with a fatalistic fury—it seems that the goopy black substance spewing from Evil Big Bird's amputated wing may be poisonous. Just as suddenly, he hits a different key and the game freezes. He turns to me. "She told you?"

"In a way?"

"What the fuck. She said she would strangle me with my own tongue if I ever brought him up again."

"We're talking about Becks, right? Because that seems a bit gruesome even for her."

I half expect Squirrel to respond with something snide, but instead he hunches in on himself. "She gets touchy, when it comes to Faras."

"Were they, um . . ."

"Boning each other? No. I didn't pick up on that, anyway."

Not entirely reassuring. Although, also, none of my business. "Where is he now? Faras?"

"Dead." And then, before I can start freaking out: "If we're lucky."

I gaze at Squirrel, the rounded carapace of his back, his hands gripping the edge of the desk like he's holding fast in a dark current. "Why do you say that?"

"He was a real piece of shit." Squirrel pulls himself in until the armrests of his chair bump against the desk. "Whatever. Can you leave now? I need to finish stealing the Scrolls of Tiranium before the sun sets and the wraiths come out."

———————

Becks says, "None of that proves he killed Pradeep."

"It doesn't," I agree. "It sets us up for proving he did."

Her eyes narrow in that way that makes her look like a particularly vicious cat. "No."

"You don't even know what my plan is."

"A confession."

Well, that's Detective Methodology 101. "Not the specifics."

"You'll bring up Drew Wilkins first, to throw him off-balance. Then Triple-Helix. You'll ask him why he lied, what else he's hiding. Try to get him upset enough he can't keep track of his story and incriminates himself. Actually, you're probably hoping he'll feel so guilty he just admits to the whole thing."

I say, "Can you read everyone's minds, or just mine?"

The corner of her mouth curls up. "I know you by now."

Something about the way she says that, or maybe it's how she's looking at me, pulls me back to the night of the concert. I'm unprepared for the regret, how it hollows me out for an instant. If Julia hadn't interrupted. Or if I had done something different, like asked her to stay on—

"Anyway, it won't work."

And we're back to our regularly scheduled programming: Becks fortified behind the immaculate surface of her desk, and the prickle of frustration, all too familiar, at how sure she is about everything, including that any idea I propose must suck. "Why not?"

"He's not the type to lose control."

"You've only met him twice! I've been looking at mandalas with him for weeks."

"I recognized what sort of person he was right away. The only way he'll confess is if we can trick him into it. Lead him to believe we have more evidence than we really do, until he says something that corroborates our theory."

I smile at her.

"What?"

"You said *our theory*."

"I . . . did," she says, like I've told her I spotted a rat in the lobby. She picks up the book on her desk—William Gibson's *Neuromancer*, one of the few times I've seen her read science fiction—and puts it down again. "It's really yours. You figured out how Matthew was using Triple-Helix. That's the key to the crime."

"I would never have put it together without those *Mansfield Herald* articles."

"It was the information you got that—" She stops. "This is a waste of time. Back to your plan."

"Our plan," I say. "And what do you think about calling this Operation Galatea?"

XII.

I TURN LEFT onto Bay Ridge Avenue and cycle through the underpass beneath the Shore Parkway, past a deceptively cheery mural of sharks and seahorses floating against a backdrop of submerged houses. The pier stretches out ahead of me on the other side, and I find myself thinking that it looks like a wide concrete gangplank.

I emerge from the shadow of the tunnel onto the bike path. It's all sky and water out here, textures of blue and gray, the cars whooshing by like they're trying to provide an appropriate soundtrack for this maritime scene. From where I am, the Verrazzano-Narrows Bridge looks like it's assembled from threads and matchsticks. I get off my bike and check Finders Keepers.

My brother has always been a proponent of process, of routine, of laying down a track and following it, over and over, until its grooves wear deep enough for you to feel like this is what you're meant to do. That hasn't changed now that he's spending his days like a misanthropic ride-hailing driver, and it's an odd little comfort. Maybe it helps me to feel like I do still know who he is. Over the last several months I've come to realize how different both my siblings are from who I've always assumed them to be, and it's been a tiny bit terrifying, like losing the ability to gauge distance or tell direction. Although the longer I'm in this verifying gig, the more apparent it is that the people you're supposed to be the closest to are the ones who are hidden from you. Look at Matthew and Pradeep.

I refocus on my phone screen. I wish I could stop thinking about Matthew, just for a little while. Ever since we learned that he had been using Triple-Helix to spy on Pradeep, I've been reexamining all the time I spent with him. My initial outreach, our walks, the things he said, the way he looked—trying to figure out if he lied about anything else and whether I failed to pick up on his duplicity sooner because, as Becks said, I was the one who recruited him. If he really could be capable of killing Pradeep. But all of that is for tomorrow. Today I need to work on some of the things I've been neglecting because, well-adjusted individual that I am, I find it easier to come up with theories of murder than to interact with my own family.

Right now traffic is even gnarlier than usual because of an accident on the Gowanus Expressway, and so Charles is still in Sunset Park—less than two miles away, but Google Maps estimates that it'll take him twenty minutes to get to where I am.

I call first. Then I text: I had a bike accident in Bay Ridge. Any chance you can pick me up? I wait two minutes, call again. Wait; call. Wait—

Charles's incoming call lights up my screen. Finally. When I answer, he says, "What are you doing?"

He sounds so distant, like he's calling from another planet. I say, "Trying to talk to you?"

"I can't talk now."

"Why not?"

"What do you mean? I'm—I'm at work."

"You didn't get my text?"

After a moment he says, "No."

Is that a lie as well? "I fell off my bike."

"What? How? Are you hurt?"

The shock cracks through the flattened surface of his voice, and something in me eases. I don't even have to fake the tremor in my question: "Could you come get me?"

"Where are you?"

"Bay Ridge. By the water, near Owl's Head Park."

"Send me your live location. Sit down; don't move. I'll be there."

When my brother's car rolls down Bay Ridge Avenue, I'm on a bench at the side of the pier, which is populated by pigeons and elderly Asian men who all appear to be members of the same e-bike fishing mafia. I watch Charles park in the underpass and get out. He's dressed in a T-shirt and jeans, and once he steps into the light I can see that he's looking . . . not good. Not in the over-worked, underslept way that's become his default over the years. This is like a psychic squid has attached itself to his soul and is discreetly siphoning it away.

He walks up to me. "What the hell happened?"

Exactly, I want to say. "I was going too fast on a turn. My knee feels a bit messed up, so I'm not sure if I can bike home, but nothing's broken."

He glances at my bike, which I've propped against the railing. I wonder if he'll ask why I'm gallivanting about on a weekday afternoon—my cover story is that I took a day off to help a friend move and we finished early—but he simply says, "Do you need to go to a doctor to get checked out?"

I shake my head. "If you don't mind dropping me off." I hadn't entirely decided how I would play this, but looking at him now, the obviousness of his lie, maybe I should just ask. "Why did you say that you were at work?"

"What?"

"On the phone just now. You said that you were at work and so you couldn't talk." I gesture at him. "But the way you're dressed. And you got here so quickly, and you drove . . . You weren't in the office."

Charles stares at me. "No," he says. "I guess I wasn't."

He moves to take my bicycle's handlebars. I get up, remembering just in time that I should be favoring one knee—and also that I can't forget which knee is fake injured; that's how the entry-level con artists are always getting caught in Inspector Yuan stories. "So why did you say you were?"

He tilts the bike upright and begins to wheel it away. "I don't think you get to ask me that."

Did I hear that right? I say, "What do you mean?"

Charles stops walking. He dips his head, as if considering how to respond. Then he says, still facing away from me, "Claudia, you're not open with me about all kinds of stuff. It's not just what happened with Aurum, how you lied about still working there after you quit. I have no idea what you're doing now. If I ask you why you're going on a long bike ride in the middle of the workday, can I trust your answer? Some of the things you've told me . . . Maybe you do it because it's easier for you to deal with the world this way. I don't know. I don't really care. But stop acting like I owe you an explanation for anything I say or do."

I feel like the water around us surged up out of the harbor and crashed down on me in a tsunami of disgrace. Everything my brother said—he's right, and the worst of it is, he can't even imagine how deep the deception actually goes, like a tunnel right to the molten center of the earth. All the pretexts I've employed in order to talk to him, to find out more about Cameron Keller and how Precision might be involved in the matchmakers' synth projects. Finders Keepers. WhatShould. Even this, now, here: I was all set to lie to him about why I was in Bay Ridge; I *am* lying to him about being injured. How did I become this person? Or have I always been this person, ready to lie and lie to get what I want, and it's only that prior to Veracity I never had to?

Or. Is it because I'm this person that I'm able to be a verifier in the first place?

Charles says, like he hasn't just firebombed any facade of good-will between us, "Let's go. I'm double-parked."

I'm so shell-shocked that I move to follow along behind him, but then a specific statement he made cuts into my memory. "Some of the things I've told you?" I say. Could he have caught on that I had my own reasons for asking about his work for the matchmakers? "Like . . . what?"

Now he half turns to gaze at me over the frame of my bike. His expression is empty, as if I'm not worth mustering any emotion for. I look for the mark on his face from the time we were kids and our mother backhanded him, her fury and her wedding ring gash-ing him open; it's a long healed-over scar that you notice only if you know exactly where it is.

He says, "What you said about Jessie."

"Jessie?" But all I said was that I'd met up with her, she thought Charles was working too hard, the cautionary tale of Cameron Keller. What would make Charles think any of that was false? "I don't . . ."

"You knew that she had decided to leave me."

Oh. Oh, fuck. His meeting with Jessie last week; she must have told him. For the briefest instant I think about denying it—my word against hers, no way to prove which of us is telling the truth—but I have to stop lying to my brother. "She was the one who asked me not to tell you," I say, and boy, does that sound like the limpest excuse since the Big Bang. Of all the people to be betrayed by: Jessie! "She thought you had enough going on with work. We thought. But—what was the point of her telling you that I knew, when—it wasn't like it made a difference, or—"

"She didn't mean to," he says. "I asked her to meet me, to talk about . . . doesn't matter. She got the impression you *had* told me, said some things that didn't make any sense. I said I didn't understand. It all . . . kind of came out." He pauses. "When she realized, she really defended you. Said she shouldn't have put you in the position she did."

His tone sounds singularly unimpressed. I say, "Do you think I should have told you, then?"

"Not that. I would have preferred it if you did, but . . . that's not what." He knuckles his forehead. "You fed me all that bullshit. What she really wanted was to spend more time with me. That's why she talked to you. When you knew—not just that it wasn't true, but what the truth was. The complete opposite." Charles shakes his head, and now he looks faintly baffled. "Why did you do it? You felt bad for me? Or did you think it would be fun?"

"No."—and now I remember everything else I did say, and how easily. "No! Of course not."

"Then why?"

"I knew she was important to you, and I thought—" What? That maybe I could nudge them toward a different outcome. That Charles would never find out. That it would do no harm. "It was stupid. I'm sorry."

He stares at me for a second longer. Then he says, "It doesn't matter now."

In the car he keeps the windows down, and the trafficky commotion of Fifth Avenue mixes with the music he's playing—one of his alt-rock bands, dreary and angsty in equal parts—to create a noise fog. I wish I could tell him there's no need to discourage conversation like that; I'm not up for it myself.

The street gets a bit quieter once we're out of Sunset Park and driving alongside Green-Wood Cemetery. We pass the entrance to the cemetery, and I twist around to look at the intricate rise of the sandstone gates and the lawns stretching away on either side, like a pocket of Victorian England magicked into postmodern Brooklyn. As I'm sitting back in my seat, my brother says, "I'm not at Precision anymore."

All I hear at first is his voice, the fact that, thank god, he remains willing to speak to me, and then the sounds harden into their meaning. I wait an appropriate length of time for someone who has not already deduced that information. "What made you decide to leave?"

He laughs. "They fired me."

"They fired you?" If Charles had said he came across a document detailing the matchmakers' master plan for world domination, it would have been less shocking. "Why?"

"Consistent underperformance."

"That's so crazy. Are you going to contest it?" I say, all indignant, until it occurs to me: I *don't* want Charles at Precision, in charge of Cameron Keller's old projects, clueless about the machinations going on around him. "Although you're better off not being at a place like that. It's their loss."

He glances at me and then back at the road in front of us. "You have no idea what I might have done."

"You were working all the time! I bet they wanted to get out of paying you severance. Maddie's old company did that to one of her coworkers. Or—do you think they were just being racist? In which case, you should definitely report them to someone, I don't know who, but—"

Charles says, "I was on probation. Had been since February."

He sounds almost defiant, like he's challenging me to object. I look at him, that familiar profile, the wall of his forehead and the nose that Coraline always says makes him look like a koala, his lips tight like driving through Park Slope is a test of concentration. The memory of long-ago violence slanting across his cheek, and for a moment that's all I can see. "What happened?" I ask.

He hits the button to roll up the windows. After the street

noise has faded out, he says, "A client complained. They said they wanted a stronger lead. Someone who *actually knew what they were doing*."

I think of Jessie saying that Charles had almost skipped out on our *tuan yuan fan*, the way he abruptly left the table to answer a call. "Was this around Lunar New Year?"

"It was going on then."

I want to ask why he didn't tell us, but it's not as if I don't know. Our mother would have annihilated him with her scorn; and even if she hadn't been around, it must have felt like too large of a failure to admit to.

"I thought I could still fix it," says Charles, like he heard my question. "I asked for more time, but someone at Mosaic spoke to someone up top at Precision and made it sound like . . . I don't know."

Mosaic? That's not a name I've heard of, in the matching industry or otherwise. I say, "This is the project that you said Cameron Keller passed on to you when he left?"

"Yeah. My group head swapped me out, and the new lead came in and saw how bad things were. And he told everyone. Not surprising. He had to cover his own ass, and none of this was his fault."

So that was why I couldn't access the Project Tahiti file on Charles's computer: he had been taken off that matter. "But it wasn't yours, either. Could you have let people know, at that point, about what Cameron had done?"

"Blame a dead guy? That would have looked even worse."

I obviously never met Cameron Keller, and know hardly anything about him apart from the clinical circumstances of his death and his secret identity as synth conspiracy whistleblower, but right then I despise him, dead or not, for what he did to my brother. I wonder if he weighed the damage to one person's career against his self-imposed mission to sabotage the matchmakers, or if he didn't think about Charles at all. I'm not sure which would have been worse.

As we approach the next intersection, Charles signals to turn left, and I realize that we're less than ten minutes away from my place. It's strange: I can't wait to get out of the car and away from all the lies I've told my brother, and at the same time I wish I could sit here with him forever, an eternal liminal space. (Although then we'd seriously have to reassess the music selection.) Maybe that's why Charles has been driving around so much.

That thought prompts me to ask, "So . . . what do you think you'll do now?"

He shrugs. "Haven't decided."

A couple of blocks later: "Maybe I should ask that chatbot."

"What chatbot?"

"You told me and Cor about it. People type in questions about what they should do and get advice."

I pause. "WhatShould?"

"Is that what it's called? Do I just go to the website?"

"Have you set up an account?"

"You need an account? I thought you could just start asking questions."

If he didn't open the Wallpath account, then . . . Coraline? Once I think that, I remember: *wallpath* was a Coraline original, a confusion with *warpath*; also, how my gleefully obnoxious nine-year-old self laughed at her for that mistake. I slide lower in my seat, until the seat belt is practically garroting me. Claudia Lin, shitty sibling exemplar.

Charles adds, "I guess that makes sense. I'm sure they want to track what people are asking."

That night I write two emails.

The first is to Coraline's ex Lionel, literary master of appropriation. I begin by congratulating him on the *New Yorker* piece, since lifelong dream and all, then express my disappointment that he appears to be building his career out of other people's stories, both real and fictional. I say that I came across a short story that contained striking similarities to his piece in *Zinc Cabin* and paste the most egregious examples (helpfully collated by TCAP). I tell him that I'll contact the author about this, as well as the magazines in which he's had the undeserved fortune to be published, unless he does two things: one, stop writing any more fiction that's in any way based on my family; and two, apologize to Coraline for what he has done.

After I click SEND, I log out of Gmail and in again, to my other account. I go to my *Drafts* folder and open up the email I started a few days after I last saw Amalia. Current iteration:

> *Happy Tuesday!* [No longer accurate, although if I dither much longer it will once again be.] *There's an art show on the High Line that reminded me of Norah Simmons when I walked by.*

I do wish I had slept with Amalia that night, for all the reasons I'd like to sleep with a pretty girl who smiled at me like she was looking forward to taking me apart and putting me back together again. And at the same time I'm glad I didn't, because I suspect doing so might have shunted us down a path we wouldn't have turned back from, and I'm not sure if that's what I want—

I hear the front door open and then slam shut again. There's a scuffling of footsteps, the slurry voices of people who are trying—not trying to be quiet. Guess Benny is staying over tonight. The sound moves past my door like a messy, eager creature and into Max's room. I'm thinking that I should excavate the earplugs I bought soon after they started dating, but then Max puts on one of his French indie pop albums and all is subsumed in shimmery guitar chords and the languid vocals of someone who sounds like she's been chain-smoking since age thirteen.

I turn back to my laptop. She feels like a sunny morning, Amalia, bright and lively and easy to enjoy. Entirely different from . . . well, someone else. The Mason Perry case is almost four months closed by now; and, in any case, she's no longer with Mason. Maybe now we can begin the way we should have all along.

I type, Would you like to go see it with me? and click SEND before I can change my mind.

XIII.

MATTHEW ESPERSEN JOINS ME in front of the large cloth painting that I'm squinting at. "A lot going on," he says.

When I turn, he looks the same as he always has. Watchful, aloof, glow-in-the-dark pale; someone who remains cloistered from the rest of the world wherever he goes. An observer, not an actor. Maybe I'm wrong and Pradeep's death *was* just an accident, as Drew Wilkins's was. Maybe we can still trust Matthew after all.

I say, "I can't tell who the good guys are." The faded canvas is teeming with figures, human and fantastical, set against a backdrop of green mountains and curlicued clouds. There are a lot of bared fangs and severed heads being brandished about, but one thing I've learned from these Rubin visits is not to judge a creature by how scary it looks.

"That might depend on whose side you're on."

I glance down: Matthew's hands are empty. "You weren't able to . . . ?"

"They made me put my bag in a locker."

I exhale. "Oh. Good. Should we go get it?"

"When we head out." He leans in to scrutinize the bottom right corner of the painting, where a monstrous red being is chasing after a pair of understandably panicked humans. "Let's Meet terminated someone on Friday."

My insides ice up. "*Terminated* as in—"

"They fired him."

Right: what that term means in the employment context, at least in the overwhelming majority of circumstances. I think briefly of Charles, who never responded to my text from last night thanking him for driving me home. At least I saw that he read the message.

Matthew says, "He was in IT. My division."

This time my apprehension feels like a gradual frost, crackling out toward my skin. "What happened?"

"All we've been told is that this person no longer works for Let's Meet, and if he reaches out for any reason we should let HR know. But I can make an educated guess." He straightens, keeping his gaze on the painting. "I've been using his credentials."

"Oh," I say. "Shit."

"Yes. They've been put on notice. They know that there's a party trying to find out more about their synths. Hopefully they think it's another one of the matchmakers."

"He lost his job because of us."

Now Matthew looks at me. "He'll find another."

"That doesn't matter," I say. "He shouldn't have . . . He didn't deserve that."

"Many people don't deserve what happens to them. This is nothing."

I think of Somnang's handler telling him about the fate of the Vietnamese family who kept him safe from the Dream. *A spot of nasty business*, he says, and then, *Sorry, old boy*, like Somnang is the one suffering the loss.

Matthew says, "I apologize."

"What?" I say. "What for?"

"I took the precaution, which, as this shows, was warranted. But Let's Meet should never have picked up on what I was doing in the first place. Either I wasn't being careful enough, or they're more competent than I gave them credit for." He shakes his head. "It will be too risky to continue looking into the twins from within the company. We'll have to find other, external sources of information."

In a way, we're already prepared for this: our base case is that, by the end of the afternoon, Matthew will be lost to us as an asset. Even if it turns out he's innocent, or I'm unable to elicit a confession, he's not going to want to stick around a bunch of people who accused him of murder.

First, though, I need to get ahold of that hard drive. "The .alt files may give us some ideas on that front." I gesture toward the gallery exit. "Should we . . . ?"

He turns without speaking. As I walk behind him I itch to look over my shoulder to see if Squirrel, who has been inspecting the row of sculptures along the far wall of the room, is following. In the Symposium song "Eurydice Gets Mad," Orpheus is portrayed as an ass for being unable to follow the one very simple instruction, but right now, I feel like I can see where the guy was coming from. (Pun unintended.) Sometimes you just want to make sure.

At the lockers, Matthew takes out a small black backpack and nothing else. He slings one of the straps over his shoulder.

"It's, ah, in there?" I ask.

He nods. "How are your allergies today?"

This isn't one of our codes, is it? We've gotten lazy about using them, and I've forgotten everything by now except *I couldn't sleep last night*, which means either that we're being followed or that we're *not* being followed.

"I thought we could go for a walk."

"Oh—sure!" I say, relieved that I'm not going to be indicted as a completely inept spy. "It's been better these last few days, after all the rain we've had."

Outside, the sky has a dark, seething look to it. Matthew leads us west on Seventeenth Street. We pass a furniture store, every one of the half dozen pieces on display looking as expensive as it does uncomfortable; apartment facades in varying shades of brown; a nail salon with a solitary customer being attended to by a diminutive Asian woman. It's clear that he has a destination in mind. Might as well investigate my other theory along the way.

"I've been wondering how you came to learn about our organization," I say. "Who we really are, and what we're doing."

When he speaks, he sounds like he's still swimming back up from the depths of some private thought. "The data breach," he says. "Last January. It started with that."

Is he referring to a breach at Let's Meet? That would be very interesting, since—officially—the company is the only one of the Big Three never to have experienced a data breach, a fact it likes to bring up in its advertising. "Why did you draw a connection to us?"

"It didn't seem to make sense, what the hackers did. They had access to over ten thousand subscriber accounts, but they only took information from around a hundred subscribers—and not what you usually see. They didn't touch names, addresses, credit card data, any of that. Instead it was things like responses to Let's Meet questionnaires or messages on ChatNow. Information about the type of person the subscriber was that wasn't public facing. I was part of the team set up afterward to look into this and how to prevent similar incidents in the future, and at some point someone said that it had to be the Romantick. She was joking, but in a way that sounded like she half believed it could be true."

I allow myself an instant of satisfaction that I called the Romantick correctly. "Are there other people at Let's Meet who share your view of the Romantick?"

"A few. They think there's more to the cover story—or they would like there to be."

"Really?"

"Just because you work in matching doesn't mean you don't wish there were a better way."

Maybe . . . but what? Whoever you happen to meet at school, or work, or your neighborhood bar? Friends of friends of friends? The serendipity of a gaze met across a crowded room or subway car? I've never tried matching for myself—it felt too deliberate for my taste, and too effortful—but I can see how there's something thrilling about the possibility that you could meet anyone out there: anyone at all. In theory, at least. In practice, our clients like to set assorted parameters for those they would consider dating, effectively funneling an ocean of opportunity into the dimensions of a fish tank.

I ask Matthew, "What would this better way look like for you?"

"If I knew," he says, "I probably wouldn't be here."

Fair enough. From what the Romantick have said, it doesn't seem like they have any grand ideas beyond hearkening back to a golden age of face-to-face encounters mediated by proximity and chance. I'm always suspicious when *the way things used to be* is the proffered solution to a problem—for the subgroups of people stranded on the banks of that era's mainstream culture, it tends to be a rockier, less hospitable situation. Although maybe that's part of their cover story as well.

"So the way the breach was carried out made you think the Romantick might have been involved. What did you do after that?"

"I started following the blog. I went to events, listened to what people were saying. It took a while. Eventually I figured out what was the Romantick and what was the dream." He glances at me; I put on my best neither-confirm-nor-deny expression. "I spoke to someone—I don't know his name—and he said he would reach out when the time came."

I feel a drop of what I can only hope is water on my head. I look up to check—mystery liquids dripping on you is a health hazard on New York streets. Another drop, splat in my eye. It's starting to rain. I tug the hood of my sweatshirt over my head. Matthew doesn't seem to notice.

"When was that?" I ask.

"Five months ago."

Right after he and Pradeep broke up; three months before my message appeared in his Ballsy inbox. That explains his lack of surprise when I told him about Silent G potentially being a fake profile, and his readiness to help.

We cross Tenth Avenue, and I wonder if we'll climb the stairway up to the High Line. Instead we continue on beneath its steel girders. We walk by a block of warehouses and reach the West Side Highway with five seconds left on the WALK sign. Matthew quickens his pace. "Let's cross."

"Really? Why don't we wait—?" But he's already striding on. I sigh and scramble after him.

The light turns green while I'm still a foot from the sidewalk, and the cars go for it like this is the F1 and not a road barriered with stoplights every other block. I lunge to safety. Ahead of me Matthew is walking south on the bike path, a behavior I despise in pedestrians. At least it's empty, given the weather and the fact that it's midafternoon on a weekday. I jog up to him and ask, "Do you really have the hard drive?"

He doesn't look at me. "You don't trust me?"

"I don't understand why you still haven't handed it over."

"Bike path! Fucking morons."

A cyclist in a neon-yellow poncho flaps past us. Why are bik-

ers such self-righteous asses? I shout, "We know that!" Ugh—my
nickname should be King of Sub-par Comebacks.

Matthew says, "There's something we need to talk about first."

I guess this is where he wants to know more about what we,
as in the people he believes to be some kind of Romantick strike
force, are planning to do with the digital twins. I run over what
Becks and I agreed we would say: collect evidence, monitor for
sabotage opportunities, no details. "What is it?"

We've reached Gansevoort Street, across from the jutting rise of
the Whitney Museum. Matthew steps off the bike path and onto
the pedestrian walkway, which, for this section of the Hudson
River Park, runs right along the water. The only people around
are a couple of committed joggers. They pass us, and Matthew
turns onto a small pier that squares out over the water. Most of it
is taken up by a fenced-off playground comprising colorful climbing structures and Astroturf. The northwest corner has been built
as a ship's prow that looks out toward the New Jersey skyline, a
wooden platform with low, curving walls. Matthew walks toward
it. I stay behind him, watching that backpack jostle against his
shoulder as he moves. What if I grabbed it and ran?

"I don't blame you."

I'm evaluating the odds of Matthew being able to catch up to
me—unlike Pradeep, he seems like someone who's unused to reg-
ular physical activity—and so my response is both lackluster and
a beat delayed: "What?"

He climbs the set of low stairs into the prow and walks to the
end of it, where its two walls meet in a point. I've just stepped up
myself when he turns and says, "Not trusting me."

There's a sudden wet chill on my skin, as if my clothes were
soaked through and not simply perfunctorily damp. Is that
possible?—has he been an agent for Let's Meet from day zero? For
an instant all I can think about is how Becks will lord this over me
until the end of time.

He places one hand on the railing on top of the prow. His other hand is fisted around his backpack strap. "Did Pradeep tell you I was the first person he matched with?"

Or maybe this isn't about Let's Meet. "He didn't."

"Sometimes I thought he was with me only because he didn't know anything else."

Coming from any other acquaintance, that statement would be an expression of startling vulnerability. From Matthew Espersen—it feels like he's flayed off his skin and presented it to me. I find myself saying, "Pradeep showed us a picture of the two of you, from his birthday. He looked very happy."

The rain beads on Matthew's face as he says, "That was our last visit to the High Line."

By the time I remember what he's referring to—how Pradeep refused to return after they ran into his coworker there—he's speaking again. "Two months later he told me he was getting married. A woman he hadn't even met yet. She was the right age, the right family, the right caste, the right . . . everything. He said he had no choice, this was something he had to do, but it wouldn't change things between us. We could continue on as we were. He said that like he believed it. I knew it was impossible. And I almost said yes."

He says all this like he's reciting a speech that he's been rehearsing for too long, waiting and waiting for an opportunity to deliver it, and it's only when he stops that I realize. This is Matthew Espersen's version of an admission.

Except—why now? I think back to our last meeting, the way he pushed to be included in our (well, the Romantick's) plans. What happened since? He swapped out the hard drive. Let's Meet fired his colleague.

And Squirrel and I broke into Pradeep's Triple-Helix account.

Right. Matthew hadn't deleted that account but, as Squirrel noted, he wasn't stupid, either. He knew he was leaving a hole that he could someday fall into if he wasn't careful. He would have taken measures, such as an alert if anyone else ever tried to log in. And, in this case, he would have seen that the device being used to log in was one that had permission to do so. He would have thought of the phone he handed to me two weeks ago.

Which leaves me standing here with a man who has killed once before, possibly twice, on an empty pier with the rain slanting in at us over the water.

And I *still* haven't wrangled that hard drive from him, dammit.

What I do next isn't inspired by an Inspector Yuan technique or a Somnang maneuver. It's lifted straight from the Mother Lin manual of emotional manipulation and control. "I get it," I say. "Sometimes you meet someone and you'll do anything to be with them."

Matthew says again, "It was impossible."

"It must have been hard to realize that you meant so little to Pradeep." I'm familiar enough with him by now to notice the twitch in his posture, and I almost apologize. Instead I say, "Even what a random person from work might think. That was more important to him than the truth of your relationship."

Now I do apologize, in the privacy of my mind. To Pradeep. Of course it's not that simple. I remember when I was fourteen years old and hanging out with my neighbor's granddaughter over summer break, how the smell of her hair and her smile when I did something goofy and every brush of her shoulder against mine made me feel like I was coming apart inside. If I hadn't read *Annie on My Mind* at the Queens Public Library and walked out holding its promise of a happy ending like a talisman—if I hadn't grown up in New York versus any number of less diverse, cosmopolitan, no-one-cares-what-the-fuck-you-do places—if I hadn't watched my siblings with my mother and figured out early on that living my life in pursuit of anyone else's approval was a fast track to misery—if, if, if. I lucked out, that was all; and still I've never been able to say to my mother that I'm gay.

"He was going to get married," I say. "Have kids, buy a house, build the dream American life. And you would have been the dirty little secret he indulged in whenever he wanted a break from that life."

Matthew is three feet away, maybe four. Enough distance for me to scurry out of the way if he goes into berserker mode, although from the defensive hunch of his shoulders, and how he's clinging to the railing like he's afraid a wave will slap him overboard, I don't think he will, not if I play this right. I have the tip of the blade balanced between his ribs, and all I have to do is lean in. I can hear my mother's voice: *You must really love him. Letting him treat you like a dog he plays with and then kicks out of the house.* She said that, and a lot more, the time she found out Coraline was seeing a married man, until my sister got up from the table and ran to the bathroom to throw up. Our mother had something to say about that, too. Coraline and our mother—

I put a pin in that particular grenade to focus on the situation at hand. "You must have really loved him," I say, and shit, it's uncanny how much like my mother I sound. Maybe that's what makes me stop, or maybe it's the way he keeps blinking like the rain has fatally obscured his vision.

Matthew hoists himself up to sit on the railing, facing me, in a manner that looks at once very awkward and completely unafraid. He shifts his backpack onto his lap, crosses his legs at the ankles, and says, "That was why. I couldn't let him be so unhappy for the rest of his life."

"Why . . . what?"

He ignores the question, which I'll admit was about as obvious as the bloody handprint in *Inspector Yuan and the Eight Immortals*. "It was the best I could do for him."

"That wasn't your call to make." I can hear the anger in my voice and I try to tamp it down, but it's calcified. "Pradeep could have changed. Or found some way to be happy."

"No," he says: a final judgment. "He wouldn't have. Eventually it would have destroyed him. I knew . . ." He pauses. "I knew."

"Like you knew with Drew Wilkins?"

The shock in his face makes me think of a wild animal lured momentarily into the light before it darts back into the safety of darkness. "Drew," he says, like he's been waiting twenty years for permission to say his name again. "I did know. But that was different."

"You were in the car with him when he died. You killed him and made it look like an accident. Twenty years later you did the same thing with Pradeep. For the entire length of Pradeep's bike route, there are only three spots where the shrubbery at the side of the path is thick enough to hide in, and where Pradeep crashed is one of them." From here on out it's conjecture, but I've done my diligence, cycling-related and otherwise, and I feel confident enough about the contours of how this went down. "You hid and waited for him to approach. You knew when he would arrive because you were tracking him through Triple-Helix. At the right time you stepped out and pushed him."

I'd considered the other possibilities: that Matthew had distracted Pradeep or otherwise led him to swerve without physically touching him; or, alternatively, that he had used some kind of weapon, a stick or a baseball bat, to actually hit Pradeep. The former felt like it would involve too much uncertainty for someone of Matthew's temperament, though, and to rule out the latter I'd reached out to a journalist I knew with NYPD contacts to see if he could check the police report on Pradeep's death for me. Michael Lindenberg had confirmed that Pradeep's only injuries were those consistent with him falling off his bicycle at high speed. He had also asked if this was related to the matchmakers, and I'd been able to rationalize my answer as *no*.

"He didn't die right away," I say. This detail hadn't made it into the news articles. "He was knocked out from the fall, but he froze to death hours later."

Matthew looks down at the bag in his lap. "I would like to modify our agreement," he says. "I'll give you the hard drive, and you'll leave the story of Pradeep's death alone."

"You're trying to trade me the truth about Pradeep's murder for a stolen piece of hardware?" I say. "That's . . . kind of insulting, actually."

"Pradeep Mehta was a happy, successful man. Loving family, promising career, beautiful fiancée. The dream American life." Matthew raises his gaze back to me. "That's how the world remembers him. And that's what Pradeep would want. You know that. While he was alive that was all he cared about. What's the use of revealing the lie now? Exposing to everyone what he tried so hard to keep hidden."

"It's still murder," I say. "Justice still needs to be done."

Miraculously, that doesn't come out cheesy at all.

Matthew says, "I agree."

I stare at him: Where is this going?

"I didn't mean this as a trade." He hefts up his backpack with one hand. "More as a . . . bonus. I thought of this, from the very beginning. Actions have consequences. I will face mine. But Pradeep—you see what I mean, don't you? He's gone. This story is the only thing left of him."

I hear myself say, "I know. But . . ."

He nods. "Then you'll understand."

He winds up and flings the bag—not at me but wide, to my right. I leap toward it like the indoctrinated Ultimate enthusiast that I am. My fingers close around fabric, and I get that tiny thrill of having aced a catch, just as Matthew lifts his legs and tips back and lets gravity drop him headfirst into the Hudson. I hear the thud of one hard surface hitting another and then, almost like an afterthought, a splash.

No. No, no, no.

When I run to the railing, I notice a distant tugging in my ankle, like a toddler trying to get my attention. I must have landed wrong; I'll deal with that later. I lean over one side of the prow. Matthew is a clump of debris below me, bobbing between two of the broken wooden pillars that poke up here and there through the surface of the water. Facedown, not moving at all—he must have knocked his head against the wall as he fell. Maybe he did it on purpose, a mirroring of how Pradeep died. Focus, Claudia. He's still alive; he's been in there for less than thirty seconds. It's a major plot point in *Inspector Yuan and the Blood Pearl*: how long it takes a person to drown. Fucking focus. I can still get to him. I swing a leg up to climb over the railing.

Something—someone—grabs me from behind and pulls me back. My heart jumps up into my mouth. I swallow it back down again and commence flailing as vigorously as I can with both arms trapped against my sides.

"Calm the fuck down."

I keep going until my brain catches up and places the voice, along with that just-as-familiar scent. I sag against her, suddenly emptied out. "Matthew," I say. "We have to save him."

Becks says, in my ear, "Squirrel's called 911. We need to leave before the authorities arrive."

I try to turn around to face her, but she continues to keep me pinned as I am. No surprise that Becks Rittel would be excessively adept at restraining holds. "They're not going to get here in time. I can do this. Let me—"

"Are you fucking crazy? There's no way you're risking your life like that."

"I'm a good swimmer. And all I need to do is get him to one of those pilings. We can hold on until help comes."

I feel the breath of her sigh against my cheek. "He chose this, Claudia."

"But I . . ." I said all those cruel things, coolly, deliberately, with the aim of cutting him open. Bleeding him out, if I had to, so he would confess.

"Do you hear that?"

At first there's only the indifferent swish of the water around us, the constant traffic bass. Then, faint but unmistakable, the frustrated scream of first-responder sirens in New York City, and the long blare of a fire engine.

"We're going. We do not want to be connected to the death of a Let's Meet employee who's been sneaking trade secrets out of the company."

From where I am I can no longer see Matthew Espersen, the pale glint of his scalp, the windbreaker he always wears, the narrow logs of his legs. I don't say anything.

I feel Becks's arms loosen around me, the warmth against my back recede. I just have time to wish she hadn't let go quite so soon before I hear her say, "What the *fuck*."

I turn. "What is it?"

Instead of answering she continues to look around, and I do as well. At the emptiness of the pier, the playground, the walkway beyond—and the prow that we're standing in. Matthew's backpack, which I dropped on the ground just a few minutes ago, is gone.

PART FOUR

PART FOUR

I.

People I ~~Know~~ Knew Who Have Died

1. Grandmother on Mom's side (knew by affiliation, since I never met her)—respiratory failure
2. Grandfather on Mom's side (same)—some kind of cancer
3. Helena's sister when we were in ninth grade—hit-and-run
4. Sarah Reaves—murder by poisoning
5. Cameron Keller—murder (most likely) by poisoning
6. Pradeep Mehta—murder by assault
7. Matthew Espersen—suicide by drowning

II.

I DON'T GO BACK to Veracity for a week.

It turns out I did mess up my ankle, which I realized that afternoon on the pier when Becks and I started to walk away and I let out an entirely involuntary yelp.

Becks stopped and stared at me.

I balanced myself on my other leg. "It's nothing," I said, when in fact the attention-seeking child from earlier had returned with a red-hot poker that they were jabbing through my ankle every time I tried to put any weight on it. "I just need to go a bit slow."

"We can't afford to go slow." She spread her arms wide. "Put your arm around my shoulders."

"I don't . . . what?"

"Just do it. Jesus Christ."

And that was how Becks literally swept me off my feet like we were rehearsing an unacceptably contrived scene in a rom-com and conveyed me over to where Squirrel was waiting for us. Going pretty fast, too—she overtook the park janitor who was trundling along ahead of us with his big rolling garbage bin, the only person still out and about now that the rain was coming down on us in diagonal gray sheets. I tried to focus on not focusing on how close my face was to the crook of her neck, or how I could feel the steady, rapid movement of her chest against my side, or how achingly good she smelled, or any other sensory aspect of the experience.

Squirrel was on the other side of the West Side Highway, idling on Jane Street in the car he had borrowed for this occasion and refused to tell us from whom. When we got in, Becks told Squirrel to bring me home.

"I'm fine," I said, "really."

Squirrel said, over the disturbingly phlegmy noises of the engine, "Traffic is going to be a fucking nightmare."

"Nothing the self-proclaimed GOAT of *Race to the Death* can't handle, I'm sure," said Becks.

I said, more loudly, "Also, we have to get the hard drive back."

"We have a bigger issue," said Becks. "Who took it, what they know, and what they want."

We stop-started our way through Lower Manhattan and into downtown Brooklyn as Becks monitored Citizen for updates on police activity around Pier 51 at Hudson River Park and Squirrel swore vociferously at every double-parked car in our path. When we finally reached Gowanus I asked them to drop me off outside my building, but Becks insisted on coming in with me. She helped me up the four flights of stairs, excavated a bag of peas and carrots from the freezer for an ice pack, installed me on the couch, scowled down at me, and said, "Take a week off."

"That's excessive," I said. "My ankle is sprained, not missing."

She was leaning next to Max's painting of Holly Golightly and Jay Gatsby, and it made me remember the last, and first, time she had been in my apartment. To ask me—without asking, of course—if I wanted to know the truth about the verifiers and join the effort against the synths. Six months and a lifetime ago. It seemed incredible that there had ever been a point when I had moved so obliviously in the world.

I heard Becks say, almost like a response to what I was thinking, "A lot just happened." She shifted away from the wall. "It'll be good for you to have a break from this shit show. Go . . . eat some pancakes and read some implausibly coincidental mysteries. Or whatever else you do in your free time." From her tone, it seemed like she expected watching paint dry to top the list.

I opened my mouth to object, and the image of Matthew Espersen tumbling off the railing spliced through my mind, his feet in the air like he was somersaulting into the sky—and then gone. I shivered.

"Are you cold?" said Becks.

"No. I just—"

Both of our phones buzzed at the same time. It was Squirrel, saying that if Becks wasn't down in five minutes he was leaving.

"Son of a bitch. As if he has anything better to do with his time." Becks jabbed out a response to our group chat that communicated with even less politeness what she'd just said and slid her phone back into her pocket. "I'll cover your active matters while you're out."

"That's going to be too much work."

"We won't take on anything new until you're back. I'm also much more efficient."

I bent forward to adjust the kitchen towel that I was using to keep a pound's worth of frozen vegetables wrapped around my ankle. "I have two open diligence reports."

"Three. Your report on Robert Vinley is overdue. Here—I'll do that."

Becks knelt down by the couch and retied the towel as if in a demonstration of her statement about efficiency. She rested her hand on my shin, a calming pressure, before she looked up at me. "You okay," she said, at once a statement and a question.

I nodded. "You should go so you can make Squirrel drive you all the way back to Tribeca. I'm sure he'll love that."

When she opened the door, I felt the impending solitude crowd in, a strange suffocation of absence. Max wouldn't be home until evening, if he was coming back at all and not spending the night at Benny's; and even if he walked in right now, there was no way I could tell him that I'd just accused a man of murder and then left him to die.

"Becks."

She turned, her hand letting go of the doorknob, the slightest drawing together of her eyebrows. If I asked her to stay, I was fairly sure she would, and not even give me shit about it. But how weak would that look? Nothing had even happened to me.

I said, "What are we going to do now?" Matthew dead, the hard drive stolen, Let's Meet alerted to the fact that people were snooping around its digital-twin project. I like to think I'm an optimist, but it all seemed bleaker than Christmas Eve in Alaska.

After a moment she said, "We'll talk about it in a week."

She left, and seconds later my phone screen lit up. Work is off-limits. But if you need something, call/text anytime.

———————

I message my family group chat to say that I'll have to miss our mother's birthday dinner because I sprained my ankle in an Ultimate game. It's a relief to be able to Houdini myself out of that obligation, but in a wretched way, like I'm bowing off the stage without putting the sawed-up magician's assistant back together again.

The only person who replies is my mother. Do you have enough food? I can bring for you. Reading that ties a little bow in my throat. I tell her there's no need, I'm well taken care of by delivery apps and my roommate. (The latter bit being true whenever Max is actually around, voluble with sympathy and insisting on fetching me beverages so my ankle can stay hydrated.) She would disapprove of the apartment's disheveled condition, the grubbiness of the neighborhood, how I've taken to showering once every three days. Plus, I'm not letting my mother within baiting distance until I've regained some emotional equilibrium.

The lack of response from Charles and Coraline—not that surprising, given where I left off with both of my siblings. But as each day lightens and then darkens again, and still nothing from them, I can feel myself heavying, like I'm absorbing all that silence as some strange sort of punishment. I try looking them up on Finders Keepers, which is how I realize that my access to the app has been disabled. Same with Match Insights, WhatShould, and all the other programs we use at Veracity. Figures that Becks would find a way to enforce my mandatory leave of absence.

So I spend my time lying on the couch with my brain plugged into one classic murder mystery series after another: audiobook format, which has the dual benefit of requiring less mental effort while also blocking out my personal soundtrack of recrimination. I sleep a lot, albeit terribly; I keep having dreams where I'm underwater all knotted up in kelp, struggling to pull free before I run out of air. I hate how predictable my subconscious is sometimes. Becks texts every forty-eight hours to say that I better be laying off that ankle, and each time I think about calling her and don't. I think about texting my siblings and don't. I try meditating once, for all of forty-five seconds. I reflect on the cosmic justice of being felled by a real injury after I so blithely faked one. I look for more audiobooks.

And, once I've reconciled myself to the fact that I'm not going to hear from Charles, I text Jessie. I tell her I know she broke up with my brother and ask how he took the news; I say he isn't really speaking to me right now, after he found out that I was aware of how Jessie felt all along.

She calls me a few hours later. "Did Charles tell you that I broke up with him?" she asks.

"I . . ." Now that I'm thinking about it, I don't recall Charles specifically saying that. But everything else he said, about Jessie already having decided to leave him—that must have been what happened. "Did you not?"

"He preempted me," says Jessie, and I can hear that wry smile of hers flickering in her voice.

"As in—" I stop. "You're not saying . . ."

"He asked to see me. All of a sudden. We met, and he said he thought it would be better if we broke up. I assumed you had decided to tell him about our conversation, that was why. I said as much, and . . . my assumption turned out to be wrong. I'm sorry." Jessie pauses. "That sounded a bit egotistical. It's not that I don't think Charles could ever want to break up with me, but the way he said it—I had the impression that he didn't. That it was something he felt compelled to do."

"He would never have wanted to break up with you." The way my brother talks about Jessie, the way he looks when he does— I feel certain of that. "I don't understand what he was thinking."

"Do you know about the situation with his job?"

"They terminated him. Those bastards. But what does that have to do with the two of you?"

Her sigh brushes against my ear. "He said he wasn't sure what he was going to do next, what his options were, how long it would take him to find a comparable job or if he even would, and I shouldn't be burdened by all of that."

I say, "Not like I have a lot of experience with relationships, but that sounds like the opposite of how things should work. People don't break up because something bad happens to one of them."

"Of course not. And I said that to Charles, that I would never think of breaking up with him so I wouldn't have to deal with him going through a rough patch. If anything, I would want to be there for him, to support him through it. Because I cared about him."

"What did he say?"

She sighs again. "That I was ready to leave him even before all of this anyway, so now I should go ahead and do so."

After we hang up, I flop back across the couch into the by-now-permanent hollow that my body weight has indented into the seat cushions and wonder what Jessie would have done if Charles hadn't known about how she truly felt. Would she have told him she would stay, out of concern and obligation; or would she have allowed him to break up with her, relieved at the exit opportunity? I suspect that if I asked Jessie, she might not be sure herself. Not without a digital twin that she could run through that exact scenario, to find out what choices she could have made and the outcome of those choices. Then I'm thinking about the digital twins, really thinking about them, for the first time since—I say it aloud, despite what feels like a jellyfish thrashing around in my stomach—"Matthew died." I say it again, staring up at the horrendous paint job our slum landlord did on our ceiling: "Since Matthew died. Fuck."

I sit up: I need to do something semi-productive to try to feel a tad less hopeless about the state of the universe. Work may be off-limits, but looking into Mosaic, the client Charles mentioned in connection with Project Tahiti—I can convince myself that doesn't count as work. Also, if I don't get off this couch I'll start developing bedsores.

I hobble into my room and open my laptop and get to researching. I find a Mosaic Group listed under *Select Representations* on Precision's website, but the description of both the company and Precision's work for it is unintelligible, perhaps intentionally so: *Leading solutions firm Mosaic Group engaged Precision across multiple projects to enhance critical data integration and validation processes, pro-*

tocols, and capabilities, laying the foundation for Mosaic's sustained and scalable growth.

Mosaic's own website is equally abstruse. It describes Mosaic's business as *developing cutting-edge platforms and applications for organizations seeking to operationalize data insights and transform decision infrastructures*, and invites interested parties to contact Mosaic's product management team for more information on its offerings. Its mission statement—*enabling tomorrow's solutions to today's problems*—sounds like something Oscar Wilde might have come up with on an off day, clever without actually making much sense.

I bookmark the relevant pages, take screenshots, and send everything to my work email for later. There's an IYKYK sheen to all of this, like one of those stores in Soho with no signage, two pairs of shoes on display in a cavernous white space, and a line of people waiting outside. The question I can't answer yet: *Is* there anything to know?

———————

Amalia responds to my High Line invite halfway through my Week of Malaise. She would love to, she says, just let her know when would work for me.

Reading her message makes me feel like I'm on a seesaw: fluttery up, jarring down. It's exciting to hear from her, and I would really like to see her again. Talk about art and books and theater over dinner at another neighborhood restaurant. Flirt with our gazes and our gestures, waiting to see who will touch whom first, both of us knowing the other wants to. Find out more about who she is beneath that jaunty demeanor, what she's like, what she wants.

Except. I already know who Amalia Suarez is. I studied her profiles, her résumé, her interests, her routines. I tracked her whereabouts. I wrote a report on her. Not only that: I've been deceiving her about myself from the very first thing I said to her, from the name I go by to my opinion of the Somnang Files to my fantasy dating life. Really, anything that might ever happen between us was foreclosed the day Mason Perry sauntered in and asked Veracity to verify his girlfriend. Pretending otherwise—it's selfish and dumb, and I really need to try harder not to be either of those things.

I can't tell Amalia the truth and I can't keep lying to her. I'd like to apologize, but then I'd have to explain what for. All I can think of to do, in the end, is disappear.

III.

WHEN I RETURN TO WORK, I learn from Becks that the *New York Post* ran a piece on Matthew's drowning. "Only because he did it in the Hudson," she says. "Name recognition." There's a big picture of the pier, the emptiness of the playground looking especially sinister beneath the headline "Hudson River Claims Another Life." The text itself is brief, which I'm glad for: the incident took place off Pier 51, an anonymous 911 call alerted the police, the man was dead by the time they arrived, no foul play was suspected.

The one other public mention of Matthew's death flagged by Squirrel's Google Alerts is a brief obituary that appears in the *Mansfield Herald* and on Legacy.com. I find out that Matthew was the third of four children, an uncle to seven nieces and nephews. Both of his parents, as well as a stepmother, are still alive. He always felt so alone; it's strange to think of him as having been surrounded by people, albeit from a distance—it seems everyone else in his family stayed in Mansfield and its environs, apart from one intrepid sibling who moved all the way to Lincoln. And now he's back in Mansfield as well. According to the obituary, he'll be buried in the town's cemetery, along with Drew Wilkins.

A few days after that obituary is published, Jemma Milkbank emails me. It's a tiny shock, seeing her name again in my inbox. She says that she's very sorry to hear about Matthew's passing and asks if I could give her a quick call. *Whenever is convenient for you.* I almost delete the message without responding—there's no point now in talking further about Matthew, or Drew, or what might have transpired between them—but that would be a lousy thing to do. I'm the one who pulled Jemma back into the past, asked her to remember. The least I can do is listen.

I try her that afternoon, half hoping she won't pick up, but she does. After telling me again about how sorry she is, she says, abrupt, "When we spoke."

Eventually I say, "Yes?"

"Do you think Matt was already considering ending his own life?"

"We don't know if it was a suicide."

"To drown like that? How could anyone believe that was an accident?"

I don't say anything.

Jemma says, more quietly, "I can't help thinking if that's why he told you about the *Herald*. Asking you to tell me that he appreciated what I'd done. It was all connected for him."

"I'm sorry. What was connected?"

"It was so long ago. People don't even remember Drew anymore. At the time it felt like no one could ever forget him."

Matthew's face when I brought up Drew Wilkins; the way he said Drew's name. Suddenly I need to know if I'm right, or if I accused Matthew of this terrible thing he never did. "Drew's death," I say. "That wasn't an accident, either. Was it?"

The silence is an ocean in my ear. I think of the Hudson River emptying itself out into New York Bay, everything it holds subsumed into the salt water of the Atlantic.

"I can't answer that," says Jemma. "It was just the two of them in the car. Matt stuck to his story, and the sheriff didn't push him on it. Even though, the way the car swerved, and Drew's condition . . . I suppose everyone thought, what was the point. He was gone anyway."

"Drew's condition?"

"He was an addict. Opioids. Might as well call a spade a spade now. His parents were checking him into a rehab facility later that week."

"Drew . . . He . . . wasn't going to Florida State on a baseball scholarship?" The question sounds impossibly inane when I say it.

"Not anymore. Did Matt tell you he was?"

"I read it in your article."

"Of course," she says. "The school counselor. She did say that. It was all true, what everyone said—that was who Drew had been, before the drugs took over. He was this perfect boy, you know? Everyone loved him. The idea of him. I just wrote the story the way all of us wished it could have turned out."

The other thing I learn from Becks is that, while I was out, Wallpath finally posted a query to our mirror version of WhatShould. "You can get that from Squirrel," she says. "Or tell him to delete it. Or whatever else you want to do with it." I had let her know, after my Bay Ridge excursion, that the WhatShould account we'd been monitoring didn't belong to my brother after all, but to my sister; she spared me the snark, which only made me feel crappier about how I'd messed up.

Becks adds, preempting me, "I haven't read it. And I made

Squirrel promise not to, on pain of his current *Ashes* quest becoming irretrievably fucked up."

I've been wondering for so long that I ask the question without even meaning to: "Who *is* this video game wizard of yours?"

Her mouth opens like she's still deciding how to respond. Then she says, "My sister's kid."

Ten more questions spring up to replace the first, like a hydra of curiosity, but I've realized that, for Becks, telling me something about herself is akin to leaping out of a moving car, a feat she has to recover from before attempting it again. "That's cool," I say.

"They're a real brat." She takes a step back from my desk and says, as if it's a logical conclusion, "You'd probably get along."

I ask Squirrel for the log of Coraline's chat with WhatShould. There's a chance this is about Lionel, and if so I want to make sure the worm didn't squirm his way out of our deal. Lionel's reply to my email was more defensive than the Hindenburg Line: utter coincidence, of course he would never, artistic integrity, he couldn't possibly be blamed if his subconscious surfaced up to him something he had once read or heard, I knew nothing about the similarity of literary styles. He closed by saying that, while he had done absolutely nothing wrong, he would acquiesce to my demands because he was aware of the damage that even unfounded accusations could inflict.

Squirrel sends over the file while I'm reviewing a new target's matching profile, and I toggle over on my computer to open it. My gaze takes a microsecond to alight on the block of text at the top right half of the screen: What should I do if—

At the next two words my brain short-circuits. When I can think again I keep going, word to word to word, like I'm crossing a plank bridge strung up between two cliffs and any of its slats could break apart beneath my feet at any time. And then all at once I'm on the other side, and everything has changed even though nothing has.

What should I do if my father
disappeared on me 15 years ago and
now he's come back saying he's sorry
and can explain why he left and really
wants to be a part of my life again?

Below that is WhatShould's mini-essay of a response, a garble of *do unto others* and *forgiveness* but also *accountability* and *emotional safety*, followed by a time stamp showing that Wallpath left the session. No clues, then, as to how Coraline is feeling or what she's inclined to do. Whether she even plans to tell the rest of us.

The full Lin family reunited? There is no fucking way we will survive that.

IV.

AT OUR NEXT GALATEA MEETING—which we've moved into Veracity's conference room given that the Nest is, in Becks's words, unfit for human occupancy—we discuss who could have taken the hard drive and why.

Squirrel reports that he's been staking out the hacker forums, and no queries on Reflect, .alt files, Pygmalion, or anything related have been posted. "There's no way a third party figured it out on their own. Even I needed an assist. Tiny one."

"That points to Let's Meet being behind this," says Becks. "Either they knew Matthew was leaking information, or they suspected."

I say, "Wouldn't they just have fired him, like the other person?"

"If I were them, I would want to see who Matthew was meeting up with first. They had him followed. The opportunity came up and they grabbed the bag." An entire mountaineering crew could vanish into the crevasse between her eyebrows; I know she's still upset about the backpack being taken on her watch. She says, "I kept track of everyone in the vicinity. Two . . . I'll be kind and call them 'runners.' They went past the pier, one heading north and the other south. A third person walking her dog. Also going south. That was it. None of them was anywhere in sight. Even if they'd doubled back while we were looking out at the water—which couldn't have been for more than five minutes, at most—we should have seen them when we turned around. The place was empty."

"The answer," says Squirrel, "is always teleportation."

I've tried to keep from thinking too much about what happened on the pier. My memory of those events feels all sharded up now, like a sheet of glass I smashed on the ground. The wetness of the rain on my face, a clinging coldness, the backpack slamming into my hands. Matthew's expression as he fell. Becks's arms cinched around me. The sharpness of sirens, the garbage bin's wheels rumbling over concrete—

"The shoeshine boy," I say.

Becks says, "Are the three of us even in the same fucking time period right now?"

"It's from the Somnang Files, the film series that . . . Anyway, there's a shoeshine boy who's a spy for the Khmer Rouge. No one notices him because he's just in the background, doing his job, exactly as he's supposed to be."

She frowns at me.

"The park wasn't empty. Do you remember—we passed a janitor. He was pushing one of those big bins. That was when you were, uh—"

"Carrying you," she says. "Fuck. We did."

"All he would have had to do was drop the bag in the bin and walk away."

Squirrel says, "Could still have been teleportation."

I'm impressed with both the creativity of the setup and myself for figuring it out. Time to propose my alternative theory, while

I have some cred. "There *is* one other group that might have been interested in what Matthew was doing."

Becks's mouth is pretzeled like she already knows what's coming next and has to actively restrain herself from objecting.

"We heard what Matthew said about the Romantick," I say. "He was in touch with someone high up there. And he thought they were responsible for a data breach at Let's Meet. Maybe the Romantick has been looking into the digital twins as well. They had Matthew on their radar, they tailed him that day, they took the bag. Depending on how far along they are, they might already know about the .alt files, which would explain why they haven't had to ask anything on the hacker forums."

"Fine," she says.

"Fine what?"

"You can go look into the Romantick, see if you can find anything that points to them possibly not being insane."

I say, carefully, "You know, technically I don't need your permission to do that."

"Whoa," Squirrel whispers, like a particularly doltish foot soldier just informed Attila that the level of violence in his campaigns was excessive.

Becks hoists one eyebrow. We look at each other across the table. She says, "That is technically correct."

"Just saying."

"You've already started, haven't you."

I did reach out to the Romantick ages ago, while investigating Sarah Reaves's death—I couldn't find a contact email address, so I posted a comment on their blog; no one ever responded. That was back when I *would* have needed Becks's permission, which I didn't seek because she'd already told me to drop everything related to Sarah. I decide that's not what she's referring to. "I've signed up for the mailing list," I say. "I'll keep an eye out for any events they have in New York."

V.

AS A SUBSCRIBER TO Sherlock Holmes's maxim about the brain being an attic and refraining from filling it with useless facts, I generally aim to forget whatever I happen to learn about any organized sport that isn't Ultimate. Three things I do know when it comes to cricket, though, due to a generous consumption of P. G. Wodehouse and the Raffles stories: the rules are indecipherable, the players wear white, and it takes a very long time.

I show up at Van Cortlandt Park on Saturday morning a couple of hours after the first game of the season has started, according to the schedule I found on Pradeep's cricket club website. This is the longest ride I've attempted since my injury, the Hudson lapping gray on my left all the way up to Inwood, and I spend too much of it thinking of Matthew's body drifting in the water, Pradeep and Matthew on the High Line looking out at the river, the hundred times Pradeep biked this very route, and the last time he did so, whether he knew the man he loved killed him, whether he could have had any inkling why. For the first time ever I'm glad when the slopes start getting steep and all I can focus on is the lactic burn consuming the lower half of my body.

It's a beautiful late-spring day, which somehow both quietens and deepens everything I'm feeling. The sky a blue dome overhead, mild sunlight, still a crisp tinge to the air. I find my way to the cricket field, identifiable by all the men in white standing about. There are more men, also in white, sitting in lawn chairs along the side of the field, surrounded by equipment bags and drink coolers. I watch a player throw a ball across a strip of sand toward another player holding a bat, who doesn't do anything. Seems like there's a lull in the game. I lay down my bike and approach the guy in the closest chair. "Excuse me," I say.

He continues to stare raptly out in front of him. I glance at the field again: some of the players are walking around with no particular urgency.

"Excuse me?"

I'm about to give up and try someone else when he exhales and sags back in his chair, then starts like he's just noticed there's an incongruous stranger hovering over him. He looks up at me. He's a burly, bearded South Asian man in his early forties. "Yes?" he says.

"Hi!" I say. "Are you the Falcons Cricket Club?"

He shakes his head. "That's the other team."

"Oh—okay." I look around for a corresponding set of men in lawn chairs. "Where are they?"

"On the field."

"All of them?"

"They're fielding."

He says that like it's an answer to my question. I say, "Do you know . . . when they'll be done?"

A rippling of noise from the other men watching the game draws his attention back to it. He exclaims, the weave of a language I don't recognize. Then he says, sounding more chipper than he did previously, "Three or four."

"Hours?"

"P.M."

I'm relieved until I realize that would involve an even longer duration of time. "This game is going on for six more hours?"

He looks at me again, this time with a kind of revelation. "You don't know anything about cricket."

"Well," I say. "I think it's a bit harsh to say I don't know *anything*."

The man heaves himself up from his chair like he's been called upon to perform his civic duty. "Let me explain," he says, "how it works."

As he talks I watch the players move across the grass and the sand, the purposeful mystery of their actions, and think about how everything they could do out there is dictated by this set of arbitrary, uncompromising rules that they have no choice but to agree to if they want to play this damn game. I think about whether someone like Pradeep would have felt comforted or stifled by that, or not considered it at all. I think about the idea that the most restrictive forms of poetry are the easiest to write. I think about whether Matthew ever got to see Pradeep play. I think about all kinds of things instead of what my cricket Virgil is saying, basically. Luckily he doesn't seem to expect any participation from me beyond the occasional appreciative murmur.

The one piece of information I do retain is that there's supposed to be a break in the middle of the game, for the batting and fielding teams to switch positions. When that comes around I thank Sanjeev for his excellent primer on the sport; by then we've exchanged names, and he's shown me pictures of his two young daughters that make me a tad judgy about him spending eight hours of his Saturday playing cricket. Then I head toward where the other team has gathered, farther down the side of the field.

They're having a spirited discussion about, unless I'm mishearing, creases and wickets, and I feel shy about interrupting, but I really want to talk to these people who knew Pradeep Mehta, a different version of him. I pick out two men standing at the periphery, who appear to be only semi-listening, and go up to them. "Hi," I say. They both look at me like I've mistaken them for people they're not. "You're the Falcons?"

The white guy says, in a drawly Australian accent, "We are, yeah."

"Did you know Pradeep Mehta?"

At the name, both men's faces change—in different ways. The Australian looks surprised, then solemn, the way you would if a recently deceased acquaintance is brought up, someone you liked but weren't close to. The man next to him, a South Asian with round cheeks and wispy hair, stares at me like I just said I could commune with the dead. Interesting.

The Australian glances at the other man, as if deferring to him to respond. When he doesn't, the Australian says, "He used to be on our team. Really decent chap."

Now the South Asian says, "And you, you also knew Pradeep?"

I start to reply and then realize the larger conversation has stopped; everyone else is looking at the three of us. A compact man at the center of the group, who projects bossiness like a Napoleon who never invaded Russia, says, "What's going on?"

The South Asian man I was speaking to says, "She's asking about Pradeep."

The dozen or so men all go still. I can almost feel the shift in air pressure like we're in our own weather system, a heaviness closing around us. Napoleon says, "What about Pradeep?"

"He was one of my good friends," I say. "I never got the chance to see him play cricket, and afterward I kept wishing I had. I know how important it was to him. So I thought I would come watch one of his team's games. And then once I was here, I thought, maybe, I should just say hi to his teammates. We were all a part of his life."

No one says anything. I can see the man who reacted so strangely when I said Pradeep's name biting his lip, looking at me and then away again.

I take a step back. "That was it. Nice to meet you all."

A man standing next to Napoleon says, "Man, you should've come to another game. That inning was rubbish."

Someone else says, "Pradeep would have destroyed them if he was playing."

"Pradeep was our star bowler," Napoleon says to me. "Did you know he played for Gujarat?"

Now they all start taking turns to talk about Pradeep: what an exceptional player he was, how despite that he was humble and generous and the best teammate anyone could hope for, the magnitude of the loss. The fact that he was about to get married comes up a few times. It's a glossy, uncomplicated portrait—as it should be, under these circumstances. Except for that one guy who hardly says anything but keeps glancing at me like he senses the opportunity to unload the weapons-grade plutonium he has stashed in his pocket. Napoleon calls him out to me at one point—it turns out this man, Khush, introduced Pradeep to the Falcons back when Pradeep first moved to New York; they knew each other from university.

After a while I thank everyone for sharing their memories of Pradeep and say that I should let them get back to preparing for the rest of the game. As I walk away, Khush follows me. He says, his voice soft, "You said you and Pradeep, you were good friends?"

He asks the question like there's something specific he's trying to figure out, and I wonder. "We were," I say. "He was friends with my girlfriend as well." Really getting a lot of mileage out of this phantom girlfriend. "The four of us would hang out."

Khush squints at me.

I say, "Pradeep and his partner."

I let that term hang between us, fluttery with implication. He says, "That was before Pradeep got engaged."

"Yes," I say.

"Did he ever . . . talk to you about that?"

I stop walking; we're far enough away from the rest of the group now. "Not really. But I know he was in the process of"— what to say here?—"making his choices. Deciding which path he wanted to go down."

"He talked to me," says Khush. "Right before he died. We got a drink, to catch up; I hadn't seen him since he got back from India. He was in a strange mood. I was joking with him about the engagement, asking if he regretted it, how he was going to lose his freedom soon, silly things like that—and then suddenly he said I was right. He did regret it. I said what was he talking about, and he said marrying Heema would be the wrong thing to do. I said why. And he said because he liked other men."

Khush squints at me again. I ask, my chest tight with trepidation for this past Pradeep, "What did you say?"

"I said then I could see why getting married to a woman might be a problem."

My breath whooshes out in a laugh. "You weren't surprised?"

"I was shocked! I mean, we used to talk about girls we liked at school all the time. He was with the same girl for years. Everyone thought they would get married, but they broke up before he moved here because she didn't want to leave India. And then Heema—when I saw her picture, I was like, *No wonder Pradeep is marrying her, she's exactly his type.*" Khush shakes his head. "A part of me didn't believe him. I almost asked if he was sure."

"I'm glad you didn't."

"He was terrified," says Khush. "I'd never seen him like that before. Pradeep was someone who always had everything under control, right? Sometimes it bordered on insane, like with that physio-quant stuff. But this thing, whatever it was, was completely out of his control. He couldn't even tell me without— His voice was shaking. His whole body was shaking. He looked . . . I don't know." Khush's round face is creased with the memory, and it's touching, the transparency of his concern. "I thought maybe he would want to talk more about it—what to do about the engagement, for one thing—but it was like he couldn't. He just said not to say anything about it to anyone. Something about how it was going to take time. And then—" He laughs, an incredulous, high-pitched sound. "He went back to talking about bloody cricket. Who was going to win the Indian Premier League this year. And I went along. I didn't know what else to do."

"You said this happened just before he died?" I say. "Do you remember when?"

"Not more than two weeks."

After Pradeep found out about the duplicate profile. Not only that—after he came to me and Becks and we told him we couldn't help him remove it from Let's Meet. What if it was that very profile, and everything it signified, that led him to think about telling people the truth—trying for a different life from the one he had always believed he had to have?

"Do you think . . ." says Khush. "Pradeep couldn't have . . . done it to himself, could he?"

I hear what he doesn't say as well: And if he had said or done something else in that bar with Pradeep, or afterward, could he have changed that outcome? I think of Matthew sitting with his back to the Hudson River, his face wet, telling me he had only done what was best for Pradeep. It feels desolate, like understanding that I'm lost in a forest as the daylight pulls inexorably away, to know I might have been right. That Pradeep could have changed; might already have begun to change. That Matthew might have killed him for a reason that wasn't even real.

"He didn't," I say.

I expect Khush to say that I can't know this, but he sags a little like he just needed someone to say what he wanted to hear. "Of course he didn't," he says. "Of course it was just an accident."

The second half of the game begins, and I find myself staying on to watch. The bowler walks onto the pitch, and I picture Pradeep there instead, the world distilled to the weight in his hand and the man across from him, the give of the sand under his feet and the air against his face. The clarity of his purpose, the certainty of what he has to do. All he has to do.

When I turn to leave, I see a dark-haired girl in the distance on an e-scooter, and for an instant I imagine that she's Amalia. For an instant I really want her to be. She glides out of the park and across the road and down the opposite sidewalk, away from me, and becomes one more stranger I will never meet.

VI.

I'M PSYCHING MYSELF UP to start on my backlog of summary case memos when Becks torpedoes out of her office looking and sounding like she'll detonate on contact. "That motherfucker," she says. "That lying motherfucking son of a fucking bitch."

I get up from my chair so I'll be in a better position to either run or duck under my desk, depending on what the situation calls for. "Who?" She said *lying*: A target? Or a client?

My question is subsumed in a follow-up litany of invectives that Becks interrupts herself from to call, "Squirrel!"

"I think he might still be asleep. It's only eleven."

Becks takes out her phone and does some rapid tapping. Through the glass panel in the door I see the Nest light up; simultaneously, music bursts from the speakers in the room, classical and thunderous, the Beethoven symphony I can never remember the number of. I bet Squirrel is regretting setting up that remote-controlled office system. Then she marches over and flings the door open. I can see Squirrel curled in his usual corner, looking like a puffy worm in his sleeping bag. Not even a twitch. I'm impressed.

Becks shouts at me over the music: "Get his narcoleptic ass up. Meeting in my office in five."

It's more like fifteen by the time I shake Squirrel into sentience, prevail on him to brush his teeth and deodorize his armpits, and push him into Becks's office. Becks has turned one of her two monitors around to face out on her desk. She's standing before it, arms crossed. When we join her I see a news headline at the top of the screen—*Identity Verification Start-up Strikes Deal with Big Three*—and the picture of a young white dude who looks like any number of Google Image search results for *tech start-up founder*. It's an article from the *Match*, one of the industry news sources that Becks continually harangues me to keep up with. I skim the first paragraph. A company called Checkmark is partnering with the Big Three matchmakers to verify subscribers' online-dating personas, apparently through the assertory usage of buzzwords like *AI* and *machine learning* and *pattern recognition*.

I look closer. "Is that . . . ?"

"Fucking right it is," says Becks.

I stare at Mason Perry's face, and the image of him sitting across from us those several months ago presses up as if against fogged glass, waiting to be recognized. His satisfaction when we called him on his lie, speculating on how we had found out, watching for our reactions. Even before that—the sense I had that he was playing a role, that he and Amalia didn't fit together like he claimed they did.

"It was all fake," I say.

Becks says, "He was scoping out the competition. Trying to learn how we did things. Dicking around with us, thinking he was so fucking smart." She makes a noise that sounds like rage distilled. "If I ever see him again I'm punching that shit-eating grin off his face."

All those weeks I spent believing I was verifying Amalia, when really Mason was verifying us. Those little tests to see if we could indeed track our targets the way we assured our clients we could: turning off Amalia's phone, creating a false discrepancy in her schedule.

Amalia. She must have been in on this. Which means—

A hole gapes wide in my stomach and begins to fill, a cold, unbearable trickling. Her hand looping my wrist, the low notes of her voice in my ear. Was that the reason she kissed me, so she could laugh about it with Mason afterward? Holy shit I am an ass. I think back to the first time we met, at the Somners of Gotham screening. She was the one who had introduced herself. Sat next to me; started talking to me. I'd imagined I was learning about her and Mason's relationship, and all the while she was playing me like a concert pianist at a charity recital. (*You know, I'm starting to think you* are *a detective*—argh!)

"*Triangulating the truth across social media activity?* Does this guy understand what a triangle is? What a fucking joke." Squirrel has hunched himself disconcertingly close to the monitor screen, blocking the rest of us from view. He turns his head, continuing to read, and adds, "Is his name for real? Isn't there a TV detective with that name? Claudia—this seems like the kind of useless shit you would know."

I say, eager to extricate myself from the cringe-chamber of my memories, "Perry Mason, and the show is based on—"

Becks says to Squirrel, "*You're* a fucking joke. How did you miss this?"

"Wrong question. I didn't. This was announced two hours ago, and when I check my crawlers all the news about it will have been pulled and consolidated."

"Not the thing with the Big Three, you dumbass. The company itself. Checkmark. Fuck, even the name is embarrassing. It was set up last year."

"Do you know how many shitty businesses are being set up all the time?"

"Of course I know, and if any of them have backers like Chase Mitson and Indus Ventures on their cap table, then we need to be watching them. Not the other fucking way around."

Becks says that and the temperature of the water swilling around inside me drops by another ten degrees of horror. If Amalia has been pulling a *Spy vs. Spy* on me, then our encounter at the Whitney wasn't a coincidence after all. She must have followed me and seen an opportunity to talk to me. And that sense I've had these past few months, every now and then, of being watched—perhaps I was, by Mason or Amalia or someone else who worked for them. The girl I saw at Van Cortlandt Park just last weekend. Could that actually have been Amalia?

But how? Squirrel regularly scrubs our phones for any potentially suspect software or data, to the point of what I would call neurosis if I weren't aware of what geolocation apps can do. Even if Amalia had succeeded in planting a tracking device on me the first time we met, I'd changed my clothes any number of times since, especially as the weather warmed from winter to spring. It wasn't like placing a tracker on a car or a . . .

"I'll be right back!" I say.

I hear Becks saying, "If this is one of your harebrained ideas—" and Squirrel saying, "She just wants attention. She's feeling left out of the conver—" and then I've sprinted out of Veracity and the front door closes behind me.

———————

When I wheel my bicycle out of the elevator, I see Becks sitting in my chair in the front office. She scowls at me through the glass and starts to rise. I put my finger to my lips—it's occurred to me that whatever tracker Amalia installed might have some sort of recording capability.

Becks's expression right then is almost worth getting scammed by the Mason and Amalia show. I crouch down next to my bike, the way I recall Amalia doing that evening in the East Village when she unfolded her e-scooter, and gaze at the underside of the seat. Nothing. I'm at once relieved and worried that maybe I'm losing my mind. But when I run my fingers across the plastic I can sense the slightest protrusion, like a wide, flat button stuck in place, and both my relief and my paranoia burgeon like competing algae blooms at a phosphate party.

While Squirrel removes the tracker and brings it into the Nest to study it, I tell Becks about running into Amalia at the Norah Simmons show. "We talked for ten minutes, max. About art." I should mention the part about giving Amalia my email address. The way Becks is staring at me, though, like I have snakes coming out of my ears—I can't. Instead I say, "I'm sorry. I should have brought this up when—"

"What do you think she wanted?"

"I don't know." The only thing I can think of is that Amalia wanted to see how a verifier would handle the situation of being recognized by a target—in which case, it's a minuscule comfort that I completely flubbed Veracity's protocol. Except if that was all, she wouldn't have come up with a pretext to obtain my contact information. Or reached out repeatedly. Or spent an evening with me. That, there's no way I'm telling Becks. Right now I would forfeit a chunk of my brain to permanently remove what happened that night from my recollection.

Becks's mouth twists like she's stopping herself from saying what she wants to say, which means it must be lethal indeed.

"I'm sorry," I say again.

A tight shake of her head, like I'm holding out the currency of a state that's been rendered worthless by hyperinflation and all-around mismanagement. "It's done." She takes a breath. "They could have been the ones who stole Matthew's backpack."

I blink at her. I did ride to the museum that day, as usual. From there Matthew and I were on foot, but if someone had been physically watching they could have followed us to the river.

She says, as if she can see my train of thought creaking along, "Assuming that was an occasion when they were tailing you in person. Which is possible. From the tracker they would know that you had been going to the Rubin every week. They might have realized you always met with the same person. Maybe they even found out who Matthew Espersen was, that he worked for Let's Meet. And they wanted to find out more about the connection to Veracity."

"If the hard drive is with Checkmark," I say, "do you think they'll be able to figure out what it contains? They won't be able to open the .alt files, not without the Pygmalion program."

"They can always look at the source code," says Becks. "Squirrel did it, which means a kindergartener could."

I say, "We know where both Mason and Amalia live . . ."

"No. Jesus Christ. You are not doing any more breaking and entering."

"Does that mean you'll do it?"

That gets me one of her vicious-cat glares. "First, we haven't confirmed they're the ones who took it. Second, if they did, it's probably at their office—which we don't know the location of—and not one of their homes. Third." She takes out her phone and taps at it. "As I thought. The numbers they gave us are not showing up on Finders Keepers. Much as I despise Mason Perry, I'm guessing he had the sense to also set up temporary addresses."

She's right, of course. I have to keep reminding myself: nothing I believed about Amalia Suarez was real.

Becks says, "We have some advantages. Checkmark has a publicized partnership with the Big Three. And they managed to get some well-known VC investors on board, god only knows how. They have a reputation to maintain. If it got out that they infiltrated a competitor, lied about who they were to try to learn trade secrets, put a tracker on an employee there . . . that's not a company anyone wants to be associated with."

I say, "But exposing them like that would bring Veracity out into the open."

"Yes."

"You and Komla always said the only way Veracity could work is if we remained invisible."

"We also always knew Veracity wouldn't last forever."

The meaning of her statement drifts against me like a stealthy iceberg, and I feel myself, ever so slowly, starting to sink. "You did?"

Something flickers in her expression, too quick for me to place. "You know that as well. It's too risky, what we do. The tools we use. The ways we have to lie. Sooner or later, all of that will catch up to us. We just need to make sure we stay ahead until we've neutralized the synths."

"We can change our methods. We don't have to . . . Wait. You said. So you agree? About the synths?"

She grimaces at me. "That's what Veracity was set up for. I was hoping we would have more time. But if a fucking Mason Perry can find out about us . . . we're already not as invisible as we should be."

The ocean floor rises up at me, a dark, silent certainty, but—not yet. I don't have to think about it just yet. "So what do you think we should do?"

"Let's send them a message," says Becks.

———————————

When I leave Veracity that evening, I cycle up to Midtown East. Indus Ventures's office commands the twenty-second floor of a stolid gray building at the corner of Lexington and Fifty-Sixth. I enter the lobby and ask the security guard behind the reception counter if this is 700 Lexington Avenue. He glances up from his phone, clocks me as someone not worth being helpful to, and resumes scrolling. I can see his phone screen reflected in his glasses, twin miniatures: he's looking at potential matches on Soulmate.

He says, an afterthought, "Nope."

"Thanks," I say to his bald spot, and walk out having pasted the tracker to the underside of the counter.

VII.

AT FIRST IT LOOKS LIKE a black plastic bag hanging from the handlebars of my bike, which I parked this morning at its usual spot on the corner of Harrison and Greenwich when I arrived at work. I hurry over, equally appalled by what I'm already envisioning the contents of that bag to be (random trash, rotting leftovers, feces—this is New York, there's no bottom to the filth) and the fact that my bike is apparently so beat up as to appear abandoned.

Then the realization explodes like a time bomb against my sternum. It's Matthew's backpack.

I slow my pace and look left and right like I'm, very belatedly, checking for traffic. I dropped off the tracker less than twenty-four hours ago; this must be Checkmark's response.

On one side, coming toward me: two women pushing strollers and chatting while their respective children strain to wallop each other from their straitjacket seats. On the other, heading away: a man walking a shag rug of a dog. I reach my bike and glance over again to see the dog pivot and squat next to a lamppost. Its owner

pulls a grocery bag out of his pocket and follows, coincidentally-
or-not turning to face in my direction. Which seems likelier—
live, very noisy children as props, or canines trained to defecate
on command?

Or maybe it doesn't matter. I can count on being watched.
Question is, is this a détente or a *fuck you*?

I check the bag's front and side pockets first: empty. Before I
unzip the main compartment I give it a subway groper's once-
over, just in case some sicko has dropped in a dead rat or a live
tarantula. Through the canvas I can make out the defined edges of
a square package—certainly large enough to contain a hard drive.

I reach inside and take out a box that looks like it could have
been procured at any Chinatown bakery, a bright red lid and Chinese characters in gold and a graphic of mandarin ducks. I ease the
cover off and look down at . . . mooncakes.

Not even fancy mooncakes. These look like the boring traditional kind, round and dense, a glossy brown crust, Chinese characters printed on the top. There are four of them, each in its own
plastic wrapper. When I pick one up I see that the wrapper has
been opened and the mooncake cut into quarters. Same for the
other three. I would've done the same, to check if there was anything relevant contained within them, a message or something
else that would reveal the location of the hard drive.

So that's why whoever took Matthew's backpack has returned
it. They're hoping I'll have some idea what these mooncakes are
about.

I replace the box in the bag and turn around to head back up to
Veracity. Maybe I do.

———————————

It's forecast to rain later in the week, and when I wake up on
Thursday morning the world outside my window—uninspiring

at the best of times, a landscape of automotive repair shops and plastic bag warehouses and eternal, accursed road construction—is a melty gray canvas. I roll over and check my phone. Our plan is predicated on the weather being crappy in exactly this wet, blustery fashion, to minimize the odds of us being tailed or at least make it maximally annoying for anyone doing so, but a part of me still sighs to see the text from Becks: We're on.

Gil Hodges Community Garden is half a mile from my place, up Third Avenue and right on Carroll Street. I spend too long ascertaining that every single one of the umbrellas in the apartment is irretrievably busted and then dash out. I make it there by 8:45, fifteen minutes after the garden opens. From a block away I can see the car that Squirrel was driving on the day Matthew died (I can think this now with only the tiniest of flutterings in my rib cage) parked on Denton Place at the corner where the garden entrance is. I get closer: Becks and Squirrel looking extremely comfy, and unequivocally dry, from what I can see through the mini-waterfall rushing down the windshield. Becks is sipping at her thermos; Squirrel has reclined his seat all the way back. I squelch past them and into the garden.

It's a small space of paved walkways and raised vegetable beds and wooden tables and benches. Once I enter I can see that I'm the only person here, but I do the round anyway, in case someone is committed enough to be hiding within the profusion of leaves climbing the wall that borders the back of the garden. Then I text Becks and Squirrel to come in as well.

We meet in the center of the garden, on the platform that I once told Matthew would be my choice of a dead drop in the city. Squirrel is in his usual baseball cap–tracksuit combo. Becks, on the other hand, is wearing a heavy military jacket over coveralls, and her hair hangs in a tight braid down her back. She looks like a cross between an army combat instructor and the guest celebrity on a garden makeover show. She frowns at me. "What?"

"Nothing," I say. "I brought the rulers"—borrowed from Max's art supplies; I told him I needed to measure some family photographs I wanted to get framed for my mother, which I immediately regretted because the lie of it just accentuated what a bad Chinese daughter I was. "So we'll each take one side?"

Squirrel says, "Someone needs to keep watch."

Becks says, "It's dirt, not radioactive waste."

"I have a thing against worms."

The platform is raised an inch above the ground on three sides. Becks and I start across from each other, using the rulers to sweep the space beneath the platform. The ground is swampy from all the rain and gives off a dark, mulchy smell. As I slither along I can feel my conviction ebbing away into the muck. Maybe Matthew was just looking to hand off some extra pastries since he didn't plan to be around to enjoy them himself. Maybe the hard drive was in the bag after all, and Checkmark swapped it for the mooncakes to mess with us. Maybe—

I hear Becks say, "There's something here. Fuck—I can't fucking reach it."

I sit back on my heels and find myself pondering the mystery of how she's able to look so poised while turtled in the mud, cheek grazing the soil, swearing like she has a daily quota she needs to hit. Then she straightens up, and I feel my heart jolting like its own recalcitrant creature—not at what she's holding in her hand, a slim rectangle wrapped in black plastic, but at the rare gleam of her smile and the way the golden rope of her braid has fallen over her shoulder.

"Got it," she says.

VIII.

I LEAVE THE GARDEN FIRST, retracing my route on Carroll. Two minutes later, Squirrel will get in his car and drive to Red Hook, and at the same time Becks will order a Lyft to bring her to the office.

I was originally going to go home, but once I get to Third Avenue I change my mind and head for Groucho's instead. I've always wanted to be one of those people who get to enjoy a leisurely weekday breakfast amid all the beleaguered nine-to-fivers, and this is my chance. Becks and I cleared our schedule for Operation Gardener; I have no client meetings or observations today, and no reports due until the start of next week.

The diner is as empty as I've ever seen it, so I slide into the booth in the back that Max and I probably have squatters' rights to by now. While I wait for my blueberry pancakes I check my phone. Messages from Squirrel and Becks: he's in the process of copying over the contents of the hard drive; she's gridlocked on the Brooklyn Bridge and griping about the city's asinine decision to turn one of the lanes of traffic into a dedicated bike path. Neither of them thinks they have been followed.

I type, Same. I'm considering including a defense of the Brooklyn Bridge bike lane in my reply when, in the periphery of my vision, I sense someone sitting down at the other side of the table. Stet that.

Amalia Suarez pushes the dripping hood of her parka off her head and smiles at me. "Hey," she says.

My first instinct is to scamper out of the booth and safely away from that amused, knowing gaze. My second instinct is to knock over my mug of tea in such a way as to spill lukewarm English Breakfast across her lap. I hold on to the edge of the bench seat until embarrassment and anger curdle together into some version of resignation, and then ask, "Got caught in the rain?"

She makes an *unfortunately* face. "Not as bad as you, though. Did you fall in a patch of mud?"

Fair enough. "I crawled through it."

My server stops at the table and unloads two plates of pancakes, along with utensils and a crusted jug that may be holding last millennium's maple syrup. I'm wondering if I should clarify—I've reached the stage of hungry where turning down an extra entrée feels like a grievous mistake—when Amalia says, "I asked for the same thing you ordered. The way you talk about food, I know you have good taste."

I think of us leaning forward to hear each other through the noise of Sawadee Thai, her asking if I wanted to try her dish, us laughing at each other's jokes. "Why did you . . ."

I stop: I'm not sure what, exactly, I should ask. Or if I even want to hear the answer.

"Kiss you?" She looks at me through her eyelashes. "I really wanted to."

I focus on cutting into my pancakes, watching the steam rise. This would be easier if I wasn't still attracted to her. Arguably, more so now that I know she's really a cunning operative with a hidden agenda, which maybe seems a bit self-sabotaging.

She says, "Why did you go to the play with me?"

I'm about to say something glib about my Jane Austen fetish, but decide to try a tactic my mother uses sparingly but devastatingly: emotional honesty. "I thought it'd be a chance to get to know you better."

Amalia's smile shrinks away. She picks up the napkin bundle of her fork and knife, starts to unwrap it.

"We read about Mason Perry's new company," I say. "Checkmark. Sounds exciting."

"It won't go anywhere."

She says that like we're talking about a plan to provide free universal health care. I ask, surprised, "Why do you say that?"

"A verification service that's funded by the matchmakers, endorsed by them, officially working with them? People will never trust it. They know that Checkmark's priority isn't monitoring for truth, it's helping the matchmakers look good."

"But the matchmakers want accurate information from subscribers as well. Without that, the premise of matching doesn't work."

Amalia tilts her head. "You sound like you believe the matchmakers can really tell us whether two people are right for each other."

I'm reminded of our exchange at the Bunker, right before the show—and in my mind a long row of dominoes starts toppling toward a conclusion that I can't quite see, not yet. "I don't know," I say. "A lot of people seem to think so."

"How about this. Do you believe they should?"

Should: the soft, seductive depth of that word. It feels like part of the problem—one group deciding on how things should be for everyone, another group disagreeing. Meanwhile, I don't even know what *I* should do about my family, this partiality for aggravating women that I'm discovering I have, or any of the rest of my own crap.

I say, "If you didn't think Checkmark would work, why did you spy on Veracity?" I find myself adding: "On me?"

She sits back. "You spied on me first."

"That's . . . different. I was helping my client to verify if his match was being truthful."

"By lying to me. Ironic, no? Claudia?"

I consider saying that my engaging with her was in fact unsanctioned, but that might sound even worse. "Jiayi *is* my name."

"The way *hapjackflappiness* is your email address."

"Come on," I say. "The two of you came up with a scheme to find out how Veracity worked so you could set up a competitor, and you're trying to guilt me about giving you a secondary email?"

"Mason found out nothing about Veracity." Amalia takes a bite of her pancakes and lifts her eyebrows in appreciation. As she reaches for the syrup jug, she adds, "But I can't say the same about myself."

The final few dominoes clack into place and I can trace the pattern now, how it spirals in upon itself. "Checkmark—it was your idea, wasn't it?"

She beams like her faith in me has been rewarded. "I'm flattered," she says, "but it was a group effort."

"You don't care about verification. It's a way to get access to the matchmakers. You wanted Mason to front it so your . . . group can stay hidden."

"Also, Mason, he's perfect to play the part of a tech start-up founder. His opinion of himself is so high you can see it from outer space."

Now that we're on the subject of Mason Perry—I know I shouldn't care about this, but I do, so I ask, "Were the two of you really dating?"

She shakes her head. "Not into guys. And even if I were." She pauses. "I'm being unfair. For a straight white cis male with a trust fund, Mason is . . . he's all right. Enough to make me feel bad sometimes."

She stops and glances down at her plate as if she wishes she hadn't revealed that. I sip at my tea, cut another wedge of pancake, let the silence sit between us: this is something I can use.

"It started with Lucinda Clay."

Luckily I'm still chewing, and so have a few extra seconds to decide on my response. I swallow and say, "The executive at Soulmate?"

"Former, now," says Amalia. "She ran one of Soulmate's highest-priority projects. We were surprised when she left so suddenly. There were a lot of stories about why, and this agency called Veracity came up. We thought it would be a good idea to look into an organization that could get rid of one of the smartest and most powerful people in the industry."

Truth is, Lucinda Clay's position at Soulmate was a lot more precarious than Amalia seems aware of. But no harm in letting her think the verifiers carried out a bigger coup than we did.

"When Mason and I were refining the business proposal for Checkmark, I told him there was a company already operating in the online identity verification space. He was the one who suggested we do some corporate espionage."

"And what did you find out?"

"Let's see. In addition to helping your clients find out if their dates are lying, you also spend a lot of time talking to an insider at Let's Meet who has expressed skepticism about the matchmakers and a readiness to help the anti-matching cause."

"Spent," I say.

She inclines her head. "Matthew Espersen was passing you information about the digital twins, wasn't he?"

"That's what . . ." I'm about to say, *the Romantick believes?* when the way she's looking at me, and the mention of Matthew, reminds me of his comment during our final walk, as the clouds massed above us like a celestial army was preparing for war. *Eventually I figured out what was the Romantick and what was the dream.* "Is that what the Dream believes?"

Amalia laughs, a bright, delighted sound. "Well done."

"You gave me the clue the first time we met. When you asked me if I thought the Dream was a group rather than any one person. Why?"

"I hoped we'd be able to talk about it someday," she says. "Along with everything else."

"Everything else?"

"The matchmakers' use of their subscribers to develop artificially intelligent agents, and their plans for those agents. Let's Meet's digital-twin model and, before that, the big-data model that Soulmate—that Lucinda Clay—was working on. Both of which I'm guessing you're familiar with."

I don't say anything, but I'm feeling pretty chuffed that I was right about the Romantick after all. It would have been such a waste for a wacky, cultlike group to turn out to be nothing other than a wacky, cultlike group.

"I'm also guessing," says Amalia, "that you agree we have to take action before everything goes up in flames. For now, we can still tell whether we're interacting with another person when we go online. Enough of the time. Even if they're lying about who they are, what they want, all the stuff you verifiers claim you can suss out—they are still people. They're walking around somewhere with synapses firing and hearts beating, typing out those lies on their phones. If the matchmakers succeed in producing their agents at scale and releasing them, forget about all that. You won't be able to know whether anyone you talk to, unless you're staring them in the face, is a real human being. Can you imagine? The kind of uncertainty and mistrust that will create?"

What she's talking about—it goes beyond companies trying

to manipulate consumers and outcomes. This would be a full-on collapse of social norms and expectations, of our digital systems and infrastructure, of how we have come to live in the world of the Internet and the smartphone and a trillion online profiles. And it doesn't sound nearly as insane as it should.

"You're way better at the doomsday scenario than I am," I say, more faintly than I would like.

"I've had practice."

Amalia leans forward, resting the points of her elbows on the table. Now she'll ask me to share what the verifiers know about the twins. In a way, she's entitled to the information; we have what we do only because Matthew thought we were the Romantick. But after everything she's done, can I even trust her with it?

"Join us."

Or . . . that.

She watches me with a gravity that she's never shown until now, and it makes me wonder how much of the Amalia Suarez I've seen so far has been an act, if this is who she really is.

I say, "To stop the synths?"

She shakes her head. "It's too late for that," she says. "We're going to have to free them."

ACKNOWLEDGMENTS

It's a strange, semifantastical feeling to work for years on a story, not knowing if it will ever amount to anything other than an excessive number of Word files hidden on my hard drive—and then to find out, as that story is finally making its way into the world, that it's not over: I get to continue writing about the verifiers and the Lin family, at least until AI starts doing a better job of it. (In two months I may come to regret this joke.) I'm still not sure what alchemy was wrought for it to happen, but for that, the insights into character and plot, and so much else, thank you to Julie Barer, agent extraordinaire.

There can be no finer editor for all Veracity-related shenanigans than Anna Kaufman, so thank you for signing on to another Claudia Lin investigation. I'm grateful for your partnership, and there's no way I could have figured out this book without you.

Thank you to the Vintage team for the thought, care, and enthusiasm that you have invested in *The Rivals*: Jennifer Barth, Kelsey Curtis, Lisa A. Davis, Christine Hung, Anne Jaconette,

Vi-An Nguyen, Kayla Overbey, Lyn Rosen, Nancy B. Tan, Christopher Zucker.

Thank you to all the readers who found something in *The Verifiers* to respond to, who reached out to ask if there'd be a sequel or to correct historical inaccuracies or to just say hi. It's a privilege to write for you.

Thank you to my friends for your kindness, generosity, sufferance, and support; I'm incredibly lucky to know you and have you in my life. Special thanks to Nate Bethea for the *Trashfuture* interview; to Cathy Sweetser for a wonderful LA visit marking the end of an era and the beginning of another; to Ray Liu for marshaling troops to my events; to James Church and Aseem Sood for offering and/or agreeing to read the draft, and also for helping to make the day job more fun (fifteenth floor forever); and to Maryam Menon and Elaine Phua for always making time and never losing touch.

My family has been a constant source of love, strength, hilarity, and assorted strong emotions. Pek Beng Choon, Cheo Hock Kuan, Pek Li Jun, and Pek Wenjie—I could never thank you enough.

Angela Yuan and I met before I succumbed to owning a smartphone, but I would swipe right on you every time.

THE VERIFIERS

Claudia is used to disregarding her fractious family's model-minority expectations: she has no interest in finding either a conventional career or a nice Chinese boy. She's also used to keeping secrets from them, such as that she prefers girls—and that she's just been stealth-recruited by Veracity, a referrals-only online-dating detective agency. A lifelong mystery reader who wrote her senior thesis on Jane Austen, Claudia believes she's landed her ideal job. But when a client vanishes, Claudia breaks protocol to investigate—and uncovers a maelstrom of personal and corporate deceit. Part literary mystery, part family story, *The Verifiers* is a clever and incisive examination of how technology shapes our choices, and the nature of romantic love in the digital age.

Fiction

VINTAGE BOOKS
Available wherever books are sold.
vintagebooks.com